"A brilliant, multifaceted, and completely original book about how a distinguished professor of Russian literature decided to retool his pedagogy in accordance with the latest findings in evolutionary and cognitive science to teach Russian language and literature to underserved, minority, inner-city high school students. Bethea's generous goal was to allow them to have the same powerful, life-altering experience he did when he learned Russian—a language with which he had been completely unfamiliar—and discovered that it revealed a new world and 'added a different gear' to his brain. In light of today's debates about 'cultural appropriation,' the decade-long success of Bethea's initiative is especially noteworthy because it demonstrates the necessity of deep engagement with cultural alterity to achieve optimal personal growth. Part memoir, part bridge between Snow's 'two cultures,' part paean to the enduring genius of Russia's national writer, Alexander Pushkin, this is an essential book for our times."

—*Vladimir Alexandrov, B. E. Bensinger Professor Emeritus of Slavic Languages and Literatures, Yale University*

"A fascinating account of how, in teaching Pushkin, one might also teach students to think about citizenship, risk, evolutionary neuroscience, and language itself. Exemplary readings of major texts are embedded in this book, which is pedagogical in multiple ways. I envy David Bethea the chance to have learned so much from students in the Pushkin Project."

—*Stephanie Sandler, Harvard University*

"This book is testimony to an astonishing hybrid. On one side Alexander Pushkin, Russia's foundational poet of genius and an octoroon; on the other, an American professor and born teacher who devotes a decade of his life to making Russian culture inspirational for young people from minority backgrounds. Prompted by creative visions as vast as those of Charles Darwin and Iain McGilchrist, all the while urging us on with his trademark faith in 'co-evolutionary spirals' that pit literature against despair, David Bethea, in this very bad time for our Russian brand, has given us a moving memoir of poetry, sociobiology, civic conscience, and pastoral care."

—*Caryl Emerson, Princeton University*

D1562590

"*The Pushkin Project* is both an inspiring memoir of Bethea's work building an educational program for children from underprivileged communities and a remarkable essay on literature and evolutionary thought. At the center of it all are Bethea's captivating readings of Pushkin's classic works, in the form of lesson plans that will be useful to educators in any high school or university. Written in an engaging manner, probing deep questions of cultural history and educational philosophy, this is a book that effortlessly and gracefully appeals to multiple audiences."

— *Kevin M. F. Platt, Professor of Comparative Literature and Russian and East European Studies, The University of Pennsylvania*

"Such a lucid and immersive narrative about a most improbable and imaginative project! I learned so much about Pushkin and inner-city culture, and the evolutionary drumbeat resonated throughout. Bravo to David Bethea, his adventurous students, and their fascinating encounters with poetry and transcendence."

—*Ursula Goodenough, Washington University, author of* The Sacred Depths of Nature: How Life Has Emerged and Evolved

"David Bethea has combined his love of Pushkin and the Russian language with his knowledge of evolutionary biology and his deep reading in other areas to devise an educational project unlike any other. The Pushkin project is unique and is dedicated to helping Black and Brown teenagers learn about another language, another culture, and a different way of seeing the world. I highly recommend it."

—*Henry L. Roediger, III Professor of Psychology at Washington University in St. Louis and co-author of* Make It Stick: The Science of Successful Learning

"This book is the best news for the field. It mixes eye-opening readings of Pushkin through the lens of evolutionary biology with something that is constantly, but I dare say especially currently, much in demand: a sense of purpose. In engaging and subtle prose, Bethea tells the story of the experience teaching Pushkin to students from Black and Brown communities, and in doing so, reminds us that the opportunity to turn our studies into something meaningful—not just for us but also for the people around us—is always at hand."

— *Daria Khitrova, Harvard University*

The Pushkin Project

Russia's Favorite Writer, Modern Evolutionary Thought, and Teaching Inner-City Youth

The Pushkin Project

Russia's Favorite Writer, Modern Evolutionary Thought, and Teaching Inner-City Youth

David M. Bethea

BOSTON
2023

Library of Congress Cataloging-in-Publication Data

Names: Bethea, David M., 1948- author.
Title: The Pushkin project: Russia's favorite writer, modern evolutionary thought, and teaching inner-city youth / David M. Bethea.
Description: Boston: Academic Studies Press, 2023. | Series: Evolution, cognition, and the arts | Includes bibliographical references.
Identifiers: LCCN 2023024140 (print) | LCCN 2023024141 (ebook) | ISBN 9798887192017 (hardback) | ISBN 9798887192024 (paperback) | ISBN 9798887192031 (adobe pdf) | ISBN 9798887192048 (epub)
Subjects: LCSH: University of Wisconsin--Madison. Pushkin Summer Institute. | Russian language--Study and teaching (Secondary)--United States. | Pushkin, Aleksandr Sergeevich, 1799–1837--Study and teaching (Secondary)--United States. | Russian literature--19th century--Study and teaching (Secondary)--United States. | Summer schools--Wisconsin--Madison--Case studies. | College preparation programs--Wisconsin--Madison--Case studies. | Teaching--Methodology. | Education--Philosophy. | Social evolution.
Classification: LCC PG2069.U68 B47 2023 (print) | LCC PG2069.U68 (ebook) | DDC 891.71/3--dc23/eng/20230714
LC record available at https://lccn.loc.gov/2023024140
LC ebook record available at https://lccn.loc.gov/2023024141

ISBN 9798887192017 hardback
ISBN 9798887192024 paperback
ISBN 9798887192031 ebook PDF
ISBN 9798887192048 epub

Book design by PHi Business Solutions
Cover design by Ivan Grave
On the cover: "Pushkin and B.B. King," an anonymous graffiti in Kharkiv, Ukraine, 2008 (fragment).

Published by Academic Studies Press
1577 Beacon Street
Brookline, MA 02446, USA

press@academicstudiespress.com
www.academicstudiespress.com

For the students of the Pushkin Project:
May you find new ideas and new forms of creativity
no less inspiring than those of the poet.
"Глаголом жги сердца людей"
(Burn the hearts of the people with the word).

And for Kim, Emily and Nate, Charlie and Colin:
And the end of all our exploring
Will be to arrive where we started

Graduation Ceremony, Pushkin Summer Institute, July 19, 2019

Contents

Acknowledgments

I would like to thank the following individuals for their generous readings of my book manuscript, including much needed constructive criticism: Vladimir Alexandrov, Brian Boyd, Brett Cooke, Sergei Davydov, Tom Dolack, Alexander Dolinin, Caryl Emerson, Ursula Goodenough, Marvin Henberg, Anya Nesterchouk, Andrew Reynolds, Gary Rosenshield. To renowned experts Elliott Sober and David Sloan Wilson I'm also grateful: they took time from their busy schedules to explain aspects of evolutionary theory to me and they kindly provided publications of their own to elucidate certain complex issues. I'm particularly indebted to a group of alumni from the Pushkin Summer Institute for their willingness not only to read and respond to the constantly evolving text, but also to answer my errant requests for additional input regarding their student experience: Jennifer Caraballo, Anthony Carreno, Andrew Carrera, Sandy Cortez, Johana Gutierrez, Gustavo Marquez, Annette Pabello, Abril Pereznegron, Claudia Torres-Giraldo. To the members of the editorial and production teams at Academic Studies Press, including Alessandra Anzani, Matthew Charlton, Rebecca Kearns, and Kira Nemirovsky, I want to extend a special thanks: their responsiveness, verbal and design agility, and attention to detail made my work much easier and even pleasant. Here I also must mention old friend and founder of ASP (in a happy coincidence the Press shares the same initials with Pushkin!), Igor Nemirovsky, whose sustained work over the decades on behalf of the Slavic and Jewish studies fields is inestimable. Last but by no means least I want to thank my wife, Kim, who helped me live with the ideas, read every word of the work-in-progress carefully, played her part in hosting the PSI staff and students, and, most of all, made me aware of those "emergent" properties that make life worth living.

Little by little, the entire era (not without reluctance, of course) came to be the Pushkin era. All the beauties, ladies-in-waiting, mistresses of the salons, Dames of the Order of St. Catherine, members of the Imperial Court, ministers, aides-de-camp and non-aides-de-camp, gradually came to be called Pushkin's contemporaries, and were later simply laid to rest in card catalogues and name indices (with garbled birth and death dates) to Pushkin's works.

He conquered both time and space. People say: the Pushkin era, Pushkin's Petersburg. And there is no longer any direct bearing on literature; it is something else entirely. In the palace halls where they danced and where they gossiped about the poet, his portraits now hang and his books are on view, while their pale shadows have been banished from there forever. And their magnificent palaces and residences are described by whether Pushkin was ever there or not. Nobody is interested in anything else. The Emperor Nikolai Pavlovich in his white breeches looks very majestic on the wall of the Pushkin Museum; manuscripts, diaries, and letters are valuable if the magic word "Pushkin" is there. And, the most terrifying thing for them is what they could have heard from the poet:

> *You will not be answerable for me,*
> *You can sleep peacefully.*
> *Strength is power, but your children*
> *Will curse you for me.*
> (Anna Akhmatova, "A Word about Pushkin")

Preface

———

They come from poor Hispanic and Black neighborhoods in the west and south of Chicago. They come to learn. They are sixteen to eighteen years old and rarely if ever have been outside of the city. In fact, one kid, let's call him "Osvaldo," has never visited the Navy Pier. "Jose" mentions how as a grammar-schooler he saw a gang member shot and killed at a bus stop by the park where he lives. "Elijah" muses in a private moment while eating pizza at a picnic how it sucks not to have a father. And then there is "Kayla" who asks for help on her college admissions essay that tells the story of how she was sexually abused by her father and is trying her best to deal with it.

Their realities cut close to the bone and are never far from the streets. "Carlos" has helped his mother get his drunken father to bed every night since he was seven. In his world this is just a fact of life, nothing worthy of special comment. His mother is a cleaning lady. Unassuming, hesitant in public. He remembers how she quietly sings her Mexican tunes as she moves around the apartment doing her chores in the morning. She never learned English well, just enough to get around stores and do her job, but her example is the compass that keeps her son on course when he moves out among the dangerous currents of ghetto life.

Where to begin to teach these young people? Where to begin to learn from them? How can a white professor who has spent forty years in college classrooms find the right communicative tools to meet these youngsters *on their terms*? To interact with them not in order to bring high culture to the masses, an activity that increasingly resembles a fool's errand these days, but to participate in a reimagining of the educational process, one that both reflects their lived experience and broadens their perspective on the world in useful ways? In short, could their story and my story possibly become *our* story?

* * *

It has been said that people love to learn from people they love. The process starts early and the logic sounds circular, but it is not. The learning takes the individual to a different place, as in the case of a child who is learning from a nurturing parent, and the site where the learning is happening is somewhere between what is known—the child trusts the parent and is familiar with the adult's behavior—and what is unknown—say, the letters of the alphabet (the child is two and a half) or a door that opens to stairs that are dangerous (the toddler is walking and into everything). The child loves the parent and associates learning with that relationship of trust, until of course she doesn't, and begins to test things on her own, either by not answering questions about the alphabet letters ("No, now I'm bored with that and want to turn my attention elsewhere") or by trying to open the door she has been told to keep shut ("Let's see what happens if I do this"). But the bottom line is the feedback loop that is learning happens in the give-and-take between these two living consciousnesses.

The idea that learning and loving are somehow intertwined is about more than that, however, and it is this excess that is the real subject of my story. The cultural products that we enjoy and that inspire us come from somewhere, and that somewhere is not only our personal creativity and agency, but also our biological origins. How is that so? The science writer Matt Ridley has argued that "cumulative evolution requires sex," by which he means that, while sex naturally occurs throughout the animal world, and while, for example, chimp parents teach their offspring to crack nuts, and thus have their version of chimp culture, what allows human culture to expand at exponential rates is *the exchange of ideas* ("ideas having sex") that then creates its own momentum.[1] Put simply, adult chimps from one group don't trade their nut-cracking technique to adult chimps from another group for something in return, but humans do trade their ideas within groups and across tribal lines. In the human realm, the increased specialization that elicited the new idea in the first place causes a knock-on effect when it goes back into the exchange process. Ridley ties the notion of progress to the "meeting and mating of ideas," especially with regard to technological advances.

In the story to follow I would like to push Ridley's metaphor in a different direction. Yes, the combinatory power of advances in technological innovation is a sexy topic. But what if this principle could also be applied to the other end of the cultural exchange spectrum—not ideas as things but ideas as essential psychic transfer, as what gets passed from person to person that allows for human sustainability? In the long run, learning is about not only acquiring the physical and material things to survive but the interpersonal, "eusocial" skills to do so. Ridley compares the head of a prehistoric spear that was made in the same fashion across hundreds of generations to the present-day computer mouse that is constructed out of many different materials and by many hands that do not know each other. What if the idea of a computer mouse could also be the idea of something not concrete and countable but still experienced as real, like curiosity about the living world, especially as that curiosity is elicited in nontangible cultural products, like a literary text, for example? In what ways can that literary text be studied not as a spearhead from the past, but as a computer mouse that speaks to us from the culturally evolved present? That's definitely a challenge, because the spearhead and the mouse are there for us to touch, while the why and the how of "life" in culture is very difficult to grasp indeed. When we venture into the abstract, we lose the sexy. Or, to put it another way, ideas about ideas, however clever, tend to lack purchase in a broader context if they strike us as not sufficiently *embodied*, not part and parcel of *who we are*.[2] Ultimately, they have to reach home to work. How, then, can our strategies for educating the young better align themselves with the human, interpersonal aspect of idea exchange and, without losing sight of the sexy, build upon it?

For my part, I believe the meeting and mating of ideas applies as powerfully to the intangible and noncountable as to the tangible and countable side of things, and obviously I wouldn't be writing these words if I didn't think it was time in our own culture for this story to be told. I also think that progress, if that term can be used at all in good faith within the realm of humanistic study, is about the compounding power of ideas that draw us in their path not toward a reshaping of human nature, which is impossible (at least in measures of time we humans can understand), but toward a continuous revisiting of learning goals and strategies that align more and more closely with the wisdom ("brain" plus "mind") of the living world in its current configuration. What if the "carrying over" (*meta + pherein*) that is metaphoric thinking really does involve actual bodies and genuine erotic attraction? That is what my favorite Russian philosopher Vladimir Solovyov thought more than a hundred years ago, long before neuroimaging suggested a connection between metaphors and sensory-motor systems. And what if the estranged couple we call "brain" (science) and "mind/heart" (humanities) tell us more about how cumulative evolution works the more we bring them, unflinchingly, into productive dialogue with each other? In practical terms, terms that take into account the education of the young, wouldn't it be more useful to look at the different worlds our bihemispheric brain-minds see— the one grasping and analytic (in shorthand, more "left-brain" dominant), the other hanging back and more broad-visioned (in shorthand, more "right-brain" dominant)—and seek out ideas and approaches that build on their continuous and dedicated arousal? This is the way I'd like to push Ridley's metaphor. It still sounds abstract, I grant you, but as I hope to show it is actually concrete, involving real people in real-life situations.

It also bears remembering that our closest relatives among the apes are the chimpanzees and the bonobos, although in species terms (the Pan genus versus the Homo genus) we split from them some six to seven million years ago.[3] Chimpanzees can be shockingly violent, up to and including castrating an opponent, and virtually all of their altercations involve fights over male territoriality and hierarchical dominance. With a high-ranking male's status goes access to females, but lower-ranking teams (normally duos) can conspire to take out the alpha if one of them wants to replace him atop the hierarchy.[4] There is no monogamy; it is more take-what-you-can when the female is in estrus. However, the males can and do perform acts of reconciliation (grooming rituals) after a skirmish, which means that, while the power hierarchies are real, the society functions. Chimpanzees know their places in the hierarchy. Bonobos, on the other hand, are more matriarchal and do not exhibit the violent tendencies toward each other that chimpanzees do. They resolve any tension through acts of rapid and casual sex or eroticized touching. This has led the primatologist Frans de Waal to formulate the basic societal difference between chimpanzees and bonobos thus: "Whereas chimpanzees resolve sexual issues with power, bonobos resolve power issues with sex."[5] In terms of Ridley's "ideas having sex" formula, doesn't this essential difference between how chimpanzees and bonobos resolve conflict, in both cases ending in acts of pure physicality, also say something important about ourselves and how we have adapted and survived? About the long arc of *human* culture? About how we resemble but are also *very different from* our sister species? And about how genuine progress for us can never be the same as brute survival?

* * *

The present book is not intended to be a scholarly tome. For forty years I have worked as a scholar of Russian literature and culture, someone who has written articles and books in which he was attempting to prove an argument buttressed by research and based on facts to a small community of similarly trained individuals. The work was entirely conceptual, in the sense that it had no practical impact on the world in which most of us live, nor was it intended to. It was, in a word, "academic." But the world has changed dramatically, and the academy has changed dramatically, and the way we think about ideas has changed dramatically too. I am writing this book because I am convinced that ideas are more like living organisms than discrete chunks of information and for that reason we have to approach them like bodies that can attach to and transform other bodies, including the interconnecting idea-bodies that are the young people we teach. Richard Dawkins's famous coinage in *The Selfish Gene* (1976) of "meme" as culture's version of gene—the "tunes, ideas, catch-phrases, clothes fashions, ways of making pots or of building arches" that get passed mind to mind, viruslike—has undergone considerable interrogation and refinement in the intervening decades.[6] One prominent voice in the discussion has been the cognitive scientist Daniel Dennett, who wrote in *Darwin's Dangerous Idea* (1995) that "the meme for education [. . .] is a meme that reinforces the very process of meme implantation."[7] Without being coy, I would like to ask what exactly does that mean in more straightforward language, language young people can understand and relate to. It should also be said that the idea of memes ("memetics") in the scientific literature has itself evolved from something particulate and bounded (for example, the "Success Kid" internet meme) to something more broadly formative in the culture. "To understand cultural evolution," writes Steve Stewart-Williams, "we need to understand which memes natural selection favors and which it discards—in other words, which memes survive in the culture and which go extinct." And "Natural selection operating on *memes* doesn't give rise to 'meme machines' exactly, but it does do something similar. It gives rise to ideas and ideologies that, in effect, convert human gene machines *into* meme machines—that is, into beings that devote their time and energy to passing on their memes: their values, their religions, their love of modern art."[8]

My larger point, however, is that machine metaphors ("meme machines"), despite their appeal for tidiness, have limited value when describing organic life, including the life of the mind. Once we've elided memes with people's "values," "religions," and "love of modern art," something has become, well, "squishy," and more is needed (see discussion in afterword). As a committed humanist, lover of Russian poetry, and scholarly agnostic, I remain skeptical that the broad population studies and "big-data" argumentation championed by the hard and social sciences get us closer to the truth of what is happening at the local level of cultural evolution. Those who study the social and natural sciences in a serious manner tend to generalize from large samples of the particular, making their way through trial and error in their laboratories and field work; those who study poetry and poetic culture, especially the culture of a national poet (admittedly a term that is not without its complications these days), tend to generalize from a different set of particulars, not those converging on a middle or average, but those of an outlier who has come to represent something more, in this case *a tradition that evolves*, because that is what seems most "alive" to them. And, as I suggested at the outset, this very "aliveness" all but disappears once we explain it in broad terms. So, without developing the narrative further at this point, I will say only that the many impressive steps forward in the study of cultural evolution, in the works of evolutionary biologists, psychologists, and anthropologists like Michael Tomasello, Peter Richerson and Robert Boyd, Alex Mesoudi, Joseph Henrich, David Sloan Wilson, Kevin Laland, and the aformentioned Stewart-Williams, parallel the shift that took place once nineteenth-century Darwinian natural selection and early twentieth-century Mendelian genetics merged in the Modern Synthesis of the 1920s and 1930s and accelerated in the population genetics of Ronald Fisher, J. B. S. Haldane, and Sewall Wright. In other words, the Darwinian algorithm for natural selection in the biological realm (variation-competition-inheritance) could now be applied to cultural formations. As Mesoudi explains,

> If culture does indeed evolve in a similar way to species, then a similar "evolutionary synthesis" might be possible for the social sciences. That is, large-scale trends or patterns of cultural macroevolution, as studied by archaeologists, historians, historical linguists, sociologists, and anthropologists, might be explained in terms of small-scale microevolutionary cultural processes, as studied by psychologists and other behavioral scientists. We can see the emergence of a unified science of culture, one that transcends traditional social science disciplinary boundaries.[9]

Mesoudi's goal for his project, nothing less than "a unified science of culture, one that transcends traditional social science disciplinary boundaries," fits aspirationally within the academic, in this case social-science, mainstream. More data, more refinement of terms, more deep diving into the Darwinian logic that changed everything.[10] But this book goes in a different direction. It recognizes the inherent power of Darwinian thought, but it also recognizes that that way of framing the world still has its blind spots and needs the humanist perspective.[11] Is there a point at which our deep diving can take us beyond a useful constraining limit, say, the cultural equivalent of the eukaryotic cell, with its parts-to-whole, inside-to-outside homeostatic dynamic, and into the cultural equivalent of subatomic particles, with their random motion no longer analyzable in terms of pattern? Adaptation in the service of sustainability in the cultural realm depends, first and foremost, on recognizing patterns and being able to act on them. Let me give an example of biological patterning that is enhanced by the humanist perspective. The evolutionary biologist Ursula Goodenough writes in *The Sacred Depths of Nature* that

> Life proceeds as a series of shape changes. We might observe three proteins fitting together to assemble a calcium ion channel that spans the cell membrane, and watch the pore of the channel expand in size to allow calcium to enter the cell from the outside. We'd next observe that the calcium flux causes an internal enzyme to change its shape such that certain pockets, previously buried in its interior, become exposed. These pockets are now

available to catalyze some biochemistry, one product of which goes on to induce yet another protein to change its shape. [. . .] And so on. Such a sequence is called an enzymatic cascade—analogous to a series of small waterfalls tumbling down a hill, each feeding the next, start to finish.[12]

Note how her metaphors—pore, pockets, waterfalls tumbling down a hill—enliven the picture, make it *mean*. What a beautiful example of form and content coming together to present the movement of life! It will be the argument of this book that certain literary texts, especially ones enhanced by the aura of their author's lived experience and thus capable of influencing, "infecting virus-like," an impressionable audience, work exactly like this enzymatic cascade, like this representation of *life happening*. Terms and phrases taken from evolutionary biology, such as "emergent," "path-dependent" "multilevel selection," will be applied to the literary texts where the patterning appears appropriate, seemingly generated from within, life-like. For our frame of reference we will steer clear of the professed intelligent designers, those who explain the enzymatic cascade with reference to a higher intelligence. Our position will be somewhere in between Marilynne Robinson's theology (we wonder at the patterning in nature and in culture without trying to outguess God) and Thomas Nagel's philosophy (there is "mind" in nature that can't be reduced to neo-Darwinian physical particulars and is still awaiting its discoverer).

This book, then, is a hybrid in terms of genre, which I'm hoping is appropriate for its time and place: its writing, and thus thinking, is neither strictly "scholarly" nor strictly "scientific" as those words are understood traditionally. In the first place, it is written for a broader literate audience, one who I hope might be intrigued by the idea and the implementation of the Pushkin Project. This audience may have an interest in Russian culture, but it need not have. In the second place, this book is written for a related but situationally adjacent audience—high school students such as I have worked with and taught over the past decade. In this respect, and taking into account that the education levels of the two audiences may not be equivalent, the book attempts to fill in the space between what my students know and have experienced up to now and what they will need going forward into tomorrow's world. Obviously, this space cannot be filled in adequately in the present tense. In my lectures and classroom discussions, which the following chapters detail, much has been boiled down and hinted at telegraphically. But I hope these bright and enterprising youngsters will be able to see in general terms where this learning process is heading and in time will be able to make more sense of it. Their responses, which I cite as thematic entry points at the outset of each chapter and return to specifically in the afterword, suggest they have. At the center of the book, in the space the students are learning about but still do not fully comprehend, are several "virus-like" idea clusters that, when put in play with each other, create the conditions for mind-blowing (as in getting outside of oneself in a good sense) experiences that should prove useful as they prepare to navigate the future: 1) a different culture (Russian) that is not theirs but that they adopt; 2) a challenging language (Russian) that is not theirs but that they learn to communicate in; 3) a cultural hero (Pushkin) who is not theirs but with whom they readily identify; and 4) a body of knowledge (evolutionary science—*but evolutionary science as understood by a humanist*) that relates points 1–3 to their lives in pedagogically convincing ways. With regard to point 4, I freely confess that I approach the mountains of highly specialized work, often dazzling beyond my ken, done in recent decades on evolutionary biology in general and the intersection of the biological and cultural spheres in particular as a layman. I'm no Jared Diamond. But inasmuch as I have succeeded in asking some useful questions, with the culture of literary art being still my primary focus and with the goal of making this art more real to these kids, I will consider the enterprise not to have been a failure.

Last but not least, I want to stress that what follows is not intended to be about the writer of these lines, at least not in a primary sense. Context is necessary, and to the extent that the social nature and underlying idea of this project involved myself I will try dutifully to provide the storyline. Likewise, as counterintuitive as it may sound, the book's aim is not to draw attention to the many outstanding thinkers who have pushed the boundaries of contemporary thought about how culture, or more specifically cultural evolution, works. Rather, it is meant to be about present and future generations embodying their own ideas, for it is to them we are passing the torch whether we want to or not. They are the story's protagonists; they are the ones who have experienced, quite literally, their own plots and their own happy and sad endings. I am confident you will find their learning experiences compelling.

CHAPTER 1

Origins

The Context

To discuss the young people who are the ultimate subject of the Pushkin Project I need to begin with the personal, for that is where the story started.

In this case, the idea originated from extended, beer-lubricated discussions in the pubs of Oxford as I was ending my tenure as statutory professor of Russian studies and fellow of Wadham College in 2011. Pubs like the Lamb and Flag, the White Horse, and the Eagle and Child (this latter a favorite of J. R. R. Tolkien and C. S. Lewis) have traditionally been the incubators of Oxford's brainchildren. One of my colleagues in the Russian area, Rob Harris, had real-world experience in business and entrepreneurship as an erstwhile Budweiser vendor (an interesting background for an academic) and helped me focus on the possible ways to bring together different parties—relevant charities, wealthy donors, senior colleagues in different colleges and campus units—to try to realize an idea that I felt needed to be born. In the years that I worked at Oxford and indeed in my previous decades at the University of Wisconsin-Madison, it had become abundantly clear that the study of humanities, by which I mean mainly but not exclusively literature, history, philosophy, language, was experiencing a seismic realignment, what philosopher of science Thomas Kuhn would call a paradigm shift, and that the expectations upon which those of us who entered the profession in the 1970s and 1980s needed to be fundamentally rethought. Change was coming from the outside in. Students tended to take humanities classes out of interest or to fulfill a requirement but not out of a potential calling. In a word, we were not where the action was.

I experienced this firsthand, if anecdotally, when serving as dean of the college at Wadham and sitting on various committees having to do with student welfare. In this capacity I came in contact with student leaders, including the president of the junior common room, an exceedingly bright and personable young man, who was reading PPE (Philosophy, Politics, Economics) and finishing his last year at Oxford. This was a kid who was clearly *primus inter pares*, with the *"pares"* already being high-flying, and he could have chosen virtually any profession as starting point. When I asked him what his plans were at the end of the school year, he said, with a wry smile that told me he knew he was going where the power was but felt a bit guilty about it, he had accepted a position at McKinsey.

And so, with this and many other examples registering on my consciousness, I gradually came to feel that something ought to be done to reorient our messaging and extend it beyond the arid confines of the contemporary ivory tower. Adapt or perish. To push against this powerful current seemed both necessary and admittedly quixotic. Part of the problem was the poisonous hot air of the culture wars and part was the economic reality that had overtaken colleges and universities in the States and the United Kingdom. The new normal was of course not all that new by then: it was dominating many professions, especially after the stock market crash of 2008. In my world, students were in effect clients, it was their "bums on the seats" that mattered, and it was a department's record of "billable hours" (it's a metaphor, but not really) that could be presented to a dean and counted on a ledger that allowed the unit to grow or shrink. The eerie sense of moving goalposts, the academy's version of Birnam Wood coming to Dunsinane, was everywhere palpable. Tenure existed, but sacred cows could still be gored. Maybe they couldn't come for you individually, at least not yet, but they could come for you as a group, as a discipline in need of downsizing. The fact that Darwin's 200th birthday arrived in 2009 amid much fanfare seemed almost fortuitous, a reminder that we, the professoriate, were also subject to evolutionary pressures, and that we needed to find a way, and fast, to work with or around the change that was defining us. In a word, our profession as humanities teachers was coming face to face with Herbert Spencer's famous description of natural selection after reading *On the Origin of Species*: "survival of the fittest." In this environment we were not particularly fit. What could we do?

The Russian studies aspect of my thinking deserves a special gloss. How exactly did I get here? I had grown up in the post-Joe McCarthy 1950s and 1960s in a middle-class WASP family. My father was a career navy officer (submarine designer), my mother a proverbial homemaker. Our longest place of residence was Newport News, VA. There were four of us siblings, all boys. Within this context, the USSR was always in the background as a kind of monolithic existential threat. The panic-stoking duck-and-cover drills in school wouldn't let us forget the Soviets' nuclear ambitions, while the Rosenberg trial (which I don't recall being aware of) made the culture at large paranoid about the spread of communist ideology. My parents shared this anti-Soviet mindset and I spent my formative years in its bubble. *But everything changed when I learned Russian.* Indeed, the very fact that I even learned Russian was one of those serendipitous happenings we look back on as life-altering. It was now the last stages of the Vietnam War and I was finishing college and needed to decide what to do about military service. I signed up with the navy, eventually making my way to Officer Candidate School (OCS) at Newport, RI. Just before graduation our class was given a test to determine if there were those among us who had the capacity to learn a foreign language, as the government needed linguists for critical language work and these screenings were a way to recruit them. Luckily for me, I scored well and was given the option of studying either Russian or Mandarin Chinese, in an intensive year's course at the Defense Language Institute (DLI), in Monterey, CA. Because I had always loved literature and had been smitten by a survey course on the Russian classics in college—Lermontov's nature-loving, human-despising Pechorin from *A Hero of Our Time* had seemed the essence of cool to me—I chose Russian. As the saying goes, I never looked back. (Ironically, I also ended up barely using my Russian for my one and only active duty posting, this to the NSA, because the war was winding down and as a cost-cutting measure I was offered an early release from the service.)

Studying Russian with native speakers for eight hours a day for forty-seven weeks, using pattern-practice drills and repeating phrases with shifting grammatical forms (primarily noun and adjective case endings and verb conjugations) until they became second nature, was an experience unlike anything I had ever known. Looking back, this approach, so hands-on and so different from old-fashioned grammar-translation models practiced in high schools and colleges at the time, shared features with the "Rassias Method" (after John Rassias) at Dartmouth. Those drills laid a solid foundation and provided the neural pathways that eventually allowed me to say things with a high degree of speed and accuracy. The experience was very intense. Many of the vocabulary items had semantic ties to the military, but we would play with them, creating phrases I remember to this day: "Well, there I've fired a shot . . . hit a duck." By learning to communicate in Russian, and in time reading more broadly and writing in Russian, I came to think in terms of "the other" to the point where I could see my own culture, including its blind spots, from the outside. That's the part that was most life-altering: it turned out that grammatical form played a role not only in what one thought but *how one thought*. Everything that came after—grad school, jobs, the decades as teacher-scholar—followed from this. And it was precisely this cognitive frisson, this sense that my brain had added a different gear, that I eventually wanted to pass on to students in a way they could use to grow up and grow out into a changing world. Looking back on it later, it struck me as not unlike the process of cooptive adaptation/exaptation: say, bird feathers as thermal insulators morphing into bird feathers as flight enablers, only in this case the mental act of learning something for practical purposes was morphing into a new mental space with an entirely different viewpoint (and once in that space I felt as though I was *embodying*[1] a new me).

It also happened that, as time passed, I became increasingly bothered by the fact that the American press greatly distorted what life was actually like for the average Russian, just as the Russian press, with the exception of the *Ekho Moskvy* (Echo of Moscow) radio station, did the same thing, but in the opposite direction. When my generation started as Russianists in the Brezhnev era, we thought the Soviet Union was forever (we were wrong), Solzhenitsyn's heroism something implicitly gesturing toward our Western values (again we were wrong), and the high modernist verbal magic and personal sacrifice for his art of someone like Osip Mandelstam breathtakingly *real* and indeed part of an ongoing tradition extending from Pushkin up to Joseph Brodsky (in this we were right). For us, Russia was the place where the lead-footed state persisted and tsars were reincarnated as first secretaries but also where great literature, and great poetry above all, still mattered. To quote again Mandelstam's friend, another great poet, Anna Akhmatova,

> He conquered both time and space. People say: the Pushkin era, Pushkin's Petersburg. And there is no longer any direct bearing on literature; it is something else entirely. In the palace halls where they danced and gossiped about the poet, his portraits now hang and his books are in view, while their pale shadows have been banished from there forever. And their magnificent palaces and residences are described by whether Pushkin was ever there or not. Nobody is interested in anything else.[2]

This tradition was palpable and it was what was best about Russia, what *deserved* to survive.

My talks with friends in Russia in the early years, which took place mostly around kitchen tables and were cloaked in fears that I was being followed by the KGB (several times I'm sure I was), confirmed this reality. Over time and dozens of visits, my personal experience of the country's mores and rhythms became second nature. I knew the Russian intelligentsia, its educated class, firsthand but also, I thought, the average Russian in the street. By now I spoke the language fluently and felt at home in a variety of situations. I visited museums, palaces, and historical sites and attended operas, plays, symphonies, circuses, public lectures, and literary readings; performed research in libraries and archives and was interviewed on television and radio; eventually owned an apartment in St. Petersburg; visited lawyers' offices to get papers stamped and signed; transferred money between banks locally and internationally; broke my finger in a fitness center and was triaged and X-rayed at a regular, which is to say, frighteningly dark and dingy, municipal clinic; and last but not least, took a gypsy cab late one night to return to my hotel on one of St. Petersburg's islands, was offered, and stupidly accepted, a drugged cup of coffee by the cab driver, was left unconscious in a deserted park after being fleeced of anything valuable (credit cards, gold wedding ring, leather jacket), was found the next day by the police after a manhunt was initiated by a former student with whom I'd been dining the previous evening, and was hospitalized for eight days while my liver was being cleansed of the drug's toxins and I was finally well enough to be flown back to the States. I knew Russia and, despite everything, I loved Russia.

Still, there was something about my love of Russia that requires a bit more information and that is perhaps difficult to comprehend for the layperson. Amid the drabness and desolation of the late Soviet era there existed in the best representatives of the intelligentsia a chasteness of purpose and a deep, abiding love of learning for its own sake that I have never observed to quite the same degree elsewhere. I would even go so far as to say that the very pervasiveness of corruption and double-dealing in the larger culture, from the one-off bribe to the traffic cop to the *blat* (pull, connections, greased palms) that make things happen at the highest reaches of government, had a hand in producing its opposite—transcendent purity and ceaseless dedication to what deserves to survive. Career-enhancing compromises with the regime were still made by many, human nature being what it is, but among the very best of a scholarly breed—individuals like the classicist Sergei Averintsev, the philologist Mikhail Gasparov, the cultural historian Yuri Lotman, and the Pushkin era expert Vadim Vatsuro—ideological matters were avoided as much as possible while the qualitative superiority of their knowledge, its astonishing depth and breadth, was universally recognized by those who encountered their work in any serious way. Often these individuals would drill down into archives to a point of such high resolution that the reader would experience not just reality, but hyperreality. They provided the contextual interstices the verbal art needed to fully come alive. For example, while laying out the historical background to Pushkin's tale "The Queen of Spades," Lotman would show the reader how a period card game like Faro could serve as a peephole into the workings of fate (as then understood) and court favoritism in Catherine's Russia (see chapter six); or, similarly glossing Pushkin's novel-in-verse *Eugene Onegin*, the scholar would explain why dueling protocols, despite their seeming barbarity, were viewed as necessary, because they could vouchsafe the restoration of an aristocrat's honor, while the court system, with its easily bribed judges, could not. Such precise and information-packed annotations grounded Pushkin's writing, made its spirit seem more, not less, real.

It has to be said, however, that something basic changed with the fall of the Soviet Union and the arrival on the scene of postmodernism in its gaudy, free-for-all glory. Social, cultural, religious, and artistic hierarchies got flipped, reshuffled, or otherwise undermined: Pushkin as cultural icon could now be mocked in the performance poetry of Dmitry Prigov; on the consumer front the Soviet gray of "Women's Footwear" (a previous sign on a store) could now be the "Colors of Benetton." Shopping for Western brands was the new opiate of the masses. The export of oil and gas and the mining of minerals, together with foreign investment in this emerging market, became the basis of the post-Soviet economy, while the oligarchs replaced the Soviet elites and an ex-KGB man who promised order replaced the falling-down-drunk Yeltsin. If Stalin could call Pasternak to inquire whether it was worth saving the life of Mandelstam, Putin now had to deal with a punk rock group named Pussy Riot that promoted gay rights and performed irreverent lyrics in a church. Authoritarianism itself had apparently caught the postmodern flu. Now of course, after February 24, 2022 and the invasion of Ukraine this "flu" looks like something much more sinister.

The Idea

But back to the idea. Why did I decide to call the undertaking the Pushkin Project? First, it had to do with the uniquely infectious poetic culture of Alexander Pushkin (1799–1837), Russia's most beloved, indeed universally recognized as most "Russian," hero from its famously literocentric past. Pushkin, much more than Tolstoy or Dostoevsky, is routinely compared in his importance to Russians to Shakespeare in the Anglophone world, but why exactly? Well, my decades-long study of Pushkin had shown me that the quiddity most defining the poet had to do not only with his art's surpassing beauty, which was very real to those who could read, and, perhaps more important, speak aloud the verses, but also with the creative way he transmuted various experiences from his life into his art. As Lotman put it, "like the mythological King Midas who turned everything he touched to gold, Pushkin turned everything he touched into creativity, art."[3] The challenge here of course, one taken up most notoriously by Nabokov in his *Onegin* translation, is: can the Pushkinian quiddity be successfully conveyed to a non-Russian audience? Then there was the second reason to connect my brainchild to Pushkin:

the fact that the poet's African heritage on his mother's side was instrumental in his sense of identity and in crucial aspects of his artistic legacy. I became convinced that this connection was fortuitous and potentially utilizable: Pushkin's life story, his unique ancestry, and his supreme ability to turn adverse circumstances presented to him by life into poems, plays, stories, and novels loved by millions could be repackaged to inspire young people from an entirely different culture, in this case American high school students from majority Latino and/or African-American populations, who may have their own challenging circumstances to overcome. Obviously, to reach today's youngsters more than the abstract idea of "Pushkin" was needed. What that "more than" entailed was key and drew more and more of my attention as matters evolved.

Over the previous decade I had read widely on the topic of biological versus cultural evolution. I had come to this topic because my disenchantment with the status quo—what was happening in the university but also in the larger culture—was forcing me to look more critically at the big picture. I needed another way to explain things to myself and to my students. The spiritual beauty of Russian culture, which one experienced on a personal level when one heard lines by Pushkin or Mandelstam, was no longer so obvious, so objectively real. It's impossible to express precisely this loss in words, to make explicit what is implicit. It's as if one wants to capture the sound and force of the exploding bullet, but one feels one is always stopping short by breaking the thing down into constituent parts.

Let me try to demonstrate with an example. It takes us into the poetic weeds so to speak, which here as elsewhere requires preparatory explanation for the students, but it is necessary to give a sense of the richness of the hidden allusions. When Mandelstam writes in 1920, "In Petersburg we will gather again / As though we have buried the sun there, / And the blessed, senseless word / We will pronounce for the first time,"[4] he ignites a fireworks of streaming, semantically loaded bits that keep discharging themselves with each enunciated syllable in the original: those that know and love Petersburg culture, the culture whose father figure is Pushkin, will meet one last time before the city enters "the black velvet of the Soviet night" (another line); the metaphorical ("as though") sun they have come to bury is Pushkin, the "sun" of Russian poetry (a whole other tradition going back to the metaphor used when Pushkin died and the sun set); the word to be pronounced like a shibboleth is both "blessed and senseless" because that is what poetic language is—sacred and literally nonsensical, non-translatable, at the same time, a combination of sound and sense that asks to be pursued but can never be plumbed to the bottom; and the word will be said for the first time because that is how the virtuous loop works—Pushkin and his tradition will come again, in the language and biographical fatedness of Mandelstam, but they will come as something completely original (another paradox). All this is uttered by the "little man" (*malen'kii chelovek*) poet who by the 1930s will be dashing about Charlie Chaplin-like (another of his avatars) trying to avoid the giant fists of Stalin and in so doing repeating in another loop, a hundred years on, the tragic story of Pushkin's Evgeny in *The Bronze Horseman* (1833), the tradition's echt-Petersburg text, who perishes after being pursued through the city streets by the equine statue of Russia's greatest tsar. These loops are about learning, making the cognitive connections, yes, but they are also about emotion. Being inside Mandelstam's trochees is like being inside a stream of music: instantly there are called up in one's mind stories from the poets' lives as well as stories from one's own life, such as the realization that the Soviet night Mandelstam is gesturing toward may be repeating itself, in a lesser key, in the postmodern night that allows Mandelstam's and Pushkin's words to be mocked, their hierarchy of existential risk turned upside down. Hence the frisson or shivering sensation announcing that one is being pulled forward by something real and something *emerging* (see below).[5]

So, this sense that the spiritual beauty I loved was slipping away pushed me to want to switch gears, to attempt to understand what, in terms of the neuroscience, is actually happening in the human brain as these lines by Mandelstam are being read. *Why* are the lines beautiful, why are they beautiful *to me*, and *can* they be beautiful *to my students*?[6] Such questions are not trivial. Iain McGilchrist, one of the principal guides helping me think my story, has demonstrated in painstakingly researched detail how hemispheric lateralization doesn't exactly cause our experience of the world, but does bring a different "us" to the things "out there" we see and attend to. Aware of how crude shorthand in this case ("left-hemisphere thinking" as compared to "right-hemisphere thinking") can be abused in the popular culture, McGilchrist is careful to point out that the two hemispheres do communicate across the corpus collosum (although that communication tends to be inhibitory[7]) and that they both compensate in the case of a stroke to the other side, but in different ways. Here he describes the elements of the right hemisphere's take on the world:

> These include empathy and intersubjectivity as the ground of consciousness; the importance of an open, patient attention to the world, as opposed to a willful, grasping attention; the implicit or hidden nature of truth; the emphasis on process rather than stasis, the journey being more important than the arrival; the primacy of perception; the importance of the body in constituting

reality; an emphasis on uniqueness; the objectifying nature of vision; the irreducibility of all value to utility; and creativity as an unveiling (no-saying) process rather than a willfully constructive process.[8]

Needless to say, no interpretation, with its left-hemisphere-dominant stab at meaning, can do justice to the experience of a poem by Pushkin or Mandelstam, while the creativity that is everywhere felt in the poem's articulation, which is also a creativity suffused with the residue of lives lived by the poets, is precisely the communicative core that is most important, that is real but incapable of being pinned down ("no-saying"), and that our students, even those who are still relatively untutored and unsophisticated, need to be made aware of, need to begin to understand.[9]

As I thought about what I had been doing for thirty-five years as a college professor I came to the conclusion that I wanted to focus less on the scholarly analysis of literary texts as literary texts, less on interpretation (theorizing plus close readings) for a shrinking audience of my peers, and more on *why* Pushkin's poetic culture was important in the first place and *how* it could possibly translate to an audience that truly needed it. With this in mind I did pretty much an about-face and turned to evolutionary biology for a place to begin a new loop. Why begin there? Because if biology teaches us anything, it is that any species can disappear. And I felt my "subspecies" (as teacher-scholar), if not my species per se, was disappearing. Any big picture describing today must begin with an a priori acceptance that, whoever we are, we can't run from biology as starting point; that we are ourselves primates who, with the help of enlarged brains and the ability, in time, to make tools, socialize with others, and especially important, deploy language, became conscious, able to self-reflect; and that the key to providing a framework for analyzing cultural products needs to have an evolutionary basis.[10] Wherever humanities studies was going, this seemed its terra firma.

Over the next little while, I read all I could about Darwin's life and his two principal works, *On the Origin of Species* (1859) and *Descent of Man* (1871), and I pondered the great naturalist's progress from the first book to the second, especially with regard to his formulations about sexual selection as opposed to natural selection (see chapter four). My interest in this latter contrast was further piqued when I listened to a dynamic young zoologist at Wadham give a talk about her research program in the tropics studying bird-calls, which are usually produced as quick-burst warnings or expressions of territoriality, and bird-songs, which can be complex and require practice and *learning* (Darwin called the latter "true song") and normally are heard during mating season, hence their role in sexual selection. That Darwin referred to birds as "the most aesthetic of animals" and that the learning they were doing to be able to sing was "costly" (the young zoologist and her team had actually dissected the brains of her bird species to tease out neuronally the call/song distinction) seemed powerfully connected in my mind with the first glimmerings of how the "artistic" appears in culture. Then I followed this up during the bicentenary year by making repeat visits to the Darwin exhibits at the Natural History Museum in London. It was also around that time that I attended a standing-room only lecture at Wolfson College to see Oxford superstar Richard Dawkins parse the last page of *The Origin of Species*, including its famous concluding sentence:

> There is a grandeur in this view of life, with its several powers, having been originally breathed by the Creator into a few forms or into one; and that, whilst this planet has gone cycling on according to the fixed law of gravity, from so simple a beginning endless forms most beautiful and most wonderful have been, and are being evolved.[11]

Obviously, for the author of *The God Delusion* (2006), "Creator" was simply Darwin's useful dodge at the time. Funnily enough, this mention of a Deity caused me to reverse course momentarily and read in a more literary direction: to wit, Gillian Beer's groundbreaking *Darwin's Plots* (1983), which probed with great subtlety and historical awareness Darwin's own language and method of emplotting the natural world and which showed how the "romantic materialist" (her phrase) patterns of his thought and writing became constitutive in some of the most important works of nineteenth-century fiction, including George Eliot's *Middlemarch* and *Daniel Deronda*.[12] Within this context I also looked at prolific author Joseph Carroll's various forays into how evolutionary biology is transmuted into literature and culture, beginning with his *Evolution and Literary Theory* (1995).[13]

Thereafter I read classics like Theodosius Dobzhansky's *Mankind Evolving* (1962) and Ernst Mayr's *What Evolution Is* (2001) and histories like Edward Larson's *Evolution* (2004). The evolution of modern evolutionary thought, as it were, the scientists' stories of dramatic discoveries alongside equally dramatic oversights and near misses, turned out to have a kind of literary, plot-rich quality to it. From Darwin's passion for collecting all manner of organic and inorganic specimens during his five-year voyage aboard the HMS *Beagle* (1831–1836), to his epochal hypothesis in 1858 about evolution by natural selection (nearly scooped by codiscoverer Alfred Russel Wallace); from obscure Moravian monk Gregor Mendel's observations on the cross-breeding of traits in pea-plants, published in an 1866 paper that was all but forgotten after his death, to the article's chance rediscovery at the turn of the twentieth century, thereby making possible the so-called Modern Synthesis (Darwinian evolution + Mendelian genetics); from the early twentieth-century mathematical models of population genetics championed by R. A. Fisher and J. B. S. Haldane, to the "adaptive landscape" metaphor devised by Sewall Wright to visualize genotype fitness; from Modern Synthesis-architect Dobzhansky's definition of evolution, in *Genetics and the Origin of Species* (1937), as "a change in the genetic composition of populations,"[14] to W. D. Hamilton's rule (1963–1964) formalizing altruism as a mathematical tipping point[15]—in short, the cast of characters and their explanatory narratives grew and grew and grew.

By the time my study had reached the latter decades of the twentieth century, the neo-Darwinian "gene's-eye view" of evolution reigned supreme. Its DNA information highway from genotype (genetic recipe) to phenotype (actual physical specimen) was viewed as a one-way street—that is, the germ-to-soma logic was virtually unquestioned,[16] while the study of epigenetics was still early stage; likewise, its seeming iron-clad position defending kin selection against group selection was widely accepted. With his take-no-prisoners polemics and celebrity, the post-*Selfish Gene* (1976) Dawkins seemed not unlike a latter-day reincarnation of Thomas Henry Huxley, aka "Darwin's bulldog." Whether E. O. Wilson's controversial (and as time would show unfairly bashed by humanists) sociobiology or paleontologists Niles Eldredge's and Stephen Jay Gould's "punctuated equilibrium," which offered a convincing revision to Darwin's gradualist evolution, from every direction came hordes of swirling facts and competing storylines. I turned to colleagues at Madison and Oxford for help in deciphering it all: Elliott Sober, a distinguished philosopher of biology at the University of Wisconsin, gave me tips on what to read and alerted me on more than one occasion to how the science of natural selection required dedicated scrupulosity in its avoidance of intentionality (something not easy for humanists), and that when nature "chose" it was simply a question of which random trait allowed the organism to gain a differential advantage compared to other like organisms—nothing more or less. While giving lectures myself, this one on Pushkin at Binghamton, I was fortunate to meet prolific author and Evolution Institute founder David Sloan Wilson, who has made a career integrating evolutionary thinking into different disciplines[17] and who explained, inter alia, how the kin selection versus group selection debate dragging on between Dawkins and E. O. Wilson had become something of a red herring in the scientific literature. By the second decade of the twenty-first century the cutting edge had largely moved on to so-called multilevel selection.[18]

With all this as background, I approached the present. I tried to maintain my own objectivity by seeking out middle ground between the reductionism, and openly stated atheism, of Dawkins and Dennett, on the one hand, and the intelligent design arguments, with their Judeo-Christian underpinnings, of those such as Stephen C. Meyer, on the other. The latter especially, in *Signature in the Cell* (2009), *Darwin's Doubt* (2013), and *The Return of the God Hypothesis* (2021), has made a well-researched case that, from the Big Bang, with its ontological status established through infinite-regress-type calculations, to the DNA strands, encoded with mind-boggling amounts of information, the origins and continuance of life on earth depend too much on "extreme fine-tuning"[19] to be anything else than the design of a higher intelligence. My own, as it were, "punctuated equilibrium" position came to the following: if there is a *primum mobile* in today's understanding of the living world, it is the notion of biological relativity, which is defined by Denis Noble as the principle *"that there is no privileged level of causation in biology*; living organisms are multi-level open stochastic systems in which the behavior at any level depends on higher and lower levels and cannot be fully understood in isolation."[20] Organisms are *multilevel* in that regardless of which level we are observing—molecule, cell, tissue, organ—there are initial and boundary conditions that serve to regulate, in a functional way, the lower-level components by higher-level properties. And they are *open* and *stochastic* because they are capable of reacting to stimuli from the outside and because these reactions are not predetermined beforehand, that is, they are randomly distributed. Even at the cellular level there is something like a "cognitive"[21] process going on, with genomes now being discussed in the scientific literature not so much as the organism's brain trust or command center, but more as its set of passive templates or data bases.[22] In other words, at every level of a living organism we encounter feedback loops that make it possible for the level to function properly.[23] And so, these feedback loops apply all the way up the line into the realm of cultural evolution,[24] only at some point their purposiveness (higher regulating lower) shifts from strictly "neo-Darwinian" (chemistry, molecular biology, DNA coding for amino acids) to "neo-Lamarckian" (social learning, construction and transmission of information through symbolic systems). That—the sense of a purposiveness to organic life that is relative without being relativistic (read: postmodern)—was my first main lesson.

Next, language, human beings' special domain, is no longer thought of, or only thought of, in Chomskian terms, as something inherent to the human mind, a universal grammar "organ" (say, something located in the Brocha and Wernicke areas) waiting to be turned on. Rather it can now be seen, as Daniel Dor has argued, as a "communication technology," the very first, that grew out of our social nature.[25] (Although Dor insists on the idea of technology as a way of linking archaic humankind with later developments like the printing press and social networks, in its original instantiation language might be better conceptualized as "technique" or social orientation, a precursor of technology.) Language allowed us, *before* individual speakers were specifically adapted for it and while we were still living in prelinguistic societies, to begin to bridge the gap between experiential, sensory perceptions (what we were seeing in the here and now at the campfire or on the savannah and communicating non-linguistically) and the imagination (what was not directly in front of us but could be pictured in the mind's eye). Plans and strategies for hunting and gathering began to be communicated socially. Dor calls this linguistically based functional capacity the "instruction of imagination." "First we invented language. Then language changed us."[26] Thus was the socially adaptive nature of what became over time all forms of language, including potentially Pushkin's poetic language, my second lesson.

Finally, as modern-day scientists have studied the shift from the purely chemical/biological to the cultural/learned, two additional areas of interest central to our discussion have emerged. First, there is the birth of the aesthetic in nature (the "evolution of beauty," as Richard Prum has termed it in connection with bird behavior), which is inextricably linked to female choice in sexual selection and which, as a crucial inflection point for the animal brain/mind in higher species, created the neural pathways that led to our interest in art or, in the case I was interested in, literary art. The female bowerbird enters the back of the variously festooned bower constructed by the male and, after pausing, *selects* the one that appeals to her as her place for mating. If she doesn't like the "boudoir" that has been prepared for her, she exits out the front before any mating takes place. In Prum's telling, aesthetic desire *coevolves* in a loop[27] involving the aroused subject and the ever more flamboyantly desired object that is not only about the passing on of healthy genes or the attracting of a protective male, which is the neo-Darwinist view, but is also, and more directly, about the arbitrary, non-utilitarian allure of the object per se (cf. the modern-day fashion industry). Here again, we might say, we come to the cognitive-emotional edge of artistically mediated perception. As an aside, the Israeli biologist Amotz Zahavi appeared to have it both ways with his famous "handicap principle" (1975), which telescoped neo-Darwinist logic within the presence of aesthetic attraction. To Zahavi, the peacock's feathers appeal to the peahen as "honest" genetic advertising because its encumbering plumage is so extravagant as to cause the female to perceive the male as being capable of "wasting" its appearance.[28]

Second, considerable attention has been paid in the literature to how the genetic and symbolic systems seem to parallel each other.[29] However, what has been less commented on is how the cybernetic/feedback-loop nature of these parallel systems also seems to hint at a "linguistic" component. If a gene's nucleotides can be seen as "letters," and if the gene itself can be looked at as a "word" (that is, it "codes" for a certain function—"make x molecule"), and if the gene in connection with other genes can produce, "sentence-like," a complex cellular function, then is this set of parallels an analogy or something more organically integral? For Daniel Dennett, the isomorphism has to do with an innate capacity to digitize: "what makes language a potent medium for the transmission of information is that it's digitized in the same way that DNA is digitized."[30] In other words, the analog data that may be cumbersome to store and preserve physically (say, Tolstoy's drafts of War and Peace) is now converted into the zeroes and ones of a lightning-fast and conveniently storable digital computer file. Thus, DNA bases play roles analogous to a human language's phonemes, while those phonemes play roles analogous to a computer language's bits and bytes. Still, how is it that the latent information in gene sequences and the implied meanings in a literary text can be stored and activated in the future?[31] My third and fourth lessons, then, by forcing me to consider the biological basis for what became in humans, over many thousands of years, the aesthetic and the linguistic, brought me back to the "right-brain" metaphorical thinking of Pushkin and Mandelstam with a renewed sense of broad horizons. The poet may want to deny biology as an ultimate cause of his or her poetry, but in the interplay of proximate and ultimate causes that brought the poem into being it seemed to me that biology— organic systems working within organic systems—was, again, a good starting point for our students.

This research into how biology and culture form a coevolutionary spiral pushed me next to consider the social level. In order to move the idea of the Pushkin Project off the drawing board of individual brains and minds, I needed to address the issue of community, the all-important context out of which the "sun" of Russian poetry rose. Here we had another ready-made parallel that could be drafted into service: the idea of Pushkin's school, the Lyceum at Tsarskoe Selo, that played such a significant role in his life. This was the bridge between the one-off phenomenon of genius (Pushkin), which we can tend to discard as an outlier, and the group or species. Regardless of the individual, it all starts with the social context of parent/alloparent and child—the toddler who mimics an action, say the tossing of a ball, that the adult is performing. Culture is initiated in humans this way. The seemingly congenital trial-and-error process that begins on the borderline of the physiological and the conscious and then expands into ever broadening circles (spirals) of learning has animated revisionary ideas like the Baldwin effect (after James Mark Baldwin, who proposed that traits enabling an organism's ability to spontaneously adapt to its environment and learn new behaviors could be gradually passed on to selected offspring as heritable substance[32]) and Jean Piaget's genetic epistemology. Writing toward the end of the nineteenth century, Baldwin was the first to champion the position that learning proceeds "from the external and social to the personal and individual" and that "higher stages [of learning] reorganize and incorporate lower stages," with the result that "adaptations acquired during the lifetime of an individual organism could play a directive role in phylogenetic evolution."[33] Likewise, Piaget's notions of "assimilation" and "accommodation" in early childhood development, which built on Baldwin's "habit" ("the repetition of what is worth repeating") and "accommodation" ("an adaptive process by which new possibilities for action are incorporated"), suggested that this back-and-forth process could produce over time the same results as biological adaptation in the species.[34] Not for nothing did Darwin, Baldwin, and Piaget develop some of their most prescient formulations by observing their own children.

Pushkin was born into an old aristocratic family on his father's side that, while by no means wealthy, endeavored to maintain class pretensions and for that reason constantly lived beyond their means. Home life was on the chaotic side. Pushkin's father Sergei Lvovich ("Lvovich" is the patronymic, "son of Lev," that goes together with the given name in polite address) was renowned for his Gallic wit and exquisite bon mots and for the fact that he could recite Molière by heart, but as a human being he was fidgety, irascible, miserly, and insubstantial. French was the lingua franca at home. The parents read French literature to their three surviving children (Olga, Alexander, Lev), but left their upbringing to foreign-born governesses and tutors. The pudgy and clumsy Alexander was the parents' least favorite child, something he felt keenly. Pushkin's mother Nadezhda Osipovna, known in society as the "beautiful creole," had a mercurial temperament and didn't like to be reminded of her African ancestry: her grandfather, Abram Petrovich Gannibal, a favorite of Peter the Great, was reputed to have been the son of an Abyssinian prince[35] and had an illustrious military career once he reached maturity in Russia, but his personal life had been stormy and marred by scandal. His son Osip, who became Nadezhda's father, was even more painful to recall, as he had left his wife and daughter to run off and marry, illegally, another woman. Unfortunately for Alexander, his recalcitrant behavior and especially his physical features, which he would refer to throughout his life as "my Negro ugliness" (*arapskoe moe bezobrazie*), annoyed Nadezhda Osipovna and caused her to impose humiliating punishments (for instance, having handkerchiefs sewn to the boy's blouse cuffs because he tended to lose them), which left a lasting impression. Luckily, the child found his own entertainment in his father's library of mostly French, often racy, literature, and refuge and warmth with his grandmother Marya Alexeevna and his nurse Arina Rodionovna. From these two women he learned Russian.

In 1811, the eleven-year-old Pushkin was taken by his uncle Vasily Lvovich to St. Petersburg to be enrolled in the Lyceum. The Lyceum was an exclusive boarding school, directly attached to the Catherine Palace in Tsarskoe Selo, the royal summer residence. It was intended for the scions of high-placed families; and it was a stroke of good luck, made possible by behind-the-scenes maneuvering, that Pushkin was admitted. Emperor Alexander I himself inaugurated the school with pomp on October 19 in the presence of the court, the faculty, and the first class of thirty students. The Lyceum was the most progressive liberal arts institution in Russia at the time; its conception was completely new, having been encouraged by the reform spirit of Alexander I's early years on the throne. Pushkin, nicknamed "the Frenchman," was a mediocre student whose main interest was to excel in fencing and pranks. Even so, the boy received at the school the best available education Russia had to offer. Like other students, he was as if inoculated here with an acute awareness of personal freedom and independence and a firm belief in his own inherent worthiness—those "natural rights" belonging to all human beings that were perhaps the most important legacy of eighteenth-century Enlightenment values to imprint its message on these young minds through lectures given by favorite teachers. Even more crucial, however, he found at the Lyceum the real home he did not know with his parents; he made lifelong friends (Anton Delvig, Ivan Pushchin, Wilhelm Küchelbecker) and spent here perhaps the happiest time of his life.

We can see, for example, how Pushkin looked to his Lyceum experience as a heartfelt homecoming in the anniversary poems he wrote regularly to commemorate the school's opening, like this one penned in 1825 when the poet, now exiled to his mother's estate in the north due to intemperate statements regarding atheism discovered in his letters, and further estranged from the father who had agreed to spy on him for the state, raised a glass to far-flung comrades from his own position of total isolation:

My friends, our union is beautiful!
Like the soul, it is as one and eternal—
Unshakable, free, and without care,
It was cemented in the shadow of friendly muses.
Wherever fate may cast us,
And wherever fortune may lead,
We remain the same: the entire world is a foreign land to us,
Our homeland is Tsarskoe Selo. (my translation)

Mythologized space ("Tsarskoe Selo"), future trials and tribulations ("wherever fate may cast us"), creativity and poetry ("friendly muses"), brotherhood and sense of family ("our union is beautiful")—this swirl of thought, sentiment, and memory formed the hatchery that, together with the precocious reading and the hurt of his upbringing at home, prepared the way for creating "Pushkin" from Pushkin.

In my own thinking, I was asking myself what it would take to create something approaching the Lyceum experience for today's kids in need. I want to stress that Pushkin's Lyceum was a phenomenon of a specific time and place and in this respect it could not be replicated. Even if we could clone Shakespeare, he would not be "Shakespeare" if he were born today. But what I was hoping was that certain learning-engendering processes could be set in motion that, organized in our time and place, would unlock creative potential—however we define "creative"—in children with their own context-specific challenges. Fortunately, we already had certain positive factors going for us. In Madison, we had a beautiful campus and the sort of infrastructure, including a pool of well-trained Russian instructors, needed for a precollege program. We also were making our first pass at a set of organizing principles and came up with seven:

1) cognitive "cross-training" to develop creativity and critical thinking skills;
2) use of biography/personal story as powerful anchor for engagement;
3) best practices in language acquisition as a skill and a new way of seeing others (and oneself);
4) integration of advanced topics in the humanities to facilitate self-expression;
5) turning personal adversity to advantage, or the secret of "experiential jujitsu";
6) learning how to learn, or developing learning skills for life;
7) learning "together" as model for mentorship and character development.

The idea within the idea was that we wanted all these seven principles to be operating simultaneously, and by so doing to create a kind of musically choreographed mix that was not linear/sequential, but continuously reinforcing in virtuous loops. Our hope was that out of our efforts would emerge a more creative learning model. In the words of education guru Sir Ken Robinson, "If you look at the interactions of the human brain [. . .] intelligence is wonderfully interactive. The brain isn't divided into compartments. In fact, creativity—which I define as the process of having original ideas that have value—more often than not comes about through the interaction of different disciplinary ways of seeing things."[36]

The Real World

But, to bring our idea to market, to give it traction in the real world, we needed something more: a plan and money. In our case, the plan was to start a series of Pushkin Project initiatives that could take hold in different high schools and eventually become scalable. We believed that teaching Russian to kids from minority backgrounds was a convincing entrée for three reasons: first, Russia was a country whose strategic importance to the United States was not going away,[37] and specialists in this area (and downstream, jobs for those specialists) were going to continue to be needed in the future; second, achieving a measurable level of competency in a language traditionally thought of as difficult would look particularly impressive on college admissions applications coming from low-income minority students; and third, Pushkin's own background and identity formation would give students something they could relate to. With regard to our finances for the project, all we had to begin with was the funding that went with my Vilas research chair at the University of Wisconsin plus some modest cash reserves from other sources that could help subsidize the first iteration of our planned summer program. In other words, the resources we had at our disposal were at best of the seed variety: sufficient to cover travel costs, a project assistant, summer teaching posts and resident counselor salaries in Madison, but not enough to pay for new positions at partner schools (a potentially large and ongoing expense). It was the eternal chicken-and-egg problem: a school needed to already have Russian instruction, something exceedingly rare in the first place, for it to even consider incorporating our version of a summer residential, "Pushkin-centered" Russian learning environment. And if no Russian was available at a candidate school, we had to convince the school administration to jury-rig something temporary to see if our idea would work.

As I was trying out my idea on friends, I made the mistake of most ivory tower-dwellers: because I thought my big idea was exciting and, like a matryoshka doll, had nested within it other powerful and mutually reinforcing smaller ideas (language acquisition, Pushkin and creativity, Pushkin and race, life on a college campus), on its own it would be simple to sell and would translate quickly into something scalable. How wrong I was! My first lesson was that the "turf" and the money that goes with that turf are already everywhere occupied. Moreover, if one does the research, one discovers that the individuals who not only conceive of but also *make happen* innovative learning structures that shift the paradigm—people like Geoffrey Canada of Harlem Children's Zone or Eva Moskowitz of The Success Academy Charter Schools—are typically visionary and "all in" at the same time. What this also means is that, with a problem as complex as K-12 education in this country, it is almost impossible to be a difference maker if one is a late arrival to the conversation and does not have the means or the influence to be heard. This was my learning curve, and it was steep.

In any event, after months of research and discussion it was finally time for us to enter the fray. We had multiple leads, but to begin with we focused on two schools: one in East Orange, New Jersey, and the other in Chicago. The reason these schools, and not others, were chosen was because they offered different entry points—different ways of addressing the chicken-and-egg problem—for growing our idea. Our experiences at these two schools taught us a lot about what is possible, and not possible, across today's secondary education landscape. In this regard our biggest comeuppance was the realization that a top-down approach, that is, one wielding influence from above to gain an audience and leverage, tends not to be successful on its own, and that a bottom-up approach, in which difference-making stakeholders at the ground level engage with other similar stakeholders, is the one most likely to make significant headway in the end. We had an "in" at the Cicely Tyson School of Performing and Fine Arts in East Orange through Lana Israel, who was friends with the famous actress and knew how much the latter cared about finding innovative ways to inspire the kids at her school. Lana put us in touch with Carl Foster, the director of the Cicely Tyson Foundation, who after consulting with Ms. Tyson agreed to a meeting in Manhattan at which we could make a pitch to her and Carl about the Pushkin Project and its potential fit for the high school that bears her name and honors her roots. The meeting took place in April 2011 and by all appearances went off successfully: Ms. Tyson knew about the poet's work and his African heritage and kindly proposed that we have another meeting the following day in East Orange with the school administration.

The administration and teaching staff at the CTS were welcoming yet understandably cautious. We were bringing something new, and, like most large urban high schools, their agendas were ostensibly settled for the year and their planning structures offered minimal space for maneuvering. The CTS, which is composed of a middle school and high school, and which serves a community that is primarily African-American, is housed in modern, immaculately maintained buildings and supported with lavish levels of technology. As we were being shown around, it was clear that both the staff and students were justly proud of their home away from home. The vibes were positive. The halls were orderly during class breaks, the then principal Dr. Stephen Cowan was cheerfully directing traffic, and discipline did not seem to be a problem. By all indications, it was an excellent high school with a strong, across-the-board curriculum, but it was also more than that. The technologically integrated classrooms and auditorium-cum-modern theater venue were all geared toward the performing arts—music, drama, cinematography, animation, drawing, and design—the cluster of subjects inspired by the school's famous patron. Ms. Tyson was present during our meeting and mentioned how she had learned about Pushkin's black heritage and his importance to Russian culture during her trip to that country. Inasmuch as everyone, staff and students alike, obviously deeply respected her (the students immediately noticed her in the hall and ran up to greet her) and inasmuch as she made the connection between Pushkin as creative black man and Pushkin as useful role model, it seemed like we began with some credit we could draw on. The administrators present expressed interest in our idea and quickly proceeded to explain the arcane nuances of New Jersey public school policy regarding hiring new faculty, since there was no one on staff who could take on teaching Russian to underclassmen, which was what we needed as a starting point.

But, after much effort and expenditure of our limited resources, this promising lead did not pan out. The story of our failure is particularly telling, as we came to the situation with enthusiasm and with an unorthodox idea that could have worked under the right circumstances, but all this had to be accepted organically into the existing culture at CTS, and that was a problem, not necessarily CTS's. First, we needed to get permission from the higher authorities (the education board) to make a temporary hire, called an Artist in Residence (AiR), who could begin to instruct interested students in *ab initio* Russian. To do that, however, we would need a prospective curriculum/lesson plan to show them what we intended to do. At this point, the Pushkin strand as pedagogical tool and the principle of cognitive cross-training had to be put on the back burner, as they were essential elements of the yet-to-happen summer residential program, while all our efforts now had to go into creating Russian instruction.

Once again, chicken and egg. The amount of money involved in the AiR position was small ($5,000), but it had to be voted on and allocated. We also had an experienced and available candidate in mind for this starting position, and we were able to present her resume together with our initial proposal, but she had to withdraw for health reasons. This pushed us to a plan B, which was a search for a properly certified individual in the local area. In the meantime, we made several visits to the CTS to present the Pushkin Project to students and their families and to interview a beginning cohort. Additional misfires from our end included sending long, instruction-filled emails (read: "TMI") to our primary contact person, a kindly senior guidance counselor, who was obviously very busy with her responsibilities and could not answer quickly, presumably because she hadn't heard back herself regarding our various queries.

My sense from all this was that we were speaking too much *our* language while not hearing sufficiently what was being said in *their* language, perhaps not a good sign in an undertaking that was all about language comprehension in the first place! The process dragged on through the fall of 2011 and into the spring of 2012. Instead of being able to create an AiR position that could meet with students four times a week and serve as a dry run for a full-time position, we were informed that we could hire someone for twice a week and that prospects for the full-time position were tenuous at best. As my colleague Rob Harris, who was handling most of the back and forth, wrote me in a moment of pique, "It appears that we request A, and sometime later we hear we are going to get B, and there is no discussion of whether we can repropose C given the rules and conditions." Rob's frustration was understandable, but looking back now at the situation I see clearly the implicit problems with the top-down approach: first, CTS had its own hierarchy of activities and its own buzzing hive life; second, this was a public school environment, and the levers moving the New Jersey school board bureaucracy had to be pulled patiently and without drama; and third, although we had Ms. Tyson's initial blessing, we were still outsiders and the blitzkrieg nature of our two-day visits did not in the end translate into a level of trust. After hiring an AiR in spring 2012 who taught a small group of kids the rudiments of the Russian alphabet and a few phrases, we dropped the program the following academic year for lack of sufficient buy-in. The short version of our amicable divorce: a long-distance relationship that fell apart because there was not enough holding the two parties together.

Our second attempt to launch the Pushkin Project was more successful. In this case we found a charter school in the Chicago area that was serving a minority, primarily Latino, community and that already included two years of required Russian in its curriculum. *This made all the difference.* The school was located in the Hermosa neighborhood of northwest Chicago, a tough area known for its gang violence (usually involving the Maniac Latin Disciples and the Spanish Cobras), but also blessed with a school, Pritzker College Prep, that featured a charismatic principal, a highly dedicated staff, and a track record of success virtually unrivaled in the Chicagoland area. By the time I met Principal Pablo Sierra and his lead Russian teacher, Phil Stosberg, in 2011, the Noble Network of charter schools had ten campuses and served 6,000 students; today they have eighteen campuses and serve 12,000 students. Penny Pritzker, entrepreneur and civic leader from a famous Chicago family, and subsequently secretary of commerce in the Obama administration, gave the school its name when she endowed it with an initial sponsoring sum in 2005. Sierra, who is of Puerto Rican descent, grew up in Chicago and was well aware of the challenges facing black and brown kids in need of better educational options. Short and powerful, he exuded confidence and an openness to new ideas at the same time. He was also someone who had walked the walk. He had tried his hand in various career options after finishing undergraduate work at the University of Illinois, eventually completing an MBA at Northwestern. Sierra's path to the field of secondary education was circuitous, but once he arrived he was passionate about it. He was hired by Michael Milkie, the superintendent of the Noble Network, and after establishing his bona fides was asked to serve as founding principal of Pritzker College Prep when the school opened its doors in 2005. Sierra had a knack for hiring and mentoring outstanding young teachers, many of whom were alumni of Teach For America (TFA). Thanks to the fact that Milkie had studied Russian at Indiana University and thought it would be a good challenge for his students to do the same at the original Noble campus (located on *Noble Street*), Sierra followed suit and made Russian a requirement at Pritzker. Needless to say, without this fortuitous circumstance we would again have been faced with an irresolvable chicken-and-egg situation.

As opposed to the Cicely Tyson School's impressive physical plant, Pritzker College Prep was housed in an old pedestrian-looking brick building rented from the Chicago Catholic diocese. From the beginning, the Noble Network campuses, whose mission was to serve poorer urban neighborhoods, were the stepchildren of the Chicago Public School (CPS) system. The fact that Noble had more flexibility in how it operated each campus meant that it was perceived as a threat to the Chicago Teachers Union (CTU) and thus, as a matter of policy, was not offered existing space within the system when the Network needed to expand. Not only did each new campus have to search out a sponsor with deep pockets, it also had to find and secure appropriate rental space on its own before it could open, and this was always a challenge.

Sierra was a creative thinker, but he was also a strict disciplinarian. He felt that the social dynamics in the Hermosa neighborhood—what the kids were learning at home when there were bad role models and in the streets when they saw childhood acquaintances joining the gangbangers—could not change unless the children's attention was radically redirected at school. Before the kids were old enough and mature enough to take responsibility and "own it," they needed to be coaxed to look at, and see, things differently. The disciplinary code at Pritzker read as follows on the 2011–2012 school website: "A well established and consistently enforced merit and demerit system ensures an environment conducive to learning. Rules and consequences are clearly communicated. Students are given demerits when they violate rules defined in the school/student/parent contract. Additionally, the strict uniform policy requires dress shoes and belts, as well as a tucked-in school polo shirt." The connection between this rare flower of a school in the midst of an urban environment where secondary education was failing and the example of Pushkin's Lyceum in which Enlightenment principles, first and foremost natural rights, were taught to a small group of fortunate teenagers amidst a sea of church-run, that is, typically obscurantist, schools in early nineteenth-century Russia came home to me. To change a group mindset, you have to start small and offer an alternative version of community. Or, to quote David Brooks, "It is an immemorial law of human nature that behavior change precedes and causes attitudinal change."[38]

In any event, as we observed students circulating through the building's aged hallways wearing maroon polo shirts with Pritzker logos and khaki pants, we noticed that they were encountering all along the way college pennants and school mottos ("Be noble!"). A tradition that jumped out at us involved the ritual of introducing a visitor to a classroom in session: the individual would knock on the door and a student representative would come out into the hall, look the outsider in the eye, and calmly explain in good English what the class was about and what was being taught on that day. At every level of teacher-student interaction stress was placed on preparing these young people to succeed in the world beyond. As their website read at the time, "Through the dedicated work of our teachers, Pritzker College Prep is the highest performing high school (as measured by ACT (EPAS) freshmen-to-junior point growth) in the entire Chicago Public School district—including the nine highly Selective High Schools. The Chicago Public School district is home to over 140 high schools." Sierra and his teachers and staff burst their buttons with justifiable pride over the fact that 94.5% of Pritzker's students were low-income, as defined by the federal poverty level, and 90% were first-generation college students, and this despite the fact that the school was non-selective and provided admission by lottery. In 2011 and 2012, the first two years Pritzker graduated senior classes, they enjoyed a 100% four-year college acceptance rate, with many students going to top public and private institutions of higher learning. "The Noble Street charter schools . . . have college-going rates that even suburban schools would envy," wrote Stephanie Banchero in *The Chicago Tribune* (January 14, 2010).

You can't step in the same river twice, but the trick is to find a different but equally promising river and to step in it a first time. As we established our relationship with Pritzker College Prep in the spring of 2012 and made plans to inaugurate the Pushkin Summer Institute that June, I kept asking myself how could our version of Pushkin's school give to these kids from the Hermosa neighborhood the kind of cultural capital that the poet and his schoolmates drew upon as they looked back on their time spent at Tsarskoe Selo. Pushkin's favorite professor at the Lyceum (the teachers were called professors and in several cases possessed professor-like qualifications) was Alexander Kunitsyn, who, "intelligent, eloquent, and highly educated," exuded *amour-propre* and never tried "to ingratiate himself with the authorities."[39] In a sketch done by one of Pushkin's classmates in which several of the professors are scampering up a plank (a kind of career ladder) to pay homage to the then minister of education Count Aleksei Razumovsky, Kunitsyn is standing at the bottom and has his back turned to the grandee.

The point is that, then as now, children know instinctively who is his own person and they respect that. "Kunitsyn taught . . . those disciplines [literally 'sciences,' *nauki*] on the basis of which the pupils learned about 'positions' (responsibilities) of the man and the citizen. These were logic, psychology, morality, private natural law, public natural law, popular law, Russian civic law, Russian public law, Roman law, finances."[40] Nowhere else in Russia were educators talking about these subjects in this way. The schoolboy Pushkin saw the connection between Kunitsyn's independence and integrity as a person and his message of the inherent right to respect of every human being, including the illiterate and downtrodden Russian serfs. It's not too much of an exaggeration to say that the moral philosophy Pushkin gleaned from Kunitsyn, once it had sunk in, played a role in helping to rid him of his frequent displays of shallowness and his eagerness to, as the Russian says, reach into his pocket for the *krasnoe slovtso*, the sparkling witticism, something that consistently got him into trouble in his youth, since his puns and epigrams were often aimed recklessly at those in authority. Kunitsyn's example inculcated in the poet the humanistic gravitas and political and social broad horizons that were so obviously lacking in his father Sergei Lvovich, uncle Vasily Lvovich, and brother Lev. As Pushkin wrote in a draft of one of his Lyceum anniversary poems: "To Kunitsyn goes a tribute of the heart and of wine! / He created us, he nurtured our flame, / It was by him that the foundation stone was laid, / By him was our pure icon lamp lit" ("19 October 1825").

And so, we proceeded into the summer hoping to nurture a few flames and light a few icon lamps of our own.

CHAPTER 2

PSI: Implementation

On Sunday, June 24, 2012, the Pushkin Summer Institute at the University of Wisconsin-Madison officially opened its doors as a six-week residential program for rising seniors from Chicago's Pritzker College Prep. Our first group of twelve was selected in consultation with the students' teachers, a pattern we would repeat as time went on. A formal application process was instituted earlier that spring. The teachers composed letters describing the students' academic and personal progress to date, and the students wrote applications telling us why they wanted to participate and providing us with samples of their written Russian. Those students who applied and were accepted to the PSI were ones we felt most wanted the opportunity and could most benefit by it. To school administrators (and eventually grant officers) we listed the program's primary goals as follows: to build and improve students' Russian language abilities; to cultivate critical thinking, reading, and writing skills; to stimulate student interest in Russia and Russian studies; to prepare students for the demands of college life; to expose students to the opportunities available at the University of Wisconsin-Madison and in the Madison community. Amongst ourselves, however, we saw the big picture in larger aspirational terms. We had a hunch that, once we saw our core principles in action, once the pedagogical strategies of cognitive cross-training, character development, and community building (the Lyceum!) began to interact with each other on a day-to-day basis, the students themselves would let us know that the summer was changing their lives in unanticipated ways, opening doors they didn't know existed.[1] (NB. Subsequently, exit interviews and follow-up communications confirmed this.) More modestly, we also believed that simply living away from home on a Big Ten campus and having the PSI's course of study recorded on one's high school transcript would be beneficial for those applying to college from our demographic.[2]

After being seen off by parents at the departure site at Pritzker, our students made the three-hour-long drive to Madison by bus. As they were minors, they needed to be chaperoned. That job fell to Pritzker colleague Phil Stosberg.

Phil had been indispensable to us that spring helping us set up the program on the Pritzker end, and he had an excellent rapport with the students not only as teacher but also as popular jazz band director. Also fortunate for us was the fact that Phil had agreed to live in the dorm with the students that first summer to ensure they were taking their studies seriously and there were no disciplinary issues. As soon as the students arrived in Madison, they were settled in their new home-away-from-home, Kronshage, one of the university's Lakeside Dorms. Their meals, beginning that evening at the opening ceremony, were served at Carson Gulley, a nearby cafeteria. Classes started the next day, Monday, and were conducted a five-minute walk away in Van Hise Hall, the campus's center for language instruction. In their welcome packets were included bright red University of Wisconsin "Bucky Badger" tee shirts emblazoned, in Cyrillic letters, with a famous Pushkin line on the back, "Burn the hearts of people with the word."

An intensive summer program like ours for high school-age students needed to provide a welcoming environment where learning could take place both inside and outside the classroom. Our senior language instructors, Anya Nesterchouk and Anna Borovskaya-Ellis, who would be with us from the beginning, found myriad ways to combine the best Russian nurturing instincts with a high degree of rigor. We wanted our curriculum and scheduling to straddle the borderline between a fun summer camp and a serious, college-like academic experience. In this connection, we blended lots of schoolwork with field trips to places like the Wisconsin State Capitol, the Vilas Zoo, and Blue Mound State Park. The University of Wisconsin-Madison campus, which extends along the shore of Lake Mendota, is lush and beautiful in the summer, while the city of Madison, with its downtown situated picturesquely between two large lakes (Mendota and Monona), is alive with outdoor activities. Favorite outings over the years for our students have included roasting marshmallows on Picnic Point (the campus's lakeshore nature preserve), watching movies on Memorial Union Terrace, kayaking on Lake Wingra (another local lake), and observing the July 4 Shake-the-Lake fireworks display from the shoreline of Lake Monona.

The residential component of the PSI was especially important to us, as it reinforced the work students did in class through nightly tutorial sessions. Tutorials were led by our residential counsellors (RCs), all of whom were current University of Wisconsin-Madison Russian majors. Students "contracted" to speak Russian during meals, group travel, and in all academic settings. The RCs not only reinforced the material covered in the classroom through the tutorials, language games, and showing of movies, they also helped the students adjust to the increased personal responsibilities of life in the dormitories as well as to the issues of time management they would inevitably encounter in college. The fact that, once we got started, most of our RCs were alumni of the summer program, and in many cases knew the students coming to us in subsequent years, added continuity and provided a growing cast of older sibling-type role models.

Because our success was directly related to the quality of our instruction and what the Brits call pastoral care, that is, being sure the kids' emotional, physical, and intellectual well-being is being attended to, we avoided trying to scale our enterprise upward with large numbers, even though there was increased demand as time went on. We found our ideal number of instructors to be four, with these rotating among two groups (of ten to fifteen people each) daily, and our ideal number of RCs was also four. Enrollments grew over the years and settled in the mid-twenties: 22 (2013), 22 (2014), 26 (2015), 26 (2015), 30 (2017), 28 (2017), 24 (2019). In years 2013–2016 the PSI also drew students from the original Noble Street campus, while beginning in 2017 it added the Noble Academy (TNA), another campus founded on Pablo Sierra's initiative and located near the site of the recently razed Cabrini-Green projects. The TNA's role as a Noble campus was unique and showed to what extent the charter school model, despite its constraints, could aim high: in this case Sierra had liaised with educators at Phillips Exeter Academy and with their input instituted their celebrated "Harkness method" of instruction as curricular centerpiece at the new inner-city campus. According to this approach, named after the oil magnate who made the initial gift to Exeter to underwrite the innovation, students sit around an oval-shaped table and direct discussion on an assigned topic while a faculty member facilitates. The result is greater buy-in and intellectual ownership on the part of the students.

Curriculum

Clearly, there are good developmental reasons for learning a new language and culture. Anyone who has experienced this knows it. Such study takes one out of one's habituated self and forces one to begin to look at the world through another's eyes. Most of our students are bilingual—fluent in Spanish and English—to begin with; their brains are ready and, cognitively speaking, eager to make this jump. In a happy coincidence, Pushkin's classmates at the original Lyceum were also bilingual, with French being the langauge of the higher classes and Russian being the language of everyday life.[3] Recent research has shown that "bilingual experience can lead to greater brain matter density and volume in regions associated with sensory processing, such as the primary auditory cortex

(PAC), as well as executive function, such as the prefrontal cortex (PFC). The behavioral correlates of these physical changes can be significant, as greater gray matter in Heschl's gyrus (in the PAC) predicts better speech perception, while the increased gray matter in the PFC is associated with enhanced cognitive control."[4] Put simply, if one is already bilingual, one has a greater capacity to learn another language.

As mentioned, PSI's academic program features both a Russian language component and a literature component. Both academic strands are conducted simultaneously over six (since 2019 five) activity-packed weeks. For Russian instruction, students meet for four hours a day in the classroom on top of study halls/tutorials in the evening lasting 1.5–2 hours. In addition to the language classes, workshops on Russian culture are held several times a week. These cultural workshops cover such topics as making *bliny* (Russian crepes), Russian superstitions, etiquette when visiting a Russian home, Russian folk music and dance, Russian rock bands, and so on. The PSI's goal in terms of linguistic competence is to advance students from the "Novice Mid" level to the "Novice High" and "Intermediate Low" levels on the ACTFL (American Council on the Teaching of Foreign Languages) scale. It is common for us to exceed these goals.

Language Instruction

An important innovation in our language curriculum was the "Passport to Russia," which was instituted in 2017. Upon entering the program, each student receives a PSI passport, in which he or she completes self-assessment forms based on weekly "can-do" statements and collected "stamps" and "visas." These self-assessments are in turn designed around weekly themes and questions: "Entry Visa / Introducing Ourselves," "Where We Live," "Our Habits," "Our Likes and Dislikes," and "Shopping in Russia: Clothes and Presents." The passport concept was created by Anya Nesterchouk, whose native competency in Russian, flawless English, prior work with nonprofit language schools, and broad experience as ESL (English as Second Language), EFL (English as Foreign Language), and RFL (Russian as Foreign Language) instructor and administrator at the University of Wisconsin-Madison made for a perfect fit. The lead instructor and curriculum designer at the PSI from its inception, Nesterchouk became the onsite director of the program in 2018.

Our curricular design for teaching Russian is grounded in the latest "Standards for World Language Education."[5] Students use Russian in the three principal modes of communication (interpersonal, interpretive, presentational) daily, both within and outside the classroom. Their activities when using the language include: engaging with topics and opinions related to their daily lives; interpreting written texts in Russian; describing aspects of Russian history, geography, and culture. Students also demonstrate an understanding of the relationship between artifacts and practices of Russian culture by exploring Russian social networking sites; shopping for and cooking Russian food; role-playing Russian customs; experiencing Russian culture through its music, movies, fairytales, and cartoons; and participating in Russian folk dancing and costume-making workshops. Extracurricular activities are normally conducted in the target language and provide opportunities to practice Russian outside class. Over time, and as our program has evolved, we have made corrections to find the right pedagogical balance for today's students between the fun of using the idioms of a new language in interpersonal communication and the grind of memorizing vocabulary lists and internalizing grammatical structures that will lay the foundation for subsequent mastery. Experience tells us that if the old-fashioned grammar-translation methodology went too far in one direction, then the modern-day communicative-competency methodology may be going too far in the other and needs to be adjusted.

Literary Studies

The literature component of the academic program centers on the life and works of Alexander Sergeevich Pushkin (1799–1837), Russia's national poet. Here it is incumbent upon me, playing the role of a modern-day Kunitsyn, to find ways to communicate the Pushkinian quiddity, the "Pushkin" in Pushkin. Over the years, my goal has been to introduce the kids to the themes and memes (the pun-based plot kernels) in the short texts we cover that are particularly "Pushkinian" and then to get the students to react to them. Principal among these are the following idea clusters: connecting inspiration to acts of language (the poem "The Poet," the first week's assignment); finding the false hero in macho behavior (the tale "The Shot," the second week's assignment); deciding between filial loyalty and mate choice (the tale "The Stationmaster," the third week's assignment); experiencing racial bias in the majority culture (excerpts from the historical novel *The Blackamoor of Peter the Great*, the fourth week's assignment); playing fairly in the game of life (the tale "The Queen of Spades," the fifth week's assignment); and weighing the cost of happiness (the short play *The Stone Guest*, the sixth week's assignment). Each Pushkin theme-meme week commences on Sunday evening when I distribute to the students a prompt sheet about the upcoming text, which has already been read. This sheet introduces ideas to be covered in the formal one-hour English-language lecture on Tuesday. The students are cued as to what to look for and how to construct a context for understanding Pushkin's ideas, language, plot, character types, and, most important, facts from his personal life that he was deploying under the surface, pushing off creatively, in his art. Often I instruct them to google certain concepts, proper names, or historical facts and be ready to discuss them at lecture.

The lecture on Tuesday typically requires that I do a pedagogical dance between informing and questioning/engaging. Depending on sleep patterns and activity levels, students can arrive in class tired or energized/alert. With the handouts I pass out at lecture, which are different from the prompts, I ask the students to read aloud certain passages from the assigned text. These readings with bolded sections and Russian language glosses demonstrate the extent to which Pushkin was embedding salient aspects of Russian culture in his linguistic play. For example, in the story "The Snowstorm," another text we read, the hero Vladimir convinces the heroine Marya Gavrilovna (Masha) to elope under the influence of French sentimental novel plots, something the mature Pushkin is making fun of. The two young people have decided Masha's parents are "cruel" (à la the French model) since they (the parents) feel Vladimir, with his low status and meager prospects, is not an appropriate match. But these Russian parents are not cruel—they love their daughter, which they show at every turn, and this makes it difficult for her to go through with the elopement, which she does anyway. "Fate" intervenes in the form of the eponymous snowstorm, which draws Vladimir and his sleigh away from the site of the secret marriage. In the meantime, the fetching bride is married by mistake to someone else, something we learn only in the story's denouement, when the actual sequence of events is finally revealed. It turns out that, as the wedding was set to take place, out of nowhere a young officer rides up, steps into the groom's position, and on a lark goes through with the ceremony. The heroine, distraught by the long wait for the hapless Vladimir, doesn't know she has married someone else until she turns to kiss her new husband. The point is that playful, irresponsible behavior, which was Pushkin's trademark as a young man, can lead to disastrous results and come back to bite one later, a prospect the poet himself was fretting about as he wrote the story on the eve of his own wedding. Be that as it may, "The Snowstorm" has a happy ending: Burmin, the more "attractive" hero, whose name derives from "storm" (*buria*), confesses to the heroine after he has become acquainted with her years later that, while he loves her, he cannot wed her. Why? Because he is secretly married to another and has no idea who or where she is. Believing they can't marry, the couple discover that they are already man and wife. Hence Burmin, the one-time rogue, ends up with the bride he was supposed to marry, which is also what Pushkin is hoping for by marrying the beautiful but young and inexperienced Natalia Goncharova.

Perhaps even more revealing than the musical-chairs plot and its authorial "tell," however, is the folk wisdom and theme-meme wordplay at work in the story: the doting parents, who are worried about their daughter when she comes down with fever in the wake of the ill-fated elopement and who are convinced her ravings mean she still loves Vladimir, agree that maybe the penniless sublieutenant isn't so bad after all and comfort themselves with the hackneyed adage "You can't escape your fated one even on horseback," which can be rendered freely in English as "marriages are made in heaven." Russians love their poet above all others because he captures so unerringly who they are, how they think, what constitutes their common humanity. Moreover, the saying is funny because that is *actually what happens in the story*. Vladimir is pulled away from Marya Gavrilovna with one hand (Pushkin the author acting as "fate") and Burmin, the better match, is pulled toward her "on horseback" with the other. *Suzhenogo konem ne ob"edesh'*: the words of the saying are said aloud by me in class and then repeated by the students. Obviously, they can't get the puns yet, but they can begin to see how the playfulness works.

The remainder of the Pushkin-strand week for the students involves drafting a two-and-a-half-page essay on the prompt and attending writing workshops held by instructors from the University of Wisconsin-Madison Writing Center. These workshops focus on different aspects of expository writing (rhetorical strategies, thesis statements, topic sentences, transitions, useful idiomatic phrases, typical errors in grammatical usage) as well as practical advice for composing a successful college admissions essay. On Thursday morning students submit the first drafts of their essays, and then on Friday afternoon they meet with the writing instructors and me to go over their work in one-on-one consults. By Sunday evening and the distribution of a new prompt the students are responsible for revising their essays based on the consults and submitting them for a grade on the assignment. Through these hands-on consultations and workshops, the PSI endeavors to sharpen the critical thinking and writing skills students will need to succeed in college. As anyone who has taught college students in recent decades knows, writing skills have deteriorated dramatically among otherwise bright and conscientious students. By the end of the PSI program the more verbally adept of our students are writing clear and persuasive essays at the University of Wisconsin-Madison college level.

Graduation Ceremony

The crowning event of the Madison PSI is the graduation ceremony, which takes place at the end of the program, the evening before the students return home. A memento of the event's celebratory atmosphere is the photo taken from the 2019 ceremony at the front of the present book. All the students dress up in their best clothes and come to the final dinner and awards ceremony abuzz with excitement. Each year, alumni from previous summers ask if they can attend and as many places as possible are saved for them at the festivities. Parents also make the trip from Chicago to see their children at the event.

The graduation ceremony is important because it weaves together the program's different strands and creates memories our impressionable charges won't soon forget. In this way, though centuries removed and in a lesser key, it replicates the ceremony at Pushkin's Lyceum when the first group of youngsters graduated from the lower form to the upper form and the budding poet read his ode-like, post-Napoleonic "Reminiscences at Tsarskoe Selo" in the presence of Russia's greatest cultural figure from the previous century, the famous odist and advisor to Catherine the Great, Gavrila Derzhavin. In Russian culture this is universally recognized as the moment when the torch of tradition was passed to the precocious fifteen-year-old and the old man Derzhavin was reputed to have exclaimed, "I have not died, this is the one who will replace me."

Once all the PSI students are seated and have settled down, the festivities begin. The evening's program typically opens with a reading of a Pushkin poem selected specifically for this year's group and their accomplishments. The poem has been printed out and is distributed to the audience. Stress marks, always a challenge for beginners, have been placed in the xeroxed copies. I lead the reading, first enunciating each line and through slight exaggeration alerting the audience to the rhythmical beats in the meter and then asking, still in Russian, that the portion read aloud be repeated in unison. Since the students have not seen this poem before, a literal translation accompanies the Russian original. Once we have recited the entire poem, which is normally on the short side, I take a few moments to explain to those present how the gist of the poem, its merging of message and sound, relates to our summer. The poem could be about the special fondness experienced by classmates for their time together at school, or the importance of being your own person ("you are a tsar yourself," says the poet in one poem). Elegantly arranged, sonorously sounding Pushkin verses exist literally for every occasion, and it is part of the charm of the evening for the visiting parents and siblings to get a feel for our enterprise by hearing their students recite.

The next section of the program is the much-anticipated announcement of awards. Before we proceed to celebrating the students' individual accomplishments we ask each teacher and resident counselor to stand and be acknowledged, often to raucous applause, by the young people they have been working with, and in the case of the RCs living with, all summer. The awards that follow identify different areas of individual achievement—highest grades in expository writing, best display of teamwork in the dorm, greatest mastery of spoken Russian, most improvement in Russian from beginning of summer, and so forth—and are presented to the students along with a special certificate designed for the occasion and a small prize. Each awardee is called to the podium and loudly recognized by the audience. The final, and most significant, award is entitled "the spirit of Pushkin": it is given each summer to the student who most embodies both the thirst for learning and the dedication to community ideals that we associate with our school and with Pushkin's poetic culture.

The final portion of the program is devoted to a presentation of the students' creative projects, which they have been working on feverishly for the last week of the session. For this event, the totality of students is divided into smaller groups, typically four to five, with each deciding among themselves which plot of a Pushkin story they would like to reenact. The groups then compete to make the most memorable video. The final products are typically campy and hilarious and often quite clever in terms of stage props and setting: gender roles are switched with boys in drag and girls in hats and fake moustaches. The central moments in the plots are acted out—duels, elopements, card games—and the key lines delivered in Russian. The students love seeing themselves on screen.

When the videos have been viewed, the official part of the program is concluded. What follows is an extended period of photo-taking in different combinations of students, teachers, and counselors. This is also the time when we, the administration, are most moved because everyone is experiencing an ending and it is not rare for the departing students to break down in tears because the summer has been such an affirming and potentially pivotal experience for them. That has always been our goal, for the key to Pushkin's poetic culture is its ability to, in the Russian, "touch the heart" (*umiliat'*), experience heartfelt "tenderness" (*umilenie*). As the poet writes in one of his last poems, "From Pindemonte" (1836),

> Marveling at the divine beauties of nature,
> and trembling joyously in raptures of *umilenie*
> before the creations of art and inspiration—
> That is happiness! Those are [true] rights . . .

After the photo session and last embraces the students are released to themselves and the counselors for a last night of pizza, partying, packing, and dorm clean-up.

PSI Abroad and Pushkin Scholars

In 2015, the University of Wisconsin-Madison became a so-called "implementing organization" for the National Security Language Initiative for Youth. NSLI-Y is funded by the US Department of State with the goal of promoting "critical" foreign language learning among American high school students. This full-scholarship program allows us to send high-achieving PSI alumni to Daugavpils, Latvia for six weeks each summer to continue their studies in the "Learn Russian in the EU" program, a comprehensive suite of language, culture, and service learning at a second level, beyond what is taught at PSI Madison. Daugavpils turns out to be an ideal setting for learning Russian: the second largest city in Latvia, it has one of the highest percentages of Russian speakers of any city outside of the Russian Federation, which also means that Russian is the language of everyday life in Daugavpils—a big plus for an immersion program. And because Latvia is a member of the European Union, US citizens do not require a visa for short-term study. Along with STARTALK, a program underwritten by the National Security Agency (NSA) for the purpose of encouraging *ab initio* study of critical languages, NSLI-Y has been an important source of external funding for the PSI.[6] Another, more recent grant (2021–) has come from the United States Russia Foundation (USRF).

Last but not least, the PSI has created a mentoring program for alumni who attend the University of Wisconsin-Madison: "Pushkin Scholars" is a special educational and social opportunity offered to the PSI's best and brightest.[7] With our faculty's detailed knowledge of PSI participants, we are in a strong position to advocate for the most successful and hardworking among them to gain admission to the University of Wisconsin-Madison and become eligible for Pushkin Scholars financial aid packages. Beginning in 2016, the administration of the PSI has worked closely with the Admissions and Student Financial Aid offices at the University to admit and fund our most promising program graduates. To date the University of Wisconsin-Madison has committed more than $1,000,000 to underwrite the education of Pushkin Scholars. Once admitted to the University of Wisconsin-Madison, Pushkin Scholars typically continue their Russian studies in our nationally recognized Flagship program, which uses its block Department of Defense (DOD) funding grant to place our students on a fast track to superior linguistic competence and a broad array of exciting in-country travel, internships, and career opportunities. Russian Flagship students combine the academic major(s) of their choice, including such recent options as criminal justice, diplomacy, and international law, with a professional level of proficiency in Russian. The PSI team also meets regularly with the Pushkin Scholar group to monitor their academic progress, celebrate their successes, and discuss their career plans.

The Students in Their Terms: the PSI Questionnaire

Since the summer of 2012, the PSI programs in Madison and Daugavpils, Latvia, have provided instruction to some 292 students. Not a large number, but not an insignificant number either. Who are these kids in terms of *their* reality?

In the testimonials presented in the appendix, but also cited selectively in the text in connection with the Pushkin readings to follow, I asked a group of our grads, a subset of whom were studying at the University of Wisconsin-Madison as Pushkin Scholars, to explain in their own words different aspects of their backgrounds and attitudes. Here is the questionnaire I sent to each of them; in the instructions I also asked that they be as specific as possible and that they feel free to be expansive where appropriate.

1. Please describe your neighborhood.
2. Please describe your family.
3. How have you been affected personally by the category of race?
4. In your childhood and early years, what do you look on as turning points in your life?
5. Which people—family and friends, teachers at school, coaches of sports teams, Sunday school teachers, scout leaders, etc.—influenced you most and why?
6. How did you learn about morality?
7. Do you consider yourself risk-averse or open to taking chances?
8. What came first, Spanish or English, and how has that affected you?
9. How much did you read as a young person and what did you read?
10. What role has music played in your life?
11. How were your days scheduled from a young age and how much free time did you have?
12. Once you got to middle school and high school, how did you react personally to the issue of "status"—who is "cool," who is "nerdy," etc.?

13. How much time did you spend thinking about the opposite sex, when did such thinking start, and what came first in your mind, schoolwork or socializing, and why?

14. How has the study of Russian, and participation in the PSI specifically, affected you academically?

15. Pushkin as a personality: interesting to you or not? Which themes, characters, plots, and word play from Pushkin's works stuck with you and caused you to think?

16. Did you learn anything at the PSI, either in a practical or an idealistic sense, that you think might help you going forward?

17. In a few words, what is the purpose of life as you see it now?

The idea in posing these questions was to see if these young people could look back at their own decision-making and at the factors that shaped their choices. They have all been asked the same questions, and in the samplings I chose to leave their responses "as is," with only slight emendations for idiomatic and grammatical correctness. I also changed their names to conceal their identities. Admittedly, this is not "big-data" social science in a sophisticated iteration; rather it is an attempt to isolate the memories of events out of which personal stories are created.

The rubrics guiding the information requested—neighborhood, family, race, turning points, influences, morality, risk-taking, language, reading, music, daily rhythms, status issues, relationships, studying Russian, Pushkin, PSI, purpose of life—constituted what I hoped to be potentially "plot-worthy" nodes, biographical intersections where personality, desire, and experience come together momentarily to resolve themselves, to give shape to students' lives. Other rubrics could have been attempted, but these seemed a good place to start.

CHAPTER 3

"The Shot": Role-Playing with Loaded Pistols

It is time to approach more directly the business of the book. Each of the following chapters makes reference to certain terms and concepts from evolutionary thought that seem particularly germane to the Pushkin text under discussion: emergent properties, adaptation, path-dependent, sexual selection, altruism, multilevel selection. Also important, I remind the students how these same concepts play essential roles in who they are and how their future lives will be unfolding. The point each time in class discussion is not how evolution *forces* us deterministically to act in certain ways, because in human decision-making choice is always present, but how it *limits our options* with regard to which actions, taken in context, make life sustainable. I'm particularly keen for the students to grasp the overlaying of the cultural realm on the biological realm as presented in imaginative literature. To put it bluntly, this is where I hope that humanistic study of the future can add to, but also in its way, go beyond anthropology proper, that is, not simply trace and historicize cultural patterns, but show how, to return to Ridley's example, the spear becomes the computer mouse, how it acquires "mind" by engaging in the exchange of ideas. What I'm suggesting is that the cultural products that will have the most value for their group, Pushkin's art being the prime example here, are the ones that remember the past in a certain way and build constructively on it.

In this chapter I aggregate three disparate idea fields around the topic of Pushkin's short story "The Shot" (1830): 1) the world the students come from, 2) the world of communication in Russian, and 3) the world Pushkin represents as understood by the students. The reason I do this is strategic. By bringing these strands together in this way, I hope to show that "natural purposiveness" and "conditioned arising,"[1] which are features of biological relativity as defined by Denis Noble,[2] can also be seen to operate in the domain of cultural learning—learning that is conscious and ever more attuned to its relation to self and world. I don't mean to imply by this that basic-level biology, say how a cell's mitochondria generate biochemical energy, is equivalent to complex cultural production, say how Hamlet's "To be, or not to be" (what Dawkins calls a meme) generates its own kind of energy in different contexts over the centuries, since clearly *much more* is going on, but that culture, including human culture, *grew out* of biology and that many of the primary patterns observable in biology are, to repeat, also observable, mutatis mutandis, in culture. This makes sense, of course, because what was originally only biology became culture through the advent, first, of awareness in the animal world, and then, eventually, *self-awareness*, or *consciousness*,[3] culminating in humans' ability to make meaning by telling stories. What was stochastic (the random stimuli impinging on a cell from outside) and what was self-regulating (how the cell adapts internally to those stimuli to stay alive) gradually, painstakingly, morphed into mind. Once again, all the intermediate steps and the vast periods of time encapsulating those steps can only be gestured at here, not described. At some point, instinct became intuition, choice became consciousness, prelinguistic signalling in the here and now became symbolic logic and language's forward-looking function as "the instruction of imagination."[4] The body is always still there, however. Metaphorical thinking, with its right-hemisphere involvement and gestalt all-present-ness,[5] is the currency that allows the world out there to attach to specific bodies. To return to Iain McGilchrist,

> Language functions like money. It is only an intermediary. But like money it takes on some of the life of the things it represents. It begins in the world of experience and returns to the world of experience—and it does so via metaphor, which is a function of the right hemisphere, and is rooted in the body. To use a metaphor, language is the money of thought.[6]

Similarly, "Pushkin" (the imagined poet) operates like the "money of thought" in the minds of our students. As cultural and linguistic phenomenon he attaches to their ideas about themselves in unexpected ways and gives them something new and exciting to trade on.[7]

Conditioned Arising and "Pushkin"

Just as the preconscious biological organism seeks to stay alive within its environment, so too does the conscious, culturally embedded organism, only the latter is always/already both an individual and a member of a group, hence social by definition and, what is key, *aware of this*. With the enhanced hominid brain's ability to interact socially, make tools, and think symbolically, the idea of "staying alive" accrues a multitude of figurative shadings to go along with the literal one. "Survival of the fittest" has been an unfortunate locution historically, as it seems to imply that strength or power is what is most important, while it is the ability to adapt to an ecological niche that is actually most crucial. In time, and especially with the advent of language and then writing, *Homo sapiens* becomes *Homo interpretans*: we make stories and then we act them out. Successful strategies for survival in the cultural realm do not typically involve hewing doggedly to a fixed set of predetermined rules, which work until they don't. Rather, they are arrived at by experimentation, under duress to perform, and like the "cooptive" model for adaptation in natural selection—recall, for example, the panda's thumb as faux opposable digit made famous by Stephen Jay Gould—they are "good enough" to work in the given situation. They are never a final solution. This also means they are "path dependent": they can proceed only incrementally, by testing out ways forward that fit specific situations (the ecological niches). In our case the strategies and the specific situations involve the PSI students—who they are at this point in their lives, where they come from, and where they see themselves going. For them, in their cultural space, the "democritization" of ecological niches is a given: Pushkin exists alongside rappers like Kendrick Lamar, Drake, and Bad Bunny. He doesn't work for them as "high" culture, a category that is increasingly attenuated in postmodern times.

But Pushkin does work for them in other ways, ways that draw attention to what *deserves to survive* evolutionarily speaking. Indeed, that is the only way Pushkin can work for this group, for this generation. As we will see, Pushkin offers our youthful readers relatable—new, different, exotic, "Russian" but, above all, relatable—storylines that oscillate tantalizingly at the pivot of the ethical and the aesthetic. Competition, jealousy, bullying, revenge, bodily ornamentation, youthful excitability, cool/hip behaviour, beauty and grace that are unearned: these have been with us, as the drivers of sexual selection (as opposed to natural selection), throughout recorded history, regardless of context. They are constants. At the same time, the poet's special manner of "attending to"—whether to language that turns back on itself and through wordplay mimics the emergence into self-awareness, to the characters formed out of the language and its literary conventions, to the stories forking in unexpected directions and placing the characters in new roles, or to the different narrative filters that challenge the meanings of the stories—this "attending to" models the game of life itself, including its call to creative behavior. And, last but not least, once the students are able to make the connection, which I help them with, between Pushkin's own history, his own choices, and their own lives, light bulbs begin to go off.

Let us now bring in some student quotes describing their neighborhood:[8]

> Issac:
> I do remember at the age of eight when I was at the park, I saw a man, gang-affiliated, be shot down at the bus stop next to the park. It was a very eye-opening experience for me.

> Juana:
> My current neighborhood is predominantly Hispanic or in the Latinx community. Most of the population is Mexican and Puerto Rican. [...] There is no diversity in my neighborhood. It is also cold. There are no personal relationships with our neighbors. [...] Additionally, my neighborhood is quite dangerous. I live close to gangbangers, which is scary and sometimes one must be careful. From time to time, there are shooting noises by or in front of our apartment. It is to the point that sometimes you cannot differentiate the sound between a shot and fireworks.

> Maria:
> I have lived most of my life in the Hermosa community in Chicago. When I tell people about my neighborhood, I simply tell them that it has changed over the years. Growing up, I always had to be careful about my surroundings. I remember waking up in the middle of the night because I heard gunshots in my alley. Even as I started high school, I was scared to walk home after soccer practice because I was afraid of being somewhere at the wrong time. My father always believed in self-defense, so he signed us up for taekwondo. We were taught from a young age to watch our surroundings and never talk to strangers.

Next, how the students look at the role of Russian:

> Isabel:
> What I liked about learning Russian is that the language took me out of my comfort zone. As a Latina, Russian was very intimidating because as a child I always heard that Russian is too hard. I took what I heard and kept it in the back of my mind. As a

child, I never got to contribute to the conversation because I was not old enough to understand (trust me, I was). When I started learning Russian in high school, I loved it because it was fun. To me, learning a different alphabet and learning the differences in the languages among the ones I know gave me an opportunity to learn in a class setting rather than in a survival mode setting. I really enjoyed speaking it because it made me feel accomplished. I was learning a language because I wanted to, not because I needed to.

Salma:

I love Russian because it is so unique, and it is something that brings me close to a small group of people. It brings forth a community full of amazing people. I started my junior year and ever since I had heard of PSI, I wanted to go so bad. I was able to go, and it turned out to be one of the best summers of my life. [...] Anytime I do something with PSI it reminds me why I fell in love with the language and why I keep going back to it. I find that when I go to Russian, I am way more involved and enjoy heading to class.

Lesly:

Little did I know that PSI was going to change my perspective about learning. I went into PSI only concentrating on the grammar and language, but I got so much more out of it. I was learning about the culture and comparing it to mine. I think the best part of the Russian language is speaking it. [...] I think that Russian has really helped me find interest in the subjects of philosophy and history. For example, "Ночь, улица, фонарь, аптека" ["Night, street, streetlight, pharmacy"—the first words of a poem by symbolist poet Alexander Blok] gives us an insight on repeated events. The idea that we might have repeated the same actions in another life is mind blowing. Whether one believes it or not, the idea is fascinating.

Nikole:

To learn Russian there is a lot of risk taking, and it is a lot more than a grade. Over time I have learned to play the system to get the grade I want. In Russian, it has always been more than a grade.

Third, the picture the kids are forming of Pushkin:

Jonathan:
Pushkin is a very interesting person because the inspiration for some of his greatest works was drawn from moments in his life, and what he created from these inspired moments is absolutely astounding. If it were not for the way he died [in a duel] he would be at the top of my list; having said that, I will place Pushkin in my mid-tier of people I would like to emulate.

Adelina:
Pushkin as a personality really interested me because in some sense he was brave. I loved reading about his flaws; however, what I really enjoyed is the fact that, behind all his mistakes, he was still a good person. I could connect with his personality because to some extent I could sense what it was like for him to feel different and unwanted. He was not the best student, but he surely was the best writer, and for me that sounds enlightening and inspiring.

Anayansi:
I think [Pushkin's] life and how people treated him because of his skin color really interests me. I feel like compared to other famous people his story is very real in the sense that I can relate to him. Being brought up as the only Hispanic in a community of white people makes me understand a snippet of how Pushkin was treated. His heritage is probably what brings me the closest to him.

Amairani:
When I started to learn about Pushkin, I was intrigued by his personality. I still remember how proud Pushkin was. He was so proud that he died in a duel. What brought me closer to Pushkin was his personality. In a way, he reminded me of my father and men who fall under the word "Machista." Like many men in my family, Pushkin loved to drink. However, outside from the drinking and the gambling, he had a soul. No man in my family would ever sit down and write poems or stories that would challenge the mind of readers.

I suggest that these quotes serve as our gateway into the imaginary world of "The Shot." Especially with regard to the latter two groups of excerpts, they make up elements of *emerging* narratives, narratives that *would not exist* without Pushkin and the PSI. As complex systems researcher and philosopher Stuart Kauffman explains this idea of emergence as it relates to organic life,

> When the heart arises in the biosphere it's a unique event and a unique structure that came to be. So it's not that the heart disobeys any laws of physics; [rather] it is the organization of the heart that allows it to pump blood, [its] structure and the propagating process, that the physicists cannot give us. [It] doesn't break any laws of physics, but the physicists can't get there. *It's emergent.* Hearts are real and you're alive because of it. [. . .] The reductionist worldview is inadequate, not stupid; we've done brilliant science with the reductionist worldview. But it doesn't cover what I've talked about. [. . .] *First, we live in an emergent universe.* Organisms are real, so are particles, but so are organisms, and so are hearts. *Second, we live in a ceaselessly creative universe, without there being a creator agent.* It is ceaselessly creative, non-ergodic [made of states that don't repeat themselves—DB], all around us, all the time, in this conversation, in this talk, and what we will say when I finish in a few minutes [my emphasis—DB].[9]

If I can manage it, I try to start off my conversations with the PSI kids within this framework: what we are attempting to grasp, but never fully succeeding, and yet not exactly failing either, is not the Brownian motion of subatomic particles, the physicists' view, but something akin to the heart's "conditioned arising" in the biosphere, as the latter applies to everything, including the life of the mind.

The *conditioned arising* for our students involves their Hermosa neighborhood beginnings as the *conditioned* part and the activities of studying Russian and learning about Pushkin as the *arising* part. Issac recounts how as an eight-year-old playing at the park he witnessed a gang-related execution at a nearby bus stop. The experience was "eye opening"; it made him aware in a way that was formative. Likewise, Juana lives near gangbangers and often hears gunfire by her apartment, while Maria recalls being awakened in the middle of the night to shots being fired in the alley beside her home and because of the constant danger was required by her parents to learn taekwondo from an early age. These young people are conditioned, taught by life, to think about survival in the most basic sense. It is telling that Jonathan, who calls Pushkin's creative work "absolutely astounding," is troubled by the poet's demise from the Russian version of gun culture; he admires the creativity in the man, but not the man's decision to allow himself to be killed in this way.

Enrolling in Russian adds an entirely new dimension to the students' educational experience. For Isabel "it took [her] out of [her] comfort zone," but then quickly morphed into something "fun," which is a turning point in a student's progress all teachers live for. Even the mention of "survival mode setting," which sounds quasi-Darwinian, suggests what the Russian class *does not* represent to Isabel: it is an escape from the—still figurative, though no less real to the teenager—"life-and-death" performance requirements of her other classes into a world where she can enjoy what she is doing and achieve at a high level at the same time. Salma found in Russian the sense of community (NB. Pushkin's Lyceum!) she couldn't find in other learning environments. Lesly came to the language thinking it was primarily a set of vocabulary words and grammatical rules and came away with an entirely different way of looking at the world, a way that challenged her own cultural assumptions and piqued her interest in philosophy and history. Likewise, Nikole found in Russian something "more than a grade."

The Plot, Part 1: Influence, Male Competition, Dueling Protocols

At its most basic level, "The Shot" is a story about insulted male pride and the desire for revenge. The narrator Lt. Col. ILP tells the tale in two stages, "earlier" and "later" accounts that reprise two duels with the same participants at two different times and places. Nobody in fact dies. Who the duelists are socially and how they comport themselves at these potentially fatal confrontations are key elements in the story. In both accounts the narration comes across as naïve: despite the fact that the military man is younger the first time around and older the second, he remains highly impressionable and tends easily to fall under the sway of others' speech (in neither case, for example, does he witness the duel, but hears about it through someone's dramatic telling). Because the narrator is so susceptible to the presence of others and to the power of personality, the story is also, and not in a secondary sense, about the *role of influence* in young people's lives. Lest we forget, imitation/influence is the equivalent in the cultural realm of copying/replication in the genetic one.[10]

Silvio is the powerful personality introduced in the first part. The hero's name is identified as foreign ("he appeared Russian, but bore a foreign name") before, some thirty lines in, it finally appears ("and so I'll call him Silvio" sounds like an afterthought). His presence in the garrison town commands the attention of the young officers for a variety of reasons: he is older ("at around thirty-five we considered him an old man"); his arrival on the scene seemingly out of nowhere is mysterious; in his previous life he was a hussar, a member of a dashing military unit suggesting social standing and possibly wealth, while in his present incarnation the ostentatiously black frock coat he wears everywhere stands out against the sea of uniforms; his supposed experience of the world in combination with his studied taciturnity cry out for a backstory; his mud-hut home, sparsely furnished and fitting his bachelor ethos, is one of the few open houses in town where the men can gather nightly to gamble and drink; most crucially, he is reputed to be a legendary duelist with a violent past, although no one knows any details. All these contradictory facts add up to creating out of Silvio something intoxicating to youth: "his habitual gloominess, severe disposition, and wicked tongue had a *strong influence* [*sil'noe vliianie*] on our young minds." In short, there is something attractive about his very "badness." The Silvio that emerges from the story is this *sil'noe vliianie*. The students and I pronounce the Russian out loud as we assemble the pieces. It starts with the language.

Lt. Col. ILP tells us that his youthful imagination in the first part is *romanicheskoe*, which has as its root *roman*, meaning both "romance" (as in "love story") and "novel" (as in "prose tale"). (By writing this and the other stories in the initially anonymously published *Tales of Belkin* Pushkin is playfully performing his "descent to prose" from his poetic origins.) The imagination of this young man is thus naively *romantic*—but not the *romanticheskoe*, with a "t," of the movement—and it is *story-generating*—it wants to know the secret that explains why Silvio comports himself the way he does. These are linguistic, and embedded cultural, details that the students, with their still rudimentary Russian, cannot know at this stage. Still, we pronounce the key phrase in unison and in addition I have an individual student read the excerpt from the handout in which the phrasing appears. The mystery in the story intensifies when another young officer, newly billeted to the garrison, becomes enraged at a nightly gambling bout when Silvio undoes his scorekeeping without comment. Inflamed by drink and his mates' laughter, the officer grabs a nearby candlestick and hurls it at the host, who just manages to step aside. Silvio, suppressing his fury, asks the young man to leave, while telling him to thank his lucky stars that this happened in his home. Everyone expects there to be a duel.

The most obvious thing about duels is that they generate plot. In Pushkin's time, the duel was the only way a person of his class could get satisfaction if he or someone close to him (say, a sister) had been insulted or dishonored. Fisticuffs or brawling was out of the question for the higher classes, as an aristocrat's body was sacrosanct and not to be touched without permission. The dueling code required that seconds conduct the negotiations of a duel's terms—time and place, type of weapon, length to dividing lines, distance between dividing lines, what happens after first individual discharges his weapon, and so forth—and that the participants not engage with the other side until the seconds, representing the interests of their parties, agree on the terms, and the duel has taken place. It was all very formal. It was also the way that aristocratic society—not the other social classes who thought the practice silly or the state who prosecuted it as barbarous—decided issues of personal offense or injustice without having to go through the corrupt court system.

Thus, a potentially lethal confrontation that proceeds according to a fixed set of rules is bound to be intriguing to a youthful (primarily "male") mind seeking adventure.[11] Here we need only recall the addictive nature of video games. Either life intervenes (the "path-dependent" steps that, once taken, enable maturity), or death (the result of an actual duel) does. The Pushkin who was a duelist numerous times in his own life and the Pushkin who is looking at the world differently now as he composes the story on the eve of his marriage in fall 1830: herein lies the dialogic interplay that is a, probably the, crucial element of discussion. Therefore, even before we start the Pushkin strand of the program, I ask the students to read a short biography of the poet, also a handout, which we then refer back to prior to each assignment. But for now we stay within the space of the story: Silvio is unique within his social set for his marksmanship, a "terrible art" (*uzhasnoe iskusstvo*) he has mastered to an uncanny degree. No one in the company would hesitate to place a pear on his head, actually, on the military cap (*furazhka*) on his head (an important distinction), and have Silvio shoot it off at a distance. (NB. This is probably an ironic allusion to the romantic Wilhelm Tell story, the point of which—its cultural substrate—the students cannot yet grasp, and so I leave outside discussion for now.)

But the duel doesn't happen. The plot diverges away from the expectations that have been planted about Silvio's dark past and the violence that seemed destined to return. The next day, the offender is still alive and, when asked, says he hasn't heard from Silvio. When they all go to visit Silvio they find him practicing his marksmanship, firing shot after shot into an ace (the playing card) glued to the courtyard gate. He doesn't say a word. A few days pass, he appears to brush off the incident as trifling, and the two make peace. For a time, Silvio's standing among the young officers takes a hit. They don't understand why the moody marksman doesn't just invoke the dueling code to take out the man who insulted him. They suspect, and in particular the narrator with his romantic imagination suspects, that Silvio may be a coward. At this juncture I suggest to the students that they remember what Silvio has been shooting at—a playing card, an ace.

The riddle of Silvio, whom the narrator still wants to believe is "the hero of some mysterious tale," continues. One day, Silvio receives a letter, reacts with unexpected animation, announces he is leaving town, and invites everyone to his place for a farewell gathering. As the party ends, he asks the narrator to remain behind: he has developed an attachment for the young man, he knows he has fallen in his friend's estimation because he didn't call the candlestick-hurling young officer out to a duel, and he wants to explain himself. It turns out that Silvio is no coward; he didn't fight because he "didn't have the right" to subject himself to possible death. What a strange way to put it! What does it mean? Well, according to the dueling code he still has a shot at his disposal to fire at a previous opponent and he cannot die in other circumstances until he has discharged that bullet. To prove the point, he removes a military cap from a box and shows the narrator the bullet hole in it slightly above the forehead. That the code, a social construct, can obligate in this way is shocking. Also shocking is Silvio's appearance as he tells his story: his face has a "gloomy pallor," his eyes are "flashing," his mouth is encircled with "thick smoke" from his pipe, with the result that he looks like a "real devil."

Next, Silvio tells his story. He begins by describing how, at a younger age, he loved "to be first" (*pervenstvovat'*). But his supremacy among his mates, who bowed to his strong personality and feared him as dueling bully (*bretteur/bretër* in Russian = someone ready to fight at the drop of a hat), and the ladies, who were drawn to his top-dog status, was shaken when a new competitor arrived on the scene. This individual outshone Silvio in every way that matters to youth: social status (he was a count), wealth, daring, wit, and physical charm/beauty. Silvio couldn't accept the eclipse of his reputation and found a pretext to provoke the count to a duel. When the count arrives the next day to the duel, which as a life-and-death encounter is by definition serious, he approaches carrying a military cap (*furazhka*) full of cherries. This of course wounds Silvio's *amour propre* still more, as even in these circumstances he cannot force his opponent to see him as a threat. The count, who doesn't seem to value his own life, plays his role to perfection. They cast lots and the count wins and is granted the first shot, which he fires through Silvio's cap without wounding him. Now Silvio can easily kill him, but the count, still unmoved, stands at the barrier calmly chewing the cherries and spitting out the pits in front of him. "You don't seem up to dying now," remarks Silvio, with as much nonchalance as he can muster, and insisting he doesn't want to hamper the count from taking his morning meal. The count answers that Silvio should do as he wishes—it's all the same to him.

Silvio lowers his pistol and decides not to shoot the count in this unsatisfying manner, to which the count replies that that too is equally acceptable to him, and that the unfired shot remains Silvio's to take anytime he wishes. The two duelists part ways. Only now does Silvio divulge to the narrator the key to the mystery: "not one day has passed since then that I have not thought of revenge." The narrator is led to believe that the "well-known person" whose whereabouts are mentioned in the letter and the count in the story are one and the same, and the time has come for Silvio to act. The final picture we have of Silvio before the first part of "The Shot" ends is him hurling his bullet-pierced *furazhka* to the floor and pacing back and forth like a caged tiger. The narrator is filled with "contradictory feelings."

Pushkin, the Byronic Role Model (and Tupac), *Obida*

The time now arrives for the students to try to figure out, with my help, the patterns and stereotypes in Pushkin's world that are shaping Silvio's behavior. I ask them to google the name "Byron" and to come to class ready to discuss the romantic poet's importance for, his *influence on*, Pushkin's generation. It turns out that Byron's special brand of romanticism, his social, political, artistic, and erotic rebelliousness, coupled with his physical beauty that was marred by a deformed foot, his mark of Cain, were cultural catnip for Pushkin and his peers. In Lady Caroline Lamb's famous phrase, he was "mad, bad, and dangerous to know," which is exactly why he was so appealing. Pushkin's older friend and early poetic model Vasily Zhukovsky had translated Byron's *Prisoner of Chillon* in 1821 and indeed visited the castle there as a sacred site when he was in Switzerland. This is relevant because by the time Pushkin writes "The Shot" in 1830 he has passed through his own Byronic phase (1821–1824), having written a series of swashbuckling "oriental" poetic tales that feature exotic settings (Russia's south as opposed to Byron's east); love affairs with fatal outcomes; and dark, alienated heroes who are meant to be read as doubles of the poet himself—all carefully calculated "Byronic" moves. But now Pushkin realizes he cannot be Byron and must be himself: he is not gorgeous the way the idol is; women do not flock to his "simian" (his metaphor) exterior the way they do to Byron's; his rebelliousness is not total and does not extend to an all-out assault on family and state. (Here I remind the students of Byron's very public separation from his wife, who thought him possibly insane, as well as his alleged incestuous relationship with his half-sister Augusta, together with his rancorous departure from England and his support for the Greek War of Independence against the British-backed

Ottoman Empire—all this versus Pushkin's ultimate desire to marry and have a family and his pride in Russian history, including the state's imperial ambitions under Peter and Catherine.) Already as early as 1823–1824, as he composes canto one of *Onegin*, Pushkin begins the process of distancing himself from Byron when he has his speaker remark that the hero of the novel-in-verse, which starts out as a Russian response to *Don Juan*, and the poet-author doing the talking-creating, are not one and the same: "That, like proud Byron, I have penned / A mere self-portrait in the end; / As if today, through some restriction, / We're now no longer fit to write / On any theme but our own plight"[12] (Falen's translation)—literally "as though it's impossible for us to write anything else except poems about ourselves." This is all meant to get the students thinking about how cultural stereotypes can be accepted, resisted, played with.

The thing about Byron, which is also the thing about youth culture in any age, is that the grievance experienced by the hero, in Russian *obida* or unjust offense/insult, is what most captivates. In a real sense Byron saw himself as the beautiful "light bearer" (Lucifer) banished to the fiery lake because God's order had unfairly created him lame. He once told his wife that he was "an avatar of a fallen angel." "Better to reign in Hell than serve in Heaven" was the motto of Milton's Satan, but Byron was the post-Miltonic real-life incarnation of that supreme rebel, and he and his romantic friends like Shelley knew it.[13] Writing in the wake of the great revolutions of the eighteenth century, he breathed himself into his plots as versions of the shadowy antiheroes of Gothic novels, like the fratricidal Father Schedoni of Ann Radcliffe's *The Italian* (1797). At the same time, he cultivated a kinship with the ultimate satanic figure of the age, calling himself archly in canto eleven of *Don Juan* "The grand Napoleon of the realms of rhyme." Thus, it could be said without exaggeration that Byron was the first modern personality *to embrace his own alienation*. Yes, he suffered because of his exilic status, but he also reveled in it. The Lucifer that is his mouthpiece in the verse drama *Cain* (1821) insinuates himself into the mind of humankind's first murderer. The secret of the tasted apple—death, mortality—is itself unjust because it is the parents who first dared to partake, whilst it is the offspring who must bear the burden. Cain's rebellious alter-ego is "Beauteous, and yet not all as beautiful / As he hath been, and might be: Sorrow seems / Half of his immortality" (I. I. 93–96). And so it is with the cursed beauty that is Byron's.

At this point I try to bring the story back to the students. I remind them of a similar doomed beauty in their world. The "Byronic hero" with his challenge to the natural order and his tragic allure has not left the scene, but continues on in the popular imagination. Consider the self-conscious blurring of "hood" experience and in-your-face art practiced by modern-day rappers like Tupac Shakur:

"It's just me against the world / Ooh, ooh / Nothin' to lose, / It's just me against the world baby / Oh, ah ah." Also not to be forgotten is the fact that Tupac died from gunshot wounds in this very blurring of art and life. He goes on:

> Can you picture my prophecy?
> Stress in the city, the cops is hot for me
> The projects is full of bullets, the bodies is droppin'
> There ain't no stoppin' me
> Constantly movin' while makin' millions
> Witnessin' killings, leavin' dead bodies in abandoned buildings
> Carries to children cause they're illin'
> Addicted to killin' and the appeal from the cap peelin'
> Without feelin', but will they last or be blasted?

It can be argued, of course, that Tupac has nothing to do with an English lord two centuries gone. But in the democratizing stream that is our culture that is not the point. What matters is what moves, what is "alive," in its niche. The students "get" Byron *through* Tupac. "But will they [the next generation] last or be blasted?" The message of nihilism and the *obida* of universal abandonment unite the two rebel poets. Lucifer's tale of natural history as an "Abyss of Space" whose only purpose is to propagate death—

> *Cain.* [...] But, spirit! if
> It be as thou hast said (and I within
> Feel the prophetic torture of its truth),
> Here let me die: for to give birth to those
> Who can but suffer many years, and die,
> Methinks is merely propagating death,
> And multiplying murder...

—becomes Tupac's "prophecy" of "dead bodies in abandoned buildings" that can't be stopped and that "carries to children" who are "illin' / Addicted to killin'."

But where then does this leave Pushkin? Pushkin initially experienced Byron and Byronism on two levels: first, as a model for political action and social behavior in real life, and second, as a model for his art. Both of these experiments turned out to be false starts, although Pushkin's southern verse narratives (his versions of Byron's Oriental tales) were hugely popular when they first appeared. As we try to connect these different levels I ask the students to recall through their reading of the poet's biography that as a young man Pushkin had a rather well-deserved reputation for making trouble. After finishing the Lyceum in 1817 he flung himself headlong into St. Petersburg social life. He enjoyed saying and doing outrageous things and on numerous occasions offended the tsar, his ministers, and polite society with his escapades. His dalliances with ballerinas and his frenetic nightlife were one thing, but his freedom-loving verse, like "The Dagger" (1821), which told of the fate awaiting despots and which circulated among radicals, was another. His dart-like epigrams mocking the high and mighty did not go unnoticed. Once at the theater he held up a portrait of Louis Pierre Louvel, assassin of the Duke of Berry, son of the future French king, with the sign: "A lesson to tsars." Another time he was reputed to have quipped, when a young bear broke off its chain at Tsarskoe Selo and ran into the park where the tsar was taking his stroll, only to be quickly destroyed: "A good man was [finally] found, but [even] he turned out to be a bear." The director of the Lyceum E. A. Engelgardt wrote of the teenage Pushkin in his diary: "His heart is cold and empty. In it there is neither love nor religion; perhaps it is as empty as any youthful heart has ever been." A troublemaker, yes, but so far, no Byronism.

The situation changed, however, when the young poet was administratively reassigned (in effect, exiled) to the south in 1820. His words and deeds had caught up with him, but he could only think about the public humiliation surrounding the rumor that he had received a flogging at the hands of the tsarist police. This was the sort of treatment to which a nobleman could not be subject (again, touching an aristocrat's body without his consent was taboo) and to suggest the opposite drove the proud and tetchy Pushkin to distraction. He may have contemplated suicide. He did not know at the time that the source of the rumor was someone he considered a friend, Fyodor Tolstoy (aka "the American"). Hence, even before Pushkin had read a word of Byron, he felt he had been betrayed and he was ready to take his revenge on the world. This large chip on his shoulder was perhaps not yet "Byronic," but it made it easier for Pushkin to try on the guise of misanthropic rebel a few months hence.

Pavel Annenkov, Pushkin's first serious biographer, suggests that the poet's penetration into the Byronic worldview was, from the start, something life-altering: "The book that they [Pushkin's friend Nikolai Raevsky-fils and Pushkin himself] chose for their practical exercises [in English] was *The Works of Byron*. Thus, the reverence for the great poet grew in Pushkin at the same time that he plunged deeper into the meaning of his ideas."[14] Moreover, since *The Prisoner of the Caucasus* (1822), Pushkin's first Byronic verse narrative, which began to be drafted in Gurzuf (Crimea), reflects the poet's direct response to the English romantic, and in particular his response to the latter's pirate tale *Corsair* (1814), we can assume the intensity Annenkov alleges was real. And so, as Pushkin was going "off his head" (his phrase) with Byron he was also beginning to *live Byronism* for the first time. The "madness," as Annenkov terms it, took two forms, each of which added fuel to the other. First, there was the *political* ferment that Pushkin experienced firsthand while visiting Kamenka, his friends the Davydovs' estate, in the Kiev (Kyiv) province, from late 1820 to early 1821. Here Pushkin participated in heated discussions about the movement for Greek independence, the political thrust of which had direct ties to Byronism. A key element of Byronism was that the social—that is, the hypocrisy of British mores and the insistence on decorum over genuine feeling—and the political—that is, the cynicism of a government that historically supported the Porte's legal status against Greek claims of outrage—went hand in hand. Excitement about the possibility of Greek independence fed in turn into the nightly debates about Russia's situation: Alexander I's own hypocrisy and fear of change; his volte-face from early liberal promise to later brittle reaction; his officer corps who after defeating Napoleon and saving Europe demanded a different world at home; the secret societies that grew up in response and that contemplated overthrowing the tsar and establishing a constitutional monarchy or even a republic (Kamenka was a hotbed of these ideas in the south); and, last but not least, what to do about serfdom and the miserable existence of Russia's vast slave-like population. Hence, in both the social and political realms it could be said that the time was ripe for *a Byronic challenge* to the status quo.

Though Pushkin was never political in a narrow or dogmatic sense he was, as Annenkov underscores, desperate to show the established warriors-cum-future Decembrists at Kamenka his bona fides. (The Decembrists were those who would revolt, unsuccessfully, against the new tsar Nicholas I in December 1825 when he assumed the throne, instead of his brother Constantine, upon the death of Alexander I.) In March 1821, right after he left Kamenka, the poet drafted a letter to friends there about his current Kishinev (today Chişinău, Moldova) impressions of the rebel movement for Greek independence. He describes in detail how the Pandur leader Tudor Vladimirescu, announcing the fact that the Greeks could no longer stand the oppression and were declaring their independence from the Turkish yoke, had left Bucharest in early February with a handful of soldiers only to see his troops swell to 7000 in a few days; how General Alexander Ypsilanti, the famous "one-armed prince" and former adjutant to Alexander I at the Congress of Vienna, had arrived in Iaşi in February, immediately took command of the city, and declared publicly that the Greek phoenix was rising from its ashes; how some 10,000 Greeks in the area, intoxicated by the idea of "freeing their ancient homeland" and playing the role of modern Themistocles, were selling family belongings in order to purchase arms and join forces with Ypsilanti.[15] It was time for this Sleeping Beauty to be revived ("'Tis Greece—but living Greece no more! / So coldly sweet, so deadly fair, / We start—for soul is wanting there," as Byron wrote in another of his Oriental tales, *The Giaour*).

That Ypsilanti proclaimed "a great power [that is, Russia] approves of this noble feat"[16] and that he was also taking command of the northern forces of the Greek insurrection movement was bound to strike Pushkin as a major historical turning point. "How he [Ypsilanti] has happily begun," exclaims the poet. "Twenty-eight years old, an arm lost [in battle], a noble goal [before him]! Now he belongs to history: an enviable lot!"[17] This is pure early romantic Pushkin getting carried away with the potential of the personal becoming historical before his eyes. He ends by telling his correspondent that Ypsilanti needs to be careful of betrayal (another Byronic theme) and that in these heightened circumstances "political murders are justified." "What will Russia do?" he wonders. "Shall she occupy Moldavia and Wallachia under the guise of peaceful intermediary? Shall we cross the Dunai as allies of the Greeks and enemies of their enemies?" Obviously, the poet could not know that in Alexander I's mind Ypsilanti had already overstepped his authority and that his use of Russia as aegis would soon be condemned by the emperor. Still, the idea that Pushkin could consciously contemplate murder for political ends shows to what extent he is caught up in the situation. At no other time in his written traces do we find him *encouraging killing* per se.

The second side of Pushkin's Byronic "madness" had to do with his plunge into the roiling brew that was Kishinev during that time. Moldavian nobles, Phanariot Greeks, Albanians, Russians, rag-tag refugees of every hue—this was the city that caught the reckless youth (Annenkov calls him a *sorvigolova*, a "hothead") in its pungent embrace. And it is here that we come face-to-face with "social" Byronism. Now Pushkin goes way beyond his previous pranks and tweaks to authority. In relations with his kindly superior I. N. Inzov it was "as though [the poet] teased the old general with pleasure," adding to his behavior an element that was "calculating and malicious."[18] Knowing Inzov's deeply religious feelings (he was a Martinist) Pushkin would start "free-thinking" conversations intended to provoke the general (happily they didn't). Annenkov then goes on to explain this "free-and-easy" quality (*razviaznost'*) as *the direct result* of "Byronism" in Russia, where, with typical Russian maximalism and without the new Russian acolytes fully appreciating the political and social context for Byron's misanthropy, young enthusiasts like Pushkin took the lessons they had absorbed from Byron's writings and from what they knew of his life to absurd lengths.

Our [that is, the Russian] version of Byronism had nothing to do either with a deep sympathy for [different] peoples or with the sort of moral and material suffering that inspired Western Byronism. Quite the contrary: instead of the former, Russian Byronism was constructed on a strange scorn—a scorn neither explained by anything nor justified by anything—for humanity in general. From the sources of Byron's poetry and his thought our foremost people extracted only a justification for unlimited caprice on the part of any blindly rebellious personality as well as the right to any sort of "demonic" indecency.[19]

While Annenkov gives numerous instances of such "indecency" (*beschinstvo*) on Pushkin's part, two examples will suffice. The first is a note (*zapiska*) in French found among Pushkin's papers. We don't know who the author is, nor can we say why exactly Pushkin kept the document. In Annenkov's view, it is possible that the *maître* in the following text (originally in French) is Pushkin himself—that is, he kept the note because he was proud of his role as initiator of these thoughts:

You, my worthy *maître*, are bold, caustic, and malicious—but that is not enough. One has to be a tyrant, savage, vindictive. I ask you to teach me that. People are not worthy of being evaluated by the sparks of feeling [they show], as I thought they might be evaluated. They ought to be weighed *by the pood*. One can subjugate them to oneself only when one becomes as much of an egoist and as malicious as they are. Only after that can one proceed to the task of assigning each his proper place. Isn't that so, my amiable compatriot, or am I wrong? Decide.[20]

The notion that human nature is base and that people exist to be bent to one's will, just as the measure of human worth is maximally crude and material (weighing somebody "by the *pood*"/"in pounds" rather than by some inner quality) and the measurer of that worth cynical and unforgiving ("caustic," "malicious," "savage," "vindictive"), is straight out of the Byronic hero's playbook. Here Pushkin is as far as possible from the character trait that defines most the second half of his career: his call for "mercy to the fallen" (from his famous valedictory "Exegi monumentum" [1836]).

The second incident is from Annenkov's rough notes for the biography and hence did not find its way into the final text. According to K. K. Danzas,

In Kishinev, while playing billiards at Fuks's coffee house, Alexander Sergeevich laughed at Fyodor Orlov, who [then] tossed him out the window. Pushkin ran back into the billiard parlor, picked up a billiard ball, and threw it at Orlov. The ball hit Orlov in the shoulder. Orlov then rushed at Pushkin with a billiard cue, but Pushkin pulled out two pistols and declared, "I'll kill you." Orlov backed off like a coward [*strusil*].[21]

Even if Danzas's story is embellished (was Pushkin really carrying two pistols around?), the idea that he could get into a brawl with the younger brother of his respected older friend and patron General M. F. Orlov, suggests how "quick at the trigger" and potentially "out of control," ready to commit *beschinstva*, Pushkin was during these months. On another occasion the poet calls out an ex-French officer (Deguilly) to a duel and then humiliates him, in typical *bretteur* fashion, for refusing to comply. Not only is this poor Deguilly accused by his adversary of bringing his wife into the affair in order to avoid the consequences, Pushkin then circulates a sketch (the only time in his career when he will use his artwork so publicly), which shows his timid opponent, now bare-bottomed, complaining that his wife wears the trousers.[22] Socially, then, this is the "Kishinev Pushkin" who strives to be as provocative as he can as often as he can. He fights duel after duel on the slightest pretense and forces Inzov to place him under house arrest multiple times; he sketches little devils at play while composing poems; and last but not least, he pens a work of the purest blasphemy, *The Gabrieliade* ("Gavriiliada"), in which Christianity's Virgin Mother is imagined as a nubile Jewess who, easily aroused, sleeps in rapid succession with the persuasive Serpent, the archangel Gabriel, and the Dove/Holy Spirit, all unbeknownst to the jealous Father.

But, having absorbed through reading and class discussion this multilayered context, the students now need to be made aware how the social and political aspects of Byronism always lead back to the poet's art, especially to its display of *personality through language*. Once again they are reminded that of all of Byron's works that were possibly influential on Pushkin's early artistic development in the south, *The Corsair* stands out as the one containing the most extensive description of the Byronic hero's *inner* world. This is the final shoe that has to drop before we can return to part two of "The Shot." What was it exactly about *The Corsair*'s hero Conrad that made him so "Byronic"? The traits that "explain" (but don't explain) Conrad in the work's opening stanzas are simultaneously ones intended to incite questioning, foreboding, mystery (again, Silvio!). This indeterminacy was key to the Byronic hero as contemporary readers perceived him. Our first glimpse of Conrad shows someone silent (this despite his author's flowing loquaciousness), solitary, and moody ("We dare not yet approach—thou know'st his mood, / When strange or uninvited steps intrude"). He cuts Juan and the crew members short when they come to report to him and attempt to give a fuller update (stanzas 6–7). Not simply a pirate captain to his crew, he is the master and they his cowed underlings, even slaves, if not explicitly, then implicitly, through the power of his personal aura (compare the control Silvio kept wanting to exert over the count). A mere look on his part is all that is required. The men address him as "Lord Conrad," which figuratively plays into his "satanic" tendencies. Again mysteriously, in a manner not justified by his less-than-extraordinary physical features (stanza 9), he bends others to his will as though they are mesmerized:

> Yet they repine not—so that Conrad guides;
> And who dare question aught that he decides?
> That man of loneliness and mystery,
> Scarce seen to smile, and seldom heard to sigh;
> Whose name appalls the fiercest of his crew,
> And tints each swarthy cheek with sallower hue;
> Still sways their souls with that commanding art
> That dazzles, leads, yet chills the vulgar heart.
> What is that spell, that thus his lawless train
> Confess and envy—yet oppose in vain?
> What should it be, that thus their faith can bind?
> The power of Thought—the magic of the Mind! (stanza 8)

By tripping almost breathlessly from one statement of self-canceling ineffability to another, by circling around a definition of this personality without getting closer to its center, the words create their own momentum. Almost like one of the crew, the reader feels overwhelmed by the rhetorical flourish ("The power of Thought—the magic of the Mind!"), but still very much in the dark. Presence is absence.

Each feature in Conrad's portrait brings out the sense of some inner hurt (again, the *obida*) corroding his original goodness/nobility. His past crimes are so terrible as to remain secret and his defiance of the status quo, or the social order, is total. As already mentioned, the defiance goes back through various Gothic villain-heroes to Milton's Satan, the fallen angel, who challenges God's order because he demands his own spiritual freedom and refuses to submit to another's (even His) will. Conrad's lip is raised in a perpetual sneer. His gaze, which others fear to meet, is Medusa-like: there is something terrible in it, but to try to spy it out only reverses and redoubles its power, thereby paralyzing the viewer. The only way to "see" Conrad is to be "unseen" (stanza 10). (This avoidance of looking back at Conrad is probably Byron's pre-Darwinian rendering of what today would be called "street" behavior: how young males in dangerous urban environments, their amygdala circuitry engaged, know what it means to maintain eye contact for too long.[23]) By commanding pirates, themselves social outcasts, he gives Satan's army a contemporary twist: "Yet was not Conrad thus by Nature sent / to lead the guilty—Guilt's worst instrument— / His soul was changed, before his deeds had driven / Him forth to war with Man and forfeit Heaven" (stanza 11). Thus he is, all at once, full of hatred for humankind's pettiness and weakness, bent on revenge (cf. Silvio's "not one day has passed since then that I have not thought of revenge"), and incapable of forgiving a slight.

> Warped by the world in Disappointment's school,
> In words too wise—in conduct *there* a fool;
> Too firm to yield, and far too proud to stoop,
> Doomed by his very virtues as the cause of ill,
> And not the traitors who betrayed him still;
> Nor deemed that gifts bestowed on better men
> Had left him joy, and means to give again.
> Feared—shunned—belied—ere Youth had lost her force,
> He hated Man too much to feel remorse,
> And thought the voice of wrath a sacred call,
> To pay the injuries of some on all. (stanza 11)

A very apt description, this, of the motivations underlying Silvio's "strongly influential" behavior.

To sum up this section, it goes without saying that a great deal of information is being presented here, perhaps too much, and, while I ask the students to be as familiar as possible with the poet's biography, I also limit class discussion to graspable talking points, which are listed in the handouts. The goal is not to make them into historians or literary critics, as they don't know enough yet (and may not ever care to), but to try to get them to see the life lessons in the cultural patterns that inhere over time, to get them started on making the connections. Just as Tupac's authenticity as "badass" street bard derives from the unique way he made poetry out of the gun violence that ultimately killed him, so too did Byron follow through literally on his words about striving to awaken beautiful Greece (the Greece of literature and imagination) from her corpse-like sleep. Only this time it was the kiss of the maiden that killed the prince. Byron gave all of himself—all of his family fortune, all of his prestige and reputation, and ultimately all of the final reserves of his youth and health—to the cause of uniting stubbornly disunited rebel forces, until it was he that was dead, at thirty-six, from fever and exhaustion, in April 1824, at Missolonghi. Byron's authenticity, like Tupac's authenticity, is intoxicating to youth. But that's just it: *to youth*. Like any intoxication, it is by definition a temporary state, not a permanent condition. If maintained too long it veers toward crapulence on the one hand or a death wish on the other. It is unsustainable. Its role with regard to survival in the cultural realm is to show, after the fact, what is too much from a species perspective. This, then, is the final layer of background that needs to be taken on board by the students, at least intellectually, before returning to part two of "The Shot."

The Plot, Part 2: The Return of the Past, Stage Props, Path Dependence

With this excursus let us now return to Silvio and the second part of "The Shot." In this section, several years have passed and the narrator has retired to the country. He lives on his modest estate and his only concerns are boredom and the dangers of taking to drink. The fairytales of his housekeeper and the songs of the peasant women have all been exhausted and he is in need of new storylines in his life. It happens that the one wealthy estate in the area belongs to a recently married countess who decides to spend time in the country with her husband, the count. Our narrator, needing some distraction and looking for an excuse to present himself, pays the young couple a welcome visit. Cowed by the opulence of the country home's interior and casting about awkwardly for an appropriate topic of conversation, he notices a painting of a Swiss landscape that is marred by two bullet holes, one planted on top of the other. This sign of evident accuracy with a firearm is something he finds easy to talk about, and so the conversation turns to the theme of marksmanship. The count says that he used to shoot but is now out of practice and hasn't held a pistol in four years. When our retired military man exclaims that the best marksman he had ever seen could knock a fly into the wall with a casual shot, his hosts are impressed and ask his name: Silvio! Thus is the story of the second duel set in motion.

Everything about Silvio's "strong influence" of Byronism in part one is turned on its head in part two. Silvio doesn't change, but the count, the cherry-munching adversary affecting Byronic cynicism and *beschinstvo*, does. The count tells the narrator how the couple was wed five years ago and removed themselves to this country house to enjoy the *dolce far niente* atmosphere of the honeymoon; this place, he says, has given him some of his happiest moments but also one of his most terrifying ones. The count's point, which is also the affianced Pushkin's as he writes the story and considers his own Byronic past, is that when he marries the countess (Masha) he suddenly has something outside of himself to live for; he is no longer "ready for death" as he was on the day of the first duel. That element of insouciant machismo no longer applies to him in the same way. It was precisely this circumstance that Silvio fixed on and was preparing himself to use as he awaited the letter telling of the count's nuptials.

The story of the second duel is told through the play between language and ritual. The duel is ritualistic in the sense that all details of the protocol established by the seconds must be observed lest the one transgressing the rules be accused of bad faith or, worse, cowardice. But when Silvio arrives at the estate his appearance takes the count totally by surprise. After being ushered into the drawing room by servants, he awaits the count, who comes home following an equestrian outing with the countess. She for her part—now the necessary complement to the count, while Silvio is always and only the unfamilied bachelor—has been left behind to walk home after a problem with her mount. Once Silvio announces himself and the count recognizes him, it is clear why he has come—to claim his shot. This causes the distracted count to break the rules of dueling and (as yet unknowingly) besmirch his honor: after they measure off a distance of twelve paces (a potentially lethal span) and the count, all the while thinking painfully of his wife, takes his position across the room before his revenant-like former enemy, Silvio convinces the count to cast lots again to decide who fires first. This change is clearly an infraction of the original protocol! But in his current state of mind the count agrees, and for a second time draws the winning lot and shoots first, with the result that the bullet doesn't hit Silvio but pierces the painting of the Swiss landscape. After this, the countess suddenly arrives and, seeing what is happening, throws herself at Silvio's feet and begs for her husband's life. Only now does the count's courage return and he demands that Silvio stop his taunting (as the count had taunted him the first time) and take his shot. At last Silvio, satisfied, fires his pistol as he exits the room, shooting the bullet directly into the hole already left by the count's first shot. The dramatic implication? Silvio *could have* executed the count on the spot, but he decides not to. Instead, his thirst for revenge is slaked completely:

"Are you going to shoot or not?"

"No, I'm not," answered Silvio. "I'm satisfied: I've seen your confusion, your faintheartedness. I forced you to shoot at me, and for me that's enough. You will remember me. I leave you to your conscience."

Pushkin lived in a time virtually without moral recourse. Force, both physical and psychological, was ever-present in the heavy hand of state rule, in the tsar's "Third Section" (security police), in the censorship of the Church, in the corruption of the courts, and in the brutality of serfdom. As already mentioned, the duel was an atavistic attempt, based in chivalry and aristocratic pride, to demand satisfaction for a transgression of one's personal honor. Its idea was to use violent means to address a situation that both parties agreed could not be resolved otherwise. Pushkin's own psychology, to judge by how he tells this story with its "before-and-after" sequence, comes down right in the middle of the duel's confused etiology. Part of him is the gloomy Silvio, his earlier self, role-playing the Byronic hero because he can't stand to be disrespected and because male competition always breeds new challengers; another part is the count who now is trying to enter another stage of life, is blest with a beautiful wife and potential family, but has this previous shot hanging over him; and a third part is the impressionable narrator who is fascinated by the strong romantic personality and is drawn to emulate him, but still has mixed feelings about his hero's attitudes and actions.

In the unsurpassed *Onegin*, which Pushkin had been writing for more than seven years from the time of the initial Byronic rage to the present moment of sober stock-taking, the hero kills his best friend, the young poet Lensky, in a duel over a trifle: Lensky angers Onegin because he persuades him to come to a name-day party for Tatiana, who still carries a torch for Onegin (as he does for her, although his Byronic cynicism will not let him admit it) and who grows embarrassed when he appears, at which point the awkward situation causes Onegin to provoke Lensky by flirting with Lensky's fiancée, Tatiana's sister Olga. The challenge (*kartel'*, from French) that the naive Lensky then conveys to Onegin sets in motion the dueling protocol that cannot be stopped. Tchaikovsky's music, we recall, distills and accentuates this momentum (right-brain involvement = it's no longer "about" the people, it feels now like it *is* the people, their living selves) when it is added to the words. By the time he writes the dueling scene Pushkin has participated in a number of duels himself; he describes with withering irony, and presumably some self-loathing, how society's view of itself is the spring that turns this wheel once the challenge has been laid down. He clearly understands that society's opinion is not worth it, but he, both as his character Onegin and as the authoring consciousness presenting the dilemma, cannot back away from the challenge. Society's hold is too strong. When Onegin kills Lensky he is devastated—his lone *"ubit"* ("he is killed") after the maelstrom of Tchaikovsky's music in the opera is the very essence of tragedy—because a beautiful young life has been snuffed out for no reason and because the affair didn't have to happen. This is the same Pushkin who a few years later will die in a duel defending his wife's honor after an arrogant young Frenchman keeps making untoward advances to her and society, gleeful at the prospect of a possible romance, and, enjoying the husband's discomfort, gossips about it.

Only now, within this larger framework, can we come back to Pushkin's language and how it communicates. If the story is about male competition and revenge, then the language, which is no longer Pushkin's earlier, more passion-filled poetry but is now his later, more ironic and life-chastened prose, must reflect this change. This is how the poetry, which is "beauty," continues in the prose, which is "reality." *The language instantiates the "path dependence" to maturity.* In other words, it (the path) can't be faked. I want the kids to understand that by making choices and succeeding in living life from the "before" to the "after" of the story they will begin to see the same patterns that the great poet did. First, what are the stage props of the drama and what happens to them over time? We recall that Silvio's "terrible art" consisted in shooting at a playing card, an ace, which he peppered with his bullets in daily target practice. We also recall that he was so adept at his art that no one among his acquaintances would hesitate to place a pear on his military cap and have Silvio shoot it off at a distance. The other stage prop is the Swiss landscape painting that the count mistakenly fires into while aiming at Silvio in the second duel and that Silvio hits again in the same spot as he departs the scene. The message is that these props are the "rhyme words" in the prose of life: they are the signs that the young narrator, and then the older narrator, is looking at actions taken through a Byronic lens and only realizing *after the fact* that the props are just that—articles in a drama that is staged by society, *but that you act in,* and that, if you're not paying attention, can have harmful, even lethal consequences.

Silvio's military cap, *furazhka,* that is shot through by the count and kept as a memento symbolizing revenge (the Byronic topos) is actually a pun, again a kind of situational rhyme word, when we stop to consider it. Silvio shoots at a playing card, a *karta,* which is an ace, *tuz,* and if you combine the two words you get *kartuz,* another word for military cap. *Tuz* also means "big shot," important person, in Russian. Thus when Pushkin has Silvio take out his *furazhka,* which the narrator also likens to a *bonnet de police,* and then has the Byronic hero make the cap the pivotal item in his tale, to the point that he hurls it to the floor prior to leaving to face the count a second time, all the while pacing back and forth like a caged tiger (again, think the vengeful Conrad), the reader who knows Russian might ask why isn't this crucial leitmotif identified as a *kartuz*. The answer involves two possibilities, both of which may be correct: first, Pushkin is playing with the reader heuristically, inserting a riddle into the text that he challenges us to untangle, and thus *become aware*; second, he is implying that we, as readers and as decision-makers in life, are in thrall to subconscious patterning that we cannot see at the time and that can come back to bite us later on. This was also what Pushkin was afraid of on the eve of his marriage: could his own rash behavior as a young man, not unlike the count's brazen cherry munching (also out of a *furazhka*) at the first duel, come back to harm him now that he was trying to start a new period in his life? But what happens to the stage props in the story is that they, including Silvio himself, are all *shot down*. That is what happens to false stereotypes. The Swiss landscape (Schiller's *Wilhelm Tell*, Byron's *Prisoner of Chillon* and *Manfred*), which in Russian is *kartina* (another play on *karta*), is shot through twice, and the loner Silvio disappears from the count's life only to die a "romantic" (but seemingly useless) death at Skulyani fighting for Greek independence alongside Ypsilanti (a Byronic fate). The count is allowed to live, but he is chastened, "left to his conscience" both for breaking the rules of dueling and for not respecting the value of life in the first place.

Pushkin's story is not about altruism or the emergence of morality in an obvious sense. That is never Pushkin's way. The count and the countess are presented as generous, amiable people, but their behavior is otherwise not remarkable. They are not particularly outer-directed or self-effacing, which would be a strange thing to draw attention to in Pushkin's world in any event. Rather what is being described in the story is how, if one is *lucky enough* to survive to maturity and become familied, one begins to see things differently. *In evolutionary terms, the copying/replication that is chemically programmed on the genetic level (no awareness) is not the same as the imitation/influence that one engages with, eventually making one's own, on the cultural level (self-awareness).* One is not only the bird whose sole attention is directed at the seed in front of it that it intends to pick up in its beak (left-hemisphere involvement); one is also the bird attending to its surroundings, on guard to protect its mate and its nest, aware of others that depend on it, engulfed in a "big-picture" gestalt of simultaneous interconnectedness (right-hemisphere involvement). Pushkin's language teaches that the stage props are false, but that society's opinion still matters, that Byronism and romantic alienation are a phase to pass through, but that the place one arrives at is never a terminus. It is always "conditioned arising." After all, Pushkin still died in

a duel. He did so because he was sufficiently fed up with his situation in 1836—
Nicholas I's bordering-on-indecent attentions paid to Mme Pushkin; the same
tsar's insistence the poet remain at court as a kind of lackey (*kammerjunker* was
an assigned title incommensurate with Pushkin's age and status); his mounting
debts that could not be repaid through publishing ventures alone; his household that needed to be maintained and that was complicated by the presence of
his wife's sisters; the rumors that swirled around d'Anthès's unseemly courting
of Natalie right under her husband's nose; the idea floated even by Pushkin's
friends that the Frenchman and Natalie formed a handsome couple; the same
idea circulated by Pushkin's enemies that Russia's greatest man of letters could
be a cuckold, and so on—to repeat, all this was enough to provoke a different
outcome from the one now tormenting him. Pushkin went to his final duel with
a clear mind and a calm heart because he knew that whatever happened, either
banishment by the tsar to the country because of the prohibition on dueling
or death by his opponent's bullet, it would be preferable. In either case he will
have preserved his life's work, which in his mind could not be saved intact if he,
its author, were subject to ridicule, if Pushkin the historical person and Pushkin
the creative genius were placed in ironic juxtaposition. And if in modern times
we are liable to dismiss the entire culture of dueling as a barbaric squandering
of human potential, we need only recall the confrontation between Alexander
Hamilton and Aaron Burr in 1804, thirty-three years before Pushkin's duel,
which deprived America's young democracy of perhaps its most gifted framer at
age forty-nine. Like Pushkin, fantastically endowed but also not without flaws,
a brilliant writer and orator but also someone who could overstep society's
bounds, Hamilton would not have been "Hamilton" without this tragic bookend
to his life. If his honor was at stake, he would not back down.[24]

In the chapters to follow we will continue to track the students' responses to
"conditioned arising" in their lives through the prism of Pushkin, the Russian
language, and current ideas about cultural and biological evolution. What is
encapsulated in "The Shot"—consciousness of how the mind attends to different things as the individual's interactions with the environment change—will
be redirected elsewhere. Other of Pushkin's texts will showcase different life lessons for the students. What is the role of sexual selection (as opposed to natural
selection) in the kids' lives and how can Pushkin's take on this before it became
science, without his knowing it, explain things "for the species" presciently? Is
our individual identity more beholden to kin selection or group selection and
what does Pushkin's culture tell us about the uses and abuses of tribalism and the
future of hybridization? Is multilevel selection,[25] the ability of between-group
cooperation over time to outperform within-group competition, possible in a

sophisticated human culture aware of its own choices? How does the morality of the church apply to modern humankind and how can the Bible's storytelling be both subverted and reaffirmed at the same time? And finally, as we live in history, and change under the environment's pressure, is "speciation"—the evolution of the species into something noticeably different—still happening with us? It is my contention, which I hope to arrive at together with, and aided by, the students, that Pushkin helps us see these issues with inspiring clarity. By looking at his words carefully we really can see consciousness building on itself, creativity happening.

CHAPTER 4

"The Stationmaster":
Morality Meets Sexual Selection

———————

Two deep-seated idea clusters embedded in all human beings' personal stories are those relating to morality and romantic choice (the latter being known in evolutionary terms as sexual selection). Here our students are no exceptions. In this chapter the plan is to show first how, in the young people's own words, they understand these concepts and how they see them unfolding in their own lives. Next, we will look at another of Pushkin's short tales, "The Stationmaster," in which these issues play a prominent role but are handled, as we might expect with Pushkin, in an unorthodox way—a way that flips on its head a universally revered biblical parable, with the result that the reader is forced to consider the existential (as in "how best to survive") dividing line between familial duty, on the one hand, and romantic desire, on the other. In this respect it is an ideal text for young people thinking about the future. As with our discussion of "The Shot," the purpose in alerting the students to these ideas is not to convince them of anything, but to make them aware of the options that may await them in their own lives. Once again, the Russian language plays a key role in bringing aspects of the decision-making process to the surface.

The Students on Morality and Romantic Relationships

Let us begin by repeating our earlier practice of quoting directly from the students' biographical statements. First, how they view their initial exposure to morality:

> Ingrid:
> I learned morality through my actions. I learned not to lie when
> I was young. Once, I saw my brother lie and then smile because

he was a terrible liar. I did the same, and I as well started to laugh. My mom told me that lying was bad because it would get me nowhere. Once a lie starts, the lie cannot stop until the truth comes to light, which is true. Ever since then, I have tried to be as honest as possible. I learned morality through most of my mistakes. I never liked the feeling of doing something wrong to someone. If I do something wrong, I feel guilty immediately and it does not leave my mind until I make it right.

Elisia:

One thing that highly affected me was when I was in elementary school and all the students had parents who were alumni of that school. I will never forget my 5th-grade history fair where I put in a lot of effort on the project and the other students barely even finished it and I got a B and everyone else got an A. Things like this occurred multiple times with multiple projects and assignments. My parents even noticed how unfair it was, but they told me that, in the end, the other students were going to be the ones to suffer because they wouldn't know how to do things on their own in high school. This really paid off.

Mia:

It was during my teenage years that I started questioning morality the most. I grew up a Christian and I attended Friday and Sunday services at a nearby church. I was always a strong believer because my mother taught me at a young age to recite Bible verses and pray every night. I was involved in the dance ministry at church, so I knew I felt something when I learned about Christ. However, I would read a lot about things that were happening around the world and sometimes I would question God's existence. I would find myself conflicted by the things I learned at school and at church. I would get into arguments with people about sexuality and identity. I would not agree when the Bible said that men and women should belong only to each other. I felt that love was universal and could not be restricted. Even though I stopped attending church, for personal reasons, I continue to keep an open mind. [. . .] I would not say I am religious, but I would say I have a soul and an understanding for people and their beliefs.

Beatriz:
All I could say is that I learned morality from my family. All the times that I wanted something but couldn't get it simply because my parents said "no you can't," stuck to me and is now how I seem to think about the world. Some things should be the way they are and that's how I continue to see it.

Samuel:
I became more moral as a person after I met a friend in high school. From this individual I learned much about being an actual good person and how I think people should be treated. [...] Failure has also taught me I should be grateful for what I have and I should work hard for what I don't. There are many tools for achieving success, but it takes your own work to get the things you want.

It's clear these young people have no difficulty explaining how morality operates in their worlds. Morality is, inter alia, a response to interpersonal relations that is other-directed; that endeavors to tell the truth; that recognizes fair play; that tries to spread love; and that identifies right actions with the disciplining of self. Whether the response is a "no" to self ("don't do that") or a "yes" to the other ("think about your family or friends"), the common denominator in all these comments is one's responsibility as a social being. The young people don't ask themselves how this inner orientation came to be; they just know that it is there and that it is not to be trifled with. Much of the time they sense morality's invisible hand *before* they are able to explain it (for example, the brother smiling involuntarily when he is caught).

Next, the students' reactions to the idea of romantic relationships were surprisingly consistent and spoke volumes about how upbringing and learning affect values (what we might call, referring back to earlier discussion, the "conditioned" aspect of the students' "arising"):

Ricardo:
I did not spend much time thinking about the opposite sex or the same sex. I never really felt anything romantic towards anyone. I saw the way my parents fought, and I did not really feel like going through that with a significant other. I found it easier to just chill and not try to be committed to anyone. I thought school came first because I have a couple of childhood friends

who had kids at the age of 15 and 16, and they could not go on to accomplish anything they dreamed of. I knew I did not want to be held back by having kids. I will do that once I have accomplished goals and lived for myself.

Bernice:
I did not think about the opposite sex often. Sure, I can admit there were people who I had crushes on, but it was not a big deal. The crushes were more physical than character-related. I probably started having those innocent crushes around second grade. However, these were not something I often paid attention to. Throughout my childhood, I believed that school and family always come first. I experienced relationships through my friends' lenses when they got into romantic relationships with others. As I grew, I learned the disadvantages of having a relationship at a young age. The idea was not very appealing because I did not want anything to get in the way of my education, and I also did not want to get distracted from my goals. These mindsets came from my mother who often told me that I was too young to start thinking about boys and that I should focus on school. I agreed. Also, the idea of being an immigrant child always comes back to me and makes me realize that it may be a mistake and that I should wait till I have it all together. These mindsets are still true today. I have always been a planner, and I would rather stick to my plan before I can go a little off track.

Mireya:
Ever since I was younger, I always had the mentality that school came first, no matter what was going on around me. I think I remember finally noticing boys by 1st grade, and by 3rd grade all the girls started really talking about them. I would have crushes but never really let them affect me. I was impacted with how badly this messed with my sister's academics and I didn't want to end up like her. I think now that I am in college I kind of pay more attention to guys but not to the point where my academics are on the line.

Ana:
I was never really allowed to date in middle school. I was always afraid of disappointing my parents if I were hiding behind their

back with some boy. I had my first boyfriend in 8th grade, which was the stupidest idea because we were going to graduate. I don't think I ever paid much attention to boys until they started paying attention to me. I don't think I ever contemplated about choosing school or a boy. The answer was and will always be school. My mindset about choosing and finishing school first comes from my parents' experience. They did not have the opportunity to finish school because they could not afford it. I have been given so many opportunities to extend my intellect and I have always been grateful for that. My goal is to do all the things that they never had the opportunity to do.

Anel:
Honestly, I do not spend that much time thinking about the opposite sex. I don't feel the need to be in a relationship now or anytime soon. I see relationships more as a burden because I simply do not have time for that. I want to date to get married, and I am definitely not ready to get married. I also want to work on myself as much as I can until then. I think this mindset has come from growing up in the church and not wanting to repeat my parents' marriage. Not saying that they don't love each other, but I can see where they fall short.

Keila:
In high school thinking about having a boyfriend was always present. Since I received attention from the popular kids at school, this was a trap because it would involve falling into cliques, but by my junior year I realized that being boy crazy only distracted me from my grades. Sure enough, I was able to be ten times more focused in school. My focus in school comes from what my mother preached. From my mother I learned how important education was and how being educated was so valuable in my life. This allowed me to always prioritize my education.

Like a red thread running through these comments is the recognition that survival into the future as young people with better options in life depends on *not* getting seriously involved with the opposite sex until they have successfully done their schoolwork in the present and advanced to a later point in adulthood when they can consider "romance" as a next step. (NB. I am referring here to the majority of students whose answers to interview questions suggest they identify as heterosexual/"cisnormative.") They see how romantic attachments negatively affected friends or siblings who stopped studying or how their parents couldn't finish their education and either ended by divorcing or otherwise struggling to get along at home. Even those who did do occasional dating, like Keila, did not let it interfere with their schoolwork. In short, if we take into account that the students who qualify for the PSI tend to be self-selecting in the first place—that is, they have performed well in school up to this point (usually top ten to twenty percent) and have demonstrated intellectual curiosity and responsible work habits—then it should come as no surprise that our applicant pool is primarily populated with young people who have made the decision to pursue their education ahead of their social life. They are the ones who have begun to sort these issues out.

* * *

As a jumping off point into a discussion of Pushkin's tale I now remind the students of the protocognitive basis of all organic life, including the cellular life going on in their bodies. Why do I start here? Because there is something about the cell as bounded, autonomous living unit that is reminiscent of how a tightly structured literary text models life. Here is how oncologist and Pulitzer Prize winning medical writer Siddhartha Mukherjee describes the cell:

> A cell is not a blob of chemicals; it has distinct structures, or subunits, within it that allow it to function independently. The subunits are designed to supply energy, discard waste, store nutrients, sequester toxic products, and maintain the internal milieu of a cell. Second, a cell is designed to reproduce, so that one cell can produce all the other cells that populate the organism's body. And finally, for multicellular organisms, the cell, or (at least the first cell) is designed to differentiate and develop into other specialized cells, so that various parts of the body—tissues, organs, organ systems—can be formed.[1]

The homeostatic interplay of parts to whole and whole to parts is very much what a literary text is all about. Obviously, I don't mean by this that there are not basic, undeniable differences between the form and function of a cell and the form and function of a Pushkin tale. To begin with, one *is life*, the other is *a representation of life*. So yes, it is only an analogy. And if one sees only those differences, then the point is not worth making. But it is worth making if one sees something distinctly *life-like* in the isomorphism and that that, too, is a kind of "knowledge," more heuristic (as in asking for more) than dispositive, one can build on.

Let me go a little farther with the analogy. In the words of biochemist and "natural genetic engineering" theorist James Shapiro:

> Cells do not act blindly. We know from physiology and bio-chemistry and molecular biology that cells are full of receptors. They monitor what goes on outside. They monitor what goes on inside. And they are continually taking in that information and using it to adjust their actions, their biochemistry, their metab-olism, the cell cycle, etc., so that things come out right. That's why I use the word cognitive to apply to cells, meaning they do things based on knowledge of what's happening around them and inside of them. Without that knowledge and the systems to use that knowledge they couldn't proliferate and survive as effi-ciently as they do.[2]

This idea of a "knowing" ("they [cells] do things based on knowledge") that is always already immanent in organic life at the cellular level has implications throughout the biosphere. As philosopher Thomas Nagel might say, it is an aspect of "mind" in nature that the materialist neo-Darwinian branch of modern evolutionary biology has not yet sufficiently accounted for.[3] Hence it may also not be too much of a stretch to speak of a Pushkin tale in analogous terms: moni-toring "what goes on outside" (the context) and "what goes on inside" (the text) and making adjustments accordingly, its language seems organically "aware." Pushkin is a genius and a one-off, but he also speaks for the species through the way he models creative behavior in his art.

Moreover, this built-in awareness is not about determinism or closing the loop in how consciousness happens. I have to keep reminding the students of that. It's more about properly weighing the value of the individual, the one-and-done phenotype, against the viability of the still evolving species, for the former, no matter the romantic pathos, is always less than the latter. Pushkin understood this. As Shapiro goes on, "Genome change is not the result of accidents. If you have accidents and they're not fixed, the cells die. It's in the course of fixing damage or responding to damage or responding to other inputs—in the case I studied, it was starvation—that cells turn on the systems they have for restruc-turing their genomes." This statement goes against everything the Dawkins's "selfish-gene" theory stands for[4]: natural selection as passive, varying randomly (via mutation), wholly dependent on the one-way chemical transfer of information from the genotype (the matrix) to the phenotype (the non-repeating instance). By alerting us to the fact that the cognitive element cannot be separated out as the researcher descends below the level of the cell, Shapiro and those like him reopen these vistas to the philosophers and poets.

The Plot: A "Moral Tone" and the Parable of the Prodigal Son

"The Stationmaster" contains many of the same storytelling stratagems as "The Shot," but they are deployed to different ends. (This makes sense because both works are part of a larger collection titled *The Belkin Tales* [1830], with these and other stories playing off each other thematically and structurally—once again, to continue our analogical thinking above, the stories form into a larger "organism.") To begin with, Titular Councilor AGN is another narrator who is highly susceptible to events happening around him, only in his case what moves him is not a macho orientation toward the world but a philanthropic one. A titular councilor is someone in the middle to lower range (level nine of fourteen) of the Table of Ranks established by Peter the Great in 1722. The purpose of the Table of Ranks was to disempower the older hereditary nobility, which Peter saw as undermining his ability to reform his backward nation, and to create in its stead a new merit-based nobility that would earn their starting positions, and promotions, within the vast state bureaucracy and carry out more efficiently the tsar's policies. Naturally, considering the Russian context, the meritocratic aspect of Peter's plan had less than optimal results. From the outset, our narrator operates in a voice zone designed to whip up feelings of compassion for the plight of stationmasters—those poor souls at the bottom of the Table of Ranks who run the post houses where teams of horses are changed for the next leg of a journey. Usually, these individuals are retired soldiers one generation removed from the peasantry/serfdom. Their lives are difficult because the status of a new arrival, say that of a nobleman or high-ranking officer, can trump that of a traveler who has been waiting in line for hours for the next available horses, with the result that the stationmaster is blamed for the delay.

> Who has not cursed stationmasters? Who has not quarreled with them frequently? Who has not demanded the fateful book from them in moments of anger, in order to enter in it a useless complaint against their highhandedness, rudeness, and negligence?

[...] Let us be fair, however, and try to imagine ourselves in their position: then, perhaps, we shall judge them with more lenience. What is a stationmaster? A veritable martyr of the fourteenth class, whose rank is enough to shield him only from physical abuse, and at times not even from that. [...] Day or night, he does not have a moment's quiet. The traveler takes out on him all the irritation accumulated during a tedious ride. Should the weather be unbearable, the highway abominable, the coach driver intractable, should the horses refuse to pull fast enough—it is all the stationmaster's fault. Entering the stationmaster's poor abode, the traveler looks on him as an enemy; the host is lucky if he can get rid of his unwanted guest fast, but what if he happens to have no horses available? God! What abuses, what threats shower on his head! [. . .] A general arrives: the trembling stationmaster lets him have the last two teams of horses, including the one that should be reserved for couriers. The general rides off without a word of thanks. Five minutes have scarcely gone by when bells tinkle and a state courier tosses his order for fresh horses on the stationmaster's desk! . . . Let us try to comprehend all this in full, and our hearts will be filled with sincere compassion instead of resentment.

The narrator's tone prepares the reader to perceive a segment of the Russian population differently. The pathos permeating this initial exposition suggests that a charitable gap needs to be filled: stationmasters have tended to be viewed as bothersome background only ("Who has not cursed stationmasters?") and not as individual human beings performing a set of difficult and demeaning duties. Indistinguishable from the trials attendant on traveling the country's horrific backroads, they are nothing more than bit players in a tableau vivant of class inequality that others notice only to the extent that they are inconvenienced. And indeed, as we will soon discover, our author is the first Russian prose writer of distinction to focus attention on the "little guy." (Dostoevsky will later pick up on this.) However, Pushkin never displays sentimentality for its own sake. Just as it was with the macho values that served as starting point of "The Shot," so too will it be with the charitable assumptions initially shaping the narrator's viewpoint in this tale. As we proceed further into the plot of "The Stationmaster," we will need to be on guard against our own humanitarian biases. The "Let us try to comprehend all this in full, and our hearts will be filled with sincere compassion" may not be entirely on the level.

After lamenting the plight of stationmasters in general, the narrator proceeds to tell us a story about a specific stationmaster, Samson Vyrin. The tale begins in 1816, which by now seems well in the past, and takes place somewhere in a backwater described merely as "X" province. The younger version of Titular Councilor AGN, who occupies an even lower rank as the action commences, has had his fill of stationmasters and their now rude, now fawning, but consistently bumbling ways. Moreover, he is appearing at this station after a downpour and is grumpy and in need of a change of clothes. Two things immediately attract his attention upon entering the building: the first is the beauty of the stationmaster's daughter and the second is the set of pictures adorning the stationhouse wall. Since the understated Pushkin always selects details with care and often makes of them semantic "fuses" that ignite sound and sense simultaneously—recall the *karta* (playing card), the *tuz* (ace), and the implied or "missing card" *kartuz* (military cap) in "The Shot"—our next step is to read aloud, and slowly, both descriptions. As this is happening, the students are tasked with trying to keep in mind as many specifics as possible before considering their relation to the evolving plot.

First, the daughter is introduced:

> "Hey, Dunya!" called out the stationmaster. "Light the samovar and go get some cream." As these words were pronounced, a young girl aged about fourteen appeared from behind the partition and ran out on the porch. I was struck by her beauty.
> "Is that your daughter?" I asked the stationmaster.
> "Aye, truly she is," answered he, with an air of satisfaction and pride, "and what a sensible, clever girl, just like her late mother."

Immediately following this comes the description of the pictures:

> He started copying out my order for fresh horses, and I passed the time by looking at the pictures that adorned his humble but neat dwelling. They illustrated the parable of the Prodigal Son. In the first one, a venerable old man, in nightcap and dressing gown, was bidding farewell to a restless youth who was hastily accepting his blessing and a bag of money. The second one depicted the young man's lewd behavior in vivid colors: he was seated at a table, surrounded by false friends and shameless women. Farther on, the ruined youth, in rags and with a three-cornered hat on his head, was tending swine and sharing their meal; deep sorrow

and repentance were reflected in his features. The last picture showed his return to his father: the warmhearted old man, in the same nightcap and dressing gown, was running forward to meet him; the Prodigal Son was on his knees; in the background the cook was killing the fatted calf, and the elder brother was asking the servants about the cause of all the rejoicings. Under each picture I read appropriate verses in German. All this has remained in my memory to this day, together with the pots of balsam, the bed with the colorful curtain, and other objects. I can still see the master of the house himself as if he were right before me: a man about fifty years of age, still fresh and agile, in a long green coat with three medals on faded ribbons.

These passages introduce plot elements that, when combined, produce different potential storylines, the roads taken and not taken, in the tale to come. One suggests one set of possibilities for the Dunya-Vyrin relationship, the other another set. We don't know yet which way these details will lead, but we can be sure Pushkin will push them in a direction that challenges our expectations, which—the taking on of the challenge—is the first step toward survival in the evolutionary process. Experiment and learn. Again, recall Shapiro's micro-level formulation: "Cells do not act blindly. [. . .] They monitor what goes on outside. They monitor what goes on inside. And they are continually taking in that information and using it to adjust their actions [. . .] so that things come out right." Here the "inside" is what happens *in* the story, with regard to the characters' actions, while the "outside" is what happens *beyond its frame*, in the minds of the readers. From this point forward, Dunya's beauty will be key, as will Vyrin's self-satisfaction and pride in his daughter; the moral of the Prodigal Son parable will also loom large in the arc of all future actions. Even the fact that the pictures are accompanied by "appropriate" (*prilichnye*, as in "respectable") German verses will play a role. The bigger question is, will "things come out, right?"

What follows after this sets the ball rolling. Dunya prepares the tea and notices that the young narrator can't take his eyes off her. Her reaction is not shyness; she has spent time in her father's uncivil world (it is she who is quickly able to calm down an angry traveler with her charm), and she answers his questions without hesitation. He calls her playfully a "little coquette" (*malen'kaia koketka*). This, too, is not an irrelevant detail. Next the narrator plies Vyrin with "punch" (alcoholic, another leitmotif) to loosen his tongue and get him to share his stories. The three seem to become fast friends and the stereotype of the difficult stationmaster and the depressing station fades away. The last thing that happens before our young traveler leaves the station is that, significantly, he asks Dunya for a kiss. This moment requires discussion because in our world it is normally seen as highly improper and potentially abusive for an adult to "hit on" a fourteen-year-old girl for favors. But this is a different context, Russia in 1816, and the kiss is meant to imply an as yet undetermined balance of power. This "transaction" is also about survival instinct. We sense Dunya's vulnerability, but we also sense her resiliency and playfulness. Notice that Dunya *takes the initiative* to see the young man off:

> At last I said good-bye to them; the father wished me a pleasant journey, and the daughter came to see me to the cart. On the porch I stopped and asked her to let me kiss her; she consented . . . I have accumulated many recollections of kisses but none has made such a lasting and delightful impression on me as the one I received from Dunya.

The plot thereafter unfolds in stages, with each new stage introduced by a subsequent visit to the station by the narrator. Several years later the narrator is in the area again and recalls the pleasant, vital stationmaster and his comely daughter. He decides to drop by to see how the two are doing. Possibly by now Dunya is married. He finds Vyrin much changed—palpably older, withdrawn, sullen. He also notices that the station house has fallen into disrepair; there are no flowers in the window, and most importantly, there is no Dunya. Sensing that something is wrong and that he won't be able to get the story by simply asking Vyrin about it, he changes tactics and offers the old man some rum-laced punch: perhaps this will get him to talk. The ruse works.

Vyrin now tells the story of what happened to his beloved daughter. Everything at home rested on her. She cooked, she cleaned, she greeted the visitors, she kept everyone happy. Ladies gave her handkerchiefs and earrings; gentlemen asked to stay for supper just to get a longer look at her. "Didn't I love my Dunya, didn't I cherish my child, and didn't she have a life here?" exclaims Vyrin. "But no, you can't swear off misfortune; what is fated cannot be averted." Three years ago, a handsome young hussar named Minsky was traveling through and demanded horses. His first reaction upon learning that no horses were available was to raise his voice and his whip, but as soon as he saw Dunya he calmed down and found an excuse to linger at the station. He ordered something to eat. When Vyrin went out to see to the exchange of horses, he returned to find Minsky seriously ill. The guest had to stay the night, and the next day, with him worse, a doctor was summoned from the nearest city. When the doctor arrived he examined the patient and prescribed several days of bed rest, all the while communicating with the sick man exclusively in German. Strangely, he also joined Minsky for a hearty meal and a bottle of wine. During Minsky's "recovery" Dunya tended to him constantly, wrapping his head with a cool cloth and bringing him lemonade to drink. When it was finally time for the hussar to leave, he offered to take Dunya to mass at the other end of the village. Dunya hesitated, but at her father's urging agreed to go with Minsky. She did not return.

Almost as soon as Dunya left, the stationmaster suspected that something was amiss. As he traced her steps, he learned that she did not take mass that day and that, indeed, she continued on of her own free will with Minsky but was crying the entire way. She was clearly torn between her devotion to her father and her attraction toward a potential young lover. Now it was Vyrin who took ill in earnest and, being looked after by the same doctor, found out that Minsky's illness had been a cruel charade. Taking leave from his post and tracking down the hussar's domicile to fashionable St. Petersburg, Vyrin decided to go and "bring home [his] lost sheep." He located Minsky at a high-class hotel, and when he confronted the young man Minsky reacted in a manner consistent with his wealth and aristocratic station: he recognized Vyrin, acknowledged (though breezily) his guilt, explained that what had happened couldn't be undone, told him he couldn't part with Dunya, stuffed some banknotes into his sleeve, and quickly ushered him out the door. In other words, in this world dominated by class and power Minsky took what he wanted without compunction. The only response Vyrin could offer was a moralistic cliché: please, sir, return Dunya because "it's no use crying over spilt milk," which in Russian is more suggestive—"what has fallen from the cart is ruined [and thus can't be put back]."

Defeated in this exchange, Vyrin was ready to return to the station, but before doing so he wanted to see his "poor Dunya" one last time. That evening, after praying in church, Vyrin noticed by chance Minsky's richly appointed carriage passing in the street. It stopped before an apartment house and the hussar himself jumped out, ran up the steps and disappeared into the building. By cleverly asking some questions, Vyrin ascertained that this was where Minsky was keeping Dunya. He bluffed his way into the building and knocked at the door of the apartment in question. When the door was opened by a servant, the agitated father rushed past her and made his way to the edge of the sitting room where Dunya and Minsky were seated in this fashion:

> In the room, which was elegantly furnished, he saw Minsky seated, deep in thought. Dunya, dressed in all the finery of the latest fashion, sat on the arm of his easy chair like a lady rider on

an English saddle. She was looking at Minsky with tenderness, winding his dark locks around her fingers, which glittered with rings. Poor stationmaster! Never had his daughter appeared so beautiful to him; he could not help admiring her.

When Dunya looked up and saw her father, she fell to the floor in a faint. On this occasion Minsky was not nearly so apologetic to his pursuer. He became enraged and accused Vyrin of stalking him like an assassin. He grabbed the old man by the collar and threw him out onto the stairwell. In the end, Vyrin was forced to accept this state of affairs—the injustice of the class structure that allowed someone to first deceive him and then steal his daughter in this manner. But this stage of the story was still not quite ended. The stationmaster wrapped up his loss of Dunya in the following way:

> "It's almost three years now," he concluded, "that I've been liv-
> ing without Dunya, having no news of her whatsoever. Whether
> she is alive or dead, God only knows. Anything can happen. She
> is not the first, nor will she be the last, to be seduced by some
> rake passing through, to be kept for a while and then discarded.
> There are many of them in Petersburg, of these foolish young
> ones: today attired in satin and velvet, but tomorrow, verily I say,
> sweeping the streets with the riffraff of the alehouse. Sometimes,
> when you think that Dunya may be perishing right there with
> them, you cannot help sinning in your heart and wishing her in
> the grave . . ."

The final stage of the story involves a third visit by the narrator. Now some more time has passed and when the titular councilor returns to the site where he first met Vyrin and first kissed Dunya everything has changed. It's been a year since Vyrin has died and his station house is now occupied by a brewer. The brewer's wife tells the narrator that Vyrin died from drink. The narrator laments his wasted trip and the seven rubles it cost him to hire the horses to bring him here. It is autumn, the most dismal time in a dismal part of the country. Before leaving, however, the narrator asks the brewer's wife where Vyrin is buried and whether someone can show him the way; she offers her ragamuffin son Vanka as guide. The little cemetery on the outskirts of town where the stationmaster's grave is located turns out to be, in the narrator's telling, one of the saddest sites he has ever seen. As a place it is a fitting setting for the tears, the *slëzy*, that are the trademark of Vyrin's story. But in pointing out the grave the boy provides significant new information: the stationmaster's resting place has not been totally forgotten; in fact, it was visited by a magnificent lady sometime after Vyrin died.

> "There was a lady, though, traveled through these parts in the summer: she did ask after the old stationmaster and went a-visiting his grave."
>
> "What sort of a lady?" I asked with curiosity.
>
> "A wonderful lady," replied the urchin; "she was traveling in a coach-and-six with three little masters, a nurse, and a black pug; when they told her the old stationmaster'd died, she started weeping and said to the children, 'You behave yourselves while I go to the graveyard.' I offered to take her, I did, but the lady said, 'I know the way myself.' And she gave me a silver five-kopeck piece—such a nice lady!"

After lying prone for a long time on the stationmaster's grave, the lady rises, goes into the village, and makes a donation to the priest, gives the boy a silver five-kopeck piece, and departs. This information causes Titular Councilor AGN to change his mind about the futility of his final visit. He too gives the boy a five-kopeck piece and no longer regrets either the trip or the seven-ruble expense.

In presenting the plot of "The Stationmaster" I have gone into more detail than is normally the case because the "facts" of the plot do not work their magic unless they are interpreted both figuratively and literally, ironically and "on the level." I warn the students about this and I ask them various questions before we get going to be sure they have taken in as much of the storyline as possible. The force field spreading out between the literal meaning of Vyrin's and Dunya's story and its blurred, semantically shaded opposite is precisely where the learning and conceptual experimentation take place that are essential survival skills. By parsing Vyrin's and Dunya's actions, as well as the narrator's responses to those actions, the students can test themselves on where they come down on the issue of what are the limits, if any, to parental love, filial devotion, and exogamous (marrying/mating outside one's social group) desire.

The irony in the storyline becomes immediately discernible once I ask the students to keep the parable of the Prodigal Son in mind as they analyze Dunya's choices as seemingly wayward child and Vyrin's reactions as doting parent. First, Dunya is not a son, but a daughter, and her options, given her social class and sex, are even fewer than those open to Vyrin. Here we notice that the father's feelings for his offspring are perhaps forgivable, but they also tend to reflect back on himself (he brags about her "*s vidom dovol'nogo samoliubiia*," literally "with an appearance of self-satisfied pride/vanity") and do nothing to promote the girl's personal growth and independence. Her role in the station house is to perform the same chores as her mother. Second, Dunya is given no patrimony, no "bag of money," that she then squanders among "false friends" and "shameless" lovers. Indeed, despite the ambiguity of her relations with Minsky, she is never presented as displaying anything approaching the "lewd behavior" in the parable's second picture. When Vyrin does find her, she is not dressed in rags sharing provender with swine, but attired and bejeweled in the latest fashion. Third, Vyrin does not act as the kind father waiting at home in the parable; instead, he flips roles and he goes out looking for his "lost sheep" (from another parable!) in the story. And fourth, when this "prodigal daughter" finally does return home she is not greeted by the forgiving father but by his silent, "judging" grave.

I ask the students to consider again Vyrin's social class and where the moral precepts in the story are coming from. Vyrin is not educated and the pictures depicting the Prodigal Son's pathway from greedy adolescent to contrite young man are accompanied by "decorous German verses," which the stationmaster cannot read. Here we also remember that it was German that Minsky and the doctor spoke in order to trick the stationmaster about his guest's fake illness. In other words, neither the parable as pictured on the wall nor its linguistic glosses help Vyrin in his search for his daughter. He ignores what the parable is instructing the "good" father to do, that is, wait at home for the son to return and forgive him if he does so, and, moreover, in his ignorance he is taken advantage of by others who use their superior knowledge (the German of the "decorous verses") against him. This is, of course, completely unfair and is the basis of the tears shed by the stationmaster later in his telling and the sympathy that the narrator feels for him as he listens.

But there are various conflicting emotions taking place in this word-picture of Vyrin and his plight, and that is where Pushkin's irony and the need for conceptual experimentation on the reader's part come in. Just as James Shapiro argues for a "cognitive" basis to the smallest unit of life, a basis that is immanent and inseparable from the cell's functional needs, so do evolutionary biologists and primatologists like Frans de Waal see *morality as growing out of the animal world* and not being superimposed on it from outside or above:

> Our best-known "moral laws" offer nice post hoc summaries of what we consider moral, but are limited in scope and full of holes. Morality has much more humble beginnings, which are recognizable in the behavior of other animals. Everything science has learned in the last few decades argues against the pessimistic

view that morality is a thin veneer over a nasty human nature. On the contrary, our evolutionary background lends a massive helping hand without which we would never have gotten this far.[5]

And

> This brings me back to my bottom-up view of morality. The moral law is not imposed from above or derived from well-reasoned principles; rather, it arises from ingrained values that have been there since the beginning of time. The most fundamental one derives from *the survival value of group life* [my emphasis—DB]. The desire to belong, to get along, to love and be loved, prompt us to do everything in our power to stay on good terms with those on whom we depend. Other social primates share this value and rely on the same filter between emotion and action to reach a mutually agreeable modus vivendi. We see this filter at work when chimpanzee males suppress a brawl over a female, or when baboon males act as if they failed to notice a peanut. It all comes down to inhibitions.[6]

If we think about Vyrin's actions in the story and apply de Waal's lens to them, other considerations emerge. To begin with, the "well-reasoned principles" of the church, however revered and practiced over generations, may not work in certain situations. Experimentation may be needed if survival is at stake. The hallmarks of morality—empathy, fair play, reciprocity, compassion, altruism, sacrifice for the group—may not be enough if the self is in danger of disappearing entirely. That is Dunya's quandry, which her father, who loves her dearly but blindly, cannot see. She is everything to her father, but she has no life of her own, which Pushkin characteristically leaves unsaid (just as he does about the *kartuz* in "The Shot"). When I discuss this with the students I ask them questions that bring out a more "Dunya-centric" view of the plot. The most linguistically telling moment in "The Stationmaster" is when the narrator explains the stationmaster's mistake in letting Dunya go in the following way: "Later the poor stationmaster could not understand how he could have permitted Dunya to go off with the hussar; what had blinded him?" In Russian the "what had blinded him" is rendered literally as "how the blindness had come upon him." It's an impersonal construction. The word for stationmaster in Russian is *smotritel'*, or "he who looks after"—that is, a kind of "watchman." Vyrin believes he has not looked properly after his daughter and that by mistake he has let her get away, but that is not what the morality of the tale is really about. The father is smitten by the daughter's beauty and cleverness, but in his pride he can see her only in her role as housekeeper, station ornament, and charmer of disgruntled travelers. Through the narrator Pushkin presents Vyrin's case in a sympathetic light. Our students virtually unanimously are on the side of Vyrin when we begin to discuss what has happened. But then we consider Dunya and her life choices, and the range of morally acceptable positions expands. Morality and fair play exist *in the balance* between the individual and the group.[7] The point is that this is all there already, in what linguistically is the equivalent of a "cellular level," in Pushkin's puns and plot construction: initially, our sympathy for the abandoned father leads us in one direction, which is reinforced by the narrator's rhetorical embellishments ("the poor stationmaster" and so on), but then the play with words, including the "blindness" that obstructs the "watching" man's vision, leads us in another direction.

Sexual Selection

The other "bottom-up" shaper of emotional and cognitive responses to the story is sexual selection, a term Pushkin would not have used, but which he implicitly understood. Now I ask the students, especially our female students, who are trying to develop their own skill sets to survive in a complicated world, to imagine themselves as Dunya. What are Dunya's realistic options given her station in life? Lest we forget, Pushkin has given Dunya a peasant name; she is not called Natalya or Olga; thus, everywhere she goes in life those who pay attention to social hierarchies will know her first by what her name suggests. This would not be much different from a young female today with a name like Juana or Jayla as opposed to Jane or Joan. Dunya is the underdog. In the story she makes a miraculous transformation from *devochka*, generic "girl," to *barynia*, "married lady of rank," although, again, there is no evidence in the text that she and Minsky have married. This transformation is highly improbable, but Pushkin brings it to life against the odds, and in the constant shadow of the Prodigal Son parable. Why? First, because the poet's creativity is always on the side of young life emerging,[8] and of the experiments and risks taken that end up bearing fruit. Finding the right rhyme word in a poem, the one that brings together in an *Aha!* moment both the sound and sense of things in a new way, is just another version of this same instinctive move. But here, the poetic texture of life arriving on the scene is transposed to a prose plot and the story of a lower-class girl with limited prospects. This is where our current understanding of sexual selection comes in.

Minsky has the wealth and social status, but it is *ultimately Dunya who chooses him*. She is the one taking the risks. Her moment of decision, captured in her hesitation to leave with Minsky when he offers to drive her to the church, is a crucial inflection point in the tale. Dunya is clearly depicted as an attractive person *and* a good person. When she leaves her father and the church-related moral code his world represents (the pictures on the wall) and chooses to go off with Minsky and the sexual attraction/mate choice he represents, she does not cease to be good. This is the lesson the students will have to internalize. But more is needed before they can understand.

Choosing a mate with whom one will have children is the most awesome decision one can make in life, with the burden for that awesomeness falling disproportionately on the woman. Matters are further complicated by the fact that sexual intercourse itself is an event so suffused with primal feeling that it is seemingly without mind. As the comic stereotype goes, this is especially true of the male side. Still, even with this implicit asymmetry, or power imbalance, it can be argued that evolution has been able to do its work. Just as morality has grown slowly but surely out of the animal world (de Waal), so too has our hominid sexual behavior, with its patterns of courting/withholding, displaying/concealing, importuning/retreating, been adapted over time into something resembling a teetering balance. Likewise, over the millennia, the idea of the sex act—not necessarily how it was performed, but how it was imagined—evolved into more than the "beast with two backs" (*Othello*) and the female's role into more than that of unwilling body upon whom sex is performed. Recent forays into evolutionary biology tell us, for example, that the female's capacity for arousal is more varied than thought previously.[9] Here, biology and culture are in a kind of tug-of-war, with the male who needs to guarantee paternity in order for his genetic material to make it to the next generation restricting female access to other donors *through culture*, including the taboos and prohibitions that insist on monogamy. Sex is of course still sex, and sex-related dehumanization and violence still happen in the world, and too often. But two things can be true at the same time. (As an aside, this is usually a good place for me to provide some commentary to the students on just how thoroughly schooled Pushkin himself was in Ovidian *ars amatoria*—the intricacies of male-female sexual negotiations cited in connection with the eponymous hero's social training in *Onegin*. Indeed, from his adolescent years on, the poet enjoyed sex's "mindless pleasures" early and often, even contracting venereal disease, probably with ballerinas or actresses, and in his twenties he fathered an illegitimate child with a peasant girl, Olga Kalashnikova, and was forced to turn to his friend Prince Vyazemsky for help in finding a place for her and the child. He thus clearly saw aspects of the hussar Minsky in himself and by today's standards would definitely be considered a player.)

As with so much else having to do with the discovery of the immanence of our animal nature, it all goes back to Darwin. And perhaps the most important shift in Darwin's thinking as he progressed from *On the Origin of Species* (1859) to *Descent of Man* (1871) was his honing in on the role of sexual selection, as opposed to natural selection, in the evolutionary process. "Sexual selection depends on the success of certain individuals over others of the same sex in relation to the propagation of the species; whilst natural selection depends on the success of both sexes, at all ages, in relation to the general conditions of life."[10] Using birds as his most vivid examples, Darwin showed that in certain animals with sufficiently developed nervous systems and cerebral capacity what tended to happen with regard to the propagation of the species was that choices were made that were "aesthetically motivated," having to do with physical ornamentation and allure, or song or dance, rather than strictly pragmatic, or having to do with protection (the strength or combative ability of the male) or health (no obvious disease, or what later generation scientists would describe as the choice of "good" genes). This distinction is all the more important because subsequent history has, with few exceptions, given Darwin's own thoroughly thought-through judgments and observations about what was at work in sexual selection short shrift. Beginning with Victorians like St. George Mivart and Alfred Russel Wallace, Darwin's codiscoverer of natural selection, and continuing up through present-day (largely gene-centered) neo-Darwinians,[11] it has been broadly assumed that sexual selection is really a subset of natural selection, which is to say, all mating choices made by animals, including humans, are determined primarily by the practical benefits brought by the impregnating male to the receptive female. According to the Wallace/neo-Darwinian line of thought, the adaptations that happen randomly and then are selected for preserving in subsequent generations because they provide a survival benefit are what count in the natural world, hence the idea of *natural* selection. Genetic mutations ("allele frequencies") affecting trait distribution that help a species to survive (when they work) or cause them to die out (when they don't)—think the famous example of different finches' beaks in the Galapagos—should be considered the transactional items of record in the evolutionary process. Sexual selection, to the extent that it exists, and the neo-Darwinians by now admit that it does, is still only natural selection by another name.

But Darwin's description of the astonishing displays of the male Argus pheasant and the equally astonishing responses of the female Argus pheasant to those displays makes the hard-science (micro-level-upward) attempts to treat this interaction as purely practical, only about "honest" advertising of health and security, and not about an ever more extravagant beauty, seem stubbornly wrong-headed and purblind:

> I know of no fact in natural history more wonderful than that the female Argus pheasant should be able to appreciate the exquisite shading of the ball-and-socket ornaments and the elegant patterns on the wing-feathers of the male. He who thinks that the male was created as he now exists must admit that the great plumes, which prevent the wings from being used for flight, and which, as well as the primary feathers, are displayed in a manner quite peculiar to this one species during the act of courtship, and at no other time, were given to him as an ornament. If so, he must likewise admit that the female was created and endowed with the capacity of appreciating such ornaments. I differ only in the conviction that the male Argus pheasant acquired his beauty gradually, through the females having preferred during many generations the more highly ornamented males; the aesthetic capacity of the females having been advanced through exercise or habit in the same manner as our own taste is gradually improved.[12]

The economy of mating sequence that Darwin observed so brilliantly here, which we could render in shorthand as "increase in male ornamental beauty leads to increase in female interest/receptivity," shifted the focus to the female for the first time. No longer was it simply the "aggressive" male mounting the "passive" female because it was time to mate and the urge was there, which would be how natural selection explained it in the Victorian era; now it becomes a function of female choice precisely because this is what the female *desires*. Moreover, the change over time in the male Argus pheasant's appearance, the plumes that have become more and more magnificently patterned, have done so *in response to* the female choosing the more extravagant over the less extravagant, because that is what arouses her, which also means that the males with "lesser" plumes are rejected, and fall away as suitors when their heritable material is not passed on. The male's beautiful wings and the female's discriminating glance are engaged in a coevolutionary dance that, in big-picture terms, changes everything. It didn't matter whether sexual selection had emerged out of natural selection during evolution's broad sweep. What mattered was that sexual selection was pushing species development in another direction, one that was qualitatively different.

Darwin could already see in his time that large swaths of human culture, including the fashion industry and the arbitrary, non-utilitarian nature of "style" (compare: "in the same manner as our own taste is gradually improved"), come down to female choice and an arousal that has its origins in sexual selection.

Yale ornithologist Richard Prum builds in fascinating ways on Darwin's original formulations and pushes them further still. Through extensive fieldwork and laboratory study he makes the case for a science more attuned to how animals, in this case birds, experience the aesthetic in nature. Whether describing in minutest detail aspects of avian anatomy or analyzing birds' social behavior across a bewildering array of species, Prum probes the moment when the animal world begins to discern the "artistic," when biological morphology and female mate choice come together to reveal the first glimmerings of "mind" in nature.[13] For example, the male bowerbird constructs an elaborate bower for the female made of brightly colored objects and twigs that is tantamount to a miniature throne room. The interested female then comes through the "back door" and tries out the throne to see if it appeals to her. If it doesn't, she exits out the front of the bower structure; if it does, she remains in place to mate.

> Essentially, the evolutionary function of the bower is to provide a setting for aesthetic evaluation that also protects the female from "date rape" . . . Because bowers function as both *objects* of choice and *enhancements* of the freedom of choice, they create a new kind of ever-escalating, aesthetic evolutionary feedback.[14]

Prum's and others' research indicates, moreover, that this exercise of choice is deliberate and based on a careful winnowing process. In short, the "ladies" are "shopping for" a male that pleases them:

> Most females visited a number of males over a series of days and then returned to revisit a smaller number before finally selecting one of those for their mate. Their choices were strongly skewed toward those males with better-constructed and more highly decorated bowers. These revolutionary data are a strong indication that female bowerbirds make their aesthetic mate choices based on a pool of interactive, experiential data, rather than in response to a simple, hardwired cognitive stimulus threshold.[15]

But perhaps Prum's most spectacular example of how biology prepares the way for culture's appreciation of art and beauty involves the anatomy of waterfowl and certain duck species' practice of rough sex. As with Argus pheasants and bowerbirds, female ducks choose their mates based on a coevolved calculus of plumage, song, and display. It turns out that non-territorial, non-monogamous (hence sexually indiscriminate) male ducks—for example, Muscovy ducks, pintails, ruddy ducks, mallards—often surround females in greater numbers and force themselves on them in coercive acts of copulation that in human culture would be called rape. It also happens, as one of Prum's colleagues Patricia Brennan discovered in her research, that the male drake's penis (ninety-seven percent of birds do not have penises) is extremely long in comparison to the actual size of the duck and when extended during copulation is flexible (not hard), corkscrew shaped, and designed to enter into the female in a counterclockwise motion as it seeks out the ovum. But, at the same time, the female's anatomy, which is constructed equally fantastically in an intricate clockwise fashion, makes it challenging for the male's sperm to find its way to the egg, especially if the "intromission" is unwanted:

> Once Brennan was able to examine the vaginal anatomy of a number of breeding ducks, what she found instead of simple tubes were vaginas that had a series of dead-end side pockets, or cul-de-sacs, located near the cloaca at the bottom of the reproductive tract. Further up the reproductive tract, she saw a series of twists and turns in the vaginal tube. Interestingly enough, these twists were *clockwise spirals*, in the *opposite* direction of the counterclockwise-spiraling duck penis. [. . .] Brennan showed that the longer and twistier the penis, the more complex the vagina, with more dead-end pockets and upstream twists—and vice versa: the shorter the penis, the simpler the vagina.
>
> But what was the cause of all this anatomical variation? The key insight was that there was a correlation between the more highly elaborated genital structures and the social and sexual lives of the species who possess them.[16]

And:

> How is it, then, that the mate the female chooses can manage to overcome the twists and whorls of her defensive anatomy? How does voluntary sex differ from forced? [. . .] [Brennan's] duck-farm observations revealed that when female Muscovys were actively soliciting copulations, they assumed the conspicuously

horizontal precopulatory display posture, dilated the cloacal muscles, and released copious amounts of lubricating mucus. It seems clear that females can make the reproductive tract a fully functioning and welcoming place when they want to. [...]

What are the ridiculously long penises of these ducks *doing* inside the female's body? The answer turns out to be, "It depends." If the copulation is solicited, then clearly the female is in for the full ride. These penile structures can easily penetrate to the upper reaches of her reproductive tract if only momentarily. [...] However, by being overwhelmingly successful at bottling up the penis during forced intromission, and preventing the vast majority of attempts at forced fertilizations, female ducks have managed to maintain the advantage in the sexual arms race.[17]

Once again, in shorthand, females *who have chosen males they want* are also able to thwart the attempts to impregnate of the males they don't want. Discrimination or aesthetic judgment based on beauty/attractiveness trumps physical force, although violence can still certainly be there in the behavior of the frantic males competing with each other to pass on their genetic material.

Dunya's Choice

These two value force fields—morality and sexual selection—are at the heart of "The Stationmaster" and Dunya's difficult choice. This is yet another reason why our students need Pushkin, because he presents these issues in a terse story form that communicates intellectually and touches emotionally at the same time. It is "infectious" in the sense Tolstoy meant when describing good art. While most children want to eventually, but sometimes sooner than is wise, assert their independence from their parents and venture out into the broader world to make their way and prove themselves, they also don't want to hurt their parents while doing so. This desire not to hurt is primarily moral—the socialization they have learned growing up in the family, going to school, attending church, joining clubs, playing sports, and so forth. At the same time, another desire that adolescents on the verge of adulthood experience is sexual. And in this instance they face the problem that Dunya faced: how to fit one's psycho-physiological need for a lover, and ultimately one's choice of mate, into the larger picture of living a good life. Pushkin captures this agonizing decision-making process through the eyes of the father as well as through the eyes of the sympathetic narrator.

When Vyrin sees Dunya caressing Minsky—it is she who is physically playing with his dark curls—we are witness to all the power and beauty of this mate choice in a minimum of words (Pushkin's signature) that only brings out the pain of the father and the sexual attraction, even obsessiveness, of the young couple more forcefully. Once again, the crucial scene:

> Dunya, dressed in all the finery of the latest fashion, sat on the arm of his easy chair like a lady rider on an English saddle. She was looking at Minsky with tenderness, winding his dark locks around her fingers, which glittered with rings. Poor stationmaster! Never had his daughter appeared so beautiful to him; he could not help admiring her.

Why would Dunya be looking at Minsky tenderly and touching him in this way except that *she loves him*? Sex has been portrayed for long portions of cultural history as the man being "in the saddle," the king who is "reigning" and "reining" the female body politic. But here it is Dunya who is in control; she sits on the arm of the chair like a "lady rider on an English saddle." Minsky is situated not above her, the mount, but below her, as though he is the one being ridden. Her beauty is culturally mediated, cloaked in the "latest finery" and ornamented with glittering rings—signs of social status that make her more desirable. But she understands (and Pushkin understands) that, for young life to emerge, her beauty needs to be joined with Minsky's dashing vitality and social capital, while the father, who has the strong moral claim, can only look on in misery.[18]

In the human realm it is not the drab female who chooses the fantastically accoutered male. Roles have largely reversed, while gender, a wholly subjective category that is not the same as biological sex, enters the picture.[19] Over millions of years evolution has built out an entire ecosystem between the human mind's imaginings and the sex act: skin can serve as ornamentation (tattoos) just as the add-ons of dress and jewelry can; what one doesn't show can create as much of a come-on as what one does show. As Freud tells us,

> The increasing concealment of the body which goes along with civilization keeps sexual curiosity awake which seeks to complete the sexual object through unveiling its concealed parts in imagination. This curiosity can be diverted to artistic efforts ("sublimation") if its interest is turned away from the genitals to the total appearance of the body. The tendency to linger at

this intermediary sexual game of the sexually accentuated gaze is found to a certain degree in most normal individuals; indeed it gives them the possibility of directing a certain amount of their libido to higher artistic aims.[20]

For Freud art exists as diversion, foreplay ("sublimation") thought up by humankind to entertain itself when not engaged in sex. Words in their way work like the presence or absence of clothing to arouse and make us curious. But that is only part of the story. The Dunya of "The Stationmaster" not only survives, she survives, one might say, *beautifully*. She survives as a woman making tough choices, a woman who may be aware of her own beauty (the "little coquette" of the first scene) but who is not sentimental about that beauty. Freud's explanation of art is too "masculine," too focused on why a (presumably male) artist needs words to turn his interest "away from the genitals to the total appearance of the body" (is this even an idea that a woman could come up with?) and thereby "direct a certain amount of his libido to higher aims" (this in itself sounds like the sperm of a Mallard drake trying to find its serpentine way to the ever remote egg). Natural selection moves forward passively, stumbling onto ways to survive without thinking about it, but sexual selection, because it chooses based on what it wants, *makes itself aware of itself as it decides*. It also is linked to the birth of artistic representation, however the overreaching Freud ("I am by temperament nothing but a conquistador," he once wrote) might describe the latter, because artistic representation, when done well, gives us the sense of life emerging, which involves sex, to be sure, but is also more than sex.

Human life emerging is mind and body acting in concert and moving about in the world in ways that balance morality and sexual selection against each other, for the sake of the species. The reason the narrator was pleased by the ending to the tale provided by Vanka was because it reinserted a moral counterweight to the earlier scenes of Dunya choosing her own desires over her father's. The story needs the lad's vivid description of the lovely lady who comes to visit the stationmaster's grave. Pushkin, in his playful seriousness, tells a modern parable of the Prodigal Son that is turned upside down in every way: son is daughter, daughter is not prodigal, father turns to drink and becomes "prodigal" himself, daughter returns home to father too late, father doesn't forgive child ("you cannot help sinning in your heart and wishing her in the grave"), and so on. The church's prescriptions don't help when applied narrowly. But the essence of a moral worldview is retained. Dunya does feel guilty that she abandoned her father and she knows that her happiness—the well-heeled *barchata* ("little masters/nobles"), the nursemaid, the lapdog, the impressive carriage—has been purchased at a cost. She shows this by tipping Vanka and making an offering at the church. "'What sort of lady?' I asked with curiosity. 'A nice [*slavnaia*] lady,' replied the urchin." We never find out whether Minsky and Dunya have wed, as Pushkin refuses to close this moralistic loop. Common-law marriages between noblemen and women outside their social class did happen; in any event, it is beside the point. Pushkin, who had difficult relations with his own parents, wrote this story on the eve of his marriage to one of the most beautiful young women in Russia, Natalia Goncharova. He too was trying to find a balance between a past littered with mistakes of prodigality and the prospect of married life and new family. And he was writing these efforts into "The Stationmaster" by giving his heroine *agency*—something he would do increasingly with the female characters of his mature period.[21]

Like Dunya, the students in the Pushkin Project usually come from humble beginnings. Pushkin knew that his most ardent admirers were his female readers and he wanted his writings to teach them things about life. In his otherwise difficult childhood he had been lovingly looked after by two women: his nurse, Arina Rodionovna, a serf woman who entertained him with her storehouse of Russian fairytales; and his maternal grandmother, Marya Alekseevna, who had raised Pushkin's mother while weathering a bad marriage and who impressed her grandson by speaking in an old-fashioned way. Both women provided refuge for the boy when his mother grew impatient with his recalcitrant behavior, and Pushkin in turn loved their authentic ways and valued their attachment to him despite his ugly-duckling status in the family. In fact, he was so fond of his nurse that he gave her to his favorite heroine Tatiana in *Eugene Onegin*.

In closing, let us not forget that Titular Councilor AGN was only too happy to ask the fourteen-year-old Dunya for a kiss as the story opens. Her beauty was there for the taking and, like any average early nineteenth-century Russian Mallard duck, he was ready to pounce. Dunya's only way out of her situation was by leveraging her cleverness and good looks to get a foothold in something better. It was a risk and she could have failed but Pushkin decided to write his Cinderella story in this way because Dunya's beauty was not skin deep. Pushkin believed in beauty. Minsky seems like a cad, but maybe his worth, despite the way that he treats Vyrin, lies precisely in the fact that he valued Dunya's beauty for what it was and he made her the mother of his children. Dunya's story is a fairytale, at least with regard to her unlikely success, and Pushkin clearly enjoyed turning the church's preachings on their head in this way, but the larger point is the good Dunya's beauty does *for the species*: when she tells her children to wait patiently in the carriage and behave themselves, one senses she is a good mother, and that her and Minsky's "mixed" heritable material will produce good outcomes.

Our students, fortunately, are not typically faced with a dilemma like Dunya's and have already weighed up the advantages and disadvantages of becoming familied prematurely and decided against it. But, going forward, it is hoped that the full import of Dunya's gamble, its troubling "morality versus sexual selection" nexus, will not be lost on them.

CHAPTER 5

The Blackamoor of Peter the Great: Identity, Creativity, Homecoming

———

> I went to a predominantly white middle school. I did not realize how certain people felt about minorities until I was classified as one myself. I think with being Hispanic comes this stigma that I am uneducated, lower class, and can be seen as undocumented (this has never happened to me). I think I spent a lot of my life running away from this stigma.
>
> (Vanessa, former PSI student)

Virtually all the young people who participate in the Pushkin Summer Institute are either Latino or African-American. They understand implicitly what it means to be looked at differently because of race, which, despite our program's good intentions, is something they can't help but experience as soon as they leave diverse and urban Chicago and come to study in mostly white and rural Wisconsin. Group identity is perhaps the most complex, and vexed, issue facing humankind today. It goes to the threat of tribalism and all the violence and misery that happen when in-group fears are stoked and acted upon through mob rule, from pogroms and lynchings to ethnic cleansing in Bosnia, Rwanda, and Myanmar. It touches on virtually everything involving human interaction. We are born into a family, which gives us our first identity, in the sense of the social bonds tying the individual to the larger unit. But then, at the same time, that original unit also partakes of racial, ethnic, and religious (or non-religious: atheists can also form groups) identities that the individual child takes on, like it or not. Add to this a sexual identity that is potentially loaded with "propagation of the species" import, and we immediately see how inherently complicated the picture is before we have even started. Are all of these characteristics equally significant in determining who an individual is? Is one more important than another, and if so, why? The key here is that, with regard to these primary, or maybe better "primal," identities, the individual does not choose any of them. They are assigned at birth. And so, the question at the heart of this chapter: what sort of heuristic toolbox can we give the students that will aid them, over time, in forming their own stable identities—identities that acknowledge this non-negotiable substrate of race and ethnicity and yet also afford them the best chance of surviving in a world where everything is always/already mediated by biology and culture? This is where we need Pushkin and his art, in this case *The Blackamoor of Peter the Great* (1827).

If the amygdala is the part of the brain that is engaged when we experience the flight-or-fight syndrome, then it is also true that the triggers that turn these circuits on very often have to do with these most deep-seated identities and the circumstances in the environment threatening them. How we get from the *emotion* of fear or aggression, with the limbic system engaged because there is an actual threat in the immediate environment, to the *feeling* of fear or aggression, which can be consciously imagined and does not require that the threat be physically present, is a contested area of modern psychology.[1] But whether the emotions are "hardwired" in the limbic system or whether they are cognitively "constructed," art can play a valuable role in our understanding. Art provides a framework, or "schema," that allows us to become "mindful" of how we have processed these fight-or-flight emotions in the past. (Of course, it goes without saying that if one is a potential victim of a genocidal act it does not matter what the function of art is in evolution's broad sweep; what matters is survival in the most basic sense, which is why the amygdala is activated in the first place.) Beyond this initial, generalized framing of the problem, however, how do we begin to get at the biological and cultural workings of group identity behavior *before* we look at Pushkin's prescient response in his verbal art?

Kin versus Group Selection and the Mystery of Altruism

A good place to start is the mind-boggling complexity of what evolutionary biologists term "kin selection" versus "group selection" as models for explaining altruistic behavior. Altruism is the holy grail of evolutionary biology. It is an extension of morality's "fair play" in that it takes the other into consideration, but it pushes the idea of reciprocity further by having it perform an act that benefits the other by being potentially disadvantageous to itself.[2] Looked at this way, it is what most separates us and our nearest higher order mammalian relatives behaviorally from the rest of the animal kingdom. Altruism, in short, had to be accounted for. In the second half of the twentieth century, kin selection came to hold sway among most evolutionary biologists with an interest in genetics because it posited a "causal"[3] connection between altruistic actions and individual, as opposed to group, advantage (a seeming paradox) and did so using mathematical formulas and statistical analysis. But the transition from the study of genes, which typically involved mathematics and was most highly developed in the discipline of population genetics, to the study of altruistic behavior, which struck most scientists originally as being a bridge too far, did not happen overnight. It took someone like the great naturalist W. D. Hamilton, who was most himself when swimming against the current, to write in his now classic, but originally rejected, article "The Evolution of Altruistic Behaviour" (1963),

> As a simple but admittedly crude model we may imagine a pair of genes g and G such that G tends to cause some kind of altruistic behavior while g is null. Despite the principle of 'survival of the fittest' the ultimate criterion which determines whether G will spread is not whether the behaviour is to the benefit of the behaver but whether it is to the benefit of the gene G; and this will be the case if the average net result of the behaviour is to add to the gene pool a handful of genes containing G in higher concentration than does the gene pool itself. With altruism this will happen only if the affected individual is a relative of the altruist, therefore having an increased chance of carrying the gene, and if the advantage conferred is large enough compared to the personal disadvantage to offset the regression, or 'dilution', of the altruist's genotype in the relative in question.[4]

Notice that the focus here is on behavior that benefits gene G, not the individual carrying gene G. This logic then became the basis of "Hamilton's rule": a costly action is performed if $C < r \times B$, where C = cost of fitness, r = genetic relatedness between actor and recipient, and B = fitness benefit to recipient. Thereafter leading science writers of the "gene's-eye view" camp like the rhetorically dazzling Richard Dawkins picked up on Hamilton's rule, hotly disputing the validity of the group selection model while building the case in favor of kin selection, since these measures (cost, relatedness, fitness benefit) affected, first and foremost, *the individual.*[5] Or so it appeared at the time. But science moves forward and a change in context can reshuffle the deck.

Multilevel selection, which is a later offshoot of the previously disparaged group selection, is a kind of selection acting on traits for their survival benefit that looks at different "cuts" (between-group versus within-group) at the same time. One level of selection may be on "particles" (individual traits); another level of selection may be on "collectives" (groups). The average fitness of a collective of particles and a collective of collectives can be segregated out and measured by deploying covariables and multiple regression analysis.[6] In prominent philosopher of science Samir Okasha's formulation, "In a multi-level setting [...] it is possible that a character-fitness covariance at one hierarchical level may be a side effect or by-product, of direct selection at a *different* level (higher or lower)."[7] Thus, the idea of covariance, which is designed to measure the relationship between two random entities (here the character/trait and the organism's fitness), suddenly conjures up a kind of four-dimensional chess match, with the different levels and the different pieces at the different levels all attacking and retreating at the same time. (The chess match is just a metaphor, but perhaps not so inappropriate under the circumstances: altruistic trait versus selfish trait, individual trait versus group trait, side effect versus direct selection, within-group versus between-group—the head spins.) As Okasha argues further,

> Such "cross-level by-products" lie at the heart of the levels-of-selection problem; they show that Price's equation is not an infallible guide to determining the level(s) of selection. The key question becomes: when is a character-fitness covariance indicative of direct selection at the level in question, and when is it a by-product of selection acting at a different level? Many of the criteria proposed in the literature for how to determine the 'real' level of selection can be understood as attempts to answer this question.[8]

And so, to evolutionary biologists who spend their professional lives investigating this problem of the links (covariance) between the ability of a species to survive (fitness) and the relationship of altruistic traits at the individual and group levels to that survival, it all comes down to causality versus correlation. "Causality" may appear more "real," more "true" in a scientific sense, but it can never seem to break free of its embeddedness in statistical correlation.

Okasha sums up:

> Recently, a number of authors have argued that the opposition between kin and multi-level (or group) selection is

misconceived, on the grounds that the two are actually equivalent. [...] Proponents of this view argue that kin and multi-level
selection are simply alternative mathematical frameworks for
describing a single evolutionary process, so the choice between
them is one of convention not empirical fact. This view has
much to recommend it. [. . .] However, the equivalence in
question is a formal equivalence only. A correct expression for
evolutionary change can usually be derived using either the kin
or multi-level selection frameworks, but it does not follow that
they constitute equally good causal descriptions of the evolutionary process.

This suggests that the persistence of the group selection controversy can in part be attributed to the mismatch between the
scientific explanations that evolutionary biologists want to give,
which are causal, and the formalisms they use to describe evolution, which are usually statistical. To make progress, it is essential
to attend carefully to the subtleties of the relation between statistics and causality.[9]

In other words, with regard to the complexities of multilevel selection, even the
data-driven scientific community cannot agree on one scenario. Often it seems
to come down to semantics. Steven Pinker, for example, who is more empirically
inclined, denies prima facie the validity of group/multilevel selection and insists
that the only valid discussion should be at the gene-centered/natural-selection
level: referencing higher-level cultural traits ("cultural evolution") is tantamount
to mixing apples and oranges.[10] This sort of "frameshifting"[11] up and down
levels, Pinker would say, is not playing the scientific game fairly. But, as Thomas
Kuhn first suggested with his notion of "incommensurability" between competing paradigms in *The Structure of Scientific Revolutions* (1962), two frameworks
for understanding the same thing can coexist and be viewed as equally proba-
tive.[12] This means a kind of "Bermuda Triangle" of scientific reasoning has been
entered. The higher the resolution of the picture the more, not less, the indeterminacy of outcome. Here again we seem to have gone down a rabbit hole
and arrived back at a place not unlike the cell's so-called "cognitive" response to
stimuli within and without researched by James Shapiro. This "knowing how"
quality, this built-in ability to navigate the different levels of the biosphere, from
the internal and individual to the group and social, is what fitness as Darwin first
introduced it is all about. And this includes the survival benefits of morality and
altruism in humans.

The larger point, of course, is that the patterns in our biology are also patterns that reappear in our conscious, culturally mediated social lives. The existence of such patterning has led network and biosocial scientist Nicholas Christakis to focus on a "suite" of cultural universals that are "written in the ink of our DNA": capacity to have and recognize individual identity, love for partners and off-spring, friendship, social networks, cooperation, preference for one's own group (in-group bias), mild hierarchy (relative egalitarianism), social learning and teaching.[13] "These features arise from within individuals but they characterize groups. They work together to create a functional, enduring, and even morally good society." At the same time, "these traits are supported by still others that are expressed on a more individual level, such as a need for transcendence or a sense of purpose; a capacity to make or appreciate art and music; and a desire to tell or hear stories."[14] In the long run, between-group cooperation will outcompete (without eliminating) within-group competition and aggression, once the dif-ferential fitness of the former is sufficiently recognized as succeeding against the latter. (To be sure, we can also destroy our species, but that possibility has always been there.) This is what a scientist-philosopher like Pierre Teilhard de Chardin, codiscoverer of the Peking Man, had in mind with his concept of Omega, the point at which human consciousness, moving faster and faster yet turning ever backwards to reflect on itself, becomes "hyper-personal"—both fully aware as the individual mind and fully aware as social groupings of individual minds.[15] It's like the superorganism of E. O. Wilson's eusocial ant colonies, only the individuals don't include sterile, zombie-like workers.[16] It's definitely a utopian vision for now, but just think, for example, how much our world has changed in just a few short decades because women, and women's viewpoints, are more integrated into the workplace, and because men have learned how to help out more at home. The process is bumpy with lots of backsliding and bad behavior but that's because we're viewing things from inside of what's happening, and because what's happening at the species level doesn't care what's happening at the individual level, and finally because it is a process that has just begun, while evolution measures change in millions of years. The reason we feel that things are speeding up is that cultural evolution operates at orders of magnitude faster than biological evolution.

Now, I have taken the time to explain multilevel selection in boiled-down form to the students because conceptually it seems intriguingly analogous to a Pushkin text. Perhaps, once again, we are dealing with a "frameshift" to a differ-ent cultural level? In any event, at this point I ask the students to consider two clusters of information: first, how the category of race affects them personally; second, how Pushkin the creative personality experienced the same issue in his life and how, becoming more "mindful" of it, turned it into a survival strategy in his art, and *as his art*. If the idea of survival in "The Stationmaster" involved Dunya's being aware of her own beauty and cleverness ("the little coquette") and using it to make a good mate choice, then in *The Blackamoor of Peter the Great* the idea of finding the right place for oneself involves something like the opposite: a recognition that the majority culture tends to look at the always visible markers of racial difference as "ugly," because that is what majority cultures (or groupings in nature) do—they reject what is not "theirs," and that the best response to this within-group tribalism is to act creatively and to make something in return that is viable, "beautiful" in a new way. In this sense, creativity in the cultural realm is like sex in the biological realm (recall Matt Ridley's "the mixing and mating of ideas") because it generates new life by bringing together opposites.

The Students on Race and the Pushkin Connection

Now, students' own perceptions and experiences of the category of race in their own words:

Javier:
I believe race plays a big role in society and always will whether people agree or disagree because race is something that makes us different. I believe race will always be seen as something central to the problems we as a species have. I personally do not think a lot about race anymore because it just is what it is, and I do not believe the idea of races affecting human life will be gone in my lifetime, so I just need to adjust and understand that there is a hierarchy of race in our society and that will not change in the foreseeable future.

Cynthia:
I have been strongly affected by the category of race. Before coming to the United States, I only identified as "X" [= someone from a major Latin American country Y]. There was no discussion about whether I was Latino (or Latinx, which is politically correct today) or Hispanic. When children in my school would ask me, "What are you?" I would answer, "I am X." They would ask, "what is that?" This took a toll on my identity because, as a second grader, I felt that my identity as "X" was not considered

important to others. Among these interactions, children and adults would just assume I was Mexican. Even today, people assume I am Mexican. Not long ago, my Lyft driver asked my friends and me, which part of Mexico we were from, without asking where else we could have been from. I think about this all the time, [and] as you can see, I am trying to correct myself about what terms I should be using. Now, society has indicated that I am Latino or Hispanic first, and then whatever identity comes in next. When I would take state tests during elementary school, there was one question that I had to fill out about race: What is your race? There were only 5 options that I was given: White, Black, American Indian/Alaska Native, Asian, or Native Hawaiian/Other Pacific Islander. I could not identify with any of these options, so by default I chose white. My thought process was: 1) I do not know what the last three options are, so I will not consider them; 2) I am not white, but I am also not black; 3) the Spanish conquered Y, so by default I will just put white. Now that I think about it, I believe it is rough to force a second grader to choose their identity through 5 options. As much as I keep learning, I am still asking myself these questions. I am still asking if my history matters, if my DNA matters. I know I am part Asian because some of my ancestors come from China, but this is something that I just learned, and my family does not talk about it. Do I identify as Asian? No. The United States has structured the system so perfectly that people assume who you are and who you are not through phenotype or physical characteristics. I know little about the Chinese culture, except the food. I guess one can say that knowing Chinese food is one way I practice one of my cultures. I guess I am at fault for picking and choosing my identities. When I am in an environment that is predominantly Latinx, I say I am "X." When I am in an environment that is predominantly white, I say I am "X" because I try to stop myself from giving in to the Latinx identity only. The Chinese identity is not something I really use, unless I am with someone that identifies themselves as Chinese. It is almost like cherry picking. The term Latinx is a panethnic term that is only used when the system wants to group cultures that identify as Latin American in origin or descent. As much as I love coming together as one identity, it has hurt me because even though I feel like there are times when we should all identify as one, since that is more effective than being in just multiple little groups (for example, when protesting), there are also times when other cultures "take over" (I do not know how else to put it; I don't mean it in a bad way) and then my identity just stays in the shadows. This conflict between identities is what makes me miss Y more because, personally, this was not something I expect to be confused about.

When I came to the US as an immigrant, I thought that the only things that were consistent in my life were my family and my proud identity as "X." There were times when I was ashamed. I still do not understand why, but for some reason I was. This shame still has some side effects. There are times I do not know how to interact with my own culture. There are times when I feel like I am not "X" enough and I have been "white-washed" or "no longer 'X,'" as other fellow "X"'s have told me. This has led me to do more things to prove that I am still "X," but, slowly and slowly, I have come to terms that I don't need to prove my identity to anyone. Sometimes I stay with that mindset, sometimes I just resent my family for making me move here. This is still a battle that I face every single day. I try to look at the good outcomes, but sometimes I just look at the bad. I know I am working hard to get to a place where my identities will not be shaken by anyone or any system.

Rosalia:

I knew that attending the University of Wisconsin-Madison would be tough, not only academically, but because I only made up 2% of the population. However, I did not know that "race" would play a role in my everyday life. I always felt like I needed to prove how "smart" or how "educated" I was to my peers. I would think that by getting into the school, it was enough, but unconsciously I knew that students, peers, and faculty saw me as a "free ride student." Maybe these thoughts were just in my head, but I always felt like I needed to make an effort to make friends in my classes while it came easily to others. I am not a person who is timid and I love socializing with people. I am currently reading a book, *The Struggle of Latino/Latina University Students* by Felix M. Padilla, and a quote that stood out to me most was, "Latino/a students are burdened by the same affirmative action stereotype which African-American students believe to be continually held against them." By presenting this quote, I am not saying that I have the same struggle as my African-American peers, but it is similar. That is why, when I go to a Latinx event, I feel most comfortable. I am a firm believer in looking for the good things when there is so much negativity. I think that my hard work in high school and other aspects of my life placed me in this university for a reason. I think I was fortunate enough to have counselors that saw my potential and gave me an opportunity to do things my parents always wanted to do themselves. I also think that being 2% makes me essential to generations of Latinx students on campus to come.

Stephanie:
Race is a crucial part of my identity. When asked to check a box for any document, I often hesitate what race I belong to. You see, as a Hispanic/Latina, I have always debated with what race, given what is provided, I am part of. Rather of thinking of it as race, I think of my ethnicity/nationality. I truly believe that race is a social construct, something created, but which many still abide by. Being part of a predominantly white institution, I have experienced what race means to many. Being part of the minority group, I have been looked at as different, I have been asked highly inappropriate things about my identity, and even had derogatory terms be used towards me. I used to really believe what others said about me and began doubting my place on campus. When first arriving to campus, my ethnicity was something I always thought about, but now that I have learned how to respond to people's ignorance, I don't think of it as much. Though I have had some negative experiences, all from classmates, I am hopeful that in a couple of years race and categorizing people by their ethnicity will not be a thing. I am hopeful that everyone will be able to celebrate their identity without fearing the response from others.

Vanessa:
I think my whole life I have been affected by race because I come from a multiracial background. I feel like every place that I go I need to accommodate more for a particular race. For example,

I went to a predominantly white middle school. I did not realize how certain people felt about minorities until I was classified as one myself. I think with being Hispanic comes this stigma that I am uneducated, lower class, and can be seen as undocumented (this has never happened to me). I think I spent a lot of my life running away from this stigma. I do not want to be stereotyped this way, but what about the people that actually fit in these categories. They shouldn't be treated as any less, but they still are. Depending on who I talk to I am a different race and often times that affects how people see me. I am embarrassed to admit that when I first came to Wisconsin, I did not want my father helping me move into the dorms. I have seen how people treated him in the past, and I did not want to be treated the same way. I think I am more secure in myself now, and I do not allow people to identify me as something that I am not. Even if I am identified that way, I am secure enough in myself to not let people's comments affect me. A more recent example of how race affects me personally is I just started dating a guy from northern Wisconsin. He is from the middle of nowhere and his first real encounter with people of color was when he moved to Madison. When he would tell me about the kind of people he grew up around back home, it started to make me feel insecure about my Hispanic background. He knew I was Mexican, but he didn't know that my dad has a strong accent, that I went to a predominantly Hispanic high school, that people in Chicago do not speak the same way as people from Wisconsin. When he first met my father, I could sense the awkwardness and it could be because he was meeting my parents for the first time. But I think it also showed me that people can't control their upbringing. If I grew up only around white people and the only thing I knew about other races were the terrible stereotypes that tv/news presents, I would probably be the same way. I think there is room to change, but it is an individual task. People have to work on themselves before there is any major difference.

The obvious takeaway from these comments is that one's racial identity in its various nuances is something these young people struggle with often in their daily lives. From Javier's stoicism in the face of an unforgiving hierarchy ("it just is what it is") to Cynthia's attempts to modulate her answers depending on group dynamics ("there are times when other cultures take over"), to Vanessa's fear of being labeled low class and uneducated ("I think I spent a lot of my life running away from this stigma"), the responses suggest that the issue is always with them and gives no signs of going away. "Race" is a look and a heritable core and a social signaling system the students want to be proud of, but on occasion are ashamed of. That causes anxiety and confusion.

Now, the Pushkin connection. The poet, who was sensitive about his black features and could not forget that his mother treated him as the least favorite of her surviving children because those features reminded her, the granddaughter of a black African, of her own racial heritage, wrote a tongue-in-cheek verse epistle to one of his drinking buddies, the handsome cavalry officer Fyodor Yuriev, in 1821. In the first part of the poem the speaker describes the addressee as a favorite of Venus and lover of "Laisas" (sexually available young actresses and dancers): the goddess of love has endowed him with charm, a raffish moustache, a bright glance, an enticing smile, and a come-hither coolness that causes the ladies to flock to him. He has enough, Pushkin says. Then, however, the poet describes himself:

> But I, an eternally idle scapegrace,
> ugly offspring of Negroes,
> someone raised in wild simplicity,
> not knowing the sufferings of love,
> I appeal to young beauty
> with the shameless madness of desire.
> With an involuntary flame in her cheeks
> so does a young nymph secretly,
> not understanding herself why,
> sometimes glance at a faun/satyr.

Somehow Pushkin, in his creative laboratory, has turned his perceived unattractiveness ("ugly offspring of Negroes") into an advantage, into a positive difference-maker. He implies that this is his "real" identity in the male world of competition for females. His goat-like lower half is sexualized and morphs into his human, "mindful" upper half (the source of the clever words), but *both still form one creature*, while the beautiful nymph looks on at the monstrous composite and wants him in a way that causes her to blush.

Perhaps more importantly, this strangely appealing self-image was true not only in the reality of his art, but also apparently in the reality outside his art.

As Countess Darya (Dolly) Fiquelmont, one of the most intelligent and percep-
tive grand dames of her era, wrote in her diary,

> It's impossible to be more ugly—a blend of monkey and tiger
> in appearance. He is descended from African ancestors and has
> preserved a certain blackness in his eyes and something wild in
> his glance. When he speaks you forget about what he lacks in
> order to be handsome; his conversation is so interesting, spar-
> kling with intelligence, without the least pedantry . . . It's impos-
> sible to be less pretentious and more intelligent in the manner of
> expressing oneself.[17]

More could be added, but the message here is how Pushkin's true selfhood,
despite all preconceived notions, comes through to this observer, who also happens to be a member of the opposite sex that the poet was so often intent on
seducing: what begins on the surface, with the appearance of the monkey (a not
so complimentary rendering of the stereotype of a black man's ancestry) and
the tiger (the coiled physicality), becomes the whole person emerging from the
inside out, as it were, so by the end of the description what was ugly is now magically attractive, beautiful in spite of itself.

Pushkin's Black Ancestry: History versus Story

The time now arrives for me to ask the students to do some serious detective
work. Not an easy request given contemporary teenage reading habits. Still,
without some appreciation of history and Pushkin's place in it, they can't really
see how his time could be their time, and his racial inheritance could be their
racial inheritance. The first piece of evidence dates to 1823 and the original pub-
lication of canto one of *Eugene Onegin*, the novel-in-verse that was to become
Pushkin's masterpiece. In footnote eleven to the fiftieth stanza, the poet anno-
tates what once took place "under the sky of my Africa." The dramatic storyline
and nostalgic filter are romantic ploys to make the speaker more intriguing, for,
while the details belong to the family patriarch, the place of the patriarch's birth,
which the speaker has never visited, is demonstrably "*my* Africa":

> The author, on his mother's side, is of African descent. His great-
> grandfather, Abram Petrovich Annibal,[18] in his eighth year was
> kidnapped on the coast of Africa and brought to Constantinople.

The Russian envoy, having rescued him, sent him as a gift to Peter the Great, who had him baptized in Vilno. In his wake, his brother arrived, first in Constantinople, and then in St. Petersburg, with the offer to ransom him; but Peter did not consent to return his godchild. Up to an advanced age, Annibal still remembered Africa, the luxurious life of his father, and the nineteen brothers, of whom he was the youngest; he remembered how they used to be led into his father's presence with their hands bound behind their backs, whilst he alone remained free and went swimming under the fountains of the paternal home; he also remembered his beloved sister, *Lagan*, swimming in the distances after the ship in which he was receding.[19]

The next item, from an unfinished autobiographical sketch of 1834 detailing the Pushkin family's genealogy, gives us a similar (but not identical) picture of Gannibal's youth. Note in particular the *additions and alterations* to the *Onegin* footnote:

My mother's genealogy is even more curious. Her grandfather was a Negro, the son of a land-holding prince. The Russian ambassador to Constantinople somehow obtained him from a seraglio where he was being held as a hostage and sent him to Peter I along with two other little blackamoors. The sovereign baptized little Ibrahim [or Abram] in Vilno in 1707, with the Polish queen, the spouse of Augustus, in attendance, and gave him the surname Gannibal. At the baptism he was named Peter, but he made such a fuss about having to bear the new name that up until his death he was called Abram. His older brother came to Petersburg and offered to buy him back. But Peter decided to keep his godson nearby. Up until 1716 Gannibal never strayed from the person of the sovereign, sleeping in his workshop and accompanying him on his campaigns. After that he was sent to Paris, where for a while he studied at a military academy, entered the French service, was injured in the head *during one underground battle* (as stated in his handwritten biography) in the Spanish War, and returned to Paris, where for a long time he lived amid the dissipation of high society. Peter I summoned him back more than once, but Gannibal was in no hurry, refusing to come under various pretexts. At last the sovereign wrote him that he had no intention of compelling him and that he left it up to Gannibal's free will either to return to Russia or to remain in France, but that in any event he would never abandon his former charge. Touched by this, Gannibal immediately set off for Petersburg. The sovereign rode out to meet him and blessed him with the Peter and Paul icon, which has been kept by Gannibal's sons, but which, alas, I have been unable to uncover. The sovereign commissioned Gannibal as a lieutenant in the Bombardier Company of the Preobrazhensky Regiment. It is well-known that Peter himself was the captain of the regiment. This was in 1722.[20]

The information in these two passages came to Pushkin almost certainly not via his mother, who we have to assume did not care to be reminded of her paternal ancestors, nor via his grandmother, who married into the Gannibal family and paid dearly for it in humiliation and heartache, but via his great-uncle, Pyotr Abramovich Gannibal (1742–1826), the brother of his grandfather, Osip Abramovich Gannibal (1744–1806), and the only surviving son of the original Gannibal that the poet was able to meet. Pushkin visited Pyotr Gannibal twice; the second visit—when Pushkin was confined to his mother's estate Mikhailovskoe in 1824, during his northern exile, and his great-uncle was living out his final years nearby at Petrovskoe—is the one that concerns us. It was through the plain-spoken, vodka-swilling Pyotr Abramovich that the poet became acquainted with the so-called "German biography" of his great-grandfather, the version of the latter's life written down by his son-in-law after the patriarch's passing and based on his papers (since lost) and/or oral family tradition. As he did not have sufficient German, Pushkin must have asked Pyotr Abramovich (after plying the old man with some of his moonshine?) to dictate the text to him in Russian; the poet then copied down the latter as best he could, making calculations and notes in the margins. The slight discrepancies between the two texts turn out to be significant.

Certain motifs in these two passages are seminal to Pushkin's self-conception, among them the notions of Africa, blackness, slavery, exile, adoption, naming, the good father, and homecoming—all figuring, as we shall see shortly, in *The Blackamoor*. What exactly did Pushkin learn from the "German biography"? For starters, this life story, which, considering the source (Gannibal himself), was bound to put the best face on the past, tells us that Pushkin's great-grandfather was an "African Negro from Abyssinia, the son of a local ruler, powerful and rich, who proudly traced his descent in a direct line from the house of the famed Gannibal, the terror of Rome."[21] The mention of the Carthaginian general seems a fantastic red herring, as the surname shows up considerably later, after Abram had returned to Russia from France in the 1720's, presumably to add luster to the military man's resumé. Pushkin may have suspected this inflation of the record since he passes over it in his commentary. Still, what is most notable here are not the historical references per se but something else: the word for Negro, *arap*, is identical in sound to the Russian word for Arab, *arab* (the "b" ultima is devoiced to "p" in the nominative, so that the two words become homonyms), and the word for slave, *rab* (pronounced "rap"), is contained phonetically in the word for an African black man ("a-ráp"). These deeply embedded (one almost wants to say "magical") links between sound and sense played with Pushkin's poetic nature from early on. How do we know this? Well, right about the time when the boy Pushkin (aged seven or eight) became infected with rhymes (and reading), the following episode was recorded by a contemporary:

> In his childhood years Pushkin was not well-proportioned and possessed the same African facial features he would have as an adult. But his hair in these early years was so curly and so elegantly waved according to its African nature that once [the writer and minister of justice] Ivan Dmitriev said, "Look, this is a real little blackamoor [*arabchik*]." The child laughed and, turning to us, pronounced quickly and boldly, "At least . . . I won't be [as was Dmitriev] full of pock-marks [*ne budu riabchik*]."[22]

The boy turns to the esteemed adult and transforms, with instantaneous wit, the fixed category (the unavoidable given of "little blackamoor" [*arabchik*]) into energy-in-motion, a joke with fangs slightly bared ("someone pock-marked" [*riabchik*]). The poetic principle, the rhyme that makes *arábchik* into *riábchik*, is there at the creation of Pushkin's world and of his thoughts about his origins. It is a kind of echo chamber of alternative meanings that forever accompanies his historical situation.

The reason offered by the German biography for the seven-year-old Gannibal's captivity in Constantinople was that his father, being a vassal of the Ottoman Empire and having risen up with the other princes against the sultanate in the last decades of the seventeenth century, was forced as punishment to give his son over as a bargaining chip against possible future hostile actions. At this point, the German text is more explicit than the *Onegin* note. Significantly, it tells *why* it was Abram who was taken as hostage and not one of his other brothers: Abram's father had, as befits Muslim custom, thirty wives, but the boy's mother was the youngest and least influential of the group; the other wives and their older sons, jealous of their father's favoritism toward his youngest male offspring, plotted against their sibling and had him sent away by force on a Turkish ship heading for Constantinople. Needless to say, this story, evoking as it does the Old Testament tale of Joseph sold by his older brothers into slavery, has the kind of dramatic potential and cultural associations that will draw Pushkin back to it.

The picture gets clearer (but never totally in focus) the closer we come to Russia and the reign of Peter the Great. Abram arrived in Constantinople in spring 1703,[23] at which point he was, in the German biography's version, placed in the sultan's seraglio to be trained as a page along with other hostage youths of African royalty. Here enters the picture the mysterious figure of Savva Lukich Vladislavich (1668–1738), who, because of his Illyrian background and invaluable service to Peter, became known subsequently as Count Raguzinsky ("of Ragusa," modern-day Dubrovnik). Vladislavich was a kind of special agent or "facilitator" who could get things done in the shadows of local mores and legalities without ruffling the wrong feathers. It was he who struck the deal with the then grand vizier to have the boy abducted, along with two other young blackamoors, as a gift to, or possibly at the request of, the tsar. The record shows that Vladislavich arranged for the departure for Russia in July 1704 of three "little blackamoors," a detail Pushkin manages to include, in correction to the German text, in his own 1834 autobiographical sketch.[24] They arrived in Russia in November of the same year (not in 1705 as Nabokov guessed).[25] One of the three boys died, probably sometime after arriving, but the two who remained were black and brothers, the older one, named "Aleksey Petrov," becoming an oboist in the Preobrazhensky Regiment and soon thereafter disappearing from historical memory entirely; the younger one, Abram Petrov, becoming a military engineer and, eventually, our poet's great-grandfather.

What did Peter the Great want with these blackamoors? What role could they play at court and in the life of early eighteenth-century Russia? The most obvious explanation is the exoticism, the "chic," of possessing a young black male in one's retinue. In this respect, Abram would simply be one more addition to a court renowned for its jesters and dwarves, mock ceremonies, foreign visitors, and its penchant for the bizarre. For example, the court ledger during these years cites expenses for new uniforms for "Abram the Blackamoor" (*Abram-arap*) and "Joachim the Dwarf" (*Iakim-karl*), which gives us an idea of the African's *Kunstkammer*-style social footing. Similarly, wealthy noble households of the era might feature liveried black footmen who opened the doors for princesses and counts and rode on the floorboards of their masters' elaborate carriages— the precursors to the kitschy lamp-holding effigies known to southern households in the twentieth-century United States (and of course harking back to the antebellum days of real-life slaves). Quite likely, Peter was simply following this practice—that, at least, is Nabokov's surmise, who calls the blackamoor a "symbol of supreme luxury and grandeur."[26] But the other reason mentioned in the German biography, which Nabokov dismisses as "idiotic," may in fact be the most plausible under the circumstances, for the method to Peter's madness almost always involved some attempt to educate his countrymen and break down the barriers of prejudice and obscurantism through ridicule (a theme that arises in *The Blackamoor*):

> [Peter] wished to make examples of them [the young blacka-moors] . . . and put [Russians] to shame by convincing them that out of every people, and even from among wild men—such as Negroes, whom our civilized nations assign exclusively to the class of slaves—there can be formed men who by dint of appli-cation can obtain knowledge and learning and become helpful and useful to their monarch.[27]

One assumes it was this reason that resonated most with Pushkin, especially as Abram was soon to distinguish himself by his studies and by his love, relatively rare for the time, of books.

The details of Abram's life as Peter's subject form the most historically intrigu-ing, and factually contested, section of his biography. The tsar had him baptized in 1705 in Vilno (apparently without the Polish Emperor Augustus II's wife Christiana standing in as godmother, as in the German biography[28]) and as a result Abram became Peter's *krestnik*, or godson. The Nabokovian version is that the act of adoption on Peter's part was merely another cruel mock ceremony and that the great ruler kept Abram around as a kind of offbeat pet, thrashing him for the fun of it when the urge arose. But the truth is probably neither as grotesque and demeaning as Nabokov asserts nor as grandiose as the family telling (Abram the constant favorite) would have us think. The recorded instance when Peter gave Abram the whipping was because the tsar had been awakened from a sound sleep by his jester's loud cries and the little blackamoor had the misfortune of being the first one the tsar stumbled upon.[29] What does seem plausible is that, as time went on, Abram became something more than a curiosity to Peter.[30] In the words of the German biography,

> [Gannibal] slept in the sovereign's extra study, his workshop, and soon became on many important occasions Peter's secretary. Above the tsar's bed always hung several slate-boards . . . and

here in the dark, with no light, he would write down when inspiration came upon him important and extensive plans. The next morning his charge was supposed to rewrite these notes in clean form and, after they had been appropriately signed, send them to the collegia [ministries]. . . . The monarch became convinced of the youth's abilities.[31]

This is a particularly charged moment in the biography because it is here that Pushkin reworks the German original into something more succinct and poeticized:

Gannibal, inseparable from the emperor, slept now in the latter's study, now in his workshop, and soon thereafter became his privy [*tainyi*] secretary. The sovereign always kept a slate-board above his bed; during the night he would write down thoughts that came to him, and then in the morning Gannibal would rewrite them and send them to the various collegia. With each day the sovereign became more convinced by the gifts of this youth.[32]

Now the boy becomes "inseparable" from the emperor; his role is that of "privy secretary" (a then non-existent position that looks forward to a high title in Peter's 1722 Table of Ranks—"privy councillor"); he is trusted enough to send out the sovereign's orders and requests without accompanying signature; the tsar's appreciation of Abram's talents grows "with each day"; and the blackamoor possesses not merely "capabilities" (*sposobnosti*) but "gifts" (*darovaniia*)—a stronger, more loaded term.[33] Clearly, this revision has great mythopoetic potential: once again, it suggests the story of Joseph, who, having been betrayed by his brothers and sold into slavery, makes a new life for himself in a foreign land as close advisor to the pharaoh, whose dreams he interprets. In this way, he uses his prophetic gifts to turn adversity into triumph.

In late 1716, Abram Petrov, as he was still called, now a young man of twenty, set off for Copenhagen where he joined the entourage of Peter, who was making a European tour. He traveled there in a group of "minors" (*nedorosli*, not-quite-mature males) who had been hand-picked by the tsar to study subjects important to the country's future in various foreign centers of learning. The African remained behind in Paris when Peter left the city in June 1717. For the next five and a half years Abram lived in France. While there, he studied fortification at the École d'Artillerie in Metz and participated in the French war against Spain, during which, in an assault on the Fuenterrabia Fortress in 1719, he was seriously wounded in the head. All this is retold telegraphically in *The Blackamoor*, but the fact is that Abram's life in France was financially constrained (he is always asking for money in his letters home), and nothing like the social whirl of beautiful women and famous men (the young Voltaire, Montesquieu) sweeping up *le nègre du Czar* in the great-grandson's fiction.[34] Still, Abram did read a lot, including works outside his military training: among the books he had in his possession when he left France were tomes relating to history and travel, as well as belles-lettres (Corneille, Racine, Fontenelle). The important point here is that, even as Abram was smitten with life in the Bourbon heart of Europe, and even as he repeatedly asked to extend his stay under various pretexts, he did finally return "home," leaving Paris in October 1722 and arriving in Moscow in January 1723, to the adoptive father who had provided these opportunities, and it is this fact that impressed the eventual poet and historical thinker the most.

Russia's greatest tsar died in 1725. By the time of the monarch's death Abram had been commissioned as lieutenant (*poruchik*) in the bombardier company of the prestigious Preobrazhensky Regiment. He was no longer simply "Abramka" or "Abram the Blackamoor." With his expertise in the construction of fortresses, he made progress through the ranks, gaining more and more hands-on experience, while his star fell and rose under different sovereigns, first Catherine I (ruled 1725–1727) and Peter II (ruled 1727–1730), then Anna (ruled 1830–1840) and Elizabeth (ruled 1741–1762). The somewhat muddled family version is that Peter's former favorite, Prince Menshikov, had Abram removed from court because he feared his influence on Peter II, whom the African had tutored, and went so far as to send him all the way to Siberia with the absurd assignment of measuring the Great Wall of China. (What Menshikov actually appears to have commanded Gannibal to do was to build a fort on the border with China, in the remote village of Seleginsk.[35]) After this, while still "in disgrace" (*v opale*), Gannibal supposedly returned incognito to European Russia in hopes that the powerful Dolgoruky princes, who eventually overthrew Menshikov, would intercede for him. But Peter II died unexpectedly, Anna came to power with her German favorites, and Gannibal, still fearing arrest, was posted by his supporter General Minikh to the western hinterland near Revel (modern-day Tallinn), where he hid himself away, according to the German text, for the next ten years. (This account is not that far from the truth. A more credible explanation for the move from Siberia back to St. Petersburg and Moscow is that Minikh needed a good military engineer and had Gannibal quietly transferred to the Baltic fort at Pernov. Citing headaches as a pretext, the African was then allowed to "retire" for several years as he avoided the long arm of Anna's favorite Biron.[36]) Finally, with the ascension to the throne of Peter's daughter Elizabeth, who purged the Germans from the court and reestablished links back to her legendary sire, Gannibal was once again in favor. He quickly went through the general ranks all the way up to general-in-chief and for his loyal service was awarded estates in the Pskov and Petersburg provinces. A stunning rise for the boy who began as an *арапчонок* ("little blackamoor")! He retired in 1762, during the abortive reign of Peter III, and lived until 1781, well into the glory years of Catherine, dying at the ripe age of eighty-five.

These are the principal contours of Gannibal's professional biography. But there is a personal side that spoke powerfully to Pushkin as well. Eighteenth-century Russia was in the main a crude, patriarchal world, and Abram Gannibal was very much a part of that world. One can take for granted that he was beaten often as a youth for anything that could be interpreted as misbehaving or in some cases, as in the episode where a groggy Peter happens upon him, just for being in the wrong place at the wrong time. He carried these behavioral patterns with him into adult life and we can only suppose that his military background did nothing to dampen them. In later years, Gannibal was reputed to have had a harsh disposition that was prone to express itself in violence, principally toward underlings, if his wishes were in any way thwarted. Family legend had it that house servants who had the misfortune of encountering the Gannibal wrath would have to be carried out of the room when he or one of his sons were done with the flogging. Pushkin's grandmother Marya Alekseevna report-edly told her grandson that she fainted from fright the first time she looked into her father-in-law's withering glance.[37] With his aristocratic fastidiousness Nabokov interprets such accounts as evidence of Gannibal's warped, unpleas-ant character: "a sour, groveling, crotchety, timid, ambitious, and cruel person; a good military engineer, perhaps, but humanistically a nonentity; differing in nothing from a typical career-minded, superficially educated, coarse wife-flogging Russian of his day, in a brutal and dull world of political intrigue, favor-itism, Germanic regimentation, old-fashioned Russian misery, and fat-breasted empresses on despicable thrones."[38] Nabokov may have some of this right, but in the judgmental aura of his epithets he also, at least as Pushkin himself saw it, got something essentially wrong. Abram Gannibal was not typical, just as the eighteenth century was not only Germanic regimentation and fat-breasted empresses.

Gannibal was married twice.[39] His first marriage to Eudoxia Dioper, the daughter of a Greek sea captain in the employ of the Russian crown, was unhappy.[40] The couple was married in 1731 in St. Petersburg. The pretty Eudoxia had from the beginning been repulsed by Abram's external features (a motif redeployed in *The Blackamoor* when the tsar arrives to arrange a match between

Ibrahim and the cowering Natalya Rzhevskaya) and, moreover, was in love with another man, a young navy officer named Alexander Kaisarov. Eudoxia had wanted to marry Kaisarov, but Abram had made the match through the father, who forced the daughter to yield. What came to light subsequently, causing Abram much embarrassment in the burgher-ish confines of Pernov, was that Eudoxia had had at least one liaison before marriage (Kaisarov) and then continued to have others once the couple reached their new post. There is even the possibility that with one of her lovers, Yakov Sishkov, she had planned to poison Gannibal.[41] In any event, when Eudoxia gave birth to a white baby, Abram concluded that he had been betrayed and promptly constructed, at home in 1732, "a private torture chamber complete with pulleys, iron clamps, thumbkins, [and] leather whips."[42] Here the unfortunate Eudoxia was for some time imprisoned and duly punished for her domestic crime of *liubodeian'e* (fornication, promiscuousness), after which the unrelenting spouse had her further incarcerated by the state. When she was temporarily freed in 1743 and placed under the supervision of the church in St. Petersburg, she got into trouble again, this time with a certain Abumov, with whom she produced an illegitimate daughter. Eventually, years later (1753), once the divorce was legally approved, Eudoxia was forced to enter a distant convent, where she died.

Abram's second marriage was more successful. While he was still trying to expedite the separation process from Eudoxia, and before his union with her had been officially dissolved, Gannibal took up with another woman, Christina Regine Schöberg, the daughter of a Swedish naval officer. Because Christina was Lutheran rather than Orthodox, Abram was able to finagle the necessary paperwork and "marry" her in 1736. It would take until 1753, however, twenty-two years after he first met Eudoxia, to get beyond the first marriage in the eyes of the state and the church. Christina bore Gannibal some eleven black babies, one of which (the third surviving male) was Pushkin's maternal grandfather, Osip Abramovich. When Osip was first named Yanuary (Januarius), the long-suffering but sturdy Christina, whose German accent made certain words hard to pronounce, was reputed to have said, "the black devil [*shorn short*], he makes me babies and gives them devilish names."[43] Pushkin would not have approved of the brutal treatment of Eudoxia, but neither would he have been shocked by it. He had no illusions about what took place behind closed doors on a land-owner's estate in pre-Enlightenment Russia. One thing he did take away from this story of Abram's first marriage, however: the theme of betrayal through the birth of a "wrong-colored" baby—what could be termed with no exaggeration as the poet's "Othello complex." It is not jealousy per se, the eruption of

"African passions," that is the issue here.[44] It is rather the sense of betrayed trust: "Then must you speak / Of one who lov'd not wisely but too well; / Of one not easily jealous, but being wrought / Perplex'd in the extreme." Particularly in his own later life, Pushkin would come back to these thoughts of Othello and Desdemona and to how his own marriage to a beautiful young Russian woman might be prefigured in Shakespeare's plot. Likewise, the theme of the birth of a "wrong-colored" baby will haunt Pushkin personally and will find expression in his work artistically, including *The Blackamoor*.

The next generation of Gannibals lived in the reflected glory of the "tsar's blackamoor," and they inherited both his good and bad (but mostly the latter) traits. On the military side, Abram's first son Ivan (1735–1801) was the most distinguished, educated, and personally decent. Less "African" in his external features than the other Gannibal males, he seems to have inherited more of his Swedish mother's good sense and equanimity as well. His Catherine-era military exploits, in particular his heroic efforts during the First Turkish War (1768–1774) as Russia tried to push her way south to the Black Sea, were certainly noteworthy. He became known as the "hero of Navarin" for taking the Turkish seaport in April 1770 with three ships and a 2500-man landing party after a six-day assault; then a few months later he played a crucial role as artillery commander in the famous battle of Chesme (Çeşme), in which the Turkish fleet was sunk but the flagship carrying Admiral Spiridov and Gannibal himself was blown up (although both survived). And in 1778 he was given the task of building Kherson, an entire fortified city, which he did, subsequently becoming its commander. Ivan retired in 1784, with numerous decorations and the admiration of his countrymen, at the rank of general-in-chief (like his father). His gravestone in the famous cemetery at the Alexander Nevsky Monastery reads: "Africa's heat gave him birth, the cold nurtured his blood, / He served Russia and built a path to eternity."[45] A lifelong bachelor, he tried to look after his brothers and their families, which, considering the Gannibals' dissolute behavior, was no easy task.[46]

The remaining Gannibal brothers, Pyotr (1742–1826), Osip (1744–1806), Isaak (1747–1808), and Yakov (1748–?), show a different picture, one that would have made anyone, but especially the superstitious Pushkin, very uneasy about his inherited flaws. (As is typical of the time, we know almost nothing about Abram Gannibal's surviving daughters Elizaveta, Anna, and Sofya.) Blaming his "openhearted nature" (*prostodushie*), Isaak got into so much debt he had to go to jail and leave his wife and fifteen children (!) on the mercy of the state; there is also the rumor that he murdered the widow of a priest for resisting his intentions.[47] Pushkin seems to have enjoyed the company of Isaak's sons Pavel and Semyon when he visited Mikhailovskoe after graduating from the Lyceum in 1817. Pyotr Gannibal, the hard-drinking old moor from whom the young Pushkin would learn about his mother's side of the family, had a successful military career like Ivan, being promoted in retirement from colonel to major-general. However, a small cloud hung over his reputation because some artillery shells had gone missing under his command, for which he was tried and eventually acquitted. He separated from his first wife after deceiving her and then, in a move that seems to have been typical for the Gannibal brothers, told her he was happier without her and their three children and would prefer if she lived apart from him. The obedient wife agreed (what choice did she have?), remaining behind in their home near Kazan, while Pyotr settled in with another woman at Petrovskoe. By the time Pushkin came upon him in his northern exile, Pyotr, who had marked Negroid features, was a hard-boiled bachelor in his early eighties. His patriarchal excesses could amuse the nephew because they were so radically at odds with the salon politesse of St. Petersburg, whose values Pushkin had imbibed from his youth.[48]

And finally, there is Osip Abramovich, Pushkin's grandfather. This Gannibal seems to have been the most profligate and willful of them all. What the grandson wrote about him in his autobiographical note has that special quality of no-nonsense judgment and perfect pitch toward the past we acknowledge as recognizably Pushkinian:

> This marriage was unhappy too. The wife's jealousy and the husband's inconstancy were the cause of discontent and arguing, which ended in divorce. My grandfather's African temperament, his fiery passions combined with a terrible lack of judgment [*legkomyslie*], drew him into amazing blunders. He took a second wife [Ustinya Tolstaya] after presenting a false testimony on the death of the first. My grandmother [Marya Alekseevna] was forced to make an appeal to the empress herself [Catherine II], who actively interceded in the case. My grandfather's new marriage was declared unlawful, my grandmother was given back her three-year old daughter [Pushkin's mother Nadezhda],[49] and grandfather was sent away to serve in the Black Sea navy. Thirty years they lived apart. My grandfather died in 1807,[50] on his Pskov estate, from the effects of immoderate living. Eleven years later my grandmother passed away on the same estate. Death united them. They now rest in peace together at Svyatogorsk Monastery.[51]

The grandmother in this passage is of course Pushkin's beloved Marya Alekseevna, who herself was born a Pushkin (she and her son-in-law were distant cousins) before she made the fatal step of entering the Gannibal clan. When Marya, a well-connected *baryshnia* (girl of noble birth) whose father had been *voevoda* (governor) of Tambov, and Osip Gannibal, an ex-artillery officer, first got married in 1773, they moved to the estate in Murom that the young wife had received as her dowry. The marriage was considered a less-than-ideal match on Marya's side of the family, and what happened next confirmed everyone's suspicions. Thanks to Osip's mounting debts, the couple was forced to sell Marya's place and move in at Suyda with old Abram Petrovich, who was by now enraged at his son's profligacy. Osip couldn't stand to lead a respectable life under the scrutiny of his father and soon thereafter disappeared, leaving the old man a note with the message that he was "hiding away forever." In any event, Osip later surfaced in Pskov, where he found a pretty young widow, Ustinya Tolstaya, and convinced a priest that he was a widower and that they should be married, creating yet another instance of Gannibal infidelity and bigamy. Ustinya herself seems to have gotten around (and deep into the pockets not only of Osip but the other Gannibals), appearing as one of the individuals to whom Isaak made one of his hapless loans. She was another of Osip's "amazing blunders." When Catherine finally annulled Osip's marriage to Ustinya in 1784, Marya was given a fourth of his estate, as child support for Nadezhda, along with the village of Kobrino (later exchanged for Zakharovo), where the Pushkin family would summer in Alexander's first decade. Osip passed his final "immoderate" years holed up at Mikhailovskoe, the greatest achievement of his failed life being that he fathered the daughter who gave birth to our poet.

Before leaving our discussion of Pushkin's African ancestors, it is worth noting that the poet was equally proud of both sides of his family. The patrilineal "Pushkin" side, whose story I stress less to the students for obvious reasons, went back to ancient nobility in the twelfth century, and the family's surname, deriving from the Russian word for "cannon" (*pushka*), announced both their martial spirit and their constant infighting near the Russian throne. Ultimately, the issue of race seems to have been of a piece in Pushkin's mind with the issue of class (again, he believed the Gannibals to have been descended from royalty—whether this royalty was African or Russian does not appear material). Furthermore, what Abram Gannibal *did* with the givens of his life is what inspired the great-grandson the most: he rose above the limitations of his captivity and his skin color to become a historically significant man in his own right. Thus, we can imagine Pushkin's white-hot anger when, in August 1830, he read the following in Faddei Bulgarin's newspaper *The Northern Bee*:

Someone has told an anecdote about how a certain poet in Spanish America, another imitator of Byron, born from a mulatto man or, I can't recall, a mulatto woman, tried to prove that one of his ancestors was a Negro Prince. In the town hall papers were found to the effect that in the distant past there was a court case between a skipper and his assistant over that Negro, whom both wanted to acquire, and that the skipper proved that he had bought the Negro for a bottle of rum. Did they know at the time that a connection to this Negro would be acknowledged by the poet? Vanitas vanitatis . . .[52]

Pushkin had reason to be livid. His mother was known as "the beautiful Creole" and this passage, which dismisses her as a *mulatka* ("mulatto woman"), is a direct assault on her parentage. Even more humiliating, Bulgarin snidely suggests that Abram Gannibal was of little consequence to Peter, the "skipper," as the latter bought the Negro for next to nothing ("a bottle of rum").

Pushkin could not call the scurrilous Bulgarin out to a duel for the two were from different social classes—Pushkin was an aristocrat and Bulgarin a de facto commoner (his Polish *szlachta*, or minor gentry, background did not translate into the Russian context). Nor could he polemicize openly in the press about his enemy's underhanded tricks, since nothing could be dispositive in that forum and, moreover, it would be unseemly for Pushkin to appear to give any public credence to the slander. Nor could he, given who he was both professionally and personally, simply allow the slight to pass. His answer came in the "Post scriptum" to the unpublishable (it circulated via manuscript) "My Genealogy" (1830):

> Figlyarin decided while sitting at home
> That my black grandfather Gannibal
> Was bought for a bottle of rum
> And fell into the hands of a skipper.
>
> That skipper was the same renowned skipper
> By whom our country was moved,
> The same one who powerfully set the rudder
> Of our native ship on sovereign course.
>
> My grandfather had entrée to that skipper,
> and the blackamoor thusly bought
> grew up zealous, incorruptible,
> the tsar's confidant, and not a slave.

"Figlyarin" is a play on Bulgarin's name and the Russian word for trickster/jester. According to the facts at his disposal, which had cost him some effort to unearth, Pushkin believed that his great-grandfather was not merely a decoration to Peter's world, that he was the tsar's godson, that he grew from valet to secretary to able student to military officer. He also believed that Peter came out of St. Petersburg personally to meet Gannibal when the latter returned from Paris[53] and blessed him there with the icon of Saints Peter and Paul, which supposedly remained in the Gannibal family.[54] In this respect, not only was Abram Gannibal "the tsar's confidant" and "not a slave," he was something more: the former youth received triumphantly "home" by Russia's greatest tsar, as though the latter were playing the father to a prodigal son, which recalled one of the poet's favorite, and also self-referential, stories from the Bible. "And he arose and came to his father. But while he was yet at a distance, his father saw him and had compassion, and ran and embraced him and kissed him." This is the gesture of generosity and mercy that Pushkin was trying, always unsuccessfully, to elicit from his last tsar, Nicholas I. Such, then, are the principal facts of Pushkin's black ancestry and some of the "poetic truths" he constructed from those facts.

The Blackamoor of Peter the Great

The plot of *The Blackamoor* begins with Ibrahim's (Abram's) life in Paris in the early eighteenth century. It is a world of "folly and luxury," one in which "greed for money" is "united to a thirst for enjoyment and dissipation." Ibrahim is in France to study and learn and eventually return to Russia to help Peter in the emperor's nation-building projects, but in the meantime he can't help himself and plunges headlong into the European capital's social scene. The *haut monde* dubs him, with his exotic appearance, *le nègre du Czar*. While enjoying the nightlife, Ibrahim makes the acquaintance of a married countess, with whom he falls passionately in love. Countess Leonora D. is one of the few women in society who responds to Ibrahim as something more than a celebrity. Intrigued by his looks but also by his demeanor and appealing reserve, she reciprocates and eventually they start an affair. Society gossips, which torments the lovely countess and poisons Ibrahim's happiness. Ibrahim is jealous by nature and fears the moment when the countess will tire of him and want to take on a new lover. Soon, the affair, which by society's rules is supposed to remain discreet, threatens scandal when the countess becomes pregnant. Now tongues wag even more, with men wagering whether the baby will be black or white. Finally, the countess goes into labor and delivers herself of a black baby; however, before the birth a bait and switch is arranged with a poor woman who is willing to give up her new-born, and the white infant is substituted for the black one. Leonora's husband, a complaisant nullity, doesn't have a clue as to what is going on.

Ibrahim and the countess try to go on as before. They clearly are still passionately in love, but time is not on their side. Ibrahim realizes that, given his social status and prospects, it cannot last. The countess is not built for suffering and social obloquy. The young black man goes over his options and, after painful soul searching, decides to quit France and return to Russia. The Duke of Orleans tries to convince him to remain in France, telling him that he owes Peter little and that France is a better place for him than the "barbaric" country to which he was taken from his original homeland. But Ibrahim stands firm, sees Leonora one last time, and then departs without telling her his plan, writing a heartfelt letter instead:

> My happiness could not have lasted. I have enjoyed it in spite of fate and nature. You would have grown tired of me; your enchantment would have vanished. This thought has pursued me always—even in those moments when I have seemed to forget everything at your feet, intoxicated by your passionate self-denial, your infinite tenderness. [...] Consider: should I subject you further to such agitations and dangers as these? Why strive to unite the fate of so tender and beautiful a creature as yourself to the miserable lot of a Negro, a pitiful creation scarcely worthy to be classed as human?

He makes the long journey back to Russia and is met at a post-house outside St. Petersburg by a tall man wearing a green caftan and chewing on a clay pipe. This man is Peter the Great, who has been waiting for him since the day before. Ibrahim hesitates in the tsar's presence, but the tsar quickly embraces his godson and kisses him on the forehead. As Peter takes him under his wing and shows him around St. Petersburg, the city founded by the tsar as a "window to the West," Ibrahim senses he is regaining his willpower and shedding the feelings of exhaustion and lack of purpose that accompanied him during his failed affair. Something transformative is happening within him:

> With a feeling almost of contrition, he confessed in his heart that, for the first time since his separation from the Countess D., his thoughts had not dwelt exclusively upon her throughout the day. He saw that the new way of life that was awaiting

him—the activity and constant work—could revive his soul, fatigued by passion, idleness and secret despondency. The thought of working together with a great man and, with him, of playing some part in the fate of a great nation, awoke in him for the first time the noble feeling of ambition.

What remains of the unfinished *The Blackamoor* involves scenes of local color at Peter's court. Old-fashioned Russia is being undermined by the Western reforms Peter is forcing on the country; the boyars' beards are being shaved off and their wives and daughters have taken to dressing according to European fashion and demanding more freedoms. Against this backdrop it emerges that Ibrahim would like to get married and have a family. Russia is the black man's adoptive homeland and, in order to have a foothold in this country he is helping to defend and modernize, he needs to put down roots. The difference between Ibrahim and the other young Russians Peter has sent West to get educated is that the African is obviously intelligent, accomplished, and self-effacing (and this despite his passionate temperament), while the others, including his friend from Paris Ivan Korsakov, are foppish and vain, and for this reason are mocked by Peter and his courtiers. Ibrahim's Achilles heel is his feelings for the countess, which flare up again when he receives a letter from her that has been passed on from Korsakov. These feelings are tinged by jealousy when he thinks of her with another man. Seeing Ibrahim's lonely predicament, the emperor decides to intrude himself into the situation. He notices that his godson has looked with interest at Natalya, the beautiful young daughter of a prominent boyar, Gavrila Rzhevsky, at one of the assemblies. He visits Rzhevsky and, as all-powerful autocrat-cum-matchmaker, he bends the father to his will, convincing him that, despite the "wild" exterior, Ibrahim is a model young man. Meanwhile, the comely Natalya, who it turns out has another beau, eavesdrops on the conversation and faints away, terrified at the prospect of having to marry the African. This is where Pushkin leaves off the plot without completing the historical novel.

I now return with the students to these bare-bone plot details to facilitate a more in-depth discussion of the category of race and its role as a stimulus to Pushkin's creativity. First, the significance of Ibrahim's love affair with the countess in Paris:

> The Countess received Ibrahim politely, but without any particular attention; he felt flattered by this. People generally regarded the young moor as a freak, and, surrounding him, overwhelmed him with compliments and questions; this curiosity, although

concealed beneath an air of graciousness, offended his vanity. The delightful attention of women, almost the sole aim of man's exertions, not only gave him no pleasure, but even filled his heart with bitterness and indignation. He felt that for them he was a kind of rare beast, an exceptional and strange creation, accidentally transferred to their world, and possessing nothing in common with them. He even envied those who remained unnoticed and considered them to be fortunate in their insignificance.

Particularly offensive to Ibrahim is the tendency of others to see him exclusively as the "rare beast" and flatter him and ask him intrusive questions. (As an aside, I remind the students that it is precisely this kind of behavior by perhaps well-meaning, but otherwise naïve and often racially insensitive white college kids from rural Wisconsin that annoys our newcomers when they first arrive on campus. Recall Stephanie's words: *"I have been looked at as different; I have been asked highly inappropriate things about my identity, and even had derogatory terms be used towards me."*) The countess, however, treats the young black man differently. Her way of not singling him out because of his appearance and of comporting herself with him as with any other wins him over. This "tell" is important because it goes right to the inner workings of Pushkin's creative laboratory—the moment at which his life experience spills over into his artistic inspiration.

It turns out that the special charm of Countess Leonora D. bears a striking resemblance to that of Countess Elizaveta (Elise) Vorontsova, the wife of Pushkin's superior in Odessa during the last portion of his southern exile.[55] Not only is Pushkin drawing on his own past to create a believable character in his art, one that never existed in Gannibal's biography, he is doing so while channeling *his own reactions* to how others look at him into those of his great-grandfather. It is a cliché, but no less true for being so: art works when it finds a way to speak to our common humanity or, to shift back to earlier discussion, when it shows in believable fashion a between-group perspective triumphing provisionally over within-group exclusionary tactics. According to memoirists, Vorontsova was extremely charming and youthfully attractive, warm and unaffected in her manners, and, above all, possessed of the capacity *to please*—all qualities describing the Countess D. Indeed, no one among Pushkin's romantic attachments either before or after—and there were many—was apparently more capable of inspiring not only his passion but *his trust* (hence the even greater potential pain of betrayal) than this utterly *comme il faut* society lady:

Ibrahim was often at her house. She gradually grew accustomed to the young moor's appearance, and even began to find something rather pleasant about the curly head, so black amid the powdered wigs in her drawing-room. (Ibrahim had been wounded in the head and wore a bandage instead of a wig.) He was twenty-seven; he was tall and well-built, and more than one beauty gazed at him with feelings more flattering than mere curiosity; but the prejudiced Ibrahim either did not notice this, or looked upon it as mere coquetry. Yet when his glances met those of the Countess, his distrust vanished. Her eyes expressed such charming good nature, her manner towards him was so simple and natural that it was impossible to suspect her in the least of flirtatiousness or mockery.

What is also going on here in the alembics of Pushkin's art is *the transposition of race (the black man as outsider) to class (the poet as outsider)*. One of Pushkin's defensive gestures whenever he was in a public situation with strangers and was asked about his poetry, what something meant, or how it felt to create, was to avoid the question and to become tetchy. He did so because this was his most private self, a self that could not, and as he also felt should not, be superficially shared. And this was also the same as his racial identity and the racial identity of his fictionalized progenitor: the secret of the man underneath cannot be gotten at by asking him about his black skin—he is that, but he is also more than that, and it can't be explained, it can only be felt and experienced. Pushkin came to believe that Vorontsova, with whom he was having a secret affair,[56] had become pregnant with his child near the time he was forced to quit Odessa. And while it can be disputed that the "swarthy" child (a daughter Sofya) born to the Vorontsovs in April 1825 was actually Pushkin's, what cannot be denied is that in several poems and fragments written by Pushkin that fall and winter, while he was under house arrest in Mikhailovskoe, the theme of a natural child comes to the fore. In all likelihood it is this "child of love, child of nature" (a quote from one of the works) that makes its way two years later into *The Blackamoor* as the *black* baby of Ibrahim and Countess D., a detail not present in the German biography of Gannibal available to Pushkin, except in reverse form (the rumor that the African's first wife had betrayed him by giving birth to a white baby). Just as Ibrahim would greedily reread Leonora's love letter to him after they were parted, so too would Pushkin pore over Elise's letters to him in Mikhailovskoe, burning them once he had committed them to memory. Thus we must assume that Pushkin's erotic obsession with Vorontsova, which he recasts as Ibrahim's with the Countess, was all-consuming at the time.

The embedded meaning of the Countess D. affair, one that the post-exile Pushkin kept returning to as he contemplated his need to find a wife, is that a love, no matter how passionate, that grows out of salon intrigue and has casual infidelity as its basis, cannot be sustained and is fated to fade. There is nothing moralistic in this realization; it is completely matter-of-fact. Equally determinative in Pushkin's creative rewriting of the meager facts of the German biography is the sense that at long last Ibrahim has decided to take part in another story. That story is the making of a modern Russia, which is also his author's story. He is not in it alone. It is *through Peter* that Gannibal receives all his lessons about self-esteem. Ibrahim sees that Peter cares for him as a father and treats him as someone *inherently worthy* even when *it was he* who was acting the prodigal son in France and temporizing about his return; Peter meets him at the post-house as soon as he returns home and invites him to his table as "one of us"; Peter agrees to serve as his matchmaker and sees no obstacle to amorous advancement in his African appearance.

> "Sire, I am happy with your protection and favor. May God grant that I do not outlive my Tsar and benefactor—I wish for nothing more. But even if I did think about getting married, would the young lady and her relatives consent? My appearance . . ."
>
> "Your appearance! What nonsense! A fellow like you? A young girl must obey her parents and we'll see what old Gavrila Rzhevsky has to say when I myself am your matchmaker."

In short, Peter is both tsar and "fairy godfather," the all-powerful one who can confer (or, perhaps more accurately, compel others to magically recognize) goodness and even attractiveness *from the outside in.*

But the Peter of *The Blackamoor* is still more than this, which is the final point. In Pushkin's rendering, it is thanks to him, thanks to his faith in his servant/"slave" (here there is the obvious sound-play between *rab* and *arap*), that Ibrahim can become a free man who *chooses* to return to Russia even when it may be in his interest to remain in France (the Europe the poet had many times dreamed of fleeing to). Peter, as it were, allows his godson *to adopt him* (what the French of *The Blackamoor* care nothing about), just as he gives Ibrahim a reason for living that, in time, comes to counterbalance the pain of his failed affair with Countess D. By acting the role of the good father in the prodigal son parable, which is Pushkin's fictionalization of family history, but also a fictionalization that the poet believed contained a kernel of truth, Peter presides over the change in status from adoptive to actual, "consanguineous":

> "Listen, Ibrahim: you are on your own in this world, without birth or kindred, a stranger to all except myself. If I were to die today, what would become of you tomorrow? You must get settled while there's still time; find support in new ties, marry into the Russian nobility."

> "Marry!" thought the African. "Why not? Must I be fated to spend my life in solitude, without knowing the greatest rewards and most sacred duties of man, merely because I was born under a stronger sun? I cannot hope to be loved, but that is a childish objection! How can one believe in love? How can love exist in the frivolous heart of a woman? Such charming fallacies I have rejected forever, and have chosen more practical attractions. The Tsar is right: I must consider my future. Marriage with the young Rzhevsky will unite me to the proud, Russian nobility, and I shall no longer be a stranger in my fatherland. I shall not demand love from my wife, but will be content with her fidelity; her friendship I shall acquire by unfailing tenderness, trust and devotion."

The way Ibrahim plans to make Russia his and fix in place what Peter has initiated is through the socially sanctioned ties of marriage, through family and children, through the act of putting down roots in the soil of his new homeland. One of the most meaning-laden statements ever made by a Pushkinian character, one the author himself will repeat in altered form several years later in a letter to his future mother-in-law when he proposes to another beautiful Natalya, and is finally, after difficult negotiations, accepted, is: "I shall not demand love from my wife, but will be content with her fidelity; her friendship I shall acquire by unfailing tenderness, trust, and devotion."[57] This, of course, is Pushkin, now the *born* Russian, speaking through Ibrahim, the adoptive son. He has been taught in the school of hard knocks not to trust a romantic love based on appearances as starting point: "I cannot hope to be loved, but that is a childish objection!" His ambition, which feeds his creativity and is fed by it, wants something else. Where his ancestors were apt, as warriors, to win their historical spurs through martial deeds, the descendant must do so through words, through the consciousness of being a poet. Starting out as his family's black sheep, he becomes in maturity Russia's Joseph, interpreter of national dreams.

Identity, creativity, homecoming: a belonging that accepts the self and yet also transcends the self by finding purpose. This is where cultural adaptation comes in. This is where the "Pushkinian" quiddity comes in. The themes of racial identity and mate choice are interwoven from two textual spaces *as Pushkin researches and writes them* (the historical personage Abram, the character Ibrahim) and one autobiographical space *as Pushkin has lived it* (his failed affair with Elise Voronstova). The fictional Ibrahim wants to find a mate and start a family so that he can feel at home as a Russian, and Pushkin the creator wants to find a marriageable young woman to experience a similar continuity, only one not made of words but experienced in the flesh. All this points to the idea that Pushkin's text is a participant in the cultural equivalent of multilevel selection. Curiously, *The Blackamoor* was left uncompleted by its author. We don't know why. It could have been that he lost interest, or that the subject matter was too uncomfortably personal, or that, fidgety by nature, he solved its creative challenge and didn't see the point in continuing. As I discuss it with our students, I like to think it was never finished for another reason: the continuation is happening in them, as cultural evolution, and its different endings are still being decided.

CHAPTER 6

"The Queen of Spades": Risk, Reward, Gaming Life

"The passion to gamble is the most powerful of passions."
(Pushkin)

As we come to our final chapter, let us reprise a few basic facts. First, any attempt to put in words a picture of how the world works is at best a snapshot that will soon fade and curl around the edges. In this respect, process philosophy still harkens back to pre-Socratic Heraclitus and his "everything flows." When we put together these word pictures, including the word picture that is this book, we focus and we push forward, with a left-brain orientation, a tunnel-vision "grasping" that already by definition has to ignore all else that is outside the picture's frame. Sometimes these versions of reality are so vivid and convincing we take them to be true, the way things "really are," but in the end the picture is always temporary. The edges of the picture and the edges of reality beyond the picture are never coterminous. The only way we can coax the "is" and the "ought" of Hume's guillotine onto one blade is through the Escher-like optical illusion of art, the projection of a full outside from an incomplete inside, which is why we need artists like Pushkin. Pushkin makes us believe in the reality of the optical illusion, in the static words on the page actually being able to capture something in motion and preserving it into the future. That also is what we mean when we say the best art models life.

Following this idea are several considerations related to the moving target that is our learning environment today. First, two things can be right at the same time: Pushkin is a unique artistic talent, one whose Russian/African heritage can inspire our students, but also, and no less important, he is a representative of a primate species, and species evolve. Second, his way of expressing himself creatively in his time can serve as a model for our students in their search for analogous niche positions in their time. Third, his writing, thinking, and, indeed, historically embedded being in the world are more functions of *processes* (*life cycles*) than of things (discrete events, people, physical realia), and looking at the processes that produced Pushkin is at least as enlightening as considering the finished excellence of his artistic works, although it is that excellence that most often inspires us. And fourth, as a rule, the idea of the romantic poet, what Russians call *poet bozh'ei milost'iu* (poet by the grace of God), should not be studied in isolation, as a phenomenon distinct from the poet's social (as in multilevel selection, within-group versus between-group) context.

One aspect of Pushkin's distinctive personality is his willingness to take risks: in duels, in freedom-loving verse, and at gaming tables. The work we investigate in our final chapter is his great short tale "The Queen of Spades" (1833), whose tense plot and linguistic sleights of hand have a strong appeal for our young audience. Why that is so and what cognitive circuits Pushkin's story turns on are our topics. Because the central plot conceit is a card game and a scene of high-stakes gambling its denouement, I ask the students to consider the concept of risk versus reward in their lives. Are there risks they have taken that have worked out for them? What about those that have resulted in mistakes and come back to bite them? As they look to the future, what sorts of risks are worth it ("no risk, no reward") and what are not? Pushkin's tale also turns out to be ideal hunting ground for examining afresh several issues touched on previously: How do wordplay, or verbal cues, and the idea of psychological manipulation reinforce each other? Is life a riddle or a game that can be cracked with a code? Is playing fairly in life something evolutionarily inscribed in our genes and biochemical makeup? What matters more in terms of survival skills, acquiring wealth (the power of things) or building relationships (the power of friendship/love)? Finally, as objective correlative, I act out the risk-taker's decision-making process by actually playing the game (Faro) with the students as we discuss what is happening psychologically with the characters.

The Students on Risk-Taking

Here is how several of our students think about the idea of risk-taking in their lives:

> Hector:
> Normally I do not take risks because I feel like I have never taken any risks in my life. I cannot recall a time when I've taken a risk that could have changed the trajectory of my life. I always like to

make sure that I think all my decisions through. I believe a risk worth taking is when you know that it can change your life for the better, like starting your own business. But the failure could also set you back. I think a significant risk I could take is moving to a different state with a lower cost of living, such as Texas, and leaving everything I know behind, such as job, friends and family. A risk I have seen others take is leaving school in order to start their own business or trying to become famous as a rapper or streamer. I have seen some succeed and some fail; it just depends how hard some people are willing to work.

Karina:

I consider myself both risk-averse and risk-taking. This mainly depends on the situation. I am risk-averse when it comes to people. I have struggled taking chances on individuals because I do not trust easily. People scare me and that is because of my experience as an immigrant and my relationship with entitled children. My whole life I have been surrounded with adults, so having people around my age outside of school was not common. I do not know how people around my age interact because they are so complex and make their lives harder, in my opinion. I am a complex individual who makes her life harder, as well, but I guess I can say I am more centered and more serious. Although I know I am making an unfair judgement, this judgement has sadly taken over my view and made me less social around my age group. I can hold a conversation and invest in a friendship, but I never get out of it what I put in, so the risk taker in me has slowly diminished in that respect because for me relationships are even. I would say that I am still a cordial person with everyone, but I am not investing as much as I would normally do.

Another way I am risk-averse is that trust does not come easily to me when it comes to things I know I cannot control but try to. Before taking risks, I try to control the situation because I have been able to do so in the past. For example, I never relied on my teacher for my own learning. I always took charge, was always the initiator. This mindset has always been with me since I came to America. When I relied on my family to help me with my English, they started helping me but then they stopped because they told me it was my responsibility. Although that is true, I felt like I lost the support when I needed it the most, so after that I did my own learning. I sometimes do not like the unknown because that means I cannot control it. You can say I am a control freak to some extent but that is because knowing the outcome tends to give me comfort. Not knowing stuff makes me anxious because I know what it is like not knowing things. I know what it means to feel lost in a place and not know comfort because you must be on your toes every day to survive.

I am a risk taker when it comes to my education and future. Ever since I moved to America, I began to take the initiative with opportunities that have been presented to me. When I came to the USA, I did not know how to speak English. I still remember the struggles and the daily crying, so I promised myself that those times I spent struggling would help me get more opportunities. For me, taking risks is not a choice but a need to survive. Even though I previously mentioned that I like to control things, I give myself enough space to take risks. I think a main risk that I have taken is with Russian. Before Russian came into the picture, I knew I wanted to only study political science and become a lawyer. I am passionate about justice and helping, and I wanted to study law because this career seemed to be one of the most prestigious jobs with a good income. Also, I felt like I needed this career to feel like "I made it" as an immigrant. As I kept taking Russian, I realized that there was more to life than just the standard "American dream." I finally realized that I had options besides being a lawyer or a doctor (I was not made for science). I have met so many individuals who have allowed me to network and open more doors for me than I could ever imagine. I can go to college without having to worry financially. I have been able to study abroad twice in two beautiful countries: Latvia and Russia. I was exposed to different cultures I never thought of exploring because they were "too far away," which they were not. I was able to make lots of friends who I still talk to and share similar interests. Russian has opened a side of me that I would have never discovered if I stayed in my bubble. I still want to help people and be involved with political science, and I have finally found my focus—international relations, and more specifically Russia-related. I have many dreams and goals, I am not sure with what I want to start, but I know I want Russian to be related somehow. I never knew Russian would give me these opportunities because I was taking it because (1) it was mandatory in my high school and (2) it was fun, and I like languages. I never knew I could keep it as I start building my career, which it turns out I can. [...]

In my opinion, risks that are worth taking are things that you will not regret no matter what the outcome is, whether it is a good one or a bad one, because it is a learning experience. Failures are good in life because they make you grow. I think a risk that is not worth taking is one that is up to one's discretion. If you know it is going to make you unhappy for sure, then I would not take it. A person takes risks for many different reasons, such as curiosity, experience, opportunities, etc. I am a person who takes risks out of curiosity, and I have known its ups and its downs, and I do not regret them. I may have regrets about how things could have been different, but I do not regret doing it.

In the future, I can anticipate that there will be many significant risks in my life with my education, career, personal life. I will be graduating soon, and I need to figure out what I will do after that, finding experience and jobs. I want to find my own place even though in Latino families that is not very common unless you are getting married, so I will be taking a risk with that. There will be risks in my life that will impact others, so I need to somewhat prepare myself for that and be ready to approach it.

Theresa:
I am the kind of person who will not do something unless I am almost sure of the outcome. I think that results from my past when I made plenty of mistakes taking risks on things that I later learned were not worth the consequences. It very much depends on the situation, but even when I have taken risks and failed, I think I have learned a lot from those situations. I have taken many risks with friends, relationships, academics, experiences, opportunities. I think a recent risk that I took this past semester was in my Russian class. I think it is embarrassing to admit because it was a mistake that I regret, but at the same time I think it shows how I am open to risk. Last semester in my Russian language class, we were asked to write many essays. After completing each of the essays, I sent them to my friends in Latvia to edit

them. Over time, I realize that my grades were really high on all of my essays. It makes sense because I had help from an outside source. After talking to a classmate one day later in the semester, he brought to my attention how it was unfair what I was doing and how the specifications on the syllabus stated that we were not allowed to get outside help. I just remember feeling super guilty after that for being dishonest. I had to make a decision on whether or not to talk to my TA teaching the class. By talking to him I was risking him giving me zeroes on all of the essays and me possibly failing the class. On the other hand, I was risking him finding out another way or me being left with shame. I honestly don't think he would ever have found out if I didn't talk to him. I ended up talking to him, and he was grateful for my honesty. I didn't end up getting punished, and it was a really good learning opportunity. In my opinion, it was a risk worth taking when your conscience is involved. For me, it is more important to be honest and true to myself. I think remaining true to myself is going to continue to be a risk. This can come in the form of relationships, choices, and experiences.

The Plot: Risk, Fate, the Uncanny, the Emergence of Character

The plot of "The Queen of Spades" is an intricate ticking time bomb. It reaches out to the phenomenal and historical world Pushkin was living in, and it reaches into the devices at its disposal, first and foremost aspects of its language from the micro to the macro levels, for turning on the time bomb and then waiting in tense anticipation for it to explode. Basically, what the words do is create a moving picture (again, the optical illusion) of the world of 1833: the words tell a story but they also instantiate what the story is about. Thus, the first order of business for the students and me as we begin to look at Pushkin's tale is to try to understand what the plot is telling us and *how* it is doing the telling at the same time. This cognitive move allows us to tie the story's inner workings to the outer world's baffling variety, and in this way mimic the characters' attempts to situate their actions within larger contexts. For the sake of simplicity our retelling will entail several passes: first, the characters' thoughts and actions *as they happen* and the information made available to the reader at that time, with the understanding that all will be known only at the ending; second, a return to the plot and a reexamination of it at the micro level, with a look at Pushkin's language and its ties to gaming metaphors and the psychology of risk; third, the ways in which the plot reflects the broad world beyond Pushkin's text, including parallels that are still with us today. It goes without saying that the goal here, as in the previous chapters, is not "literary criticism," but life lessons in light of evolutionary theory and practice as the latter apply to the cultural realm.

"The Queen of Spades" is the story of Hermann, a young engineer in the officer corps. The story opens after an evening of card-playing at a certain Narumov's, with the different players discussing their luck at cards. Hermann has been sitting and watching but not playing; he says that, while the game has a strong appeal for him, he can't afford "to sacrifice the necessary in order to obtain the superfluous." One of the card players, Tomsky, tells those present a story about his grandmother, the Countess, who was a big hit at the gaming tables in Paris in the previous century, sixty years ago. Beautiful, exotic, strong-willed, she was known as "la Vénus muscovite." The story has a fantastic twist: after losing a massive sum at Faro (*faraon* or "Pharaoh" in Russian) and having her otherwise normally docile husband get his back up and refuse to pay her debt, the Countess is forced to turn to a friend, the mysterious Count St. Germain, for help. St. Germain doesn't want simply to give her the money, because that will only make her feel more encumbered, so instead he provides her with a three-card formula for winning back her losses. She is to play the three cards in order, bet the maximum each time, and then agree not to play any more after that. She accepts St. Germain's offer, wins back everything, and departs the scene as instructed. Tomsky complains slyly that his wastrel father or even he himself could have used his grandmother's help on more than one occasion, but that she has always refused to share this knowledge with anyone, except for Chaplitsky, another well-known gambler, on whom she unpredictably took pity when he lost a colossal sum in his youth and was in despair. Chaplitsky too won back his losses with the three cards the Countess vouchsafed him. Everyone at Narumov's is struck by Tomsky's story. They try to explain it in three possible ways that accord with the "nature of things" at the time: "luck" says the first guest, "a fairytale" says Hermann, "powdered cards" (that is, cheating) says the third. After that the gambling party breaks up.

"The Queen of Spades," however, is not only the story of Hermann, it is also the story of Lizaveta Ivanovna, or Liza. The next part of the tale tells us about Liza and her life as the ward of the Countess. Liza is a *baryshnia*, a young lady of good family, who lives with the old Countess as her companion. But she is poor, hence her role as all-purpose vis-à-vis: she reads the temperamental Countess books and then has to answer for their defects; she follows instructions and asks the servants to prepare the carriage for an outing that the old woman then peremptorily cancels because it is too windy; she accompanies the Countess to balls at which her primary function is to tag along with young ladies to the powder room; she is prettier than her wealthy coevals and would like the chance to dance at the balls, but is mostly ignored due to her social station, and so on. The narrator calls her a "domestic martyr." At this point the Hermann-storyline reappears through a conversation Tomsky has with Liza at the Countess's. Tomsky asks his grandmother if he can introduce his friend Narumov to her at an upcoming ball. When the Countess is out of earshot, Liza asks Tomsky if his friend is an engineer. Thus does Hermann's identity (still not revealed as such) creep into the Liza-subplot, since Narumov is a cavalry officer, which fact makes Tomsky curious as to why Liza is asking. We soon find out how Hermann has entered the frame with the following description:

> Lizaveta Ivanovna remained alone [after Tomsky left]: she laid aside her work and started to look out the window. Soon there appeared from behind a corner building on one side of the street a young officer. A deep blush covered her cheeks and she again took up her work and bent her head over the [embroidery] frame.

The reader asks, *why* does Liza laugh awkwardly and avoid telling Tomsky the reason she thinks Narumov might be an engineer? The answer is that Liza has everything to lose if the Countess should find out that she has been showing interest in a young man outside of the household. This is how the gambling theme touches Liza, for it is *a huge risk* for her to initiate such relations on her own. She could lose everything. At the same time, the tale's originating riddle, the one involving Hermann's nature as he watches intently others gambling but doesn't play himself, deepens with the appearance of the unnamed young officer whose insistent presence makes Liza blush. What is Hermann doing there? *It is as if the narrator is revealing one card at a time, with the full hand not yet being formed.*

The next move comes with the game being played toward the end of part two. Now the narrator shows more of his cards:

> Once—this happened two days after the evening described at the beginning of this tale, and a week before the scene at which we stopped—once Lizaveta Ivanovna, while sitting at the window with her embroidery, by chance looked out at the street and

saw a young engineer officer standing still and training his eyes at her window. She lowered her head and again took up her work. Five minutes later she looked again—the young officer was standing in the same place. Not being in the habit of flirting with passing officers, she stopped looking at the street and continued sewing for about two hours without raising her head. Dinner was served. She got up, began to collect her embroidery and, having looked by chance at the street, again caught sight of the officer. [. . .] Two days later, leaving the house with the Countess and preparing to get into the carriage, she again saw him. He stood up against the entrance, having covered his face with his beaver collar; his black eyes sparkled from under his hat. Lizaveta Ivanovna became frightened, not knowing herself why, and trembled inexplicably as she got into the carriage. [. . .] Arriving back home she ran to the window—the officer stood in the previous place, training his eyes on her; she moved back, tormented by curiosity and troubled by a feeling completely new to her. [. . .] From that time on not a day passed that the young man didn't appear beneath the windows of their house at the appointed hour. Between him and her there were established unspoken relations. Sitting at her place of work she felt his approach; raising her head she looked at him with each passing day longer and longer. The young man, it seemed, was grateful to her for this: she saw with the sharp sight of youth how a rapid blush covered his pale cheeks every time their glances met. In a week's time she smiled to him.

It is as if a stone is dropped in the middle of a still pond and the ripples resulting from it extend in broadening circles. With this lengthy quote and *the process unfolding within it* we begin to see how the idea of gambling/risk-taking edges its way into the worlds (distinct, but now crossing over into each other) of both main characters. Based on the information that the narrator (the Pushkin voice) is releasing to us in small doses, we are not yet sure what Hermann's game consists of. Liza's game, her search for a "savior" from her "domestic martyrdom" with the Countess, seems more obvious. As far as we can tell, she is not playing Hermann. Hermann's black eyes, on the other hand, that sparkle beneath his hat, his cheeks that are covered in a blush when their eyes meet—surely some real feeling is passing back and forth here? Is the young man genuinely, as in amorously, interested in Liza or is something else going on? In this crucial ground-laying part of the tale the point of view keeps shifting back and forth between

Liza and Hermann. First, Liza avoids Tomsky's question in a cryptic dialogue devoid of narrative editorializing; next, we see through Liza's eyes how she first encounters Hermann (unnamed) as the officer standing in the street waiting for her to catch sight of him; then, also through her eyes, we see how their relations develop; and only after that does the narrator explain *why* Liza was evasive with Tomsky: "When Tomsky asked permission of the Countess to present his friend to her, *the heart of the poor girl contracted.* When she discovered that Narumov was not an engineer but a cavalry-guardsman, she regretted the fact that she had given away her secret to the flighty Tomsky with the indiscreet question." *That Liza is "the poor girl" is another card on the table. We are encouraged to empathize.*

Then the narration immediately shifts over to Hermann's viewpoint and what has been transpiring in his head when he first sees Liza. Now, little by little, we see more cards, and the more we see, the better able we are to evaluate choices when they are made down the line.

> Hermann was the son of a Russified German, who had left him a small amount of money. Being strongly convinced of the need to enhance his independence, Hermann did not touch the interest on his money, lived on his salary alone, and never allowed himself the slightest whim. However, he was secretive and ambitious and his mates rarely had the opportunity to make fun of his excessive thrift. He had strong passions and a fiery imagination, but his firmness saved him from the typical mistakes of youth. Thus, for example, being at heart a gambler, he never picked up the cards because he reckoned that his situation did not permit him (as he was wont to say) *to sacrifice the essential in hopes of acquiring the superfluous,* but at the same time he would sit whole nights through at the card tables and follow with a feverish trembling the various turns of the game.
>
> The story of the three cards acted powerfully on his imagination and didn't leave his mind for an entire night. "What if," he thought the next day in the evening, as he was wandering around Petersburg, "what if the old Countess will tell me her secret! Or designate to me the three winning cards! Why not try my luck? . . . Get introduced to her, work my way into her good graces, become, perhaps, her lover. But that takes time, and she's eighty-seven years old. She could die in a week, in two days! Yes, and the story itself? . . . Can it be believed? . . . No! Calculation, moderation, and hard work: these are my three winning cards,

this is what will triple, increase by sevenfold my capital and deliver peace of mind and independence to me!"

Only now, after the "unspoken relations" between Liza and her secret admirer have been established do we learn these additional details about Hermann. He is a cauldron of conflicting impulses and tendencies: the disciplined "German" and the devil-may-care "Russian," the patience (thrift) and the passion (wild imagination), the avoidance of the cards and the obsessive interest in them. The story of the three cards won't leave Hermann alone. The force of desire seems to take the upper hand when he suggests to himself that perhaps the Countess will reveal her secret to him—maybe he can insinuate himself into her confidence, become her lover! He is not repulsed by her eighty-seven years. This fact also tells us something. But then the tick-tock of his reasoning snaps back in the opposite direction: he realizes he doesn't have enough time to turn the Countess. And so, he focuses on the three cards (still the gambling metaphor) that have brought him this far: calculation, moderation, and hard work (his "German" virtues).

The very next constellation of thoughts and movements on Hermann's part brings the reader to the heart of the gambling mentality—*the idea of luck or fate*:

> Thinking to himself in this way, he turned up on one of the main streets of Petersburg, in front of a house of old-fashioned architecture. The street was jammed with carriages, one after the other they drew up to the lighted entryway. Each moment from out of the carriages there extended now a young beauty's shapely leg, now a heavy boot, now a striped stocking and diplomat's shoe. Fur coats and cloaks flitted by a stately doorman. Hermann stopped.

Note that Hermann *turned up* (*ochutilsia*) at "a house of old-fashioned architecture." We don't know yet that it is the Countess's. This is key because there is no logical explanation for how this happens. It is luck, or at least that is how Hermann will come to view it. Also the feet exiting the carriages attract our attention: like details foregrounded in other of Pushkin's sparsely worded texts, they would not be presented in this way unless they were freighted with a kind of meaning that will reassert itself later (think, for example, of the military cap, the bullet-riddled ace, and the Swiss landscape in "The Shot" or the elaborate description of the Prodigal Son pictures in "The Stationmaster"). This is the sort of right-hemisphere "attending to" context and the big picture that reading artistic literature trains us to do. Whether or how Hermann is paying attention to these carriages is also the question. We will come back to these feet in due course.

In any event, it is now that Hermann senses he is in the power of the uncanny:

> "Whose house is this?" he asked a policeman on the corner.
> "Countess X's," the policemen answered.
>
> Hermann shuddered. The astonishing story presented itself again to his imagination. He began to walk in the vicinity of the house, thinking about its mistress and her wondrous capability. It was late when he returned to his humble dwelling. For a long time he couldn't nod off, and when sleep finally did overtake him, he dreamt of cards, a green table, piles of banknotes and heaps of *chervontsy* [gold coins]. He played card after card, bent the edges [that is, doubled the bet—DB] decisively, won without cease, and raked in the gold and put the banknotes in his pocket. Waking up late, he sighed for the loss of his fantastic wealth, went out again to wander the city and again found himself in front of Countess X's home. It seemed that an unknown force was drawing him there. He stopped and began to look at the windows. In one of them he noticed a small head with black hair, probably bent over a book or work. The small head raised itself. Hermann saw a fresh complexioned face and black eyes. That moment decided his fate.

Like his hero, Pushkin himself was highly superstitious. The essence of superstition is that the subject *doesn't know* whether what is happening is a *coincidence*, mere happenstance that means nothing more than that, or a *coincídence*, a fantastical merging of the natural and supernatural realms. Hermann believes that something is bringing him here, to the place where the secret of the three cards resides in the person of the Countess. That's why his dreams of continuously winning become more insistent and grandiose. He also believes that the sight of the small female head is a sign, something that will help him obtain the secret without wasting time. A tipping point ("that moment *decided* his fate") has been reached, although what it is tipping *towards* we're still not sure.

Hermann sees his chance and pursues Liza. The next part details his tactical maneuvers as he enters into an epistolary romance with her. At first she rejects his written entreaties as too forward, but then over time, and under the pressure of his ardor, she yields and answers in kind. Another interesting gambit on Pushkin's part is that Hermann's feelings appear more and more genuine, that is, instead of writing as though he is copying phrases "from the German," which is how he starts, his letters become "inspired by passion," with "language uniquely his"; they express "the inevitability of his desire" and "the disorder of his unbridled imagination." Again, the reader is intrigued: who is the *real* Hermann? At last, Liza, her defenses abandoned, writes to arrange a tryst with Hermann. It is to take place in the early morning, after the Countess and she have returned from a ball. She explains in detail how he is to make his way into the Countess's house and sneak by the sleeping servants and up to her tiny bedroom. If anyone is awake and he meets them, he is to say he is asking after the Countess and then retreat when he is told she is not there. The day and time come, the Countess and Liza have left for the ball, and Hermann, on razor's edge, is successful at entering and not waking any of the household staff. The description of what is on view as he passes through the Countess's chambers is, again, loaded with the sort of detail Pushkin never includes casually:

> Hermann entered the Countess's bedroom. In front of the icon stand, which was filled with ancient icons, a yellow icon lamp flickered. Along the walls, covered with Chinese silk, faded stuffed easy chairs and sofas with puffy pillows, their gilding coming off, stood in melancholy symmetry. Two portraits, painted in Paris by Madame Lebrun, hung on the wall. One depicted a man of about forty, ruddy and stout, in a light-green uniform with a star on his chest; the other—a beautiful young woman with an aquiline nose, her powdered hair combed off the temples and decorated with a rose. Protruding out of the corners were china shepherdesses, table clocks by the celebrated Leroy, boxes, roulettes, fans, and various ladies' playthings invented at the end of the previous century along with the Mongolfier balloon and Mesmer's magnetism. Hermann went behind the screens. On the other side stood a little iron bed. To the right was a door that led into the study. To the left was another leading into the hallway. Hermann opened that one and saw a narrow winding staircase that led to the room of the poor ward. . . . But he returned and entered the dark study.

This museum-like inventory is obviously meant to conjure up the Countess and her eighteenth-century world. These items are the data of a life lived in a certain way. What connects them all is the Countess's personal aura and the choices she has made to reach her eighty-seven years. Set out here in this manner they constitute a puzzle: do the icons signify religious faith or simply traditional décor? Do the portraits, presumably of the Countess and her late husband the Count when they were younger, mean that the subjects were proud of their past together and enjoyed a good marriage (certainly not what Tomsky's story was suggesting) or that this, the wall art, was simply another de rigueur touch to go with the furnishings? And the multitude of hand-held novelties, are they gifts from admirers composing additional subplots or decorations to keep a vain old woman company? We can't know yet. But the mention of the Mongolfier brothers' hot-air balloon and Franz Mesmer's "animal magnetism" do suggest an eighteenth-century focus on unseen forces that goes with the story of the Countess and the secret cards. How much of this registers on Hermann's psyche? Given the fact that he passes through the room and doesn't stop until he has gone behind the screens and chosen which door to take after that, we have to assume he is on a mission, much like a predator in search of his prey. He is "left hemisphere" focusing, not "right hemisphere" absorbing the gestalt of the big picture. This is again key, for what literature teaches above all is to *stand back and take it all in*. Last but not least, Hermann has the choice between the two doors: the one on the left leads to Liza's room, the one on the right to the Countess's study. He looks down the hallway of the left-hand option, then pauses and enters the door on the right. Although Pushkin leaves it unsaid, we may assume that this is a second major tipping point, to go along with "that moment decided his fate."

Hermann waits in the small study for the Countess's carriage to arrive. "He was calm; his heart beat evenly, like that of a man who has settled on something dangerous but necessary." Finally, at 2 a.m. he hears the approach of the carriage's wheels. From the study he can look through the keyhole and see Liza pass by on the way to her room. The narrator states that "his heart responded with something like a stab of conscience and then went quiet. He became as stone." Next, he spies the former "muscovite Venus" as she is undressed by her maids. "The disgusting mysteries of her toilette"—the unhooking of a cap decorated with roses, a powdered wig lifted from a closely cropped gray head, a yellow ballgown stitched in silver that drops around swollen feet, hairpins falling like rain—he observes clinically. The typical formula of the voyeur, the old and the aberrant secretly viewing the young and the beautiful, is reversed. In her dressing gown and nightcap, and free of adornment, the Countess looks more her age and is less hideous. The maids leave. She now sits alone in a Voltaire chair, moving her lips, staring vacantly, and rocking left to right. Potentially "magnetized" details continue to accumulate. "One might think," says the narrator, that "the rocking of the horrifying old woman arose not by her will, but by the action of a hidden galvanism." Again: the previous century's invisible forces and a potential link to the cards?

Hermann emerges from his hiding place and appears before the Countess. She is startled out of her lethargy when she sees the stranger. Hermann tells her not to be afraid. She can make his happiness, he says, by revealing the three winning cards to him. Hesitating and searching for words, she answers, "It was a joke, I swear to you it was a joke," to which he retorts angrily that one shouldn't joke about such things. What about Chaplitsky, he asks? Confused, her facial features express strong emotion, but then she falls again into a vacant trance. Hermann becomes more insistent. For whom is she guarding her secret? Certainly not her grandsons, who don't know the value of money. But he, Hermann, does! Hermann gets down on his knees and tries to appeal to the Countess's feelings. Has she ever heard the cry of a newborn son? Can't she access that pang and with it sense how much he needs her secret? How much he and his family through the generations will honor her for it? How he is willing, in a Faustian bargain, to take any sin off her conscience and onto his own for it? The Countess remains unresponsive. Finally losing his temper, Hermann calls her a witch, takes out a pistol, and declares he will force her to answer. Terrified, for a moment the Countess appears to regain lucidity and holds up her hand as if to ward off the bullet, but then falls forward and doesn't move. Hermann discovers that she is dead.

The succeeding parts of the tale begin to create a different momentum because by this juncture certain choices have been made. We now have a much clearer picture of who Hermann is. In the next part, Hermann goes to Liza's room after his fatal encounter with the Countess. Pushkin, always playful with his epigraphs, frames this section with a line from an anonymous correspondence: "Homme sans mœurs et sans religion!" We take this to be a comment about Hermann and it is soon confirmed when he explains matters to Liza. But before that happens our attention is directed to Liza, who returns from the ball to find her secret admirer not there and has mixed feelings about the non-event. She falls into thought and recalls an exchange she has just had with Tomsky, who again has been toying with her at the ball: "'That Hermann,' continued Tomsky, 'is a genuinely romantic personage: he has the profile of Napoleon and the soul of Mephistopheles. I think that he has at least three crimes on his conscience.'" To Tomsky this is idle chatter, but what would the now dead Countess make of these words? Not only is Napoleon the romantic figure par excellence of the age, the upstart young colonel at Toulon who goes on to make his name as legendary general, he is also something else. *He is the usurper*, the one who takes the emperor's crown from the pope and places it on his own head. He is *a completely new type*, who seizes what does not belong to him—the "homme sans mœurs et sans religion." And in this respect he is not so much a point of connection between the eighteenth and the nineteenth centuries, but a dividing line separating them. The addition of "the soul of Mephistopheles" suggests that this transformation is a Faustian bargain. Whereas Goethe's Faust trades his soul to the devil for infinite knowledge, Hermann, as he expressed it in his plea to the Countess, is willing to take on any sin for a specific kind of knowledge, that of the secret cards and the wealth they confer. Liza realizes this when she sees him and he tells her what has happened:

> So, the passionate letters, the ardent demands, the daring, insistent pursuit—this was not love! Money, that's what his soul hungered for! She was not the one who could satisfy his desires and make him happy. The poor ward was nothing more than the blind accomplice of a robber, the murderer of her old benefactress.

This is Liza's moment of truth. The risk she took makes her an unsuspecting participant in the crime and she, being a moral agent, will share that guilt going forward. For his part, Hermann regrets only that the secret to the cards is lost. He is not moved by the beauty of the grieving young woman. As he sits by the window and frowns menacingly over the missed opportunity, Liza is again reminded of how much he resembles Napoleon. He then leaves the house via a secret staircase at the rear of the Countess's study to which Liza points him. Another strange coincidence occurs to him as he descends the steps: sixty years previous what fortunate young man, now long in the grave, took these same stairs away from an amorous assignation with the beautiful young Countess, who now too has joined her lover on the other side of death.

The essence of the fantastic, as Tzvetan Todorov tells us, is that "uncanny" events in a plot cannot be explained in the reader's mind as exclusively supernatural or exclusively natural. Is a character actually seeing a ghost or imagining it? This tension is precisely what dominates throughout the remainder of the tale, as Hermann appears to come more and more in contact with uncanny happenings that can't be separated from the death of the Countess and the secret of the cards she has taken with her. In other words, from now on we cannot tell if what is transpiring is due to the intervention of otherworldly forces or to the overwrought state of Hermann's psyche.

In the next part, the Countess's funeral service is announced and Hermann, hedging his bets, decides to attend:

Not feeling remorse, he could still not completely quiet the voice of conscience telling him, "You are the old woman's murderer!" Without having much genuine faith, he had a multitude of biases. He believed that the dead Countess could exert a harmful influence on his life, and so he made up his mind to attend the funeral in order ask her forgiveness.

The narrator describes with ironic distance the hypocrisy of the overly proper funeral and the pretense of grieving. It was not, as the bishop intones, "the angel of death who came upon her while she was vigilant in her righteous thoughts and awaiting her midnight groom," but Hermann. Family, guests, household servants—all solemnly take their leave of the Countess in her coffin. Hermann takes his turn last. First, he bows down in dramatic fashion next to the catafalque, then raising himself up, he leans over the coffin. What happens next is "*it seems to him*" that the dead Countess looks at him mockingly and winks with one eye. Hermann jumps back, trips on the steps, and falls to the floor. Liza, who is also at the funeral, faints and has to be carried out. The scandal interrupts the solemnity of the occasion. Among the whispers is heard the rumor that Hermann may be the Countess's natural son.

Hermann can't rid himself of thoughts of the Countess. Uncharacteristically, he gets drunk at a tavern, finds his way home, and falls into a deep sleep. Well after midnight he wakes up, or *thinks he wakes up*, and sees somebody look into his window from the street and move away. He pays no attention. Shortly thereafter he hears the outer door to his apartment open and he assumes it is his orderly returning home drunk as usual. But the person's footfall is different; these steps are short and shuffling. The door to his room opens and in comes a lady in a white dress—the Countess!

> "I have to come to you against my will," she said in a firm voice. "But I have been ordered to fulfill your request. The three, seven, and ace will win for you, in that order, but only on condition that you not play more than one card a day and that after that you not play for the rest of your life. I forgive you my death on condition that you marry my ward Lizaveta Ivanovna . . ."

The apparition leaves the way it came, doors opening and shutting and someone looking in on Hermann from the street. When he goes out into the front room to check, the drunken orderly is there and can't tell him anything. The door to the street is locked. Again, the fantastic: has Hermann really seen a ghost or has his troubled psyche seen one? Is the apparition's message of the three cards to be believed or not?

At last we come to part six, the climax of "The Queen of Spades." The opening is especially rife with details that, considering all that has come before, call out for interpretation. It is one of the most remarkable passages in all of Pushkin:

> Two fixed ideas cannot exist together in a moral nature, just as two bodies cannot occupy the same space in the physical world. The three, seven, and ace soon blocked out the image of the dead old woman in Hermann's imagination. The three, seven, and ace didn't leave his head and kept moving on his lips. If he saw a young girl, he would say, "How shapely she is! . . . A real three of hearts!" If someone asked him "What time is it?" He would answer, "Five minutes to seven." Any pot-bellied man would remind him of an ace. The three, seven, and ace pursued him in his sleep, taking on all possible guises: the three bloomed before him in the shape of a luxurious flower, the seven presented itself as a gothic gate, the ace as a huge spider. All thoughts converged on one: how to use the secret that had cost him so dearly. He began to think about retirement and travel. He wanted to pry loose treasure from enchanted fortune in the gaming houses of Paris. Chance spared him these efforts.

Lest we forget, the moral world being described here is one *in transition* from the eighteenth to the nineteenth century, something that has been planted in the reader's mind by the reinforced references to Hermann's "Napoleonic" profile. At the same time, Pushkin is never moral in a prescriptive or didactic sense. In its dry, ironic way, his text is merely observing the fact that Napoleon's role as usurper and the culture's celebration of that role have consequences for posterity, the creation of a Hermann being one of them. Hermann's decision to try *to take the secret* even when the Countess can't or won't reveal it to him (the pistol) is what most defines him. And this despite the fact that he may have bad dreams or hallucinations about what he has done, which means that he is not completely without an awareness of guilt. But those misgivings, conscious or unconscious, are not enough to stop him from proceeding with his plan. This is the momentous shift that Pushkin is getting at with his physical metaphor for a new metaphysical state: two "fixed" ideas cannot coexist in a moral nature just as two bodies cannot occupy the same space in the physical realm. This is also the culture's version of a genetic code that Dostoevsky gives to Raskolnikov (the "*raskól*" being the split in his nature), Hermann's murderous offspring in the next generation. Hermann still has a moral nature—we have to assume that the "two fixed ideas can't exist together in a moral nature" refers to him—but the point is that the choices he has made have turned that nature in a dangerous new direction. The combination of three, seven, ace has *blocked out* (*zaslonili*) the image of the Countess and the crime associated with her death in Hermann's mind. It is as if one card has been placed on top of, "trumped," another. At this point, Hermann sees the three, seven, ace everywhere, beginning with the roots of the words he utters and the mental pictures those words in turn evoke. We will come back to this linguistic/etymological substrate momentarily, but first we have to conclude the plot.

The same Narumov who hosted the gambling party at the beginning of the tale takes Hermann to a high-stakes game in St. Petersburg. The famous Chekalinsky, who is known for having the most opulent gambling house in Moscow, has brought his game to St. Petersburg. Young people visit his establishment in droves and willingly trade their interest in the opposite sex for the allure of the gambling table. With a few precise strokes, the interieur at Chekalinsky's is captured. The camera, as it were, scans through the sumptuously appointed rooms and fawning waiters, the various layers of well-born sitting and blandly passing the time (generals playing whist, others smoking and eating ice cream), until it comes to the suave host himself, who is keeping bank at the Faro table. Faro, we recall, is the most popular game of chance at the time. It is not a game of skill, but one exclusively of luck (Pushkin or Lermontov would have called it *schast'e*, "fortune"): the "punter" places his bet on a card and then the dealer (the banker) draws cards from the deck and places them one after the other to his right and his left, in that order. If the card being bet on appears first on the left, regardless of suit, then the player wins; if the card appears on the right, the bank wins.

When Hermann and Narumov arrive, the activity at the Faro table is already lively, with a crowd surrounding Chekalinsky. Up to this moment the betting has been modest, in the hundreds of rubles. Hermann proceeds directly to the Faro table and when a new deck is opened, asks to make a bet. He wagers the astronomical amount of 47,000 rubles (his entire estate, it turns out) on one card. This bet is way beyond anything anyone has seen and immediately the room is abuzz. Chekalinsky politely requests that Hermann confirm he has the funds to make such a wager and Hermann produces an authentic banknote for the full sum. Chekalinsky deals: to the right he drops a nine, to the left a three. Hermann turns over his three, takes up his bet and his winnings, now totaling 94,000 rubles, and leaves. Everyone is in shock. The next evening the scene is repeated. Again Hermann waits for a new deck and Chekalinsky graciously welcomes him. The much larger crowd is tense with excitement. This time a jack falls to the right and a seven to the left. Once more Hermann has won, his original 47,000 rubles having now quadrupled to 188,000. He calmly collects his money and disappears.

Finally, on the third night everyone is prepared for the ritual. The crowd is huge and makes way for Hermann. Chekalinsky is still smiling but looks pale. Hermann, however, seems calm and sure of himself. Both men open their own deck of cards and prepare to play. The confrontation is reminiscent of a duel.

> Chekalinsky started to deal; his hands were shaking. To the right fell a queen, to the left an ace.
>
> "The ace won!" said Hermann and exposed his card.
>
> "Your queen has lost [literally 'is killed']," said Chekalinsky kindly.
>
> Hermann shuddered. It was true: instead of an ace a queen of spades lay before him. He couldn't believe his eyes, couldn't comprehend how he had picked the wrong card.
>
> In that moment it seemed to him that the queen of spades winked and grinned. An extraordinary likeness struck him . . .
>
> "The old woman!" he screamed in horror.

In the epilogue, Hermann has gone mad and is in an asylum. His room number is seventeen. He keeps muttering senselessly to himself "Three, seven, ace! Three, seven, queen!" Liza has made a good marriage and is now helping to rear her own poor female relative. Tomsky has been promoted and is marrying the Princess Polina. In other words, life goes on.

Language and the "Subcellular" Level of Consciousness

With this detailed reprise of the plot of "The Queen of Spades," we are able to establish exactly what all the characters (inside the text) and the reader (outside the text) know at each moment that the action is unfolding. In our next look at the tale, we will examine what Pushkin's language is telling us at these different junctures when thought becomes, or doesn't become, action. If evolution happens in human beings as process *all the way down* to the subcellular level where "structure" and "change" merge, as in the Golgi apparatus and other organelles, then something similar is happening in speech at its most basic level of phonemes and allophones. Speech operates at a speed and with a complexity in an individual's consciousness that cannot be successfully parsed in medias res—*that* is the basic truth that Pushkin as poet understood in his bones prior to the discoveries of evolutionary psychology and neuroscience. Through metaphoric thinking the subject extends himself or herself out into the world and then, when the world responds, absorbs that information back into the body-mind's orbit. But of course it's not that simple. As we discussed earlier, there are metaphors and metaphors. Lateralization of brain function is there for evolutionary reasons. Ultimately, all speech has a metaphorical underpinning: there is a spectrum overarching the literal and figurative, but it is still words. Vocabulary that is denotative, and grammar and syntax that are rule-based, are normally governed by the left hemisphere, with circuits originating in the Broca's and Wernicke's areas (NB. This anatomical mapping can be flipped if the individual is left-handed). But more complex, figurative language; metaphors involving unlikely or striking tenor-vehicle combinations; prosodic devices adding a musical element; authorial tones implying irony and requiring a more "big picture," contextual feel for meaning—all these will normally need the help of the right hemisphere. Again, in Iain McGilchrist's metaphorically performative formulation,

> Language functions like money. It is only an intermediary. But like money it takes on some of the life of the things it represents. It begins in the world of experience and returns to the world of experience—and it does so via metaphor, which is a function of the right hemisphere, and is rooted in the body. To use a metaphor, language is the money of thought. Only the right hemisphere has the capacity to understand metaphor.[1]

The point about language being the money of thought is that it involves exchange, a trading of *this for that*. As metaphor researchers George Lakoff and Mark Johnson put it, "The essence of metaphor is understanding and experiencing one kind of thing in terms of another."[2] In everyday speech we don't much dwell on this exchange process. We simply take it to be real. Indeed, to think about it gets in the way. The "take it to be real," however, is a function of the left hemisphere's *grabbing hold*—its demand for logical consistency, its adherence to its rules once we enter its domain, its way of abstracting itself and assuming command.

> All of this—this grasping, this taking control, this piecemeal apprehension of the world, this distinguishing of types, rather

than of individual things—takes place for most of us with the right hand [that is, governed by left hemisphere—DB]. [...] It is also through grasping things that we grant things certainty and fixity: when they are either uncertain or unfixed, we say we 'cannot put our finger on it', we 'haven't got a hold of it'. [...] The grasp we have, our understanding in this sense, is the expression of our will, and it is the means to power.[3]

This is exactly what Pushkin's tale is telling us. The story of the Countess's secret cards captures Hermann's imagination and sets him spinning in his own outer space; outside the text the reader also can't tell what is real and what is fantasy. Hermann grasps at the story's significance, projects it forward into the world around him, and loses sight of all surrounding context except that which relates to his idée fixe. His hold on the story, or the story's hold on him, is "an expression of his will" and a "means to power." Once again, when he first finds himself in front of the Countess's house, he sees the following:

> The street was jammed with carriages, one after the other they drew up to the lighted entryway. Each moment from out of the carriages there extended now a young beauty's shapely leg, now a heavy boot, now a striped stocking and diplomat's shoe. Fur coats and cloaks flitted by a stately doorman. Hermann stopped.

The legs extending out of the different carriages, whose doors resemble the rectangular frame of a playing card, already suggest mnemonically the three, seven, and ace that will become his obsession. Indeed, the carriages themselves, *karéty* in Russian, which is also a play on *karty* ("cards"), are pulling up *one after the other*, like a sequence of playing cards. The shapely leg of the young beauty is "*stroinaia*," with the *troi* being paronomastically suggestive of *troika*, or "trey," in Russian; the "heavy boot," presumably of a military type, would look like an inverted seven as it exited the vehicle; and the diplomat's shoe would belong to a "big shot," which is also an alternate meaning of *tuz*, or "ace," in Russian.[4] In other words, well before the fact the seed *could be* planted for the three-card combination. Pushkin doesn't say explicitly it has been planted and that is the explanation. In fact, there is no editorializing whatsoever. The only hint, unspoken but no less telling, is *why these three images in this order*? It is directly after this that Hermann learns *he has turned up* at the Countess's house and feels he has been brought to this place by a power beyond his control. Although it is not said in so many words, this sensation of the uncanny is precisely what the gambler feels when he is "on a roll." What is going on here is that Pushkin is presenting the intrusion of the unconscious into the conscious world. "The unconscious, while not identical with, is certainly more strongly associated with, the right hemisphere."[5] The gambling mentality lunges at a pattern, takes it to be real, and then is consumed by it.

What I want our students to understand as we look for the rabbit hole of *language operating all the way down* is that 1) their own use of language is a cross-section in time of where they are evolutionarily, and thus they should pay particular attention to their own sense of style, because in important ways *that* is who they are (as the cartoonist Dick Guindon quipped, "Writing is nature's way of letting you know how sloppy your thinking is"[6]); 2) by studying Pushkin's language and comparing it to their own they can draw life lessons about survival in a usable, but not necessarily moralistic or narrowly prescriptive, sense; 3) the plot of "Queen of Spades" is such a powerful exemplum linguistically because it demonstrates how *things belong to processes* (remember the "processual" philosophy with which we started discussion), not the other way around—perhaps the most important life lesson they will ever learn.

Now, as we look more carefully at the different levels of language in the story, we should isolate first what jumps out as most salient: to wit, the three-card code that Hermann believes is the key to winning the game and the army of numbers and numerically related lexical items that keep hinting that the code is there but just out of reach. This echo chamber of language is an invitation to the reader to try to find the figure in the puzzle. To take a few examples (there are many),

1. The old Countess X sat in her dressing-room before the mirror. <u>Three</u> maids surrounded her. <u>One</u> held a jar of rouge, <u>another</u> [as in "a second"] a box of hair-pins, a <u>third</u> a tall cap with fiery-colored ribbons.
2. <u>Once</u>—this happened <u>two</u> days after the evening described at the beginning of this tale, and a <u>week</u> before the scene at which we paused—<u>once</u> Lizaveta Ivanovna, while sitting at her embroidery, chanced to look at the street and saw a young engineer officer standing still and training his eyes at her window.
3. <u>Three</u> days after the fatal night, at <u>nine</u> o'clock in the morning, Hermann left for monastery X, where the burial service for the dead Countess was being held.

In the first example the numbers 3, 1, 2, 3 function as ways to fix the scene in place; in the second and third examples, 1, 2, 7, 1 and 3, 9 do the same. In theory, these numbers might be combined to generate different codes, one of which *could lead* to the Countess's secret. Then there is phrasing such as "two days after the evening," "a week before the scene," and "three days after the fatal night"—are these to be read as "2+1," "7–1," and "3+1" or simply as "2," "7," and "3"? Or perhaps the author is just pulling our nose? As punters in the game that is the tale, however, we have not yet witnessed the Countess's apparition that appears before Hermann in section five and gives him the 3-7-1 (ace), combination. Thus readers, and there have been many in the scholarly ranks, who return to earlier passages with knowledge of the "correct" combination as key to Hermann's "mistake" (choosing 3–7-queen instead of 3–7-ace) are "cheating," in the sense that cognitively speaking they are not "gambling" just as Hermann himself is not really gambling, because they are trying to substitute a sure thing (the code) for a fifty-fifty chance (the Faro odds) at not getting it right. Liza, by the way, does *not* do this in her gamble on Hermann's love. But the larger point obtains: all these numbers scattered throughout the unfolding story by the ironic author, including the numbers atop each section and any numbers accompanying the epigraphs, constantly prod the reader to try to solve the riddle, *Are the three cards in the correct sequence here somewhere?* This is how the reader is drawn into the game.

The game of Faro involves choosing one card and then waiting to see on which side of the dealer, the left or the right, the card falls. The next linguistic level *going all the way down* has to do with the sounds and shapes of words. We already mentioned the *karety* versus *karty* wordplay and the images of the legs exiting the carriages before the Countess's house. The game continues when Hermann enters the house on the evening the Countess and Liza are away at the ball. Once in the Countess's chambers, he passes by the items representing the Countess's past in the eighteenth century, among them two portraits, again reminiscent of flat, rectangular, playing card-like frames (*karty*, "cards," and *kartiny*, "paintings" are etymologies Pushkin has played with elsewhere): one of a "big-shot," or *tuz* (ace), the Count; the other a beauty, *krasavitsa*, or the "queen-like" Countess in her youth. When Hermann passes behind the screens and is deciding where to go, he pauses between the door *on the left*, which leads to Liza's quarters, and the one *on the right*, which leads to the Countess's study. The doors themselves are rectangular structures whose frames are suggestive of playing cards and whose opening and closing are like the cards being drawn. Once the Countess has been undressed, she sits in a Voltaire chair, another "frame" from the eighteenth century, and rocks side to side in a "galvanic" (that is, the work of occult forces) movement reminiscent of a Faro hand. The other rectangular shapes the Countess is witnessed in by Hermann include: the coffin "from which the dead woman looked at him mockingly, winking with one eye"; the small window in his apartment "from which someone [the Countess's apparition—DB] looked in on him from the street"; and the actual "queen of spades [that] screwed up her eyes and grinned" and in which he recognized the Countess ("The old woman!").

Keeping in mind our students, most of whom are not interested in lit crit or the high-culture language games that professors play, how do we begin to move discussion to a place that engages this younger audience in their own time-space, evolutionarily speaking? We do this by showing that, while it is true the tale is elegantly constructed, and while it is also true the elaborate mosaic of numbers, shapes, and sounds mimic a kind of linguistic Where's Waldo, that may not be the only, or even the most important, reason Pushkin writes the way he does. Yes, as his letters often reveal, he does enjoy penning texts for those in his circle of friends who get his in-jokes. Yet, in his famous valedictory poem "I have erected for myself a monument" (1836), he claims that his words will be known by the Tungus, the Kalmyk, and the Finn—certainly not an appeal to elitist cultural norms. Thus, Pushkin's language is also about survival in a species sense, about making it to the next generation and living on: "No, all of me won't die—my soul in sacred lyre / Will outlive my ashes and escape decay," he says in the same poem. And that idea, how survival's tool kit changes over time, should resonate with today's young people, regardless of educational background. On the one hand, Hermann doesn't want "to sacrifice the necessary in order to obtain the superfluous," but he also wants to gamble. He can't do both *fairly*. When he wagers against Chekalinsky, he is not gambling the way a true gambler does. On the other hand, the historical Pushkin *was* a true gambler, because he superstitiously believed in fate and because he was willing to make bets that could (and did) cost a great deal, up to and including his own unpublished manuscripts. Lest we forget, he was also, to judge by his astronomical gambling debts, decidedly unsuccessful at the gaming tables. Fate, for Pushkin, was something to be approached honestly, in a "manly" fashion; one wasn't allowed to cheat it, just as one wasn't allowed to manipulate inspiration. Occult forces were absolutely real to him. In his youth he paid a visit to the well-known fortune-teller Kirchhof; as friend Sergei Sobolevsky reports, she made a number of prophesies, several quickly coming true. The final one predicted that "he would live a long time if in his thirty-seventh year a misfortune didn't happen that was caused either by a white horse, by a blonde head, or by a white man [*weisser Ross, weisser Kopf, weisser Mensch*]."[7] Pushkin was killed at thirty-seven years of age as the result of a duel with an adversary, George d'Anthès, who was fair-haired. Not dispositive? We're talking here about the mind of a poet.

"The Queen of Spades" has had such staying power over the years because, first and foremost, *its mysteries can never be resolved.* There are no keys that can pry it open and lay it bare once and for all. The idea of playing fair is embedded deep in our mammalian brains; even rats, as "affective neuroscience" authority Jaak Panksepp demonstrated, will refuse rough-and-tumble play with a fellow rat if the bigger one is too overbearing and will not let the smaller one win at least thirty percent of the time.[8] The underpinnings of morality (reciprocity) are already there in the rat behavior; juvenile rats need to learn how to play or their prefrontal cortex will not develop properly. The same with children: according to Piaget, when little kids play—say, preschool girls having a tea party—they embody the ideas (sitting around and serving tea and cakes) *before* they understand them. In this case, they pretend to be their mothers and play act without really knowing why. The ages between two and four, play- and fantasy-filled, are crucial for the process of socialization to do its work. The ultimate lesson that children learn is that life is not one particular game, but a set of games, each with its own rules, and the goal is not to win "at all costs" the particular game, although you still try your best, but to participate across a spectrum of life's games, playing fairly in each contest. It is the "meta-structure" of game-playing, which is another name for morality, that counts.[9]

This is the perspective that needs to be added to the game theory aspect (that is, how to model Hermann's card playing mathematically) of "The Queen of Spades." While Hermann pursues his obsession, and while the reader tries to find the secret card sequence in the text, an exercise in self-interested survival is going on. Paths are being tested. Is it the right door into the Countess's study and the riches to follow? Or is it the left door into Liza's quarters and the possibility of love? What is it that most propels one's attention forward? Pushkin lures us in with the magic card gambit because he knows that the attraction of the unknown coupled with our fear of it are essential drivers of story, and that survivors always have a story. But in this story Hermann is not a survivor, at least not a successful one. Why exactly? Why did the Faro "duel" with Chekalinsky have to end in the loss of everything and madness? Well, because Hermann represents something larger than himself, which we will return to momentarily, and because by 1833 winning at all costs is not a compelling story for Pushkin. By now he is familied—still a gambler *but also* a family man. He knows that all the partial codes winking at us never become complete one-to-one cribs. He also knows that life cycles, including his own, are processes leading to future generations. As he writes in his beautifully pared down blank-verse narrative "Again I have visited" (1835),

Upon the margin
That bounds my grandfather's estate, just where
The road, deep-pitted by spring rains,
Begins its slow uphill meander, there three old pines
Stand—one aside, aloof; two others closely
Entangled—here, when of a moonlit night
My horse would amble past, their soughing summits
Would greet me with fond murmur. Now along
That selfsame road I travel, and before me
Again I see those pines. They're still the same,
My ear is still accustomed to their murmur—
But near their ancient mass of branching roots
(Where once the ground was always bare and barren)
A youthful grove now vigorously burgeons,
A family of green; the shrubs crowd in
Beneath their canopy like children.
Yet their somber comrade stands apart, a lone
Decrepit bachelor, whilst all around him
Is barren as before.
                    All hail, new tribe,
Youthful and undiscovered! I'll not live
To witness your magnificent full growth,
When you will overtop these friends of mine,
And in your turn conceal their agèd crowns
From eyes of passers-by. But may my grandson
One day take in your murmured salutations
As he returns from some late cordial jaunt;
And brimming full of cheerful, pleasant musings,
May he pass by you in the midnight darkness
And spare a thought for me.
(translated by Alyssa Dinega Gillespie)

The speaker, acknowledging his own mortality ("I'll not live to witness"), is drawn to the susurrating pines and through them he greets future generations in the person of his grandson, who one day will repeat the evening ride and recall the ancestor. The two pines have become a family; they have managed over the intervening years to produce offspring underneath their canopy; and one day they too will be replaced. The "somber comrade," on the other hand, a "decrepit bachelor" who never mates, will die alone surrounded by barren ground. Either the end of the line or a belonging to process; Pushkin wrote the poem while the young Darwin was collecting different species of wildlife aboard the HMS Beagle.

To sum up, then, the one character in "The Queen of Spades" who plays the game of life fairly is Liza, because she bets the maximum with no guarantees, appears to lose, and then, in the end, with the author's typical irony, wins by finding a way (or perhaps more accurately, by being "luckily" provided a way) forward. The lead epigraph to the entire tale is "The queen of spades betokens secret ill-will (*The Latest Fortune-Telling Book*)." The ill-will, the queen turning up instead of the ace, manifests itself because Hermann tries to trick life. He opts for the right door that happens, à la the left-right movement of the Faro hand, to be the wrong door. Choosing Liza's door may not have solved all Hermann's problems (recall Ibrahim's bad luck with romance in *The Blackamoor of Peter the Great* that had a strong element of authorial self-identification), but at least it might have led to companionship and family, the two pines "closely entangled" and the "youthful grove" of green to follow. Elsewhere in his maturing years Pushkin adapts a well-known Russian proverb: "my ideal is now a wife, my desires— tranquility, a pot of cabbage soup, and to be my own boss." This is how Pushkin's tale mimics a toolbox for survival: not a system but an allegory of systems,[10] it never stops challenging the reader and yet provides a moral framework, understated to be sure, in the end. The "things," the ideas and sounds and images, that draw us to it belong to the process, not the other way around.

Risk Then and Now

I have now discussed with the students how Pushkin's language operates *all the way down* to reveal the psychological underpinnings of Hermann's and Liza's story. Sounds, shapes, numbers, wordplay—these hover between the presemantic and the semantic to suggest potentialities of meaning. How then do these same subcellular-like units, these linguistically embedded "organelles," also *reach out* to the broader world Pushkin was telling? Equally important for our purposes, how do they reach out to the contemporary world our students inhabit? I propose now in the last part of the chapter to close the loop, so to speak, but also to reopen it at the same time. We can do this by showing how Pushkin's story relates to the historical moment he and his countrymen were living through (the loop closes momentarily) *and* how it relates to our problems today (the loop reopens). We keep our eye on the idea of process.

First, we revisit in more detail Panksepp's affective neuroscientific research on the evolutionary basis of play and what the latter can tell us about the culture of Pushkin's time in general and Hermann's obsession with Faro in particular. (NB. Here I need to go into my "boiling it down" mode because the subject matter quickly gets too dense.) The structure of the higher animal brain and its primary-processing emotional circuits are homologous across different species—a fact of considerable importance because it shows how, over millions of years, evolutionary selection preceded, as in laid the "precognitive" groundwork for, individual learning (not the other way around). This, Panksepp insists, is a very big deal:

> It seems that all higher animals—by which I mean nothing more than critters with complex brains, like mammals and birds, all of which exhibit quite similar emotional and motivational urges—share very similar primary-process infrastructures in their brains. Affective-emotional behavioral tendencies seem to have been built into their behavioral repertoire as ancestral memories that generate various instinctual, emotional, and motivational urges that are accompanied by feelings—which the behaviorists merely called rewards and punishment because those could be defined by external objects and events. *The behaviorists chose to ignore the possibility that in the brain emotional circuits induced feeling states that guided behavior.* [...] It became central dogma for us that if we could activate distinct and coherent emotional behavior patterns in animals using localized ESB—electrical stimulation of the brain—especially in the same brain regions across different species, *we had evidence for the existence and location of emotional operating systems that were constructed by evolution rather than by individual learning.* And whenever one found brain sites like that, one could empirically demonstrate that they could serve as rewards and punishments in learning tasks. This means that they generated experienced states of the BrainMind. I cannot emphasize this simple fact too much, especially since so few scholars, even cognitive neuroscientists, appreciate the point: If you activate a brain system with electrical garbage and you consistently generate coherent emotional behavior patterns accompanied by affects, then *there is no other logical option but to conclude that behavioral and affective tendencies, in raw form, were constructed*

into the infrastructure of the brain by evolutionary selection as opposed to individual learning [my emphasis—DB].[11]

Next, the path from play studies as neuroscience to cultural institutions:

The BrainMind has to be envisioned as an evolutionarily layered organ system, with all higher developments still anchored to the lower primary processes of the brain. This is simply the way the brain is organized. The original foundations of mind remain critically important for the ability of higher processes to function. The play processes of the brain are delightfully representative of such complexities. Play studies have brought positive psychology one of the most important inbuilt emotional complexities that can help clarify many higher-order issues, from our love of sports to the rough-and-tumble nature of power politics. [. . .]

Many would prefer to envision our playfulness as reflecting higher mind function [i.e. the cognitivist position—DB] rather than lower, more ancient ones. The sooner we shift our perspectives, the sooner we are likely to build cultural institutions that support our joyful *lower nature*, so important for mental health, as vigorously as our *higher* cognitive *nurture* that is all too often administered in rather unpalatable ways to our children [italics in the original].[12]

Play is categorized as a positive emotion (an example of a negative emotion similarly generated through primary-processing circuitry would be panic, or separation distress, as of a young animal from its mother). Rat pups, like human children, learn through the "rough-and-tumble" of wrestling how to play with their bodies to the point where they can pin their opponents without hurting them. Females play like males, only it takes them longer to join in. The fun of the rat play ("I want more of this") is evidenced not only by the joyful chasing and pouncing, but also by the sound of chirping, in effect "laughing," measured at fifty kilohertz. When things get too rambunctious, however, complaints, with sounds at twenty-two kilohertz, and stoppage can ensue. Play, therefore, is crucial evolutionarily because it develops what Panksepp calls the "social brain":

There will be no better general answer to the question of why play evolved than the supposition that without play it would have been difficult to build in all the needed social dynamics that complex animals such as mammals need to thrive within the complex worlds into which they are born. Often social dimensions of survival vary depending on local environmental conditions, and hence the nuances of the most adaptive social dynamics in specific environments need to be learned. Thus, when I ponder such difficult issues, I suspect play is one of the major ways that the complex social brain emerges from the experiences of living within various ecological and cultural constraints. In short, much of the social brain is created by experiences, and the urge to play is a primary process that helps achieve the programming of higher brain regions, such as the neocortex, which resembles a tabula rasa of massive random-access memory banks within the higher regions of our brains.[13]

Needless to say it is a big leap from the "adaptive social dynamics" displayed in rat behavior and the role gambling and risk-taking played in eighteenth- and nineteenth-century Russia. Still, the following provides us a useful bridge from evolutionary neuropsychology to the "social brain" of Pushkin's time:

Our best hypothesis right now is that the primary-process emotional urge to play, when allowed abundant expression, helps construct and refine many of the higher regions of the social brain. Perhaps it is especially influential in refining our frontal cortical, executive networks that allow us to more effectively appreciate social nuances and develop better social strategies. In other words, play allows us to stop, look, listen, and feel the more subtle social pulse around us.[14]

The first thing we need to recognize as we move from the positive aspects of play as studied scientifically by Panksepp to the behavior exhibited by Hermann in "The Queen of Spades" is that there is nothing innocent or joyful about the game of Faro in its local Russian context. Indeed, Hermann's urge to play and win is not about learning to "more effectively appreciate social nuances and develop better social strategies." Quite the opposite. Not about fitting in, winning here is about gaining power in a competitive setting. Likewise, while the narrator is often ironic, the game itself is sinister: the queen of spades "betokens ill-will" and the filter of the fantastic makes it impossible for the reader to decide whether the dead Countess is actually winking at Hermann from her coffin (the supernatural) or whether he just imagines she does (the natural, the psychological).

The play part for the juvenile rats, which involves the full participation of their bodies together with their brains' emotional deep circuitry, has become a culturally laden "duel" between Hermann and Chekalinsky. However, rather than moving their bodies vigorously in a physical wrestling match, the two card players—presumably with their brains' emotional circuitry activated while their bodies, registering the feedback from that circuitry, move minimally—wrestle with each other cognitively and affectively at the same time, matching wits and courage. In the Russian context the "pin" of the opponent, the queen defeating the ace, turns out to be fatal. What exactly has happened?

As Yuri Lotman demonstrated in a famous article, there is a direct, one is even tempted to say, virtually *causal* link between the historical context in which Faro emerged as a favored game of the ruling classes across Russia (and Europe) and the idea of fortune or fate as the latter applied to one's position in Russian society. During Catherine's reign (1762–1794) one's ability to rise to a position of wealth and influence (we are speaking here almost exclusively of the nobility) was sorely limited. One could use family connections or one could try to ascend the rungs in the state military or civil service ladder—the Table of Ranks established by Peter in 1722 with the idea, always realized imperfectly, of creating a more service-based nobility—but, in any event, a rapid rise through merit or hard work alone was next to impossible. Also looming large in public awareness during Catherine's time on the throne was the question of her legitimacy as ruler. An obscure German princess (Sophie Friederike Auguste von Anhalt-Zerbst-Dornburg) with useful ties to European royal families, she was brought to Russia as a teenager in 1744 to become the wife of Peter of Holstein-Gottorp, heir to the throne upon the death of Empress Elizabeth (ruled 1741–1762). Princess Sophie faithfully learned the language of her adoptive country, abandoned Lutheranism for the Russian Orthodox faith, and took the Russian name Catherine. In July 1762, however, just a few months after Elizabeth had died and the new tsar had been crowned Emperor Peter III, her own imperial designs, until then sub rosa, were suddenly made public when she took part in the plot to overthrow the pro-Prussian and unpopular, but still dynastically legitimate husband she detested. Catherine's complicity in the coup d'état, which had been orchestrated by powerful court insiders, did not help her reputation as usurper. Thus her claim to power, especially in the early years, was perpetually suspect. She had to rule on her own through the relationships she built around her. Most prominent among these relationships were those with the men who became her "favorites"—her generals, advisers, and, most importantly for the blend of fact and fiction that grew up around the empress, *temporary lovers*. This idea of *the good-luck streak*, here the lover who enjoys sudden, albeit short-lived, success with "Lady Fortune" (*fortuna* is feminine in Russian), is what is crucial for the connection to Faro.

Pushkin was generally savvy enough not to try to criticize openly the tsar or the church in works he planned to publish through official, that is, censorship-guarded, channels. Thus, when we wish to understand what he thought about such outsize figures as Peter I or Catherine II we need to find those unpublished moments in his writings where he speaks more with his guard down. In 1822, during his stay in Kishinev, Pushkin made some notes on eighteenth-century Russian history that he planned to use to introduce his autobiography, but then he destroyed the larger project as a precaution in the wake of the 1825 Decembrist uprising. The only reason these notes survived is because Pushkin had handed them over to a friend for safe keeping. The picture Pushkin paints of Catherine in these powerfully worded formulations is shocking in its over-all negativity (recall that Pushkin was at his most "Byronic" in Kishinev); it is here that we find the famous phrase likening the empress to "a Tartuffe in skirts." While not stated explicitly, the connection between the corruption of Catherine's reign and the cynical atmosphere of the Countess's household in "The Queen of Spades" is obvious.

> The reign of Catherine II had a new and powerful influence on the political and moral situation in Russia. Elevated to the throne through the plot of a few mutineers, she enriched them at the expense of the people and humiliated our anxious nobil-ity. If to rule means to know the weakness of the human heart [lit. "soul"] and how to take advantage of it, then in this regard Catherine deserves the amazement of posterity. Her magnifi-cence blinded, her amiability attracted, her generosity created attachments. Her very love of the voluptuous (*slastoliubie*) affirmed this clever woman's mastery. Producing a weak murmur in the people, who were accustomed to respect the flaws in their rulers, this voluptuousness aroused a disreputable competition in the higher classes, since neither intelligence nor merit nor tal-ent was necessary to achieve second position [that is, right next to Catherine—DB] in the state. [. . .] In time history will evalu-ate the influence of her reign on morals. It will reveal the cruel actions of her despotism under the mask of modesty and toler-ance, the oppression of the people by her satraps, and the plun-dering of the treasury by her lovers. It will show significant errors in her political economy, the worthlessness of her legislation,

and the revolting falsity in her relations with the century's philosophers. And when that happens Voltaire's voice moved by flat-
tery will not save the memory of her glory from Russia's curse.
[. . .] Catherine knew how her lovers cheated and robbed, but
she remained silent. Encouraged by such weakness, they knew
no bounds in their cupidity, and a favorite's most distant relatives greedily took advantage of his brief access to power. It was
as a result of this that there appeared the gigantic estates of completely unknown families and the total lack of honor and honesty
in the higher class of people. From chancellor to lowliest clerk
everything was stolen and everything was for sale. Thus did a
debauched ruler debauch her state.[15]

Again, especially telling is the fact that Pushkin says exactly what he thinks here
(no irony!). Elsewhere he still gives Catherine and her grandees such as Potemkin
credit for their martial successes and impressive territorial expansion. But there
can be no doubt that the author of these lines disapproves of the way the celebrated
monarch (Catherine and Peter are the only two Russian sovereigns referred to by
history as "the great") wields power. In his view, Catherine has used her feminine
wiles not only to advance an Enlightenment agenda, presumably a good thing, but
also to manipulate others through a false perception of civility and charm, and
ultimately, whether intended or not, to create an atmosphere of *sluchainost'*, or
"randomness" (that is, who will be the next *vremenshchik*—another word for
someone with temporary access to power—is a mystery, depending only on her
whims and appetites), that severely frays Russia's social fabric and institutions and
fosters a universal cynicism and insecurity.

Faro, we must not forget, is a game of *chance*, not skill. The way Catherine
showered riches on her favorites was also strongly suggestive of pure chance
(being in the right place at the right time) rather than anything earned or meri-
torious. As Lotman reprises the financial costs of the favorites' temporary access
to power as reported by the French diplomat Jean Henri Castéra,

In just such a saltation-like, internally unmotivated fashion
was the process of enrichment imagined by contemporaries.
Grandiose fortunes were created in a moment, depending
on leaps of luck, in spheres having little to do with economics. According to Castéra's data, the Orlovs received 17 million
rubles from the Empress, Vasilchikov—1,100,000; Potemkin—
50 million;   Zavadovsky—1,380,000;   Zorich—1,420,000;

Lanskoy—7,260,000; the Zubov brothers—3,500,000. In total, by his reckoning, 92,500,000 rubles were granted to various favorites during the years of Catherine II's reign. To this there should also be added the grants made to their relatives, the gifts by the favorites themselves, the rents and other forms of easy enrichment. Pushkin wrote down the following conversation of N. K. Zagriazhkaya: "Potemkin, sitting with me, once said, 'Natalya Kirillovna, would you like some lands?' 'What lands?' 'I have them in the Crimea.' 'Why, on what account should I take your lands?' 'It's obvious, the sovereign will make a gift, I only have to tell her.' 'Ok, do me the favor.' [. . .] A year goes by and they bring me 80 rubles. 'Where are these from, for goodness's sake?' 'They're from your new lands; herds are roaming there and they pay you for that.' [. . .] It was at that time that [prominent state functionary Kirill] Kochubei was courting Masha [Maria Vasilievna Vasilchikova—Zagriazhkaya's niece and daughter of Catherine favorite Alexander Vasilchikov's brother]. And I said to him, 'Kochubei, please take my lands in the Crimea; they're just a bother to me.' And what do you think? In the future those lands provided Kochubei 50,000 in income. I was very happy." These huge fortunes that accumulated in various hands rarely were preserved among the direct heirs for more than two generations. *This whimsical movement of riches reminded one of the movement of gold and bank notes on green baize during a card game* [my emphasis—DB].[16]

The amount of wealth being capriciously gifted here is truly mind-boggling, even by today's standards. A ruble in Catherine's time, which was based on the price of a gram of gold (averaging seventy to eighty kopecks in the second half of the eighteenth century), would be worth today approximately fifty to sixty US dollars; this means Potemkin's fifty million would translate into two and a half to three billion dollars. If the accounting is boiled down just to the impact on the imperial treasury the scenario is perhaps even more shocking: according to contemporaries, the 92,820,000 rubles that went as gifts to, and upkeep for, Catherine's eleven principal favorites exceeded the outlays of the annual state budget and was comparable to the sum of all external and internal debt accumulated by the Russian empire at the end of her reign.[17]

And so, it is within this context of the seemingly arbitrary circulation of fortunes among hitherto obscure families and the movement of gold and bank notes on the green baize of the card table that Hermann, the "new man" with the profile of Napoleon and the soul of Mephistopheles, reenters the picture. His character is the point at which Panksepp's rats and the game of Faro as played in the Catherine era momentarily closes. By "closes" I mean the feedback loop becomes so overloaded with similar information that we converge on the domain of causality. What it takes to survive in one's "ecological niche" in Catherine's Russia is simply too dependent on the vagaries of a corrupt bureaucracy *and* too improbable in terms of the wealth creation to be considered fair play by the thinking person. The result: the thinking person acts. The rats play *until the game is unfair*, but Hermann, being the usurper and the "new man," plays *only if the game is unfair*, only if he possesses the code to win. What has happened in the transition from the biology of the mammalian brain to the cultural practice of gambling in late eighteenth- and early nineteenth-century Russia? Lotman gives a clue:

> The "probabilistic" picture of the world, the idea that life is governed by Chance, opens up before the individual personality possibilities of unlimited success and sharply divides people into passive slaves of circumstance and "persons of Fate," whose image in European culture of the first half of the nineteenth century is invariably associated with Napoleon. Such a character trait on the part of the hero requires that alongside him in the text is found a passive individual, in relation to whom the hero reveals his Bonapartist qualities.[18]

On the one hand, Pushkin understood with his finger-always-in-the-wind artistic sensibility that "probabilistically" the existing order was stacked against one. On the other hand, the only way to challenge this hyper-order where human intelligence and drive were almost always wasted was to take a chance, against the odds. Pushkin is drawn to the true gambler's spirit because at least when one is playing Faro each deal of the banker gives one a fifty-fifty chance to win at that play. Of course winning each time over numerous successive deals is less likely than winning over only a few successive deals, but in any case one is not in the hands of the state, but in the hands of "Fate." Pushkin wrote another famous line in a review of a contemporary history tome whose approach (explaining Russia's past using European models) he strongly disagreed with: "The human mind is not a prophet, but a guesser; it sees the general direction of things and can deduce from that profound suppositions, ones often justified by time, but what it can't do is foresee chance—the powerful, sudden instrument of Providence."[19]

What Pushkin's text tells us about the cultural milieu of Russia in 1833 is astonishingly prescient in an evolutionary sense, and that's what I want for the students to be able to make out for themselves. Again, not as future literature scholars, but as educated citizens aware of how science and culture are inevitably intertwined. Yes, this tale points to Raskolnikov and Sonya (Dostoevsky's Liza) and to the law student's theory of the Napoleonic superman who can wade through blood without compunction because he can. But it also points to us. Hermann acts like Napoleon in that, being a usurper, he takes what is there without looking back (his "fate-deciding" appearance at the Countess's house), *but* he does not act like Napoleon at Toulon in that there is nothing heroic in his decision to use Liza for the sole purpose of gaining access to the Countess, winning at Faro, and accumulating wealth. "The small head raised itself. Hermann saw a fresh complexioned face and black eyes. That moment decided his fate." Not exactly a world-historical turning point. Downstream Catherine's favoritism has produced a cultural subspecies in which the prototypes (Napoleon and Mephistopheles) have been debased. All heroic storyline has been drained. The Faustian bargain involves possibly sleeping with an eighty-seven-year-old. The profound knowledge of the universe being traded for is a winning combination at cards that brings piles of gold. And Liza, who unlike Gretchen doesn't even get in the way, is the means to that end.

The loop reopens a final time: before leaving the "Queen of Spades" I ask the students how they understand the game of life as it is played in the world they live in. Let us conclude by repeating Karina's answer to the question about what risks she has taken thus far in life:

> When I came to the USA, I did not know how to speak English. I still remember the struggles and the daily crying, so I promised myself that those times I spent struggling would help me get more opportunities. *For me, taking risks is not a choice but a need to survive* [my emphasis—DB]. Even though I previously mentioned that I like to control things, I give myself enough space to take risks. I think a main risk that I have taken is with Russian. Before Russian came into the picture, I knew I wanted to only study political science and become a lawyer. I am passionate about justice and helping, and I wanted to study law because this career seemed to be one of the most prestigious jobs with a good income. Also, I felt like I needed this career to feel like "I made it" as an immigrant. As I kept taking Russian, I realized that there was more to life than just the standard "American dream." I finally

realized that I had options besides being a lawyer or a doctor (I was not made for science). I have met so many individuals who have allowed me to network and open more doors for me than I could ever imagine. I can go to college without having to worry financially. I have been able to study abroad twice in two beautiful countries: Latvia and Russia. I was exposed to different cultures I never thought of exploring because they were "too far away," which they were not. I was able to make lots of friends who I still talk to and share similar interests. Russian has opened a side of me that I would have never discovered if I stayed in my bubble. I still want to help people and be involved with political science, and I have finally found my focus—international relations, and more specifically Russia-related. I have many dreams and goals, I am not sure with what I want to start, but I know I want Russian to be related somehow.

Panksepp's rats won't play if their chance of winning is less than thirty percent. The mammalian BrainMind gets it. In what ways is the game of life in modern-day America stacked against the Karinas? Fair play is built arguably into the species but the outcomes involving that emotional circuitry and the phenotype's individual interactions with the environment are not predetermined. When losing happens too often players quit. Inadequate early childhood education, the challenges of keeping families intact when they are surrounded by crime and poverty, the siren song of celebrity culture substituting for more robust values, the Pavlovian draw of social media, the American Dream as unbridled wealth creation, reality TV raising bullies and braggarts to high office—all this and more doesn't make it easy. It has been our story that "Pushkin," broadly defined as source of language, inspiring mind, and cultural symbol, provides a useful alternative. Likewise embedded in that alternative is the framework of modern evolutionary thought that has sketched out a big picture of "mind" in nature and suggested why a Russian poet is such a powerful catalyst in the process called cultural evolution. *"For me, taking risks is not a choice but a need to survive."* And: "I think a main risk that I have taken is with Russian . . . [which] has opened a side of me that I would have never discovered if I stayed in my bubble." Finally, it's a story that has brought me closer to these young people and to what it means to try to "emerge" in our contemporary American culture.

Afterword:
The Students Respond

———————

> We do not see our power until we grow from our
> ups and downs. Our arrival is out of nowhere and
> mysterious, and I think that is cruel and beautiful.
> (Lucia)

This book's narrative has tried to juggle four very different colored balls in the air simultaneously: the PSI kids and their backgrounds, Pushkin as source of cultural and linguistic energy, the why and the what of the Pushkin Project, and evolutionary thought. I have set these different storylines in motion in this way because the goal, preparing these kids for the future as educated users of culture, is in my judgment not attainable, or at least much less attainable than it should be, if any one of the balls is dropped. And by different colored balls I really mean: the individual as social creature and product of a specific context, the idea of learning that can excite one personally, the heuristic scaffolding that can make connections between the individual and that excitement, and the big-picture framework that can show how everything is related to everything else. But, the skeptical reader might ask, isn't this an arbitrary joining of incommensurables, a kind of Procrustean bed where the fit feels forced? Won't these deserving kids be helped just by learning some Russian, which is a good thing, and by reading some stories by Pushkin, which is another good thing, without the evolutionary framework? Yes. But our primary focus through all this has been *processual*: how the human cultural realm mimics the biological realm and how everything we create, including the products of our minds, is involved in its own life cycle and its own effort to sustain itself until it can't. Isn't this a framework that ought to be there as starting point along with everything else, even for those still young and inexperienced? This positioning doesn't have to assume a religious, or a non-religious or anti-religious, perspective; it only has to consider culture as an expression of organic life. Thus, all the balls need to be in motion and the hand to eye coordination seamless for a quasi-magical effect, in this case a true 'Aha!' educational experience, to happen.

Now, in this afterword, I propose to bring together briefly several of our students' final comments on what the PSI experience has meant to them and how their thinking has been influenced or adjusted by the Pushkin texts. These comments were solicited from students *after* they read an advanced draft of the book manuscript and considered its findings. I also take the opportunity here to offer my own take on the state of current evolutionary theory as it relates to humanities studies and to the education of the young.

Let's begin by looking at the following quote from Daniela:

> With regard to "The Stationmaster," I do agree that Dunya survives beautifully. I think this is what spoke out to me more. I have seen my peers grow up beautifully as well. The one thing I can say I am good at is observing individuals, and I can say that everyone [from our PSI group] has shown resilience despite some challenging college experiences so far and have made choices that are best for them and their future.

Daniela's takeaway is that Dunya "survives beautifully," which is a phrase lifted from my concluding remarks in "The Stationmaster" chapter. She then explains how this resonates with her personally (it "speaks out" to her) and how that realization also plays to her own strength as a young person trying to figure out how the world works: "The one thing I can say I am good at is observing individuals." The personal then becomes the social (the sense of community: again Pushkin's Lyceum!) when Daniela perceives Dunya's ability to survive in the way she does being repeated in her PSI classmates, who are "grow[ing] up beautifully as well" and who are "show[ing] resilience despite some challenging college experiences so far." It's not enough merely to keep alive; one should keep alive *and* do so with wit, intelligence, grace, *beauty.* Pushkin provides the spring-mounted plot mechanism, the Prodigal Son parable that is turned on its head to produce an alternative moral (*but still a moral!*), which the students are then asked to understand and, where appropriate, apply to the emerging storylines in their own lives. What does it mean if it's not the son, but the daughter? What is the father's (or Father's) proper role in the story? Is the biblical story still sacred or is it simply being made fun of and undermined? What are the situations in life when the moral trumps the sexual, or the sexual the moral? This is the "stepping back and taking in" process we want students to learn and internalize by studying literature.

Writing about the same story, Fabiola explains that

> Vyrin did not let Dunya live her own life because he was only
> thinking about himself, but I also think he did not want to be
> alone. Perhaps this interpretation is a bit different, but I will say
> that at an old age being alone is not fun. The narrator suggests
> that most likely the stationmaster died of alcoholism, but I hon-
> estly believe he died of sadness or a broken heart. [...] I do not
> think greed is necessarily bad, and I feel that Dunya would have
> not changed her decision if she could. She put herself first and
> that is selfish, but I think it takes a lot to put yourself as a priority
> when others expect you to do otherwise.

The sophistication and absence of sentimentality in these remarks are truly
impressive. The combination of Fabiola's life experience coupled with her assimilation of the Pushkin cultural substrate make for an example of written self-
expression mature beyond its years. Vyrin's situation as the abandoned parent
is fully understood and empathized with ("I honestly believe he died of sadness
or a broken heart"), but so too is Dunya's as the "selfish" child. As intellectual
hairsplitters we tend to want to nuance Dunya's dilemma, to see her as unfairly
trapped between the precepts of church morality and the undeniable need to
find a mate, so that calling her selfish seems a bit harsh. But Fabiola parses the
situation correctly for someone in Dunya's position: "I do not think that greed
is necessarily bad" and "it takes a lot to put yourself as a priority when others
expect you to do otherwise." What she is singling out is precisely *the stripped-
down morality of survival*: while in flight aboard an aircraft the rule is the adult
puts the oxygen mask on first before helping the child with it. "Greed" here
is not hoarding excess; it is managing the absolute bare minimum. This is not
selfishness for the sake of selfishness, selfishness in blind disregard of others, but
selfishness as the only realistic alternative to not having a future at all.

And now, Lucia on "The Shot":

> You mention that Silvio is introduced as a powerful personality
> and the name is identified as foreign. I think this exact moment is
> how I have felt before—a powerful personality but seen as differ-
> ent because I do not fit the standard. We do not see our power
> until we grow from our ups and downs. Our arrival is out of
> nowhere and mysterious, and I think that is cruel and beautiful.

This, too, is a striking extrapolation and application of the Pushkin message. Lucia does not fit neatly with others' preconceived notions about her. Like Silvio, whose name sounds different and is a portmanteau for "strong influence" in Russian, she comes into social situations as foreign, as other. But that does not cow her, force her to retreat. Why? Because she sees herself as a "powerful personality" whose strength is hidden *until* she notices herself "grow[ing] from [her] ups and downs." What was not there becomes there: she adapts. Again, it's the Pushkin substrate that elicits confidence and self-knowledge and catalyzes the psychic growth spurt. The last sentence captures Pushkin, his crispness and boldness, by becoming artistic in its own right: "Our arrival is out of nowhere and mysterious, and I think that is cruel and beautiful." The "out of nowhere" and the "cruel and beautiful" have the earmarks of the *creative*, but it's a creativity that comes from pushing off from Pushkin and at the same time affirming one's own prowess.

And so, what can we say in parting about this project and its place in the big picture? Well, first, as recent decades have shown, the postmodern turn in culture has been a rising tide that lifts some boats, while capsizing others. There are those among us who feel that the world is getting worse, but in fact, in terms of poverty, literacy, health, freedom, education, and demographic transition (decrease in population growth rates as economies advance), the world has improved dramatically over the past two hundred years.[1] Belles-lettres as such for the Lucias of the world will presumably not be something that occupies a relevant fitness niche, with fitness here meaning something like the necessity (for survival or success in the larger culture) of learning about a once dominant literary tradition. Those niches are either breaking up and disappearing altogether or reforming themselves into something else as we speak depending on marketplace and global positioning. Lest we forget: *if biology teaches us anything, it is that any species can disappear, but not before change and adaptation have produced new species.* The novels, biographies of famous people, and "cutting-edge" idea books we buy today are now mostly marketed for their entertainment value. What informs and educates still matters, but to a lesser extent. Democratization in culture also means entropy and leveling. The great novels of the past like George Eliot's *Middlemarch* and Tolstoy's *Anna Karenina* that people read to experience contemporary ideas and problems and to find a habitable space between the "is" and the "ought" of existence are virtually impossible to imagine occupying the same kind of fitness niche in the culture today.

Yet evolution also teaches us that, processually speaking, two things can be right at the same time: it is about the individual and it is not about the individual. As Pushkin recedes as one-off genius his life lessons for the still adapting species coming after remain. Recall, for example, the compelling story of embryology told by Dobzhansky:

> The individual begins its existence as a fertilized ovum, and proceeds to develop through a complex series of maneuvers. Body structures and functions that are formed fit together not because they are contrived by some inherent directiveness named "telos," but because the development of an individual is a part of the cyclic (or, more precisely, spiral) sequence of the developments of the ancestors. Individual development seems to be attracted by its end rather than impelled by its beginning; organs in a developing individual are formed for future uses because in the evolution they were formed for contemporaneous utility. Individual development is understandable as a part of the evolutionary development of the species, not the other way around.[2]

As presented by Darwin, natural selection is a totally passive, nonintentional process with regard to the host organism in which the adaptive changes take place. There is no "choosing." What is being selected for depends on the most sustainable way forward in the given situation (again, the "panda's thumb"). "Body structures and functions that are formed fit together not because they are contrived by some inherent directiveness named 'telos,'" but because they serve "contemporaneous utility." By the same token, but now with regard to "cultural selection," which does involve intentionality, Pushkin gives us patterns of language and thought in which "individual development seems to be attracted by its end rather than impelled by its beginning." It is this "seems," this sense of an inherent purposiveness, to which I have been trying to alert our students. Yes, the individual matters, but "as a part of the evolutionary development of the species." Think of the "little coquette" Dunya who strays from her church upbringing and the morality of the Prodigal Son parable only to return home as the successful lady and mother who, while still remorseful (still morally aware), anticipates a broader, more humane perspective for her kind.

The neo-Darwinian insistence on physico-chemical reductionism (the gene's-eye view) as the ultimate explanation for life has led philosopher Thomas Nagel to counter,

> The great advances in the physical and biological sciences were made possible by excluding the mind from the physical world. This has permitted a quantitative understanding of that world,

expressed in timeless, mathematically formulated physical laws. But at some point it will be necessary to make a new start on a more comprehensive understanding that includes mind. It seems inevitable that such an understanding will have a histori-cal dimension as well as a timeless one. The idea that historical understanding is part of science has become familiar through the transformation of biology by evolutionary theory. But more recently, with the acceptance of the big bang, cosmology has also become a historical science. Mind, as a development of life, must be included as the most recent stage of this long cosmological history, and its appearance, I believe, casts its shadow back over the entire process and the constituents and principles on which it depends. [. . .] *My guiding conviction is that mind is not just an afterthought or an accident or an add-on, but a basic aspect of nature* [emphasis added].[3]

I would only add that Denis Noble's idea of biological relativity, with which we started, or James Shapiro's notion of a protocognitive element at the cellular level are precisely those aspects of the science that need to be borne in mind when we come to the question of how human consciousness and the culture that goes with it have evolved. No more accurate definition of how culture oper-ates exists than Noble's relativity concept in biology: "there is no privileged level of causation in biology; living organisms are multilevel open stochastic systems in which the behavior at any level depends on higher and lower levels and can-not be fully understood in isolation." This is also how I asked our kids to try to understand the multilevel functioning of a Pushkin text: *its relativity (parts to whole, whole to parts) models life.* The "mind" that Nagel wants the reductionists to explain is the mind that can create something that is relative without being relativistic/"postmodern" (that is, all parts matter equally *and* they are able to adapt to random stimuli coming from outside = the "stochastic" element versus no part really matters). Where do our ideas come from? They come from *that.*

Which brings us to our final thoughts about memes and memetalk. In popu-lar culture internet memes are absolutely real, in the sense that people, espe-cially young people, see them all over the place and know what they are. They catch on like viruses and spread from brain to brain. They are witty and they are fun. Just google "distracted boyfriend" meme or "first-world problem" meme, and you will get the idea. But are these actually *functional units* that we can con-sciously construct our culture of the future around? How do our efforts to create the learning structures in the Pushkin Summer Institute look in the context of memetalk? Once again, in his original coinage, by analogy to the gene's-eye view of evolution, Dawkins proposed the following:

> The new soup is the soup of human culture. We need a name for the new replicator, a noun which conveys the idea of a unit of cultural transmission, or a unit of *imitation*. 'Mimeme' comes from a suitable Greek root, but I want a monosyllable that sounds a bit like 'gene'. I hope my classicist friends will forgive me if I abbreviate mimeme to *meme* . . . It should be pronounced to rhyme with 'cream'. Examples of memes are tunes, ideas, catch-phrases, clothes fashions, ways of making pots or of building arches.[4]

This terminological legerdemain, which seemed at once both very useful and very arbitrary, unleashed a small flood of claims and counterclaims in the literature whose history since 1976 is fascinating in its own right. Dawkins himself got into the act, first defending and refining and then ultimately allowing the concept to take on a life of its own. Famed paleontologist Stephen Jay Gould sniffed that the meme was a "meaningless metaphor" and that it would be preferable if the phrase "cultural evolution" simply disappeared from use. Over time philosopher of science Daniel Dennett became the idea's most energetic impresario with his many books and articles delving deep into the weeds of the term's possible meanings and applications from a neo-Darwinian, reductionist point of view. Dennett even posited that "the most striking differences in human prowess depend on microstructural differences (still inscrutable to neuroscience) induced by the various memes that have entered them and taken up residence."[5]

For both Dawkins and Dennett, the chief challenge for understanding the meme as the "unit of cultural transmission" hung on the transposition of "replication" from the chemical realm to "imitation" in the symbolic realm. It's ok for a tune or an idea or a clothes fashion to be copied if each time the item is identical in all respects, but is that what happens in culture, when it's the change in the copying that matters—the *difference* between the parable of the Prodigal Son in the Bible and the plot of the not-so-prodigal daughter in Pushkin's "The Stationmaster"? Is a meme an entity or a set (something with boundaries), a source of psychic energy (analogous, say, to a mitochondrion), or both? Can we call a line from a poem a meme, the poem itself a meme, the poet's life-facts (and the memes in his mind) that produced the poem together with the poem itself a meme—how do we categorize? It was thought at first that a term like "meme-plex" might be able to handle these complications, but ultimately it was a distinction without a difference. Dennett saw these problems coming and responded:

> And what he [Dawkins] proposed was that human culture was composed, *at least in part*, of elements, units that were like genes in that they were copied and copied and copied and copied and copied. And it was the differential copying, the differential replication of these items, these memes that accounted for the excellent design of so much in human culture. *And this is a very repugnant and offensive idea to many people, especially in the humanities.* They wanted to hang onto the idea of *the god-like genius creator* who out of sheer *conscious brilliant comprehension* makes all these wonderful things, whether they're poems or bridges or whatever. He was saying in effect well, yes, people do make amazing things, but if you look at the projects in detail you see that they couldn't do that if they hadn't filled their heads with all *these informational things*, which are like genes, which are also information. But they're not passed down through the germ line. They're not passed down through the sperm and the egg. You don't get them with your genes. You get them from the ambient culture, from your parents, from your peers, from the society in which you're raised. It requires perception.[6]

I have *italicized* in this passage those moments that reflect needed interventions on the part of us humanist-educators when building in the future on the real, though still partial advances of scientists and philosophers like Dawkins and Dennett. Yes, culture can be seen to be composed of memes, but notice the hedge: *at least in part*. There is an addition, an excess, that cannot be captured by memes alone as here defined. What matters for the evolutionary element in human symbolic systems is the conscious reshaping of the cultural unit, which is not only an *informational thing* but potentially an *inspirational thing*: it contains, and releases as energy, the personal, emotionally shaded residue of life experience (in Pushkin's case, his own difficult relations with parents, his love of female beauty, and his realization that fair play should be extended to women and their choice of sexual partner), so that the "differential copying," in order to be meaningful, has to be appealing not only to the mind, but to the heart, the emotions. Dennett dismisses with glib sarcasm the *conscious brilliant comprehension* of *the god-like genius creator* (such as Pushkin), whose mind is inhabited by memes coming from every which way and who is thus not really responsible for the fitness (as in future utility) of his creations. But would it be accurate to say that Pushkin didn't know what he was doing with the Prodigal Son parable? No, he definitely understood the power of the original story (perhaps his signature myth), the dense web of religious convention organizing poorly educated society in his time, and the interest he would generate in his readership by flipping the story the way he did. Where Dennett is correct and the traditional approach of humanist-professors is wrong is their (our) tendency to want to hang on to the idea of the genius creator as the primary mover of culture. That may have worked for Pushkin's time, but it doesn't any longer, at least not to the same extent.

Let us humanities types freely acknowledge that Dawkins and Dennett have gotten a great deal correct. Their focus on cybernetics and on the "digitizing" parallels across machine/computer, human/phonetics, and chemical/genetics languages seems too real to be ignored. They force us to think outside of the box. Their contributions have much to recommend them as building blocks for the future. Dennett sums up,

> A better question is whether memetics can provide unified explanations of patterns that have been recorded by earlier researchers of culture but not unified or explained at all. I have claimed that the meme's eye-view fills the large and awkward gap between genetically transmitted instincts and comprehended inventions, between competent animals and intelligent designers, and it fills it with the only kind of theoretical framework that can nonmiraculously account for the accumulation of *good* design: differential replication of descendants. [. . .] The issue should not be whether Dawkins, when introducing the concept, managed to articulate the best definition, or whether I or anybody else has yet succeeded in coming up with a bullet-proof formulation. The issue is—as it usually is in science—whether there are valuable concepts and perspectives emerging from the explorations to date.[7]

Still, two final corrections to Dennett's memetalk are in order. First, the necessary adjustment by Steven Pinker:

> A complex meme does not arise from the retention of copying errors. It arises because some person knuckles down, racks his brain, musters his ingenuity, and composes or writes or paints or

invents something. Granted, the fabricator is influenced by ideas in the air, and may polish draft after draft, but neither of these progressions is like natural selection. Just compare the input and the output—draft five and draft six, or an artist's inspiration and her oeuvre. They do not differ by a few random substitutions. The value added with each iteration comes from focusing brainpower on improving the product, not from retelling or recopying it hundreds of thousands of times in the hope that some of the malaprops or typos will be useful. [. . .] The striking features of cultural products, namely their ingenuity, beauty, and truth (analogous to organisms' complex adaptive design), come from the mental computations that 'direct'—that is, invent—the 'mutations,' and that 'acquire'—that is, understand—the 'characteristics'.[8]

This description of "focusing brainpower," of the creative person "knuckling down," "racking his brain," "mustering his ingenuity," and then "composing or writing or painting or inventing" something seems much closer to how a multilayered meme works than the idea of change through copying errors. As should be clear by now the sorts of memes that Pushkin marshals in his stories—think the Byronic hero, the sentimental plot, the biblical parable, the game of chance—are more than traditional motifs or themes. They are bundles of moving parts and sources of linguistic and psychic energy that can release their magic in different, unexpected directions. For the planning that went into the Pushkin Project, this correction still seems essential.

And second, the points made by Eva Jablonka and Marion Lamb dovetail neatly with Pinker's and go further still:

The problem with the kind of autonomy posited by the meme-talk is that the active biological-psychological-cultural *agent* disappears. It cannot. Ideas are generated, edited, and reproduced as part of the development of groups and individuals, and these sociocultural developmental processes impinge on the transmissibility of the ideas and the precise content and form of what is transmitted. [. . .] But an even bigger problem is that the transmission of ideas, patterns of behaviors, skills, and so on involves several types of concurrent and interacting learning processes. Focusing on one aspect will not lead us very far. It is the non-automatic and non-rote aspects of symbolic transmission—those

aspects that involve directed, actively constructed processes—
which are the most dominant and interesting in the generation
and construction of cultural variations. And these aspects are the
ones that are so often ignored or dismissed. [...] Symbolic variation is directed in three ways—it is targeted, it is constructed,
and it is future-oriented.[9]

The sort of existing meme manipulation and new meme creation that Pushkin
was involved with in his thinking and writing and that we encouraged our students to be aware of fulfills *the directedness* of symbolic variation perfectly: *"it is
targeted, it is constructed, and it is future-oriented."*

Finally, and not merely as afterthought, the postmodern culture we are living
in is confusing for everybody, not least for those of us whose job it is to educate the young. As shown in the recent documentary film "The Social Dilemma"
(2020), the way we experience our high-tech digital world today is with the aid
of algorithms that tailor the information coming to the recipient via the internet specifically to that individual, with the result that we are increasingly going
down rabbit holes created out of our own interpretation of a fact pattern, which
the media platforms then feed back to us by giving us more of what we want.
This is full-on democratization, only the people, the *demos*, are both the predator
and the prey. The platforms do what they do because this algorithm-enhanced
process is monetized: the more sophisticated the algorithm and the more powerful the digital technology the more revenue is generated for the advertisers.
The process seems even more rigged if we take into account that young minds,
which we as educators should be looking out for and teaching how best to learn,
are searching for meaning from within a limited experiential base that is increasingly constituted with the quasi-magical (as in technologically "cool") help of
these very same algorithms. Thus, what were once large swaths of shared values and traditions are pulverized daily into billions and trillions of emotionally
charged—because individualized, dopamine-propelled—bits of information
that don't cohere socially—which is also, and not just by the way, the design of
the business plan—and that impede the process of learning in a well-designed,
heuristically anticipatory fashion. (As I write this, I should report that many
of the young people I have been teaching recently in the PSI have difficulty
focusing.) This, where we are now in our own culture's life cycle, is what I would
like our students in the PSI to be most aware of as they look back on their study
of the phenomenon of Pushkin, his personality, his language, and his stories,
and as they prepare to be lifelong learners. At the end of our chapter on "The
Queen of Spades" we commented on the parallels between rat culture of play

and human culture of play: Panksepp's rat pups refused to play if the bigger pup did not allow the smaller pup to win the wrestling match at least thirty percent of the time, and in Russian culture of the late eighteenth and the early nineteenth centuries the punters in a game of Faro preferred that game to others because it offered a fifty percent chance of winning against the dealer when the chance of winning significant financial and status rewards in the larger game of life was virtually nil. What would the rat pups and the Faro punters say about their ability to "freely" choose to play in our twenty-first-century social media game?

Appendix:
The PSI Questionnaire

---

1. Please describe your neighborhood.
2. Please describe your family.
3. How have you been affected personally by the category of race?
4. In your childhood and early years, what do you look on as turning points in your life?
5. Which people—family and friends, teachers at school, coaches of sports teams, Sunday school teachers, scout leaders, etc.—influenced you most and why?
6. How did you learn about morality?
7. Do you consider yourself risk-averse or open to taking chances?
8. What came first, Spanish or English, and how has that affected you?
9. How much did you read as a young person and what did you read?
10. What role has music played in your life?
11. How were your days scheduled from a young age and how much free time did you have?
12. Once you got to middle school and high school, how did you react personally to the issue of "status"—who is "cool," who is "nerdy," etc.?
13. How much time did you spend thinking about the opposite sex, when did such thinking start, and what came first in your mind, schoolwork or socializing, and why?
14. How has the study of Russian, and participation in the PSI specifically, affected you academically?
15. Pushkin as a personality: interesting to you or not? Which themes, characters, plots, and word play from Pushkin's works stuck with you and caused you to think?
16. Did you learn anything at the PSI, either in a practical or an idealistic sense, that you think might help you going forward?
17. In a few words, what is the purpose of life as you see it now?

1. Neighborhood

Oswaldo:

I was born in the Hermosa neighborhood and moved to the Logan Square neighborhood at the age of 5. Both neighborhoods are predominantly Hispanic and black. I constantly saw violence growing up whether it be theft, murder, whatever—all being caused by gang-affiliated crime. [...] During my childhood my block was between two rival gangs, so I often could not play outside after a certain time and I also could not go to the park a block away from my home.

Juana:

I have lived in 3 neighborhoods. The first was in a big port city in Latin America. There the neighborhood was very bad and had a high delinquency rate. You don't really need to research statistics when you live there. However, no one really messed with my family because we were all very close as neighbors. Also, my uncle was very intimidating, so no one really wanted to get on his bad side. Everybody knew me and I knew everybody. Everybody was invited to everything, even when no one invited you in the first place. This neighborhood was a place that I keep close to my heart because it gave me a pretty nice childhood up to the age of 7. [...]

I also lived in my grandparents' neighborhood in Chicago: Hermosa. Most spoke Spanish, so it was not hard to adjust. This part of my neighborhood was quite calm and a little social, but not compared to my first home. It was predominantly Hispanic and Latinos. [...] This neighborhood really showed me how cold the interactions were between people in the US. I did not know my neighbors and my neighbors knew little of me. [...] I do have to give my neighborhood credit. The people in my neighborhood did create a carnival once a year for a few years, but then they stopped, and things turned cold again. This neighborhood was significant, and I miss it because I spent my golden childhood years (7–13) there.

My current neighborhood is predominantly Hispanic or in the Latinx community. Most of the population is Mexican and Puerto Rican. [...] There is no diversity in my neighborhood. It is also cold. There are no personal relationships with our neighbors. [...] Additionally, my neighborhood is quite dangerous. I live close to gangbangers, which is scary and sometimes one must be careful. From time to time, there are shooting noises by or in front of our apartment. It is to the point that sometimes you cannot differentiate the sound between a shot and fireworks. There is not much of a community. People are nice but distant.

There is no trust, which is interesting because as a minority, there should be a sentiment of unity as a support system for each other.

Veronica:
We lived in this apartment for a while until [. . .] my parents started having a lot of money issues, and we could no longer afford to live there. My sister had finally moved out with her boyfriend. [After that] we moved into a small one-bedroom apartment in a not so good neighborhood. Now it is just my parents and sometimes me who live in that apartment.

Maria:
I have lived most of my life in the Hermosa community in Chicago. When I tell people about my neighborhood, I simply tell them that it has changed over the years. Growing up, I always had to be careful about my surroundings. I remember waking up in the middle of the night because I heard gunshots in my alley. Even as I started high school, I was scared to walk home after soccer practice because I was afraid of being somewhere at the wrong time. My father always believed in self-defense, so he signed us up for taekwondo. We were taught from a young age to watch our surroundings and never talk to strangers.

2. Family

Jose:
Both of my parents immigrated to the US and after a time became legal citizens. They are both from poor families in Mexico. They came to the US and gave birth to me immediately. They then worked tiring jobs. My father was a construction worker for the last 30 years while my mother worked on and off jobs in the school system. I only have a younger brother. [. . .] I saw alcohol abuse going on at home because my father would come home drunk 6 out of 7 days a week for a very long time. I often would have to help my mother carry him in the house starting at the age of 8. I did not have many healthy male role models to learn from growing up.

My mother was always a positive example for me because she took a lot of mental and physical abuse. She also had to get over some big humps. She did not know English, she was timid, did not know how to drive or do anything. She learned all of this through sheer willpower. That is something that I think about a lot.

Isabella:

My family is a Spanish-speaking household. English is spoken among my siblings, but it is rare. [. . .] I live with my parents when I am in Chicago. My father works as an Uber driver and my mother works as a janitress in a gym. They are both very hard workers and try to support us as much as possible in any way possible. My family is very united. Every Sunday we eat breakfast together and dedicate that time to catch up. We are all really involved with each other's lives. We are a very vocal family. We often disagree because we have different points of views; however, we have all learned to respect each other. There have been rough times that we have gone through as a family, including a potential separation, but we worked together to stay connected and fight for the unity for our family, and in this we succeeded.

As a child who grew up in a financially unstable household, I also learned to make decisions on how I should spend my money by learning the difference between want and need. I was an aware child. No one had to tell me what situation I was in because I always knew. These experiences made me more mature and allowed me to grow faster than my peers, which made me feel different. Because I was already speaking like an adult to my family, it was hard to interact with kids my age because they were not talking about debt or financial struggles. We all had different topics of conversations in mind. As a result, I am more comfortable speaking with adults rather than people my own age, which is still true today.

Fabiola:

The first family I can actually remember was just my mother, her two bosses, their daughter, and me in a pretty well-off part of the city. During this time, my mom was babysitting for a white family who in turn paid her and let us live in the second-floor apartment in the two-flat they owned and lived in. My mom was basically a live-in nanny, but we had a very good life there. I went to a Catholic school, was enrolled in summer camps, and best of all I was able to be around my mom almost all the time since her job was at my own home. I would see my dad once in a while on weekends and maybe sleep over his house once or twice a month, but at that time, I wouldn't really say he was part of my family.

I think being alone with my mother for most of my life has had a big impact on me. My dad's side of the family isn't really the best influence on anyone, and my siblings were raised in that environment and to this day I am glad I wasn't. We are polar opposites in that I am very independent, and they are not. I am the first one to go to college and do things on my own whereas to this day they are older and still depend on my dad. I was raised around a very educated family and seeing my mother as a single mother striving to make my life better had a huge impact on me. When I was younger my mother never asked for anything from anyone, which is how I turned out to be. I truly believe that I would be a completely different person if my mom and dad did not get divorced when I was younger.

Erica:
The person who influenced me the most growing up was my mother. [...] Over the years, I stopped looking at my mother as my "mom" and started considering her as my best friend. She was always a source of advice that I could rely on. The best advice that my mom ever gave me was about the nine fruits of the Holy Spirit. She would tell me that I should always live life through Galatians 22. When she told me this for the first time, its importance didn't yet click in my head. She would tell me that I should plant good everywhere I go. She would remind me that planting good seeds rewards you with good crops. I am not perfect, and I make mistakes, but following this advice has given me so many opportunities.

3. Race

Javier:
I believe race plays a big role in society and always will whether people agree or disagree because race is something that makes us different. I believe race will always be seen as something central to the problems we as a species have. I personally do not think a lot about race anymore because it just is what it is, and I do not believe the idea of races affecting human life will be gone in my lifetime, so I just need to adjust and understand that there is a hierarchy of race in our society and that will not change in the foreseeable future.

Cynthia:
I have been strongly affected by the category of race. Before coming to the United States, I only identified as "X" [= someone from a major Latin American country Y]. There was no discussion about whether I was Latino (or Latinx, which is politically correct today) or Hispanic. When children in my school would ask me, "What are you?" I would answer, "I am X." They would ask, "what is that?" This took a toll on my identity because, as a second grader, I felt that my identity as "X" was not considered important to others. Among these interactions, children and adults would just assume I was Mexican. Even today,

people assume I am Mexican. Not long ago, my Lyft driver asked my friends and me, which part of Mexico we were from, without asking where else we could have been from. I think about this all the time, as you can see, I am trying to correct myself about what terms I should be using. Now, society has indicated that I am Latino or Hispanic first, and then whatever identity comes in next. When I would take state tests during elementary school, there was one question that I had to fill out about race: What is your race? There were only 5 options that I was given: White, Black, American Indian/Alaska Native, Asian, or Native Hawaiian/Other Pacific Islander. I could not identify with any of these options, so by default I chose white. My thought process was: 1) I do not know what the last three options are, so I will not consider them; 2) I am not white, but I am also not black; 3) the Spanish conquered Y, so by default I will just put white. Now that I think about it, I believe it is rough to force a second grader to choose their identity through 5 options. As much as I keep learning, I am still asking myself these questions. I am still asking if my history matters, if my DNA matters. I know I am part Asian because some of my ancestors come from China, but this is something that I just learned, and my family does not talk about it. Do I identify as Asian? No. The United States has structured the system so perfectly that people assume who you are and who you are not through phenotype or physical characteristics. I know little about the Chinese culture, except the food. I guess one can say that knowing Chinese food is one way I practice one of my cultures. I guess I am at fault for picking and choosing my identities. When I am in an environment that is predominantly Latinx, I say I am "X." When I am in an environment that is predominantly white, I say I am "X" because I try to stop myself from giving in to the Latinx identity only. The Chinese identity is not something I really use, unless I am with someone that identifies themselves as Chinese. It is almost like cherry picking. The term Latinx is a panethnic term that is only used when the system wants to group cultures that identify as Latin American in origin or descent. As much as I love coming together as one identity, it has hurt me because even though I feel like there are times when we should all identify as one, since that is more effective than being in just multiple little groups (for example, when protesting), there are also times when other cultures "take over" (I do not know how else to put it, I don't mean it in a bad way) and then my identity just stays in the shadows. This conflict between identities is what makes me miss Y more because, personally, this was not something I expect to be confused about.

When I came to the US as an immigrant, I thought that the only things that were consistent in my life were my family and my proud identity as "X." There were times when I was ashamed. I still do not understand why, but for some reason I was. This shame still has some side effects. There are times I do not know how to interact with my own culture. There are times when I feel like I am not "X" enough and I have been "white-washed" or "no longer 'X'," as other fellow "X"'s have told me. This has led me to do more things to prove that I am still "X," but, slowly and slowly, I have come to terms that I don't need to prove my identity to anyone. Sometimes I stay with that mindset, sometimes I just resent my family for making me move here. This is still a battle that I face every single day. I try to look at the good outcomes, but sometimes I just look at the bad. I know I am working hard to get to a place where my identities will not be shaken by anyone or any system.

Rosalia:

I knew that attending the University of Wisconsin-Madison would be tough, not only academically, but because I only made up 2% of the population. However, I did not know that "race" would play a role in my everyday life. I always felt like I needed to prove how "smart" or how "educated" I was to my peers. I would think that by getting into the school, it was enough, but unconsciously I knew that students, peers, and faculty saw me as a "free ride student." Maybe these thoughts were just in my head, but I always felt like I needed to make an effort to make friends in my classes while it came easily to others. I am not a person who is timid and I love socializing with people. I am currently reading a book, *The Struggle of Latino/Latina University Students* by Felix M. Padilla, and a quote that stood out to me most was, "Latino/a students are burdened by the same affirmative action stereotype which African-American students believe to be continually held against them" (Padilla 12). By presenting this quote, I am not saying that I have the same struggle as my African-American peers, but it is similar. That is why, when I go to a Latinx event, I feel most comfortable. I am a firm believer in looking for the good things when there is so much negativity. I think that my hard work in high school and other aspects of my life placed me in this university for a reason. I think I was fortunate enough to have counselors that saw my potential and gave me an opportunity to do things my parents always wanted to do themselves. I also think that being 2% makes me essential to generations of Latinx students on campus to come.

Stephanie:

Race is a crucial part of my identity. When asked to check a box for any document, I often hesitate what race I belong to. You see, as a Hispanic/Latina, I have always debated with what race, given what is provided, I am part of. Rather of thinking of it as race, I think of my ethnicity/nationality. I truly believe that race is a social construct, something created but which many still abide by. Being part of a predominantly white institution, I have experienced what race means to many. Being part of the minority group, I have been looked at different, I have been asked highly inappropriate things about my identity, and even had derogatory terms be used towards me. I used to really believe what others said about me and began doubting my place on campus. When first arriving to campus, my ethnicity was something I always taught about, but now that I have learned how to respond to people's ignorance, I don't think of it as much. Though I have had some negative experiences, all from classmates, I am hopeful that in a couple years race and categorizing people by their ethnicity will not be a thing. I am hopeful that everyone will be able to celebrate their identity without fearing the response from others.

Vanessa:
I think my whole life I have been affected by race because I come for a multiracial background. I feel like every place that I go to I need to accommodate more for a particular race. For example, I went to a predominantly white middle school. I did not realize how certain people felt about minorities until I was classified as one myself. I think with being Hispanic comes this stigma that I am uneducated, lower class, and can be seen as undocumented (this has never happened to me). I think I spent a lot of my life running away from this stigma. I do not want to be stereotyped this way, but what about the people that actually fit in these categories. They shouldn't be treated as any less, but they still are. Depending on who I talk to I am a different race and often times that effects how people see me. I am embarrassed to admit that when I first came to Wisconsin, I did not want my father helping me move into the dorms. I have seen how people treated him in the past, and I did not want to be treated the same way. I think I am more secure in myself now, and I do not allow people to identify me as something that I am not. Even if I am identified that way, I am secure enough in myself to not let people's comments affect me. A more recent example of how race affects me personally is I just started dating a guy from Northern Wisconsin. He is from the middle of nowhere and his first real encounter with people of color was when he moved to Madison. When he would tell me about the kind of people, he grew up around back home, it started to make me feel insecure about my Hispanic background. He knew I was Mexican, but he didn't know that my dad has a strong accent, that I went to a predominantly Hispanic high school, that people in Chicago do not speak the same way as people from Wisconsin. When he first met my father, I could sense the awkwardness and it could be because he was meeting my parents for the first time. But I think it also showed me that people

can't control their upbringing. If I grew up only around white people, and the only thing I knew about other races were the terrible stereotypes that tv/news presents. I would probably be the same way. I think there is room to change, but it is an individual task. They have to work on themselves before there is any major difference.

4. Turning Points

Issac:
I do remember at the age of 8 when I was at the park, I saw a man, gang-affiliated, be shot down at the bus stop next to the park. It was a very eye-opening experience for me.

Angelica:
My life completely changed when I moved to Chicago. First of all, when I arrived to Chicago I thought that we just went to visit my mom's family on a vacation. As months passed, I realized that this was no vacation but a permanent stay. I was devastated because I missed my family and friends. My childhood ended early. [...] Immigrating to a different country is rewarding and traumatizing at the same time. That event changed my whole life because it changed the way I viewed myself in society. I went from being the majority to being the minority in just a few hours. For example, when I first arrived to America, I could immediately tell I was different. I noticed that I did not look like others.

Cariana:
One event that really altered my life as a kid was my parents' divorce. My parents separated when I was in 7th grade. It was a very hard time because I was witnessing my parents falling apart. Because I was the eldest, I had to make sure that I could help my sisters as much I could. I remember being distracted in school because all I could think about was what was happening at home. It was even more difficult needing to grow up so fast within that year. As soon as my parents separated, my mother started to work even more. I had to learn how to cook and keep things neat around my home. It was harder for me to even find time to be with my father. It shattered my world knowing my parents could never be together in the same room without tension. When I entered high school, it was even harder trying to play the role of "mom". I would come home from practice exhausted and still need to make food for my sisters and me. I would have so many sleepless nights, but through all this, I grew up.

Bryanna:
The most impactful moment in my walk with God was when He literally saved my suicidal sister's life. She attempted to kill herself so many times. But for some reason He just wouldn't let her die.

Manuel:
The thing that changed me the most was the divorce of my parents. That event changed and influenced my whole life. It was very difficult but it allowed me to become strong to face other challenges.

5. Influences

Rueben:
I found a male role model in my childhood basketball coach. He was also a first generation Mexican-American and he was exactly what I needed in my life—a man from whom I can learn moral values while still being an active kid. I played on his basketball team from 1st to 8th grade. He would invite the team over to his house for cookouts and he took us to U of I to meet his son and show us that we can make something of ourselves. He also would be there for us when we needed him. In high school I would be his assistant coach for his middle school boys, and I saw myself shaping into a person I could be proud of.

Diana:
My dad and mom always inspire me to work harder. They were not born into privileged families, but they always made sure they helped their family in any way they could. They have always been workers. They always make sure we have everything we need, and I will forever appreciate their actions. They influence me to be the better version I can be. They are my number one fans and always support me to do my best. They tell me to follow my dreams and do whatever makes me happy. They encourage me to try new things and get out of my comfort zone. They are honestly my heroes. My older brother also inspires me to never give up. When we first arrived to America, he sacrificed his education in order to support the family. Now he is going to college and working hard at the same time. He never gives up and always supports me in any way he can. He always puts others first before himself, which I strongly respect. My second-grade teacher (Ms. XXX) strongly influenced me when I was mostly struggling in my childhood. When I entered second grade, I did not speak English. She was my first American teacher. Luckily she spoke a good amount of Spanish, which

allowed me to survive second grade. She always encouraged me and helped when I needed it the most. She always said I was her favorite student because I always worked hard. The truth is that she inspired me to work harder because she always said she believed in me, which is what allowed me to get better at English. My Russian instructors (Mr. XXX and Ms. XXX) have also strongly influenced me because they taught me what it is like to work hard and to believe in myself. They supported me in various ways and provided me with resources to better myself as a person and as a student. They encouraged me to pursue my dreams while challenging myself. They are hard workers and very caring people. They are the type of people that inspire me to do great things for myself and others.

Gabriela:

I played volleyball from 4th grade to 12th grade and through all those years I only had one influential coach, who was my high school coach. Her name was Ms. XXX and I felt that if ever needed advice or anything I could go to her. Sophomore year is when I got really close to her because I went through a lot of issues with one of my friends who tried to commit suicide. Ms. XXX was very understanding about my situation. She taught me a lot about perseverance and hard work. She always believed in me even when I felt like I didn't even believe in myself. Another influential teacher I had was Mr. XXX. He was my high school band teacher and ever since I met him, he was a huge supporter of mine. He always thought highly of me and because of that I never wanted to let him down. He was one of the first figures of authority in my life that not only taught me as a student but who took all my advice into consideration and applied most of it. He had a lot of trust and put me in a ton of leadership positions. He was always very passionate about his work which in turn made me want to have as much drive and passion toward my own future career. The biggest thing that has stuck with me thanks to Mr. XXX is his phrase "it's only awkward if you make it awkward." This has honestly helped me a lot and whenever I feel weird or awk-ward, I say this in my head and it honestly eases up situations. My best friend XXX is also a huge influence in my life. She is one of the few people that will straight up tell me what I need to hear, not what I want to hear. She is someone I can count on to not judge me when I mess up. She has been my best friend since my junior year of high school and it seems that no matter how far we are or how long it's been since we've seen each other, things never change. She taught me how to not care what others think and I truly believe I am most like myself when I am around her. My mom is obviously a huge influence on my life and everything I do is for her. I want to be someone she is proud of and I want to be able to provide and give her the world when I am able to. She has taught me to be who I am and one thing I always keep in my mind is "you are not better or less than anyone. Remember that you are on the same level." I think this has really helped me stay humble and nonjudgmental towards others around me.

Rachel:
It is pretty typical for people to say this but my mom is one of the most influential people in my life. For a long period of time, she was my best friend. She was and still is my go-to person. And let me tell you, I literally tell her everything. I tell her things that a kid my age would never tell their parents. My mom has earned my trust through her love and trust. She spent most of my life teaching me to be independent. Also, by allowing me to learn for myself and not being overly protective when I did mess up she has encouraged me to trust her that much more.

6. Morality

Ingrid:
I learned morality through my actions. I learned not to lie when I was young. Once, I saw my brother lie and then smile because he was a terrible liar. I did the same, and I as well started to laugh. My mom told me that lying was bad because it would get me nowhere. Once a lie starts, the lie cannot stop until the truth comes to light, which is true. Ever since then, I have tried to be as honest as possible. I learned morality through most of my mistakes. I never liked the feeling of doing something wrong to someone. If I do something wrong, I feel guilty immediately and it does not leave my mind until I make it right.

Elisia:
One thing that highly affected me was when I was in elementary school and all the students had parents who were alumni of that school. I will never forget my 5th-grade history fair where I put in a lot of effort on the project and the other students barely even finished it and I got a B and everyone else got an A. Things like this occurred multiple times with multiple projects and assignments. My parents even noticed how unfair it was, but they told me that in the end, the other students were going to be the ones to suffer because they wouldn't know how to do things on their own in high school. This really paid off.

Mia:

It was during my teenage years that I started questioning morality the most. I grew up a Christian and I attended Friday and Sunday services at a nearby church. I was always a strong believer because my mother taught me at a young age to recite Bible verses and pray every night. I was involved in the dance ministry at church, so I knew I felt something when I learned about Christ. However, I would read a lot about things that were happening around the world and sometimes I would question God's existence. I would find myself conflicted by the things I learned at school and at church. I would get into arguments with people about sexuality and identity. I would not agree when the Bible said that men and women should belong only to each other. I felt that love was universal and could not be restricted. Even though I stopped attending church, for personal reasons, I continue to keep an open mind. [...] I would not say I am religious, but I would say I have a soul and an understanding for people and their beliefs.

Beatriz:

All I could say is that I learned morality from my family. All the times that I wanted something but couldn't get it simply because my parents said "no you can't," stuck to me and is now how I seem to think about the world. Some things should be the way they are and that's how I continue to see it.

Samuel:

I became more moral as a person after I met a friend in high school. From this individual I learned much about being an actual good person and how I think people should be treated. [...] Failure has also taught me I should be grateful for what I have and I should work hard for what I don't. There are many tools for achieving success but it takes your own work to get the things you want.

7. Risk-Taking

Hector:

Normally I do not take risks because I feel like I have never taken any risks in my life. I cannot recall a time when I've taken a risk that could have changed the trajectory of my life. I always like to make sure that I think all my decisions through. I believe a risk worth taking is when you know that it can change your life for the better, like starting your own business. But the failure could also set you back. I think a significant risk I could take is moving to a different state with a lower cost of living, such as Texas, and leaving everything I know behind, such as a job, friends and family. A risk I have seen others take is leaving school in order to start their own business or trying to become famous as a rapper or streamer. I have seen some succeed and some fail; it just depends how hard some people are willing to work.

Theresa:

I am the kind of person that will not do something unless I am almost sure of the outcome. I think that results from my past when I made plenty of mistakes taking risks on things that I later learned were not worth the consequences. It very much depends on the situation, but even when I have taken risks and failed, I think I have learned a lot from those situations. I have taken many risks with friends, relationships, academics, experiences, opportunities. I think a recent risk that I took this past semester was in my Russian class. I think it is embarrassing to admit because it was a mistake that I regret, but at the same time I think it shows how I am open to risk. Last semester in my Russian language class, we were asked to write many essays. After completing each of the essays, I sent them to my friends in Latvia to edit them. Over time, I realize that my grades were really high on all of my essays. It makes sense because I had help from an outside source. After talking to a classmate one day later in the semester, he brought to my attention how it was unfair what I was doing and how the specifications on the syllabus stated that we were not allowed to get outside help. I just remember feeling super guilty after that for being dishonest. I had to make a decision on whether or not to talk to my TA teaching the class. By talking to him I was risking him giving me zeroes on all of the essays and me possibly failing the class. On the other hand, I was risking him finding out another way or me being left with shame. I honestly don't think he would ever have found out if I didn't talk to him. I ended up talking to him, and he was grateful for my honesty. I didn't end up getting punished, and it was a really good learning opportunity. In my opinion, it was a risk worth taking when your conscience is involved. For me, it is more important to be honest and true to myself. I think remaining true to myself is going to continue to be a risk. This can come in the form of relationships, choices, and experiences.

Karina:

I consider myself both risk-averse and risk-taking. This mainly depends on the situation. I am risk-averse when it comes to people. I have struggled taking chances on individuals because I do not trust easily. People scare me and that is because of my experience as an immigrant and my relationship with entitled children. My whole life I have been surrounded with adults, so having people around my age outside of school was not common. I do not know how people around my age interact because they are so complex and make their lives harder, in my opinion. I am a complex individual who makes her life harder, as well, but I guess I can say I am more centered and more serious. Although I know I am making an unfair judgement, this judgement has sadly taken over my view and made me less social around my age group. I can hold a conversation and invest in a friendship, but I never get out of it what I put in, so the risk taker in me has slowly diminished in that respect because for me relationships are even. I would say that I am still a cordial person with everyone, but I am not investing as much as I would normally do.

Another way I am risk-averse is that trust does not come easily to me when it comes to things I know I cannot control but try to. Before taking risks, I try to control the situation because I have been able to do so in the past. For example, I never relied on my teacher for my own learning. I always took charge, was always the initiator. This mindset has always been with me since I came to America. When I relied on my family to help me with my English, they started helping me but then they stopped because they told me it was my responsibility. Although that is true, I felt like I lost the support when I needed it the most, so after that I did my own learning. I sometimes do not like the unknown because that means I cannot control it. You can say I am a control freak to some extent but that is because knowing the outcome tends to give me comfort. Not knowing stuff makes me anxious because I know what it is like not knowing things. I know what it means to feel lost in a place and not know comfort because you must be on your toes every day to survive.

I am a risk taker when it comes to my education and future. Ever since I moved to America, I began to take the initiative with opportunities that have been presented to me. When I came to the USA, I did not know how to speak English. I still remember the struggles and the daily crying, so I promised myself that those times I spent struggling would help me get more opportunities. For me, taking risks is not a choice but a need to survive. Even though I previously mentioned that I like to control things, I give myself enough space to take risks. I think a main risk that I have taken is with Russian. Before Russian came into the picture, I knew I wanted to only study political science and become a lawyer. I am passionate about justice and helping, and I wanted to study law because this career seemed to be one of the most prestigious jobs with a good income. Also, I felt like I needed this career to feel like "I made it" as an immigrant. As I kept taking Russian, I realized that there was more to life than just the standard "American dream." I finally realized that I had options besides being a lawyer or a doctor (I was not made for science). I have met so many individuals who have allowed me to network and open more doors for me than I could ever imagine. I can go to college without having to worry financially. I have been able to study abroad twice in two beautiful countries: Latvia and Russia. I was exposed to different cultures I never thought of exploring because they were "too far away," which they were not. I was able to make lots of friends who I still talk to and share similar interests. Russian has opened a side of me that I would have never discovered if I stayed in my bubble. I still want to help people and be involved with political science, and I have finally found my focus—international relations, and more specifically Russia-related. I have many dreams and goals, I am not sure with what I want to start, but I know I want Russian to be related somehow. I never knew Russian would give me these opportunities because I was taking it because (1) it was mandatory in my high school and (2) it was fun, and I like languages. I never knew I could keep it as I start building my career, which it turns out I can. [...]

In my opinion, risks that are worth taking are things that you will not regret no matter what the outcome is, whether it is a good one or a bad one, because it is a learning experience. Failures are good in life because they make you grow. I think a risk that is not worth taking is one that is up to one's discretion. If you know it is going to make you unhappy for sure, then I would not take it. A person takes risks for many different reasons, such as curiosity, experience, opportunities, etc. I am a person who takes risks out of curiosity, and I have known its ups and its downs, and I do not regret them. I may have regrets about how things could have been different, but I do not regret doing it.

In the future, I can anticipate that there will be many significant risks in my life with my education, career, personal life. I will be graduating soon, and I need to figure out what I will do after that, finding experience and jobs. I want to find my own place even though in Latino families that is not very common unless you are getting married, so I will be taking a risk with that. There will be risks in my life that will impact others, so I need to somewhat prepare myself for that and be ready to approach it.

8. Spanish versus English

Gladys:
My childhood ended early because I had to take on the responsibilities of learning a new language and supporting my family in any way a seven-year-old could. [...] It was hard to communicate with others because I could not understand them, and they could not understand me. There was a language barrier. Even if they did understand me, there were times where kids would take advantage of their power over me and use it to create their own entertainment. Through these

experiences I learned that I was always going to be different and that I should only rely on myself. I was independent in everything I chose to do. When I was learning English, I only relied on myself to learn, which I successfully did. I am an independent learner. I gained so many skills. I became the translator, the tech girl, and the resource of my family. If I did not know something, I made sure I learned it, so I could aid my family. I learned to fix a computer, so my family would not always have to pay someone to get it repaired. I learned to work with phones better, so I could teach my parents how to use the current smart phones. I learned to master the subject in school better, so if my siblings had a question, I could help them.

Melanie:
I come from a multi-racial household. My mom is Slovak and Polish while my dad was born and raised in Mexico. Being multi-racial has allowed me to be immersed in more than one culture growing up. My mom's first language was Polish, and when my parents first met, my dad spoke little English, so my mom was forced to perfect her Spanish. The other influences on my language were my great-aunt, who lived on the second floor of my house and who only spoke Polish her whole life, and weekly church services, which were in Spanish. At a young age, I spoke Spanish and understood a vast amount of Polish. There were years that I attempted to speak Spanish, but I remember getting made fun of for having a "white" accent. That was the end of my attempt to speak any Spanish. Anytime someone spoke to me in Spanish, I would simply pretend to not understand.

Graciela:
Being the first one in my immediate family to learn English (in third grade to be exact) is something that played a huge role in who I am today. Having to struggle day and night to speak a language that everyone around me seemed to already have mastered put me down. It honestly took a lot out of me to keep practicing and not give up in school. This is something that I keep very close to myself. I really have been the most determined person, especially when it comes to my education, beginning with that school year.

9. Reading

Carlos:
I did not like reading at all because I was not very good at it, but my mom made me read because she knew I needed to excel as a reader in order to be successful. I enjoyed reading comic books. I read my first one at the age of 7 and ever since

then I read all kinds of superhero comics, whether it be DC or Marvel comics; they just stuck with me because most heroes have tragic backstories which make it empowering to see how these people do wonders in the world.

Adela:

As a young person, I read a lot. Even when I did not know English, I had a dictionary next to me and translated the sentence from English to Spanish, so I could understand what the book was saying. I read anything that I could get my hands on. I would often go to the library and check out some 10 books and read them. I read fiction, nonfiction, fantasy, textbooks, biographies, horror, and mystery. These books took me to a whole new world that allowed me to escape from the current one. I realized that I enjoyed books that had hidden messages because, to me, that was more meaningful and added a whole new layer to the stories. One book that I still remember from my childhood is *The Giving Tree* by Shel Silverstein. This book taught me about human greed, flaws, and virtues. The more I read the more I realized that characters in fiction allow us to view human nature through different lenses. Another book that I still remember is *The Secret Soldier: The Story of Deborah Sampson* by Ann McGovern. It influenced me to take action in what I believe to be right for myself. I still have these books in my possession to remind me how literature affected me as a child and does so to this day.

Kiara:

When I was younger, I used to read a lot. When I hit high school, I stopped being interested in books because I finally had a lot more friends and I focused more on music. I used to read a lot of young adult fiction and most of the books I read were cheesy and along the lines of a less popular girl who found someone who liked her who was pretty much her polar opposite. I used these books as an escape in middle school because I got bullied a lot. I used to be called all types of names and was bullied mainly for being overweight. These books were a way of escaping, and when I was younger I kind of hoped that one day what happened in the books would happen in real life.

Marbella:

As a kid, I would read a lot because it was a requirement. I started to enjoy books a little more during my sophomore year [of high school]. I found interest in books that were associated with topics of today's news. The books I enjoyed most were *Fahrenheit 451*, *Hunger Games*, *Divergent* and *The Handmaid's Tale*. I think that these books interested me because they were all based on utopian societies. I would like to imagine myself in the character's shoes. This may sound a bit odd, but I think this is the reason why I am able to respect and understand other people's perspectives. When I would imagine myself in these extreme scenarios that the characters were facing, I would try to think what I would do differently and what the outcomes would be if that were the case. It has been harder for me to pick up a book and read it lately because my attention has been directed to other things. I recently picked up *Looking for Alaska* by John Green, an author I have always been fond of. I love his writing because he takes his time to develop his characters. He gives them personality in the most incredible way.

Lissette:
I spent a lot of my childhood reading. I really enjoyed Greek and Egyptian mythology. I enjoyed reading fiction. I would spend days locked up in my room until the book was finished just to read it all over again because I was so sad when it got to the end. I also really liked dystopian books and fiction overall. In high school, I started reading a lot of character development books, and I read my Bible everyday (I don't know if this counts, but I read it every day so that I am not blindly believing). I enjoy reading character development books because they help me work through the trauma that I grew up with. They also help shape me into the person that I want to be. Another therapeutic tool that I use on a daily basis is journaling. I journal every day at least once but on a harder day more than that.

Tiana:
Growing up I never really liked reading. A huge part of this was because I never really understood what I was reading, especially when I read in English. However, whenever I did read, it was usually for school or a book that was gifted to me. A book that I have read many times and still make sure that I read again at least once a year is *To Kill a Mockingbird*. It honestly amazes me how a single book can reveal so much truth about our society.

10. Music

Luis:
Early on in life I found music to be an escape for when I was going through some stuff. I did not really play an instrument growing up; I preferred singing or just listening to music. I listen mainly to rap just because that is what I grew up around, and it is something that I feel can both relax me or pump me up.

I also do enjoy Spanish music that my mom played when I was younger. I do not really remember the genre, I just remember hearing it every Saturday morning: my mom would wake us up to its sounds as she was cleaning and then she would make us clean. It is just the way Mexican moms work because every other Hispanic kid will tell you that is how it is at their house. You can quote me on that. As I listen to music, I drift to a whole other place which is why I lean on music to get me through days now that I am in college.

Adelina:
Music has heavily impacted my world. I was raised with Latin music. Music is part of my culture and has affected how I interact with my culture: through dancing. Music is the only thing that keeps me sane. I play the flute, alto saxophone, and prima domra. Music is almost an escape from the world and its problems. I listen to all different genres, except country (I do not like country music). Music has always created a safe place where I can lower inner walls and truly be myself. When I listen to music, I mainly focus on the beat. I always pay attention to the beat and go along with it. I sing the beat, or I tap my pen/pencil. My mind just pays attention to the beat and makes me feel calm and at peace. It is a time when my mind tries to think or review my life. Those are the times I do my best thinking. Music has been a coping mechanism that I have used to de-stress and a time where I do not have to worry about anything else. My mind just calms down.

Talia:
Music has always been around me since I was little. I played the flute since 3rd grade and when I got to high school, it was a huge focus of mine. If I ever had a rough day or felt down, or I needed time to relax, the band room was like my sanctuary. It was the one place where I felt I fully belonged. I listen mainly to Billie Eilish, some rap, and any Latin music. I usually choose the music depending on my mood. If I feel more energized, I listen to upbeat music, but if I'm having a harder day, I listen to sadder music. Most of the time I think about things going on in my life at the moment. But sometimes when I listen to music past experiences that relate to the songs come to mind.

Aimee:
I would say that I always have a variety of music I listen to. When I am doing homework, I normally listen to classical music or jazz. When I am with family, I usually enjoy listening to Latin music like reggaeton, bachata or cumbia. When I am with friends, I love listening to R&B, hip-hop or rap. When I listen

to Spanish music, I feel alive. I want to dance to it all day long. I am a bit pickier when it comes to R&B and rap because sometimes artists make music that I can't exactly relate to or make sense of. For example, when I listen to a Drake song like "Sandra's Rose" I'm able to enjoy it because he raps about his success. He gives his mom credit for his fame because she is his biggest support system. But when I listen to "Work" by Drake I don't enjoy it because it repeats that same word until it wears you down.

Joselin:

I grew up playing musical instruments my whole life. My mother was a musician. She played the piano and the violin. Growing up I played the piano, then the flute, and in high school I played the oboe. Music was an escape from my crazy reality. It was an escape from family struggles, school, and the stress that came with daily life.

Jailene:

Music has always been essential in my life. Most of my family members at some point in their life were part of a musical group, so I always grew up listening to someone play an instrument while someone else would sing. Music, as I learned, always teaches me new lessons and continues to open my mind. Most of the music that I listen to is Latin music, R&B, or Hip Hop. I either listen to music to dance to or listen to actually listen and learn, which is where R&B and hip-hop come in.

Anthony:

Music has played a big part of my life. I played trumpet my four years in high school and it has brought me my best years in life. I truly did enjoy it. I mostly listen to rap nowadays. When I'm listening to music, I imagine scenarios or I dream of things in my own life that are similar to what the song is saying. When a song is sad, I think of something that has happened to me that was sad. If the song is about love, I think of the one person I care about.

11. Daily Rhythms

Adrian:

School took up most of the day, then I would play basketball for 2 hours after school, so I was kept busy, which was for the better because I was not out on the streets doing things I should not. I was not free until 9 pm: I would get home at 5, change clothes, take a shower, then have dinner, and finally do homework. As soon as I became free I would either watch some basketball games or play video games. I really didn't watch much TV unless LeBron James or the Bulls were on. Video games were great for me because they allowed me to relax and enjoy myself after a very long day.

Alyssandra:

Apart from school, my days were not very scheduled. I would usually get involved with after-school programs because I wanted to improve in academics. When I got home at the end of the day, I would eat and then do homework. I would usually watch TV because I wanted to get used to listening to English, which is why my parents let me watch a lot of television. I would mostly watch Disney Channel and Nickelodeon. [. . .] Other times, I would go to the park or play outside. I was always an outdoor person and bored when at home. My parents did not allow me to play videogames because my siblings were addicted to them, and they did not want me to go through the same thing. My dad thought videogames were a waste of time. Today, I still do not play.

Daisy:

I was always involved with something when I was younger. I was either in camp all day during the summer, in ballet and ice-skating on the weekends, or in clubs and sports during the week. Even though I did all this, I still had a lot of free time. Once I got into high school my schedule became a little easier, yet still very packed. I focused on sports and music, which took up most of my after-school time and weekends, and I went to the gym after school almost every day. These were things that my friends also did, so we had similar schedules and sometimes participated in similar things. I never got into videogames and rarely watched television. To this day, I'm not a huge fan when it comes to TV.

Ruby:

At a young age, I already had a schedule. During school days, I would go to school and then on Monday, Wednesday, Friday and Saturday I would go to taekwondo. The days I did not have taekwondo, I would spend at the YMCA in Mozart Park. During the summer, my mom would sign us up to day camp at the YMCA or at the Boys and Girls Club. Even in the summer, I would have taekwondo or dance class. I was always involved in something and I was never really at home. I thank my mom for involving me in so many things as a kid because these activities helped me receive my liberal education. Because of this I learned to manage my time wisely and to take on so many things at the same time.

Apryll:
Growing up I had very little free time. My mom put me in every activity that she could think of. I played just about every sport: volleyball, ballet, baseball, floor hockey, gymnastics, swimming, ice-skating, and more. The free time I did I have I would spend at the library with my family. We rarely watched TV or spent time at home.

12. Status Issues

Erik:
I did not really care much for status because I treated everyone the same and I spoke to everyone even if they seemed like a nerd or a cool kid. I have always been fair with getting to know people and not judging them because I do not know what they have been through, so there is no reason to add another unnecessary burden on someone who might be going through something. I have never really felt like an outsider because I participated in many different activities. I always had a place where I felt welcomed.

Jocelyn:
Once I got to middle school, I was really affected by "status." For some reason, being nerdy was portrayed as bad because that meant you were "weird." The people who were considered cool were the students who did sports. I never fit in with people my age because they had different priorities than I did. I always studied because I wanted to get the best grades. I always tried hard in everything that I did because I loved doing a good job. To me, being popular was not important, but it did affect my daily life. Because I was considered "weird/nerdy," people would bully me and hide my textbooks. This was a constant thing. I would not find my textbook for weeks or even months. I never truly understood why I got bullied if I never really messed with anyone in my classroom. I just did my own work. People would also bully me when I had braces. It made me uncomfortable not being able to fit in because it gave my peers another reason to target me. School then became an uncomfortable and unsafe place for me. In order to avoid my classmates, I used to eat my lunch in the classroom with a friend and play chess. At school, I never wanted to be popular; I just wanted my classmates' respect. Popularity was so important to them that it affected the way they acted around everyone else. It was a very uncomfortable situation that I am glad I never had to go back to. High school was quite different. Popularity was not a big deal there because no one truly focused on that aspect. There were

people quite known, but they were not a huge topic in the school since everyone focused on their own business. I did not mind that people did not like me because it was not a big deal. There was still respect maintained among peers. Middle school and high school were two different worlds for me.

Alejandra:

In middle school, I wanted to be popular so bad. I believed that being skinny was the key to it all. I remember vowing to myself that once I hit high school, I would be popular and prove everyone around me in middle school wrong. In my head at the time, this was really important to me, but once I got to high school it all changed. Once I met friends that were truly my friends and started knowing people and joining clubs, I realized it wasn't as important as I thought. In high school I felt that regardless of what people thought my status was, I had great friends who didn't care. As high school went on, I got more comfortable with the idea that I am not the same as others and that if they don't want to accept me that is on them, not on me. That was hard to learn in middle school, but I'm glad it finally registered in high school.

Anaise:

In middle school, I was a complete nerd. People would come up to me and ask me to help them with their homework. I never really cared about appearance until I got older. While every other kid had Jordan's or Nikes, I had Sketchers or shoes that were "affordable." I outgrew my clothing very fast and my parents sometimes couldn't afford to buy me new clothing. We would spend some Sundays at the thrift store shopping for gently used clothing that we could wear out. By 7th grade, I started to care a little bit more about my appearance, so I would save up my allowance to buy the shoes that were in style. I started to feel more comfortable with myself by the time I got to high school. I was never a person that really cared about what people thought of me as long as I knew I was being true to myself. In high school, I would say I was a bit more popular because I was involved in sports and I would talk to everyone. Now that I am in college, I love building friendships everywhere I go.

Korayma:

Once I transferred into a middle school where all the students seemed to be the smartest, I soon learned how difficult cliques were. I never was sporty, or artistic, nor was I the smartest. I soon learned that I really didn't fit into any of their circles. Thankfully, to my surprise, I was able to make it in high school with a great, positive mentality. Going into high school I promised myself that I would find what was interesting to me and not to everyone else. I promised myself that I would not fit into what everyone else said. Though during my freshman year this was hard, I soon was able to avoid being part of cliques and tried out different things. My curiosity led me to who I am today: I allow my ideas to be formulated into reality over and over again.

13. Relationships

Ricardo:
I did not spend much time thinking about the opposite sex or the same sex. I never really felt anything romantic towards anyone. I saw the way my parents fought, and I did not really feel like going through that with a significant other. I found it easier to just chill and not try to be committed to anyone. I thought school came first because I have a couple of childhood friends who had kids at the age of 15 and 16, and they could not go on to accomplish anything they dreamed of. I knew I did not want to be held back by having kids. I will do that once I have accomplished goals and lived for myself.

Bernice:
I did not think about the opposite sex often. Sure, I can admit there were people who I had crushes on, but it was not a big deal. The crushes were more physical than character-related. I probably started having those innocent crushes around second grade. However, these were not something I often paid attention to. Throughout my childhood, I believed that school and family always come first. I experienced relationships through my friends' lenses when they got into romantic relationships with others. As I grew, I learned the disadvantages of having a relationship at a young age. The idea was not very appealing because I did not want anything to get in the way of my education, and I also did not want to get distracted from my goals. These mindsets came from my mother who often told me that I was too young to start thinking about boys and that I should focus on school. I agreed. Also, the idea of being an immigrant child always comes back to me and makes me realize that it may be a mistake and that I should wait till I have it all together. These mindsets are still true today. I have always been a planner, and I would rather stick to my plan before I can go a little off track.

Mireya:
Ever since I was younger, I always had the mentality that school came first, no matter what was going on around me. I think I remember finally noticing boys

by 1st grade, and by 3rd grade all the girls started really talking about them. I would have crushes but never really let them affect me. I was impacted with how badly this messed with my sister's academics and I didn't want to end up like her. I think now that I am in college I kind of pay more attention to guys but not to the point where my academics are on the line.

Ana:

I was never really allowed to date in middle school. I was always afraid of disappointing my parents if I were hiding behind their back with some boy. I had my first boyfriend in 8th grade, which was the stupidest idea because we were going to graduate. I don't think I ever paid much attention to boys until they started paying attention to me. I don't think I ever contemplated choosing between school or a boy. The answer was and will always be school. My mindset about choosing and finishing school first comes from my parents' experience. They did not have the opportunity to finish school because they could not afford it. I have been given so many opportunities to extend my intellect and I have always been grateful for that. My goal is to do all the things that they never had the opportunity to do.

Anel:

Honestly, I do not spend that much time thinking about the opposite sex. I don't feel the need to be in a relationship now or anytime soon. I see relationships more as a burden because I simply do not have time for that. I want to date to get married, and I am definitely not ready to get married. I also want to work on myself as much as I can until then. I think this mindset has come from growing up in the church and not wanting to repeat my parents' marriage. Not saying that they don't love each other, but I can see where they fall short.

Keila:

In high school thinking about having a boyfriend was always present. Since I received attention from the popular kids at school, this was a trap because it would involve falling into cliques, but by my junior year I realized that being boy crazy only distracted me from my grades. Sure enough, I was able to be ten times more focused in school. My focus in school comes from what my mother preached. From my mother I learned how important education was and how being educated was so valuable in my life. This allowed me to always prioritize my education.

14. Studying Russian

Daniel:

I love learning everything about Russian—whether it be the literature, culture, or language itself. I strongly dislike the cases in Russian as well as all the exceptions that exist in the Russian language. I think reading and speaking came to me the easiest just because I am great at pronunciation and reading. Listening is very hard for me because Russian is spoken so fast, while Spanish and English are very slow and smooth languages, in my opinion. I do not think there are many connections [between learning Russian and learning other subjects] because most other subjects come very quickly and easily, while Russian requires a lot of time and effort, which is why I find it so difficult.

Isabel:

What I liked about learning Russian is that the language took me out of my comfort zone. As a Latina, Russian was very intimidating because as a child I always heard that Russian is too hard. I took what I heard and kept it in the back of my mind. As a child, I never got to contribute to the conversation because I was not old enough to understand (trust me, I was). When I started learning Russian in high school, I loved it because it was fun. To me, learning a different alphabet and learning the differences in the languages among the ones I know gave me an opportunity to learn in a class setting rather than in a survival mode setting. I really enjoyed speaking it because it made me feel accomplished. I was learning a language because I wanted to, not because I needed to. Yes, I had to learn the language well in order to get a good grade, but I also think that I could have done minimum work and still pass. Russian has given me the space to feel vulnerable and learn from my mistakes.

PSI really reinforced my interests in the language. Before the program, I thought that Russian was only a high school thing and I wouldn't bring it to college with me. However, PSI made me realize that I truly wanted to build a career that was centered around the Russian language. PSI in Madison gave me the platform to get more comfortable with my speaking. PSI in Latvia gave me the platform to immerse myself more in the language and culture. Honestly speaking, PSI in Latvia entirely reinforced my interest in the language because it gave me a sneak peak of what I would like to do with my life: diplomacy. I struggled a lot with Russian. To me, speaking and listening came easiest because of my previous experience learning English. Reading and writing were the hardest skills to develop because sometimes I really had to think what case certain words had.

However, this is what made me work so hard. The connection I noticed between how I learn Russian and how I learned other subjects is that I took my time to learn the language. I found myself more intrigued and learning to understand, not so much learning to get a good grade.

Salma:

I love Russian because it is so unique, and it is something that brings me close to a small group of people. It brings forth a community full of amazing people. I started my junior year and ever since I had heard of PSI, I wanted to go so bad. I was able to go, and it turned out to be one of the best summers of my life. I met so many amazing people and the teachers were fantastic. I truly believe that that is the best my Russian has ever been in all categories. Anytime I do something with PSI it reminds me why I fell in love with the language and why I keep going back to it. I find that when I go to Russian, I am way more involved and enjoy heading to class. There have been few classes that I can say I have gone to and looked forward to going to the way I enjoy going to Russian class. I feel like I am strong at reading, writing, and listening but not at speaking because I don't get enough practice with it.

Lesly:

When I first started learning Russian, I found it very difficult because I couldn't find a connection to it. I decided to join PSI because I knew that I would be taking IB [International Baccalaureate] Russian. Little did I know that PSI was going to change my perspective about learning. I went into PSI only concentrating on the grammar and language, but I got so much more out of it. I was learning about the culture and comparing it to mine. I think the best part of the Russian language is speaking it. Most of the words I learned sounded very familiar to words I knew in Spanish. I think that Russian has really helped me find interest in the subject of philosophy and history. For example, "Ночь, улица, фонарь, аптека" ["Night, street, streetlight, pharmacy"—the first words of a poem by symbolist poet Alexander Blok] gives us an insight on repeated events. The idea that we might have repeated the same actions in another life is mind blowing. Whether one believes it or not, the idea is fascinating.

Nikole:

The Pushkin Summer Institute is actually what sparked my desire to learn Russian. The only reason why I signed up for the PSI in Madison was because I had gotten my first C ever in Russian, and I was looking for an explanation to give to colleges to justify my C. I think I initially received a C because I was so afraid of making a mistake, and that was all I seemed to do in class. I used to dread going to Russian and would have panic attacks before, after, and during class. I enjoyed the Pushkin Summer Institute because it was low stakes. The non-judging aspect of classrooms allowed me to move past my insecurities and really learn.

The PSI Abroad is where I learned the most Russian. It makes sense because of the language immersion. After endless nights of speaking Russian with my host mom the listening and speaking came easier to me than reading and writing. I think this is more because of my lack of grammar skills. I wish the local summer program had focused more on the grammar even though it was nice to learn the topic vocabulary.

To learn Russian there is a lot of risk taking, and it is a lot more than a grade. Over time I have learned to play the system to get the grade I want. In Russian, it has always been more than a grade. When I forced myself to like it, that is when I started to get better grades and do better overall.

15. Pushkin

Jonathan:
Pushkin is a very interesting person because the inspiration for some of his greatest works was drawn from moments in his life, and what he created from these inspired moments is absolutely astounding. If it were not for the way he died he would be at the top of my list; having said that, I will place Pushkin in my mid-tier of people I would like to emulate. He revolutionized Russian literature and he is an international icon to the point that Hispanic teens read about him every summer. I have never heard of such a program for any other poet or author. Pushkin is truly a one of a kind writer. His African descent did not register with me much because I did not see him as an African Russian man, but I just saw him as a poet. His ability as a writer overshadowed all else. The theme of the role of fate in Pushkin's works is what may have affected me the most because it furthered my disbelief in faith. I believe we all create our own path and fate. Nothing is set in stone until it is in the past. So now I do not stop trying to do something until I know it is over.

Adelina:
Pushkin as a personality really interested me because in some sense he was brave. I loved reading about his flaws; however, what I really enjoyed is the fact that behind all his mistakes, he was still a good person. I could connect with

his personality because to some extent I could sense what it was like for him to feel different and unwanted. He was not the best student, but he surely was the best writer, and for me that sounds enlightening and inspiring. I think Pushkin stacks up against other famous writers whom I admire and would like to emulate because the stories he wrote are very relatable. His writing gave me a glance of life—not everything has a happy ending. His writing also provided me with additional lenses to approach literature and the deeper meaning of a story. I could easily connect to the characters he depicted. He inspires me to try and touch others the way he did and still does with me. He demonstrates how no one is truly perfect and he portrays the inner desires that some people may have and deny saying. I think Pushkin's ethnic/racial heritage did draw me closer to him, but it was not the main reason why I became interested in him. On the other hand, his heritage did surprise me since I had assumed being Russian meant being fully Anglo, but that was only because I did not have much exposure to the Russian culture and its history. I did find some comfort in his heritage because it made me realize that I could learn Russian and read Russian literature like anybody else.

The themes, plots, characters, and linguistic play in Pushkin's works did sink in and became things that I often think about when it comes to literature and personal life. The actions in a story like "The Queen of Spades" did teach me about psychology, morality, and creativity. I learned about what it means to be a true gambler and how that involves taking risks, and how difficult those risks can be because of the character's thought processes. [. . .] The connection in my mind between Pushkin's Russian and my learning of the Russian language helps me interact with both because I am better able to understand the decisions Pushkin made to write certain stories and enrich them with his word play. It is all quite fascinating.

Anayansi:

I find Pushkin very interesting. I think his life and how people treated him because of his skin color really interests me. I feel like compared to other famous people his story is very real in the sense that I can relate to him. Being brought up as the only Hispanic in a community of white people makes me understand a snippet of how Pushkin was treated. His heritage is probably what brings me the closest to him.

Amairani:

When I started to learn about Pushkin, I was intrigued by his personality. I still remember how proud Pushkin was. He was so proud that he died in a duel.

What brought me closer to Pushkin was his personality. In a way, he reminded me of my father and men who fall under the word "Machista." Like many men in my family, Pushkin loved to drink. However, outside from the drinking and the gambling, he had a soul. No man in my family would ever sit down and write poems or stories that would challenge the mind of readers. Although I found the themes very important in Pushkin's stories, I was more intrigued with his creativity. The one story that stands out to me is the "Queen of Spades" because in it Pushkin creates symbolism that helps set up the ending of the story.

Martin:
Pushkin is interesting and has a cool outlook on certain things. You are able to see that through his writings. He has a certain style that makes you question the message he's putting into his works. His ethnic/racial heritage does not really register for me. The lessons from Pushkin's stories are something I still remember to this day. I believe that I have learned from them. The morality of Pushkin's works and the Russian that he uses is interesting. I feel there is much undiscovered content that we need to look into.

16. PSI

Priscila:
I think the aspects of the PSI that have stuck with me as guideposts or ideals going forward are the resources that allow us to develop our language skills, the support system offered during and after the program, and the ability to accept when we make mistakes and how that is okay because we can still improve ourselves.

Nadia:
I think the biggest thing I took from the PSI was the connections and relationships I made with teachers and even other students in my cohort. PSI always makes me fall back in love with Russian even if it feels like I have fallen out of love with it. PSI is what has motivated me to try and make a change in the education system through my major.

Daniela:
PSI was one of the greatest decisions I have ever taken. It helped me build friendships that I will carry throughout the rest of my life. Without it, I would have not fallen in love with learning the language. I carried this very experience with me to Latvia, where I fell in love even more.

Grecia:
I think what has stuck with me from the PSI is that it is fun to learn Russian, and as long as I keep that mindset, I will have a reason to persist.

Tiana:
During the span of six weeks I learned so much. I honestly learned a lot about being independent and about having distance between myself and my family. Some of the most important benefits of the program came from interacting with new people. Additionally, the connections I made with students and staff still continue to guide me as I face the challenges of college life at UW.

Jahson:
PSI has taught me mostly what it would be like to go away from home and study. In this way it prepared me for college. I am very grateful for that.

17. Purpose of Life

Justin:
I do not believe there is a purpose to life. I think we are just insignificant conscious beings who make the best out of what we have.

Lorena:
As I see it now, the purpose of life is to do what makes us happy, to connect with others who are different from us because that is the way to create unity out of our differences, and to continue learning because we will never know everything. I think in general these ideas can be the purpose of life. However, my purpose is to learn as much as I can, help and advise as much as I can, be happy as much as I can, and earn as much as I can. I want to make a difference like Pushkin did. Pushkin made a difference through his writing. I am trying to find how I can make a difference through my own work. I still do not know what that looks like, but I am working toward it.

Tamia:
The purpose of my life is to help students that are thought of as stereotypically bad students or troublemakers and get them the help they deserve in order to make their dreams a reality through their education. I want them to feel like they belong in college and not that they need to be on the street.

Gissele:

The purpose of life, I would say, is to influence everyone around you, create memories, take risks, mess up, learn and oversee your life. Do the things you love to do because you want to, not for money or fame, but because it gives you pleasure. Have no limits and live as you please; after all, you're the one living it.

Nathalie:

When you ask me what the purpose of life is, I believe I have a religious purpose. With regard to a secular outlook, I think the purpose of life is to make the most of every situation because you are never going to get it back. Making the most of every situation means working hard, enjoying the moment, laughing, and knowing that some way, somehow everything is going to work out, so there is no point in dwelling on the things that cannot be controlled.

Cristal:

The purpose of life for me is to continue learning, growing, and helping. My goal is to open a non-profit community center where I will be able to guide the youth into the best future possible. By being able to provide the youth with all the tools possible, I will be helping others in the way I would've loved being helped with the college process.

Miguel:

The purpose of life depends on who you are. One purpose could be to make the world a better place; another could be to do the opposite. I think deep down that the purpose is to always be learning and seeking knowledge because knowledge is infinite.

Notes

___

Preface

1 Matt Ridley, "When Ideas Have Sex," https://www.ted.com/talks/matt_ridley_when_ideas_ have_sex/transcript?language=en. More detail is found in Matt Ridley, "The Evolution of Culture," in Matt Ridley, *The Evolution of Everything: How New Ideas Emerge* (New York: Harper, 2015), 82–85.

2 "Embodied cognition" involves at least three ways of framing body-mind interactions: 1) the "embodiment thesis," 2) the "extended mind thesis," and 3) the concept of "situated cognition." All three approaches make features of cognition dependent on certain characteristics of the physical body, but in the second case the idea of mind is extended beyond the brain and even the body out into the world, while in the third the concept of knowing is made inseparable from doing (here the links with John Dewey and American pragmatism become obvious). There is a huge amount of research on this topic engaging multiple disciplines, but we will only touch on it lightly here. See "Embodied Cognition," Wikipedia, https://en.wikipedia. org/wiki/Embodied_cognition.

3 This is a very approximate number. While "original divergence" from the "chimpanzee–human last common ancestor" (CHLCA) may have occurred as early as thirteen million years ago (Miocene), hybridization may have been ongoing until as recently as four million years ago (Pliocene). See "Chimpanzee–Human Last Common Ancestor," Wikipedia, https:// en.wikipedia.org/wiki/Chimpanzee%E2%80%93human_last_common_ancestor.

4 On how bully behavior is dealt with in groups see especially Christopher Boehm, "Bullies: Redefining the Human Free-Rider Problem," in *Darwin's Bridge: Uniting the Humanities and Sciences*, ed. Joseph Carroll, Dan P. McAdams, and Edward O. Wilson (New York: Oxford University Press, 2016), 11–28; and Christopher Boehm, *Moral Origins: The Evolution of Virtue, Altruism, and Shame* (New York: Basic Books, 2012), 66–70.

5 Frans De Waal, *Mama's Last Hug: Animal Emotions and What They Tell Us about Ourselves* (New York: Norton, 2019), 198.

6 Richard Dawkins, *The Selfish Gene* (New York: Oxford University Press, 1976), 192.

7 Daniel C. Dennett, *Darwin's Dangerous Idea: Evolution and the Meanings of Life* (London: Penguin, 1995), 364–365.

8 Steve Stewart-Williams, *The Ape that Understood the Universe: How Mind and Culture Evolve* (Cambridge, UK: Cambridge University Press, 2018), 14.

9 Alex Mesoudi, *Cultural Evolution: How Darwinian Theory Can Explain Human Culture and Synthesize the Social Sciences* (Chicago: University of Chicago Press, 2011), xii.

10 See, for example, David Sloan Wilson, *Evolution for Everyone* (New York: Delta, 2007), 193: "Evolutionary theory provides a common language that can erase the distinction between the hard sciences, the social sciences, and the humanities."

11 The position Owen Barfield formulated in 1965 still resonates today:

> The hypothesis of chance has already crept from the theory of evolution into the theory of the physical foundation of the earth itself; but more serious, perhaps, than that is the rapidly increasing "fragmentation of science" which occasionally attracts the attention of the British Association. There is no "science of sciences"; no unity of knowledge. There is only an accelerating increase in that pigeon-holed knowledge by individuals of more and more about less and less.

Owen Barfield, *Saving the Appearances: A Study in Idolatry*, 2nd ed. (Hanover: University Press of New England, 1988), 145.

12 Ursula Goodenough, *The Sacred Depths of Nature* (New York: Oxford University Press, 1997), 30.

Chapter 1

1 See endnote 2 above in the preface.

2 Anna Akhmatova, "Slovo o Pushkine," in Anna Akhmatova, *O Pushkine* (Leningrad: Sovetskii pisatel', 1977), 6–7.

3 Iu. M. Lotman, *Pushkin: Biografiia pisatelia. Stat'i i zametki 1960–1990. "Evgenii Onegin". Kommentarii* (St. Petersburg: Iskusstvo-SPB, 1995), 388.

4 Here and elsewhere translations are mine unless otherwise indicated.

5 "Arthur M. Jacobs, an experimental psychologist and professor of experimental and neurocognitive psychology in Germany, examined a number of methods and models that were being used at the time [2015] for investigating the neural bases of poetry. The new research was suggesting that poetry, more than any other literary form, demonstrates 'the complexities with which our brain constructs the world in and around us, because it unifies thought and language, music and imagery in a clear, manageable way, most often with play, pleasure, and emotion.'

In 2017, a group of psychologists, biologists, and linguistic experts from the Max Planck Institute in Germany aimed to understand this by studying the physiological effects of poetry. First, they measured skin variability to look for peak emotional responses, like chills or goosebumps, which are physical phenomena indicating states of high emotional and physiological arousal. They gave participants new poems that they had never read and allowed them to self-select a few, and the results were unequivocal. All participants experienced chills, while 40 percent showed goosebumps on video monitoring that took place during the study.

Next, they put participants into an fMRI machine to understand what was happening in the brain as these peak emotional experiences were taking place. This time, the team selected all of the poems in order to test the effects of reading the poetry for the first time. The subcortical areas of the basic reward system lit up. Reading poetry, in fact, lights up some of the same parts of the brain as listening to music. It provides a familiar rhythm that taps into something more ancient in us. So, even though poetry is words, it reaches beyond language. [...]

Our brains are hardwired for the rhythms and rhymes of poetry, lighting up the right side of the brain, while a poem that truly resonates with us does so at a neurological level by stimulating the areas of the brain that are associated with meaning-making and the interpretation of reality. Poetry, at a cognitive level, can help us make sense of the world and consider our place in it. [...] Rhyme and rhythm have been shown to intensify emotions at a neurochemical level as poetry activates brain areas such as the posterior cingulate cortex and medial temporal lobe, which have been linked to the default mode network and introspection." (Susan Magsamen and Ivy Ross, *Your Brain on Art: How the Arts Transform Us* [New York: Random House, 2023], 53–55)

6 For the neuroscience on how our brains combine different intakes to create an aesthetic moment, see the section on the components of "The Aesthetic Triad" (i.e. our sensorimotor systems, our reward system, and our cognitive knowledge and meaning-making) in Magsamen and Ross, *Your Brain on Art*, 15–19.

7 "Two competing hypotheses have been proposed on the emergence of functional lateralisation based on the structure of the corpus callosum, the most considerable inter-hemispheric connection. The inter-hemispheric independence hypothesis suggests that, during evolution,

brain size expansion led to functional lateralisation in order to avoid excessive conduction delays between the hemispheres. Accordingly, functionally lateralised regions will be connected less strongly via the corpus callosum than non-lateralised regions to make processing of lateralised functions more efficient. The inter-hemispheric competition hypothesis proposes that functional lateralisation arises from the competition between the hemispheres that inhibit each other via the corpus callosum. As functionally lateralised regions would need to inhibit the opposite hemisphere more than non-lateralised regions, they could be more connected by the corpus callosum." Vyacheslav R. Karolis, Maurizio Corbetta, and Michel Thiebaut de Schotten, "The Architecture of Functional Lateralisation and Its Relationship to Callosal Connectivity in the Human Brain," *Nature Communications* 10 (2019): article no. 1417, https://www.nature.com/articles/s41467-019-09344-1/. Iain McGilchrist (see below) obviously follows the second ("inhibitory") hypothesis and brings a great deal of evidence to bear in support of it.

8 Iain McGilchrist, *The Master and His Emissary: The Divided Brain and the Making of the Western World* (New Haven: Yale University Press, 2009), 177.

9 McGilchrist is particularly useful on the connections between music as music (how neurologically we experience it) and metaphorical thinking. See, for example, ibid., 96, 41, 470 n135.

10 "Biologically we are just another ape; mentally we are a whole new phylum of organism." Terrence W. Deacon, *The Symbolic Species: The Co-evolution of Language and the Brain* (New York: W. W. Norton, 1997), 862.

11 Charles Darwin, *On the Origin of Species* (New York: Modern Library, 2009), 648–649.

12 See also George Levine, *Darwin the Writer* (Oxford: Oxford University Press, 2011).

13 In addition to Joseph Carroll's *Evolution and Literary Theory* (Columbia: University of Missouri Press, 1995), see his *Literary Darwinism: Evolution, Human Nature, and Literature* (New York: Routledge, 2004), *Reading Human Nature: Literary Darwinism in Theory and Practice* (New York: SUNY Press, 2011), and his edited volumes: Joseph Carroll, Dan P. McAdams, and Edward O. Wilson, eds., *Darwin's Bridge: Uniting the Humanities and Sciences* (New York: Oxford University Press, 2016); and Joseph Carroll, Mathias Clasen, and Emelie Jonsson, eds., *Evolutionary Perspectives on Imaginative Culture* (Cham, Switzerland: Springer Nature, 2020). Carroll is especially useful for the way he foregrounds literature's biological embeddedness. He begins *Evolution and Literary Theory*, for example, by listing the four biological concepts governing his literary theory: 1) that most important is the relationship between the organism and its environment; 2) that innate psychological structures— perceptual, rational, and affective—have evolved through an adaptive process of natural selection, and that these structures regulate the mental and emotional life of all living organisms, including human beings; 3) that all "proximate causes" or immediate human motives are regulated by the principles of inclusive fitness as "ultimate cause"; and 4) that representation, including literary representation, is a form of "cognitive mapping." Carroll, *Evolution and Literary Theory*, 1–2. Carroll also provides, inter alia, a helpful (though I assume not dispositive) corrective to Steven Pinker's point that the pleasure afforded by literature is a nonadaptive bypoduct (Stephen Jay Gould would term it a spandrel) of higher cognitive processes:

> The argument I am making for the way literature grounds itself in elemental motives and basic emotions suggests a different hypothesis about its psychological function. Literature is satisfying—moving or disturbing—not in the degree to which it fulfills fantasy expectations— though it can do this—but in the degree to which it provides a sense of psychological order. [. . .] Through literature and its oral antecedents, we recognize the elemental structures of human concerns in our own lives, and those of others. We filter out the trivial and the tangential aspects of experience and see into the deep structure of our nature. And we not only "see"—not only understand objectively. Through stories and verse and dramatic enactments—whether written or oral—we realize our deeper nature in vividly subjective

ways. Through such realization, we situate ourselves consciously within our environments and organize the feelings and thoughts through which we regulate our behavior. Literature produces pleasure, but it is not merely a "pleasure technology" equivalent to recreational drugs. It is one of the primary means through which we regulate our complex cognitive machinery. It contributes to personal and social development and to the capacity for responding flexibly and creatively to complex and changing circumstances. (Caroll, *Evolution, Human Nature, and Literature*, 115–116)

14 Theodosius Dobzhansky, *Genetics and the Origin of Species* (New York: Columbia University Press, 1982 [orig. 1937]), 12.
15 "When the genetic relatedness (r) of a recipient to an actor, multiplied by the benefit (B) to the recipient, becomes greater than the reproductive cost (C) to the actor, or rB>C." "Kin Selection," Wikipedia, https://en.wikipedia.org/wiki/Kin_selection.
16 This germ −> soma directionality as a law of inheritance in animals was first discovered by August Weismann, the German evolutionary biologist (1834–1914). The "Weismann barrier" is "the strict distinction between the 'immortal' germ cell lineages producing gametes and 'disposable' somatic cells in animals (but not plants), in contrast to Charles Darwin's proposed pangenesis mechanism for inheritance. In more precise terminology, hereditary information moves only from germline cells to somatic cells (that is, somatic mutations are not inherited)." "Weismann Barrier," Wikipedia, https://en.wikipedia.org/wiki/Weismann_barrier.
17 See, for example, *The Literary Animal* (Evanston: Northwestern University Press, 2005), which David Wilson edited together with his student Jonathan Gotschall.
18 This is not to suggest that multilevel selection is now universally accepted in the scientific community. It still has its prominent naysayers, including Richard Dawkins. As E. O. Wilson, writing in 2016, summed up recent developments,

> this formulation [that is, multilevel selection] recognizes two levels at which natural selection operates: individual selection based on competition and cooperation among members of the same group, and group selection, which arises from competition and cooperation between groups. Multilevel selection is gaining in favor among evolutionary biologists because of a recent mathematical proof that kin selection can arise only under special conditions that demonstrably do not exist, and the better fit of multilevel selection to all of the two dozen known animal cases of eusocial evolution. (Edward O. Wilson, "The Meaning of Human Existence," in *Darwin's Bridge: Uniting the Humanities and Sciences*, ed. Joseph Carroll, Dan P. McAdams, and Edward O. Wilson [New York: Oxford University Press, 2016], 6)

I return to multilevel selection and its potential applicability to cultural products, including Pushkin's literary texts, in greater detail in chapter five.
19 See, for example, "Extreme Fine-Tuning—By Design?," in Stephen C. Meyer, *Return of the God Hypothesis: Three Scientific Discoveries That Reveal the Mind Behind the Universe* (New York: HarperOne, 2021), 146–163.
20 Denis Noble, *Dance to the Tune of Life: Biological Relativity* (Cambridge, UK: Cambridge University Press, 2017), 160; my emphasis.
21 On the idea of the "cognitive" as it applies to cellular activity see especially the work of distinguished chemist (and perhaps not by chance erstwhile English major?) James A. Shapiro, whom I cite elsewhere in the text. See the following endnote.
22 Cf. Noble, *Dance*, 171–172; James A. Shapiro, *Evolution: A View from the 21st Century* (Upper Saddle River: FT Press, 2011), 1–6; and Suzan Mazur, *The Paradigm Shifters: Overthrowing 'the Hegemony of the Culture of Darwin'* (New York: Caswell Books, 2015), 10–21.
23 As recent process-oriented philosophers of biology Daniel Nicholson and John Dupré put it, "If the living realm is indeed processual, then we should consider the central explanandum

of biology to be not change but stability—or, more precisely, stability achieved by activity, that is, by change." Daniel J. Nicholson and John Dupré, eds., *Everything Flows: Towards a Processual Philosophy of Biology* (Oxford: Oxford University Press, 2018), 14.

24 On the major researchers in the area of cultural evolution (such as Richerson and Boyd, Mesoudi, Tomasello, Henrich, D. S. Wilson, Laland, Stewart-Williams), see the preface.

25 Daniel Dor, *The Instruction of Imagination: Language as a Social Communication Technology* (New York: Oxford University Press, 2015), 1–2.

26 Ibid., 4.

27 Richard O. Prum, *The Evolution of Beauty: How Darwin's Forgotten Theory of Mate Choice Shapes the Animal World—and Us* (New York: Doubleday, 2017), 63.

28 See "Amotz Zahavi," Wikipedia, https://en.wikipedia.org/wiki/Amotz_Zahavi.

29 To be sure, in terms of evolutionary timelines symbolic systems, thanks to the element of human decision-making and choice, operate more forcefully and much more rapidly, than genetic ones. See, for example, Eva Jablonka and Marion J. Lamb, *Evolution in Four Dimensions: Genetic, Epigenetic, Behavioral, and Symbolic Variation in the History of Life*, rev. ed. (Cambridge: MIT Press, 2014), 4: "With the emergence and elaboration of the symbolic systems, even the genetic system has taken an evolutionary back seat. Throughout human history, adaptive evolution has been guided by the cultural system, which has created the conditions in which genes and behavior have been expressed and selected."

30 Daniel C. Dennett, "Memes 101: How Cultural Evolution Works," https://bigthink.com/videos/daniel-dennett-memes-101.

31 Jablonka and Lamb, *Evolution*, 220–222.

32 As J. Mark Baldwin wrote,

> There is a class of modifications which arise from the spontaneous activities of the organism itself in the carrying out of its normal congenital functions. These variations and adaptations are seen in a remarkable way in plants, in unicellular creatures, in very young children. There seems to be a readiness and capacity on the part of the organism to "rise to the occasion," as it were, and make gain out of the circumstances of its life. [. . .] What is the method of the individual's growth and adaptation as shown in the well-known law of "use and disuse"? Looked at functionally, we see that the organism manages somehow to accommodate itself to conditions which are favorable, to repeat movements which are adaptive, and so to grow by the principle of use. (J. Mark Baldwin, "A New Factor in Evolution." *The American Naturalist* 30 [1896]: 443–444, https://www.journals.uchicago.edu/doi/epdf/10.1086/276408)

The process sounds Lamarckian but is actually neo-Darwinian.

33 Robert H. Wozniak, "Consciousness, Social Heredity, and Development: The Evolutionary Thought of James Mark Baldwin," *American Psychologist* 64, no. 2 (2009): 96–97.

34 Ibid.

35 This version of Pushkin's matrilineal genealogy has been thoroughly revised in recent decades. See, for example, Dieudonné Gnammankou, *Abraham Hanibal: L'aïeul noir de Pouchkine* (Paris: Présence africaine, 1996).

36 Ken Robinson, "Do Schools Kill Creativity?," Ted Talk, April 22, 2013, https://www.ted.com/talks/sir_ken_robinson_do_schools_kill_creativity.

37 As I write this, at the beginning of 2023, more than ten years into our program, this still holds true despite (or should it be *because of*?) horrendous recent developments in Ukraine, beginning on February 24, 2022.

38 David Brooks, *The Second Mountain: The Quest for a Moral Life* (New York: Random House, 2019), 182.

39 M. Basina, *V sadakh litseia. Na bregakh Nevy* (Moscow: Detskaia literatura, 1988), 33.

40 Ibid., 33.

Chapter 2

1 A clarification is useful here. A good example of a project that applies evolutionary tenets to improve a specific social situation is David Sloan Wilson, *The Neighborhood Project: Using Evolution to Improve My City, One Block at a Time* (New York: Little Brown, 2011). The Pushkin Project is organized rather differently: its goal is to teach the students of PSI how the different levels of a specific culture interact and interpenetrate while also alerting them to their own placement within a cultural evolutionary framework.

2 See, for example, our first-year video: "Why This Program," PSI Madison, https://pushkin. wisc.edu/psi-madison/psi-madison-program-overview/why-this-program/.

3 My thanks to Professor Brett Cooke for drawing this parallel to my attention.

4 Viorica Marian and Sayuri Hayakawa, "Why Bilinguals Experience the World Differently: Multilingualism Alters What You See and Hear," https://www.psychologytoday.com/ us/blog/language-and-mind/201906/why-bilinguals-experience-the-world-differently. The research on the topic of bingualism is considerable. See, for example, the journal *Bilingualism: Language and Cognition*, edited by Jubin Abutalebi and Harald Clahsen and published by Cambridge University Press.

5 "World-Readiness Standards for Learning Languages," ACTFL, https://www.actfl.org/ resources/world-readiness-standards-learning-languages.

6 Due to the invasion of Ukraine in February 2022 we cannot predict what will happen to this program in the future.

7 "Pushkin Scholars," PSI Madison, https://pushkin.wisc.edu/psi-madison/psi-madison-pushkin-scholars/.

Chapter 3

1 Noble, *Dance*, 176.

2 See ibid., 160–186.

3 "All sexual eukaryotes are aware of their environment, potential mates, and potential pathogens. In addition, early members of the animal radiation devised the neuron, a cell type specialized for awareness, and this made possible the avenue of awareness called consciousness" (Goodenough, *Sacred Depths*, 90–91).

4 Dor, *Instruction*. For an excellent recent account of the complex evolutionary history from primitive nervous systems to human consciousness, see Joseph LeDoux, *The Deep History of Ourselves: The Four-Billion-Year Story of How We Got Conscious Brains* (New York: Penguin, 2019). As LeDoux summarizes,

> Some species exhibit even more complex forms of behavior that depend on cognitive capacities. Here, cognition will be used to refer to the ability to form representations and use them to guide behaviour—as when you refer to a mental spatial map when planning a route and using the plan to drive to your destination. [. . .] The more sophisticated the cognitive capacities of a species, the greater the ability of its members to transcend survival—to act for the sake of living in a particular way, rather than merely for the sake of remaining alive. (LeDoux, *Deep History*, 34)

5 See chapter 1 in this book, 8–9 and endnotes 7–9.

6 McGilchrist, *Master*, 115.

7 LeDoux in *Deep History* gives an excellent blow-by-blow presentation of how the animal world progressed from its beginnings to consciousness in human beings. See, especially, parts 9–13: "The Beginning of Cognition," "Surviving (and Thriving) by Thinking," "Cognitive

Hardware," "Subjectivity," "Consciousness through the Looking Glass of Memory" (LeDoux, *Deep History*, 204–311).

8 For more examples see the Appendix to this book.

9 Stuart A. Kauffman, "Reinventing the Sacred," https://vimeo.com/105980303. See also Stuart A. Kauffman, *Reinventing the Sacred: A New View of Science, Reason, and Religion* (New York: Basic, 2008), 34–39.

10 Dennett writes most explicitly about the distinction between copying (gene) and cultural imitation (meme) in *Darwin's Dangerous Idea*, 373: "I want to propose a framework in which we can place the various design options for brains, to see where their power comes from. [...] I call it the Tower of Generate-and-Test; as each new floor of the Tower gets constructed, it empowers the organisms at that level to find better and better moves, and find them more efficiently." The phrase "better and better moves" implies that the meme changes as it is copied, thus it is not merely replicated.

11 See Jonathan Gotschall's fascinating *The Professor in the Cage: Why Men Fight and Why We like to Watch* (New York: Penguin, 2016). His chapter 2 on dueling and bullying ("Monkey Dance," 33–61) is particularly germane in the context of what drives Silvio, the Count, and the narrator in "The Shot." Pushkin's own fatal duel against d'Anthès is discussed on p. 48.

12 Alexander Pushkin, *Eugene Onegin: A Novel in Verse*, trans. James E. Falen (Oxford, UK: Oxford World's Classics, 1998), 29.

13 As Shelley describes Byron's worldview, based on conversations they had in Italy, in 1818, in *Julian and Maddalo* (wr. 1818–1819, pub. 1824), "[B]ut pride / Made my companion take the darker side. / The sense that he was greater than his kind / Had struck, methinks, his eagle spirit blind / By gazing on its own exceeding light." Julian is the idealistic, but still atheistic rebel Shelley, while Count Maddalo is the cynical, existence-rejecting Byron.

14 P. V. Annenkov, *Pushkin v aleksandrovskuiu epokhu* (Minsk: Limarius, 1998), 113–114.

15 Ibid., 136–137.

16 Ibid., 136.

17 Cited ibid., 137.

18 Ibid., 126.

19 Ibid.

20 Ibid., 126–127.

21 B. L. Modzalevskii, *Pushkin i ego sovremenniki. Izbrannye trudy (1898–1928)* (St. Petersburg: Iskusstvo-SPB, 1999), 482.

22 Abram Efros, *Risunki poeta* (Moscow: Academia, 1933), 89, 220–222.

23 See, for example, Gotschall, *The Professor in the Cage*, 56–59.

24 Again, see ibid., 33–61.

25 See chapter 1, endnote 18 in this book. Kin selection, group selection, and multilevel selection, which I take up in more detail in chapter 5, are all terms that have generated considerable controversy in the literature, which is copious. David Sloan Wilson is probably the best-known advocate for a merging of kin selection and group selection into multilevel selection. See, for example, David Sloan Wilson, Mark Van Vugt, and Rick O'Gorman, "Multilevel Selection Theory and Major Evolutionary Transitions: Implications for Psychological Science," *Current Directions in Psychological Science* 17, no. 1 (2008): 6:

> The concept of a group as comparable to a single organism has had a long and turbulent history. Currently, methodological individualism dominates in many areas of psychology and evolution, but natural selection is now known to operate at multiple levels of the biological hierarchy. When between-group selection dominates within-group selection, a major evolutionary transition occurs and the group becomes a new, higher-level organism. It is likely that human evolution represents a major transition, and this has wide-ranging implications for the psychological study of group behavior, cognition, and culture.

See also Wilson's open letter to Richard Dawkins (David Sloan Wilson, "Open Letter to Richard Dawkins: Why Are You Still In Denial About Group Selection?," Evolution for Everyone, September 4, 2010, https://web.archive.org/web/20160316234245/http://scienceblogs.com/evolution/2010/09/04/open-letter-to-richard-dawkins/); as well as his friendly debate with Tom Stoppard on aspects of altruism that get left out of scientific discussions (Tom Stoppard, David Sloan Wilson, Stuart Jeffries, "The Hard Problem: Tom Stoppard on the Limits of What Science Can Explain," *The Guardian*, May 22, 2015, https://www.theguardian.com/books/2015/may/22/the-hard-problem-tom-stoppard-on-the-limits-of-what-science-can-explain).

Chapter 4

1 Siddhartha Mukherjee, *The Song of the Cell: An Exploration of Medicine and the New Human* (New York: Scribner, 2022), 74.
2 Mazur, *Paradigm Shifters*, 14–15.
3 Thomas Nagel, *Mind and Cosmos: Why the Materialist Neo-Darwinian Conception of Nature is Almost Certainly False* (New York: Oxford University Press, 2012), 16: "My guiding conviction is that mind it's not just an afterthought or an accident or an add-on, but a basic aspect of nature."
4 To be fair to Dawkins he wrote in the foreword to the book's thirtieth-anniversary edition that he "can readily see that [the book's title] might give an inadequate impression of its contents" and in retrospect thinks he should have taken Tom Maschler's advice and called the book *The Immortal Gene*. "The Selfish Gene," Wikipedia, https://en.wikipedia.org/wiki/The_Selfish_Gene#cite_note-timesexcerpt-2.
5 Frans De Waal, *The Bonobo and the Atheist: In Search of Humanism among the Primates* (New York: Norton, 2013), 240.
6 Ibid., 228.
7 See, for example, Michael Tomasello, "The Interdependence Hypothesis," in Michael Tomasello, *A Natural History of Morality* (Cambridge, MA: Harvard University Press, 2016), 1–8.
8 Compare the section from "Again I have visited" (1835) about the young saplings (*roshcha*) growing up around the two pines (an "older couple") versus the single pine (the "old bachelor"), around which all is barren. This poem and its embrace of life cycles is also discussed in chapter 6.
9 The scientific literature here is vast. A classic text on the subject is David M. Buss, *The Evolution of Desire: Strategies of Human Mating* (New York: Basic, 2016 [rev. ed., orig. 1994]), especially the chapter "What Women Want" (31–77). See also Daniel Bergner, *What Do Women Want? Adventures in the Science of Female Desire* (New York: Ecco, 2013).
10 Charles Darwin, *The Descent of Man* (Mineola: Dover, 2010), 445.
11 Prum, *Evolution*, 28–53. "Neo-Darwinians" refers here to such scholar-scientists as, for example, W. D. Hamilton, John Maynard Smith, George Williams, Richard Dawkins, Daniel Dennett.
12 Darwin, *Descent*, 447.
13 It can be argued that Prum is being highly speculative here. Couldn't the choices about prey or the ability to negotiate hierarchies of dominance also be signs of "mind"? But I still believe Prum's research is a necessary corrective to the exclusively utilitarian approach to mate choice of the neo-Darwinians, just as I think the female's response (her calculated *choice*) to what can only be called aesthetic criteria is a crucial dividing line in this case. My thanks to Professor Tom Dolack for this observation.
14 Prum, *Evolution*, 203.
15 Ibid., 194.
16 Ibid., 167.

17 Ibid., 175.
18 "Evolution has favored women who prefer men who possess attributes that confirm benefits and who dislike men who possess attributes that impose costs. Each separate attribute constitutes one component of a man's value to a woman as a mate. Each of her preferences tracks one component" (Buss, *The Evolution of Desire*, 35).
19 Other primates also show sex-typical behavior by watching others. Frans De Waal compares these behaviors in humans, chimpanzees, and bonobos in his most recent book *Different: Gender Through the Eyes of a Primatologist* (New York: Norton, 2022).
20 Freud, "Three Essays on the Theory of Sexuality," in *The Standard Edition of the Complete Psychological Works of Sigmund Freud*, trans. James Strachey, with Anna Freud (London: Hogarth Press, 1953), vol. 7, 156–157; cited in Winfried Menninghaus, *Aesthetics after Darwin: The Multiple Origins and Functions of the Arts*, trans. Alexandra Berlina (Boston: Academic Studies Press, 2019), 28.
21 Compare Tatiana (*Eugene Onegin*), Liza ("The Queen of Spades"), Masha Mironova (*The Captain's Daughter*).

Chapter 5

1 LeDoux, *Deep History*, 350–351:

> Cognitive theories of emotion are variants of an idea proposed in 1962 by Stanley Schachter and Jerome Singer. The psychologists argued that an emotional experience is not biologically predetermined, but instead is constructed by the appraisal, interpretation, and labeling of biological, including neural, signals in light of the social and physical context of the particular experience. Although the belief that emotions are hardwired in the limbic system still dominates in neuroscience, the cognitive view of emotions has, thanks to Schachter and Singer, also been a strong force in contemporary psychology.

2 Once again, Tomasello, in *The Natural History of Morality*, is very good on the evolutionary progression from primitive human psychology to morality. He describes early human psychology in terms of three formulas that led eventually to a full-scale morality: "you > me" (sympathy), "you = me" (fairness), and "we > me" (commitment to collaborate) (78–82).
3 One needs to place "causal" in scare quotes here and elsewhere when parsing the empirical and the conceptual at the same time: "In general, we cannot directly test causal methods of the processes affecting natural populations; we can only directly test the statistical relationships that our causal models imply." Samir Okasha, "Multi-Level Selection, Covariance and Contextual Analysis," *The British Journal for the Philosophy of Science* 55, no. 3 (2004): 484. Also, "The issue [of group selection—DB] may look straightforwardly empirical—surely it is about whether a certain causal process, called 'group selection', has, or has not played an important role in evolutionary history? [...] As will become clear below, the group selection debate actually involves a curious blend of empirical and conceptual issues, which makes it ideally suited to—and much in need of—philosophical clarification." Samir Okasha, "Why Won't the Group Selection Controversy Go Away?," *The British Journal for the Philosophy of Science* 52, no. 1 (2001): 28. See below.
4 W. D. Hamilton, "The Evolution of Altruistic Behaviour," In *Narrow Roads of Gene Land. The Collected Papers of W. D. Hamilton*, vol. 1: *Evolution of Social Behaviour* (Oxford: W. H. Freeman, 1996), 7.
5 Famed geneticist, evolutionary biologist, and mathematician J. B. S. Haldane once quipped, "I would gladly give up my life for two brothers or eight cousins." The joke is about how mathematically to receive one's full genetic complement for an altruistic act, which by calculating

("two brothers or eight cousins") appears to make the act less than altruistic. My thanks again to Professor Tom Dolack for alerting me to this anecdote.

6 One such formula involving covariation is "Price's equation," which calculates how a trait/allele and its fitness relative to a subpopulation covary over time. Multiple regression analysis predicts the value of a dependent variable, in this case fitness, by using two or more independent variables. The namesake of the formula is the genius polymath George Price, whose story from leading-edge geneticist investigating the chemical bases of altruism to homeless squatter who commits suicide is told by Oren Harman in *The Price of Altruism: George Price and the Search for the Origins of Kindness* (New York: Norton, 2010).

7 Okasha, *Evolution and the Levels of Selection* (Oxford: Oxford University Press, 2006), 5.

8 Ibid.

9 Okasha, "Kin Selection, Group Selection, and Altruism," OUP Blog, https://blog.oup.com/2015/01/kin-group-selection-controversy/.

10 Steven Pinker, "The False Allure of Group Selection," *Edge*, June 18, 2012, https://www.edge.org/conversation/steven_pinker-the-false-allure-of-group-selection#22479.

11 See Okasha, "Multi-Level Selection, Covariance and Contextual Analysis," 496.

12 "Practicing in different worlds, the two groups of scientists see different things when they look from the same point in the same direction." Thomas S. Kuhn, *The Structure of Scientific Revolutions*, 4th ed. (Chicago: University of Chicago Press, 2012), 149.

13 Nicholas A. Christakis, *Blueprint: The Evolutionary Origins of a Good Society* (New York: Little, Brown Spark, 2019), 13, 16.

14 Ibid., 13 and fn31.

15 Pierre Teilhard de Chardin, *The Phenomenon of Man*, trans. Bernard Wall (New York: Harper Perennial Modern Thought, 2008), 259–260.

16 Pinker doesn't believe the gene-centered theory of insect eusociality can apply to humans. See Pinker, "The False Allure of Group Selection."

17 V. E. Vatsuro et al., eds., *A. S. Pushkin v vospominaniiakh sovremennikov* (St. Petersburg: Akademicheskii proekt, 1998), vol. 2, 140.

18 "This is the French form of the English and German 'Hannibal' and the Russian 'Gannibal' or 'Ganibal.'" See Vladimir Nabokov's notes to Aleksandr Pushkin, *Eugene Onegin: A Novel in Verse*, trans. Vladimir Nabokov, rev. ed. (Princeton: Princeton University Press, 1975), vol. 3, 389n5.

19 Nabokov's translation in Pushkin, *Eugene Onegin*, vol. 3, 389–390.

20 A. S. Pushkin, "<Nachalo avtobiografii>," in A. S. Pushkin, *Polnoe sobranie sochinenii*, ed. V. D. Bonch-Bruevich et al. (Moscow: Akademiia Nauk SSSR, 1937–1959), vol. 12, 311–312.

21 I. L. Feinberg, *Abram Petrovich Gannibal—praded Pushkina* (Moscow: Nauka, 1983), 111; for the English translation see Pushkin, *Eugene Onegin*, vol. 3, 397.

22 M. N. Makarov, "Aleksandr Sergeevich Pushkin v detstve (iz zapisok o moem znakomstve)," in *Pushkin v vospominaniiakh sovremennikov*, vol. 1, 377–383; cited in V. Veresaev, *Pushkin v zhizni*, 6th ed. (Moscow: Sovetskii pisatel', 1936), 54–55. *Riabchik* means literally "grouse," but here is clearly a play on *riaboi*, "pockmarked."

23 This currently most authentic time of arrival in Constantinople is given in M. N. Virolainen, ed., *Legendy i mify o Pushkine* (St. Petersburg: Akademicheskii proekt, 1994), 47n58 (this is the Russian version of Nabokov's Gannibal study, with the new notes being provided by N. K. Teletova).

24 Ibid.

25 Ibid., 47n62.

26 Pushkin, *Eugene Onegin*, vol. 3, 428.

27 Ibid., vol. 3, 420; Feinberg, *Abram Petrovich Gannibal*, 112–113.

28 Here Nabokov's calculations come up with the wrong date for the baptism: 1707, and not 1705 (Pushkin, *Eugene Onegin*, vol. 3, 424). The addition of the Polish queen was probably

a later fiction inserted into the German biography by its author, Abram's son-in-law Adam Rotkirch. Gannibal himself never mentioned the fact in any of his own writings. The notion seems to go back to the memoirs of Prince P. V. Dolgorukov: Georg Leets, *Abram Petrovich Gannibal* (Tallinn: Eesti raamat, 1984), 26.

29 Pushkin, *Eugene Onegin*, vol. 3, 427; Virolainen, *Legendy i mify o Pushkine*, 49n78.

30 One sign of Peter's attachment to the little blackamoor is the following bizarre anecdote recorded by Pushkin in "Table Talk" (wr. 1835–36):

> Once the little blackamoor, who was accompanying Peter I on a walk, stopped on account of a certain necessity and suddenly cried out, "Your Majesty! Your Majesty! My intestine is falling out." Peter came up to him and, seeing what the matter was, said: "You lie; that's not your intestine, it's a tapeworm." And he yanked out the tapeworm with his own fingers. The story is rather off-color, but it paints [accurately] Peter's customs. (Pushkin, *Polnoe sobranie sochinenii*, vol. 12, 157)

31 M. A. Tsiavlovskii, et al., comm., *Rukoiu Pushkina* (Moscow and Leningrad: Academia, 1935), 51–52; Feinberg, *Abram Petrovich Gannibal*, 114.

32 Pushkin, *Polnoe sobranie sochinenii*, vol. 12, 435.

33 See discussion in V. S. Listov, "Legenda o chernom predke," in *Legendy i mify o Pushkine*, 59–60.

34 Pushkin also says Gannibal lived "in the dissipation of [Parisian] high society" in his own autobiographical comments. Pushkin, *Polnoe sobranie sochinenii*, vol. 12, 312.

35 Leets, *Abram Petrovich Gannibal*, 59–61.

36 Ibid., 57–73; Nabokov in Pushkin, *Eugene Onegin*, vol. 3, 434.

37 D. N. Anuchin, *A. S. Pushkin: Antropologicheskii eskiz* (Moscow: Russkie vedomosti, 1899), 30; cited in A. Tyrkova-Williams, *Zhizn' Pushkina*, 3rd. ed. (Moscow: Molodaia gvardiia, 1998), vol. 1, 38.

38 Pushkin, *Eugene Onegin*, vol. 3, 438.

39 See discussion in Leets, *Abram Petrovich Gannibal*, 74–99.

40 Virolainen, *Legendy i mify o Pushkine*, 51n95.

41 Leets, *Abram Petrovich Gannibal*, 83.

42 Pushkin, *Eugene Onegin*, vol. 3, 434. The account is from a piece assembled by Stepan Opatovich and published in *Russkaia starina* 18 (1877): 69–78. Cited also in Leets, *Abram Petrovich Gannibal*, 83.

43 Pushkin, *Polnoe sobranie sochinenii*, vol. 12, 313.

44 As Pushkin explains (mostly to himself) in "Table Talk" (wr. 1835–1836), "Othello is not by nature jealous; just the opposite: he is trusting." Pushkin, *Polnoe sobranie sochinenii*, vol. 12, 157.

45 B. L. Modzalevskii, *Pushkin* (Leningrad: Priboi, 1929), 56.

46 Leets, *Abram Petrovich Gannibal*, 170–174.

47 Ibid., 180.

48 Ibid., 174–177.

49 Actually, Nadezhda was nine at the time.

50 The correct date of Osip Gannibal's death is October 12, 1806.

51 Pushkin, *Polnoe sobranie sochinenii*, vol. 12, 314.

52 *Severnaia pchela*, no. 94, August 7, 1830. E. O. Larionova, ed., *Pushkin v prizhiznennoi kritike. 1828–1830* (St. Petersburg: Gosudarstvennyi Pushkinskii teatral'nyi tsentr, 2001), 280.

53 As it now seems, mistakenly: Peter was in Moscow from December 18, 1722 until February 23, 1723 and therefore could not have met Abram outside Petersburg upon the latter's return as Pushkin's autobiographical note has it. Leets, *Abram Petrovich Gannibal*, 50.

54 The icon was not of Saints Peter and Paul but of the Savior Not Made By Hand (*Nerukotvornyi Spas*), *if* the icon belonging to Abram and surviving into later generations of the family is the same one Peter used to bless him. Ibid.

55 My reading of the Countess D.-Vorontsova connection, including the race-class overtones amid a scandalous affair, owes much to T. G. Tsiavlovskaia, "Khrani menia, moi talisman," in *Utaennaia liubov' Pushkina*, ed. R. V. Iezuitova and Ia. L. Levkovich (St. Petersburg: Akademicheskii proekt, 1997), esp. 348–358.

56 The fact of the affair has never been proven by external evidence, but we can assume it happened based on internal evidence provided by Pushkin's writing (for example, the "child of love, child of nature"/*ditia liubvi, ditia prirody* description of the infant Aleko holds in his arms in a discarded fragment of *The Gypsies/Tsygany*). See following discussion and Pushkin, *Polnoe sobranie sochinenii*, vol. 4, 445.

57 See Pushkin's letter (in French) of April 5, 1830 to N. I. Goncharova in Pushkin, *Polnoe sobranie sochinenii*, vol. 14, 318: "Only habit and extended intimacy can help me to earn the affection of your daughter; I can hope in time to awaken her attachment, but I have nothing with which to appeal romantically [*ponravit'sia*] to her; if she agrees to give me her hand I will see in that only proof of the calm indifference of her heart."

Chapter 6

1 McGilchrist, *Master*, 115.

2 George Lakoff and Mark Johnson, *Metaphors We Live By* (Chicago: University of Chicago Press, 1980), 5.

3 McGilchrist, *Master*, 112.

4 I am helped here and elsewhere by Sergei Davydov, "The Ace in 'The Queen of Spades,'" *Slavic Review* 58, no. 2 (Summer 1999): 309–328, esp. 317–318.

5 McGilchrist, *Master*, 98.

6 "VNM," Medium blog entry, September 26, 2018, https://medium.com/@vnm26x/writing-is-natures-way-of-letting-you-know-how-sloppy-your-thinking-is-16e6a0c16e00.

7 S. A. Sobolevskii, "Iz stat'i 'Tainstvennye primety v zhizni Pushkina,'" in *Pushkin v vospominaniiakh sovremennikov*, vol. 2, 9–11.

8 Jaak Panksepp, "Science of the Brain as a Gateway to Understanding Play: An Interview," *American Journal of Play* (Winter 2010): 264.

9 See Jordan Peterson, "Rules of the Game," https://www.youtube.com/watch?v=xC9zUdOj-mM.

10 I am helped in my thinking here by Caryl Emerson, who describes the tale as "an allegory of interpretation," in Caryl Emerson, "'The Queen of Spades' and the Open End," in *Puškin Today*, ed. David M. Bethea (Bloomington: Indiana University Press, 1993), 37.

11 Panksepp, "Science of the Brain," 255–256.

12 Ibid., 263–264.

13 Ibid., 268.

14 Ibid., 269.

15 Pushkin, *Polnoe sobranie sochinenii*, vol. 11, 15–16.

16 Iu. M. Lotman, "'Pikovaia dama' i tema kartochnoi igry v russkoi literature nachala XIX veka," in Lotman, *Pushkin*, 796.

17 N. I. Pavlenko, *Ekaterina Velikaia* (Moscow: Molodaia gvardiia and Zhizn' zamechatel'nykh liudei, 2006), 389.

18 Lotman, "Pikovaia dama," 802.

19 Pushkin, *Polnoe sobranie sochinenii*, vol. 11, 127.

Afterword

1 Max Roser, "The Short History of Global Living Conditions and Why It Matters that We Know It," Our World in Data, 2020, https://ourworldindata.org/a-history-of-global-living-conditions-in-5-charts.

2 Theodosius Dobzhansky, *The Biology of Ultimate Concern* (New York: New American Library, 1967), 25.

3 Nagel, *Mind and Cosmos*, 8, 16.

4 Dawkins, *Selfish Gene*, 192.

5 Dennett, *Darwin's Dangerous Idea*, 365.

6 Dennett, "Memes 101."

7 Daniel C. Dennett, *From Bacteria to Bach and Back: The Evolution of Minds* (London: Penguin, 2018), 241, 246–247. For a helpfully revisionary treatment of memes and memetics in the context of cultural evolution, see Stewart-Williams, *The Ape that Understood the Universe*, passim.

8 Steven Pinker, *How the Mind Works* (New York: W. W. Norton, 2009), 209.

9 Jablonka and Lamb, *Evolution in Four Dimensions*, 220–224.

Works Cited

Akhmatova, Anna. "Slovo o Pushkine." In Anna Akhmatova, *O Pushkine*, 6–7. Leningrad: Sovetskii pisatel', 1977.

Annenkov, P. V. *Pushkin v aleksandrovskuiu epokhu*. Minsk: Limarius, 1998.

Anuchin, D. N. *A. S. Pushkin: Antropologicheskii eskiz*. Moscow: Russkie vedomosti, 1899.

Baldwin, J. Mark. "A New Factor in Evolution." *The American Naturalist* 30 (1896): 441–451, 536–553. https://www.journals.uchicago.edu/doi/epdf/10.1086/276408.

Barfield, Owen. *Saving the Appearances: A Study in Idolatry*. 2nd ed. Hanover: University Press of New England, 1988.

Basina, M. *V sadakh litseia. Na bregakh Nevy*. Moscow: Detskaia literatura, 1988.

Beer, Gillian. *Darwin's Plots: Evolutionary Narrative in Darwin, George Eliot and Nineteenth-Century Fiction*. 3rd ed. Cambridge, UK: Cambridge University Press, 2009.

Bergner, Daniel. *What Do Women Want? Adventures in the Science of Female Desire*. New York: Ecco, 2013.

Bethea, David M., ed. *Puškin Today*. Bloomington: Indiana University Press, 1993.

Boehm, Christopher. "Bullies: Redefining the Human Free-Rider Problem." In *Darwin's Bridge: Uniting the Humanities and Sciences*, edited by Joseph Carroll, Dan P. McAdams, and Edward O. Wilson, 11–28. New York: Oxford University Press, 2016.

———. *Moral Origins: The Evolution of Virtue, Altruism, and Shame*. New York: Basic Books, 2012.

Brooks, David. *The Second Mountain: The Quest for a Moral Life*. New York: Random House, 2019.

Buss, David M. *The Evolution of Desire: Strategies of Human Mating*. Rev. ed. New York: Basic, 2016.

Carroll, Joseph. *Evolution and Literary Theory*. Columbia: University of Missouri Press, 1995.

———. *Literary Darwinism: Evolution, Human Nature, and Literature*. New York: Routledge, 2004.

———. *Reading Human Nature: Literary Darwinism in Theory and Practice*. Albany: State University of New York Press, 2011.

Carroll, Joseph, Dan P. McAdams, and Edward O. Wilson, eds. *Darwin's Bridge: Uniting the Humanities and Sciences*. New York: Oxford University Press, 2016.

Carroll, Joseph, Mathias Clasen, and Emelie Jonsson, eds. *Evolutionary Perspectives on Imaginative Culture*. Cham, Switzerland: Springer Nature, 2020.

Christakis, Nicholas A. *Blueprint: The Evolutionary Origins of a Good Society*. New York: Little, Brown Spark, 2019.

Darwin, Charles. *The Descent of Man*. Mineola: Dover, 2010.

———. *On the Origin of Species*. New York: Modern Library, 2009.

Davydov, Sergei. "The Ace in 'The Queen of Spades.'" *Slavic Review* 58, no. 2 (Summer 1999): 309–328.

Dawkins, Richard. *The Selfish Gene*. New York: Oxford University Press, 1976.

De Waal, Frans. *Different: Gender Through the Eyes of a Primatologist*. New York: Norton, 2022.

———. *Mama's Last Hug: Animal Emotions and What They Tell Us about Ourselves*. New York: Norton, 2019.

———. *The Bonobo and the Atheist: In Search of Humanism among the Primates*. New York: Norton, 2013.

Deacon, Terrence W. *The Symbolic Species: The Co-evolution of Language and the Brain*. New York: W. W. Norton, 1997.

Dennett, Daniel C. *Darwin's Dangerous Idea: Evolution and the Meanings of Life*. London: Penguin, 1995.

———. *From Bacteria to Bach and Back: The Evolution of Minds*. London: Penguin, 2018.

Dobzhansky, Theodosius. *Genetics and the Origin of Species*. Introduction by Stephen Jay Gould. New York: Columbia University Press, 1982 (orig. 1937).

———. *Mankind Evolving: The Evolution of the Human Species*. New Haven: Yale University Press, 1962.

———. *The Biology of Ultimate Concern*. New York: New American Library, 1967.

Dor, Daniel. *The Instruction of Imagination: Language as a Social Communication Technology*. New York: Oxford University Press, 2015.

Efros, Abram. *Risunki poeta*. Moscow: Academia, 1933.

Emerson, Caryl. "'The Queen of Spades' and the Open End." In *Puškin Today*, edited by David M. Bethea, 31–37. Bloomington: Indiana University Press, 1993.

Feinberg, I. L. *Abram Petrovich Gannibal—praded Pushkina*. Moscow: Nauka, 1983.

Freud, Sigmund. "Three Essays on the Theory of Sexuality." In *The Standard Edition of the Complete Psychological Works of Sigmund Freud*, translated by James Strachey, with Anna Freud, vol. 7, 125–245. London: Hogarth Press, 1953.

Goodenough, Ursula. *The Sacred Depths of Nature*. New York: Oxford University Press, 1997.

———. *The Sacred Depths of Nature: How Life Has Emerged and Evolved*. 2nd ed. New York: Oxford University Press, 2023.

Goodenough, Ursula, and Terrence W. Deacon. "The Sacred Emergence of Nature." In *The Oxford Handbook of Religion and Science*, edited by Philip Clayton, 853–871. Oxford: Oxford University Press, 2006.

Jablonka, Eva, and Marion J. Lamb. *Evolution in Four Dimensions: Genetic, Epigenetic, Behavioral, and Symbolic Variation in the History of Life*. Rev. ed. Cambridge: MIT Press, 2014.

Gnammankou, Dieudonné. *Abraham Hanibal: L'aieul noir de Pouchkine*. Paris: Présence africaine, 1996.

Gottschall, Jonathan. *The Professor in the Cage: Why Men Fight and Why We Like to Watch*. New York: Penguin, 2016.

Gottschall, Jonathan, and David Sloan Wilson, eds. *The Literary Animal: Evolution and the Nature of Narrative*. Evanston: Northwestern University Press, 2005.

Hamilton, W. D. "The Evolution of Altruistic Behaviour." In *Narrow Roads of Gene Land. The Collected Papers of W. D. Hamilton*, vol. 1: *Evolution of Social Behaviour*, 1–10. Oxford: W. H. Freeman, 1996.

Harman, Oren. *The Price of Altruism: George Price and the Search for the Origins of Kindness*. New York: Norton, 2010.

Kauffman, Stuart A. "Reinventing the Sacred." https://vimeo.com/105980303.

———. *Reinventing the Sacred: A New View of Science, Reason, and Religion*. New York: Basic, 2008.

Karolis, Vyacheslav R., Maurizio Corbetta, and Michel Thiebaut de Schotten. "The Architecture of Functional Lateralisation and Its Relationship to Callosal Connectivity in the Human Brain." *Nature Communications* 10 (2019): article no. 1417. https://www.nature.com/articles/s41467-019-09344-1/.

Kuhn, Thomas S. *The Structure of Scientific Revolutions*. 4th ed. Chicago: University of Chicago Press, 2012.

Lakoff, George, and Mark Johnson. *Metaphors We Live By*. Chicago: University of Chicago Press, 1980.

Laland, Kevin N. *Darwin's Unfinished Symphony: How Culture Made the Human Mind*. Princeton: Princeton University Press, 2017.

Larionova, E. O., ed. *Pushkin v prizhiznennoi kritike. 1828–1830*. St. Petersburg: Gosudarstvennyi Pushkinskii teatral'nyi tsentr, 2001.

Larson, Edward J. *Evolution*. New York: Modern Library, 2004.

LeDoux, Joseph. *The Deep History of Ourselves: The Four-Billion-Year Story of How We Got Conscious Brains*. New York: Penguin, 2019.

Leets, Georg. *Abram Petrovich Gannibal*. Tallinn: Eesti raamat, 1984.

Levine, George. *Darwin the Writer*. Oxford: Oxford University Press, 2011.

Listov, V. S. "Legenda o chernom predke." In *Mify i legendy o Pushkine*, edited by M. N. Virolainen, 53–64. St. Petersburg: Akademicheskii proekt, 1994.

Lotman, Iu. M. *Pushkin: Biografiia pisatelia. Stat'i i zametki 1960–1990. "Evgenii Onegin". Kommentarii*. St. Petersburg: Iskusstvo-SPB, 1995.

———. "'Pikovaia dama' i tema kartochnoi igry v russkoi literature nachala XIX veka." In Iu. M. Lotman, *Pushkin: Biografiia pisatelia. Stat'i i zametki 1960–1990. "Evgenii Onegin". Kommentarii*, 786–814. St. Petersburg: Iskusstvo-SPB, 1995.

Magsamen, Susan, and Ross, Ivy. *Your Brain on Art: How the Arts Transform Us*. New York: Random House, 2023.

Makarov, M. N. "Aleksandr Sergeevich Pushkin v detstve (iz zapisok o moem znakomstve)." In *Pushkin v vospominaniiakh sovremennikov*, edited by V. E. Vatsuro et al., vol. 1, 43–46. St. Petersburg: Akademicheskii proekt, 1998.

Marian, Viorica, and Sayuri Hayakawa. "Why Bilinguals Experience the World Differently: Multilingualism Alters What You See and Hear." https://www.psychologytoday.com/us/blog/language-and-mind/201906/why-bilinguals-experience-the-world-differently.

Mayr, Ernst. *What Evolution Is*. New York: Basic, 2001.

Mazur, Suzan. *The Paradigm Shifters: Overthrowing "the Hegemony of the Culture of Darwin."* New York: Caswell Books, 2015.

McGilchrist, Iain. *The Master and His Emissary: The Divided Brain and the Making of the Western World*. New Haven: Yale University Press, 2009.

Menninghaus, Winfried. *Aesthetics after Darwin: The Multiple Origins and Functions of the Arts*. Translated by Alexandra Berlina. Boston: Academic Studies Press, 2019.

Mesoudi, Alex. *Cultural Evolution: How Darwinian Theory Can Explain Human Culture and Synthesize the Social Sciences*. Chicago: University of Chicago Press, 2011.

Meyer, Stephen C. *Darwin's Doubt: The Explosive Origin of Animal Life and the Case for Intelligent Design*. New York: HarperOne, 2013.

———. *Return of the God Hypothesis: Three Scientific Discoveries That Reveal the Mind Behind the Universe*. New York: HarperOne, 2021.

———. *Signature in the Cell: DNA and the Evidence for Intelligent Design*. New York: HarperOne, 2009.

Modzalevskii, B. L. *Pushkin*. Leningrad: Priboi, 1929.

———. *Pushkin i ego sovremenniki. Izbrannye trudy (1898–1928)*. St. Petersburg: Iskusstvo-SPB, 1999.

Mukherjee, Siddhartha. *The Song of the Cell: An Exploration of Medicine and the New Human*. New York: Scribner, 2022.

Nagel, Thomas. *Mind and Cosmos: Why the Materialist Neo-Darwinian Conception of Nature is Almost Certainly False*. New York: Oxford University Press, 2012.

Nicholson, Daniel J., and John Dupré, eds. *Everything Flows: Towards a Processual Philosophy of Biology*. Oxford: Oxford University Press, 2018.

Noble, Denis. *Dance to the Tune of Life: Biological Relativity*. Cambridge, UK: Cambridge University Press, 2017.

Okasha, Samir. *Evolution and the Levels of Selection*. Oxford: Oxford University Press, 2006.

———. "Kin Selection, Group Selection, and Altruism." OUP Blog. https://blog.oup.com/2015/01/kin-group-selection-controversy/.

———. "Multi-Level Selection, Covariance and Contextual Analysis." *The British Journal for the Philosophy of Science* 55, no. 3 (2004): 481–504.

———. "Why Won't the Group Selection Controversy Go Away?" *The British Journal for the Philosophy of Science* 52, no. 1 (2001): 25–50.

Panksepp, Jaak. "Science of the Brain as a Gateway to Understanding Play: An Interview." *American Journal of Play* (Winter 2010): 245–277.

Pavlenko, N. I. *Ekaterina Velikaia*. Moscow: Molodaia gvardiia and Zhizn' zamechatel'nykh liudei, 2006.

Pinker, Steven. *How the Mind Works*. New York: W. W. Norton, 2009.

———. "The False Allure of Group Selection." *Edge*, June 18, 2012. https://www.edge.org/conversation/steven_pinker-the-false-allure-of-group-selection#22479.

Peterson, Jordan. "Rules of the Game." https://www.youtube.com/watch?v=xC9zUdOj-mM.

Prum, Richard O. *The Evolution of Beauty: How Darwin's Forgotten Theory of Mate Choice Shapes the Animal World—and Us*. New York: Doubleday, 2017.

Pushkin, Aleksandr. *Eugene Onegin: A Novel in Verse*. Translated by Vladimir Nabokov. Rev. ed. Princeton: Princeton University Press, 1975.

———. *Eugene Onegin: A Novel in Verse*. Translated by James E. Falen. Oxford, UK: Oxford World's Classics, 1998.

——— [Pushkin, A. S.]. *Polnoe sobranie sochinenii*. Edited by V. D. Bonch-Bruevich et al. Moscow: Akademiia Nauk SSSR, 1937–1959.

Ridley, Matt. "When Ideas Have Sex." https://www.ted.com/talks/matt_ridley_when_ideas_have_sex/transcript?language=en.

———. "The Evolution of Culture." In Matt Ridley, *The Evolution of Everything: How New Ideas Emerge*, 82–85. New York: Harper, 2015.

Richerson, Peter J., and Robert Boyd. *Not by Genes Alone: How Culture Transformed Human Evolution*. Chicago: University of Chicago Press, 2005.

Robinson, Ken. "Do Schools Kill Creativity?" Ted Talk, April 22, 2013. https://www.ted.com/talks/sir_ken_robinson_do_schools_kill_creativity?language=en.

Shapiro, James A. *Evolution: A View from the 21st Century*. Upper Saddle River: FT Press, 2011.

Sobolevskii, S. A. "Iz stat'i 'Tainstvennye primety v zhizni Pushkina.'" In *Pushkin v vospominaniiakh sovremennikov*, edited by V. E. Vatsuro et al., vol. 2, 9–11. St. Petersburg: Akademicheskii proekt, 1998.

Stewart-Williams, Steve. *The Ape that Understood the Universe: How Mind and Culture Evolve.* Cambridge, UK: Cambridge University Press, 2018.

Teilhard de Chardin, Pierre. *The Phenomenon of Man.* Translated by Bernard Wall. New York: Harper Perennial Modern Thought, 2008.

Teletova, N. K. *Zabytye rodstvennye sviazi A. S. Pushkina.* Leningrad: Nauka, 1981.

Tomasello, Michael. *The Cultural Origins of Human Cognition.* Cambridge, MA: Harvard University Press, 1999.

———. *A Natural History of Morality.* Cambridge, MA: Harvard University Press, 2016.

———. *A Natural History of Human Thinking.* Cambridge, MA: Harvard University Press, 2014.

Tsiavlovskaia, T. G. "Khrani menia, moi talisman." In *Utaennaia liubov' Pushkina*, edited by R. V. Iezuitova and Ia. L. Levkovich, 295–380. St. Petersburg: Akademicheskii proekt, 1997.

Tsiavlovskii, M. A., et al., comm. *Rukoiu Pushkina.* Moscow and Leningrad: Academia, 1935.

Tyrkova-Williams, A. *Zhizn' Pushkina.* 3rd. ed. Moscow: Molodaia gvardiia, 1998.

Veresaev, V. *Pushkin v zhizni.* 6th ed. Moscow: Sovetskii pisatel', 1936.

Virolainen, M. N., ed. *Mify i legendy o Pushkine.* St. Petersburg: Akademicheskii proekt, 1994.

Wilson, David Sloan. *Evolution for Everyone.* New York: Delta, 2007.

———. *The Neighborhood Project: Using Evolution to Improve My City, One Block at a Time.* New York: Little Brown, 2011.

Wilson, David Sloan, Mark Van Vugt, and Rick O'Gorman. "Multilevel Selection Theory and Major Evolutionary Transitions: Implications for Psychological Science." *Current Directions in Psychological Science* 17, no. 1 (2008): 6–9.

Wozniak, Robert H. "Consciousness, Social Heredity, and Development: The Evolutionary Thought of James Mark Baldwin." *American Psychologist* 64, no. 2 (2009): 93–201.

Index

Printed in the USA
CPSIA information can be obtained
at www.ICGtesting.com
LVHW011311010524
778616LV00007B/20